Tomm looked at Hunter. They had to prove to Officer Lisa that they were from outer space, or they were *never* going to get out off this screwy planet. Hunter sighed, pulling a small white box from his pocket and activated the button on top. There was a sudden flash and a burst of green smoke. When it cleared, Hunter's flying machine was standing in the middle of the big room, seemingly appearing out of nowhere.

Lisa's jaw fell open. She turned pale. She tried to say something, but nothing came out. Catching her breath, she slowly approached the spacecraft, and touched it.

She gasped, "This can't be real . . . "

They took her at her word—and Zarex snapped his fingers. There was another burst of smoke, and suddenly the clanking robot 33418 was standing before them—all ten feet of him. Metallic muscles, arm weapons, death-ray visor. The works.

Lisa looked up at him. 33418 made an odd whirring sound.

And that's when she fainted dead away.

She hit the floor with a bang, taking several rickety chairs down with her.

"Oh great!" Zarex moaned. "*Now* what do we do with her?"

Also by Mack Maloney

STARHAWK I

CHOPPER OPS
CHOPPER OPS 2: ZERO RED
CHOPPER OPS 3: SHUTTLE DOWN

For more information visit
www.MackMaloney.com

PLANET AMERICA

MACK MALONEY

ACE BOOKS, NEW YORK

PLANET AMERICA

An Ace Book / published by arrangement with
the author

PRINTING HISTORY
Ace mass-market edition / November 2001

All rights reserved.
Copyright © 2001 by Brian Kelleher.
Cover logo by Michael Herring.
Cover art by Jean Targete.
Cover design by Pyrographx.

This book, or parts thereof, may not be reproduced in
any form without permission.
For information address: The Berkley Publishing Group,
a division of Penguin Putnam Inc.,
375 Hudson Street, New York, New York 10014.

Visit our website at
www.penguinputnam.com

Check out the ACE Science Fiction & Fantasy newsletter
and much more on the Internet at Club PPI!

ISBN: 0-441-00878-X

ACE®
Ace Books are published
by The Berkley Publishing Group,
a division of Penguin Putnam Inc.,
375 Hudson Street, New York, New York 10014.
ACE and the "A" design are trademarks
belonging to Penguin Putnam Inc.

PRINTED IN THE UNITED STATES OF AMERICA

10 9 8 7 6 5 4 3 2 1

PART ONE

While Shooting the Five-Arm

1

The secret base was located just beneath the surface of the tiny jungle moon.

It had two hidden openings: one to the east, another to the west. Both were cut out of sheer rock. The top of the base was covered by thick vegetation and hidden by a perpetual blanket of fog. Two towers poked up through this mist, guarding the entrances at either end of the base. A series of ancient ruins stood nearby, too; they masked ventilation tubes for the hidden chamber below. Other than that, the secret base was invisible.

The underground facility was large enough to accommodate an entire squadron of spacefighters. Trouble was, these eighteen combat spacecraft were no match for the calamity that was about to befall the secret base. The few hundred people inside were the last holdouts of an antiimperial faction that had once proliferated in this part of space. They had fled here after a series of battles with the hated imperial forces. But somehow the secret location of this last safe haven had been compromised. Now their enemies were about to finish them off in a most gruesome manner.

A huge mechanical battle star—the enemy's most powerful weapon—was drawing close to the tiny jungle moon. This enormous space station carried an immense death ray capable of destroying an entire planet in a matter of seconds. It could vaporize a tiny moon such as this in the blink of an eye.

The enemy death star had shown up out of nowhere. It was presently on the other side of the planet around which the tiny moon revolved. It was moving very swiftly, though, and once the mother planet got out of the way, the enemy's gigantic death ray would have a clear shot at the moon.

The rebels faced an impossible task then: trying to stop the battle star before it destroyed the tiny moon. The problem was, the rebels' rather puny spacefighters were built only for combating other spacefighters. Attempting to disable or even destroy the huge ball of metal coming their way was light-years removed from their capabilities.

Still, all eighteen of the rebel spacecraft were getting ready to launch and give it a try. The pilots all knew this would probably be their final mission. At least half the rebel spacefighters would have to be dispatched against the fifty or so opposing fighters this big, black, death station thing was known to be carrying; stopping them would be another impossible task. There was no doubt that the rebel pilots would fight the good fight, for they were known far and wide for their bravery. But the reality of the situation was clear: Against the powerful battle star and its own combat spacecraft, the rebels' valiant effort would probably end in a very brief, very one-sided contest.

There was no little chaos within the secret base now. Pilots getting strapped into their spacecraft. Mechanics doing last-second checks on the small, swift fighters. Squads of security troops rushing to their positions; robots of all shapes and sizes scurrying about as well. Above it all, a high-pitched warning Klaxon was bleating full blast.

The rebel spacefighters were lined up along a launching ramp that cut right through the middle of the subterranean chamber. Standing next to this ramp was a handful of people. One was a young woman. She was very pretty, dressed all in white, with odd, tightly woven pigtails rolled like pinwheels against the sides of her head. She was the leader of the rebels. She was known to all simply as the Princess.

Close by were two young men. One had blond hair, a flashy uniform, and a strangely blunt swordlike device stuck in his belt. He was about to climb into the last of the waiting spacefighters; indeed, he would be the last pilot to strap in. Despite appearances, he was a bit overwhelmed by the drama of the moment. He looked a bit like the Princess. Possibly he was her brother.

Next to him was an older, rakish man, more weathered than the kid. He was loading supplies onto another spacecraft, one different in shape and size from the rebel spacefighters. Though the Princess was obviously fretting about the looming catastrophe, this man was trying to sneak peeks at her shapely rear end every chance he could get. Several steps behind him was the strangest individual of all. Very tall. Weird face. Big teeth. Hair from the top of the head to the soles of the feet.

The combined whine of spacecraft propulsion units filled the chamber now. All of the spacefighters were carrying substantial weapons loads, the very last of the rebels' ammunition stores. The warning Klaxon began blaring even louder. The lights inside the hidden chamber suddenly became dim.

Then an amplified voice announced in ominous tones, "The battle star will be in attack position in two minutes. . . ."

These words sent a wave of grim electricity through the hidden base. Pilots revved their propulsion units. The first of the spacefighters began moving toward the chamber's opening. On the Princess's signal, the lead craft shot forward and roared out of the chamber, climbing through the fog into the skies beyond. It was followed close behind by the rest of the squadron, all except for the spacefighter being piloted by the kid who looked a bit like the Princess.

No sooner had the seventeen spacecraft departed when the walls of the chamber reverberated once again with the gloomy, amplified voice. "The battle star will be in attack position in one minute, fifty seconds. . . ."

The Princess looked around the nearly empty facility. She choked back a tear. She considered this tiny moon very dear to her. Soon, it would be blown to bits.

"One minute . . . forty-five seconds . . ."

She turned toward the kid's spacefighter; he was ready to take off and just waiting to have one last word with her.

"One minute . . . forty seconds . . ."

Their eyes locked—tears on both sides now. It appeared as if both were going to speak at the same time, when a very strange sound interrupted them. They turned to see a spacecraft swooping down out of the sky and heading right for the eastern approach to the hidden chamber.

What was this? Was one of their spacefighters returning to base? Why? Even extreme mechanical trouble was not an adequate excuse for avoiding combat under these dire circumstances.

But this craft was not a returning spacefighter. That was apparent almost immediately. It looked unlike any spacecraft those left inside the chamber had ever seen. It was not built in the standard triangular fashion that prevailed in all flying things throughout the Galaxy. This aircraft was slender, tubular. It had wings. Stranger still, it had wheels.

And it was traveling so fast that not two seconds after first spotting it, it was suddenly right in front of them, screeching to a halt about twenty feet from where the Princess and her party stood. A faint green mist was spilling from the tail end of its fuselage. Its rubber wheels sizzled on the chamber's damp concrete floor.

This strange craft had appeared so quickly, the chamber's security troops had had no time to react. Now, as the Princess watched, the bubble-shaped canopy on top of the winged machine popped open. Two men could be seen inside. One of them climbed out from the back of the cockpit and jumped down to the oil-stained floor below. Only then did the security troops go into action. They quickly surrounded the hissing spacecraft and seized the man who had jumped from it.

But the Princess raised her hand, freezing the soldiers in place. The man was wearing a long, brown cassock and a tight white collar around his neck. He looked up at the Princess, then bowed deeply. He was short, of middle age, probably close to 200 years old. His face was that of a weary man of faith caught in a very faithless part of the Galaxy.

Obviously, he was a priest.

"My apologies, your highness," he said now. "My friend and I are lost and we are seeking directions . . ."

The Princess stared back at him, incredulous.

"You're looking for directions?"

"We are, your highness," the priest said, finally straightening from his deep bow. "We took a wrong turn at the last star system and . . ."

She raised her hand, cutting him off.

"Excuse me, Padre," she said through gritted teeth. "Perhaps you haven't noticed, but we are in sort of a *situation* here. This base, this entire moon, is about to be blown to kingdom come, if you will pardon the expression. So forgive me if I seem discourteous, but you could not have picked a worse place to stop and ask for directions!"

The priest just stared back at her. He didn't look surprised or frightened. Just perplexed.

"My lady, we had no idea . . ." he began to stutter in reply. "Our approach was extremely speedy, and it was difficult to see what was . . ."

Just then, the mechanical voice blared throughout the chamber again.

"The battle star will be in position to fire in one minute and twenty-five seconds. . . ."

The Princess's features dropped a mile, as if all the air had suddenly been let out of her. She was no less pretty. But tears had come to fill her eyes.

"We are but seconds away, Father," she whispered. "Then it will all be over."

"The battle star will be in position to fire in one minute, twenty seconds. . . ."

The Princess looked down at the priest and added gloomily, "Perhaps your arrival here is the most opportune thing to happen. We all need some promise of salvation at this moment. Though I fear you might have come too late."

The priest glanced back at the strange craft he'd arrived in. Its pilot was looking out at him, his face barely visible beneath his enormous lightning bolt–adorned helmet. His body language seemed to be asking, "Just how lost *are* we?"

"One minute, fifteen seconds . . ."

More tears came to the Princess's eyes. Her companions looked very dejected as well.

Yet the priest was able to muster a slight, if anxious, smile.

He took a step forward. "Your highness, as quickly as you can, please tell me the details of your situation here."

She started to bark back at him, but now it was his turn to interrupt. He raised his hand gently to her lips.

"No time for that, child," he said firmly. "Just tell me: Who is trying to annihilate you and why?"

The Princess paused, but only for a second. Then she began talking very rapidly, telling the priest that she and her subjects were rebelling against a vile, merciless imperial force that sought to rule this part of space. This enemy's ultimate weapon, a huge battle star nearly as big as the moon itself, would soon be in a position to fire its all-powerful death ray at them. This weapon was capable of destroying entire planets. This tiny moon would prove no match for it.

While all these words were spilling out, the priest was holding the Princess's hand and staring deeply into her eyes. He was looking for something behind the words, something deeper within. Just as the doomsday voice announced there was but one minute left before the base would be destroyed, the priest put his finger to the Princess's lips again.

"Enough, my child," he said. "I understand the situation now, and what's more, I believe you."

She stopped only long enough to catch her breath.

"And now you will perform the last rites?" she asked, a small measure of defiance returning to her voice.

The priest shook his head. "No, your highness," he said softly. "Now, I will attempt to save you."

He walked back to the strange spacecraft and had a hurried conversation with the pilot. The pilot shrugged twice and wearily adjusted his crash helmet. The priest stepped back from the craft, and the pilot lowered the canopy again. The pilot could be seen pushing some controls in front of him.

Then, suddenly, the craft disappeared.

Or at least that's what it looked like.

Actually, the odd flying machine had exited the base so quickly, it just seemed to disappear. Its speed was so swift, it couldn't be adequately measured or comprehended by the human brain. It was that fast. No one inside the chamber except the priest had ever seen anything like it. The Princess was especially stunned.

"Your friend has left you here? To die with us?" she asked the priest.

But he just shook his head. "No, your highness," he said. "In fact, he'll be right back . . ."

And no sooner were those words out of his mouth, when indeed, the strange aircraft zoomed back through the entrance portal and was again sitting on the launch ramp, no more than twenty feet away.

"What sorcery is this!" the Princess exploded.

Her security troops surrounded the aircraft in force this time. No less than six soldiers ran forward and grabbed the priest.

But then came the sound of an incredible explosion from

above. Suddenly, the walls of the hidden base were shaking violently. The sky outside its portals turned fiery red. Billions of pieces of flaming material were streaking through the tiny moon's atmosphere, creating a spectacular if frightening light show. Then cheering could be heard from the hidden base's control center.

But what had happened?

The pilot climbed out of his spacecraft and approached the Princess. He bowed deeply as well, the proper thing to do in front of a princess—any princess.

"Your enemy is no more," the pilot announced bluntly. "You and your people are safe again."

The Princess remained frozen to the spot. She still wasn't getting the drift of all this. The pilot recognized her plight and reached into the breast pocket of his black flight suit. He came out with a viz disk.

"This will explain it all," he said.

But the Princess looked no more enlightened. She clapped her hands, and one of the chamber's robots raced over to her. She pushed the viz disk into a slot in its cranium. There was a click and a beep. Then a 3-D image sprang to life in midair about three feet from her deep brown eyes.

What the disk showed seemed to be impossible. It was a recording of a massive space battle, first involving up to fifty spacefighters, all of them belonging to the despised enemy of the rebels. This battle was being projected from the point of view of the very unusual winged and wheeled flying machine, its nose aglow with a bright red flame. Essentially, it showed a series of impossibly quick explosions; these were the enemy fighters simply blowing up as the strange flying machine twisted crazily through a small area of space just a hundred miles above the moon's surface. In the background, the black, grim-looking battle star was moving into position.

With the enemy fighters so quickly dispatched, the flying machine headed right toward the enormous ball of metal. Suddenly, it was flying through the battle star's canyon of external channels. At one point, the flying machine's nose lit up again. The rays it spewed forth went down one of the shafts adjacent to the battle star's main channel.

There was a bright flash, and the battle station was blown to bits. The explosion was so bright, it washed out the visuals for a few seconds. By the time the viz disk recovered, it was showing the strange winged craft entering the hidden chamber again. Then the disk went blank.

These images had lasted but a few seconds, and even then, it was evident that they had been slowed down to insure that they made some kind of sense.

Still it was not an easy thing for the Princess to comprehend.

"Again, what is this trickery?" she asked tartly. "This can not be real. The only possible explanation is that your flying machine is so fast it was able to destroy all of our enemy's fighters and the battle star in the barest fraction of a second."

The priest smiled and took her hand again. "That's exactly what happened, my dear," he said. "And actually in less than a thousandth of a second, as normally measured."

Just then, another announcement came over the hangar's audio system. The speaker's formerly morose tone had changed completely. It was confirming what the viz disk seemed to show. There were no more enemy fighters, no more enemy battle star. All space around the tiny moon was clear of adversaries, and the rebel squadron was returning intact as well. A great cheer went up around the chamber.

"But how?" the Princess asked, almost pleading with the pilot and the priest now. "You must tell me."

"I don't know myself, your highness," the pilot finally replied. "I am just grateful to be able to help your cause."

"But . . . you saved us all," she began stammering. "What payment could I possibly . . ."

The priest stepped forward again. "As I said before," he began. "We were looking for directions."

The Princess shook her head and quickly called for the highest intelligence officer within the hidden war chamber. He arrived a few seconds later. After a quick chat with both the pilot and the priest, the intelligence man conjured up a satchel of old star charts and handed it to them.

And finally the Princess was smiling.

"I don't suppose you want to stick around and maybe have a glass of wine with me?" she asked the pilot.

The pilot's eyes went wide. He began to reply when the priest interrupted again.

"Many pardons, your grace," he said. "But we really do have a schedule to keep."

He began bowing as he was backing up, the pilot stumbling along behind him.

"But can't we stay, just for a drink?" the pilot was asking the priest.

The priest did not reply, he simply continued nudging the pilot back toward the strange flying machine.

"Well, at least ask her why that guy is wearing a hair suit," the pilot pleaded weakly with the priest, pointing to the strange figure standing mute behind the Princess.

"I will not," the priest shot back in reply. "Some things are best left unknown."

With that, they climbed back into the odd flying machine. There was a sudden glow from its engine compartment, and then it simply disappeared again.

The Princess blinked her eyes, the kid and the other guy did as well. The goon in the hair suit let out a loud, fake growl.

The Princess looked at the viz disk and just shook her head.

"Who *were* those guys?" she whispered.

2

No one knew why Hawk Hunter's flying machine went so fast.

Its design had come to him in a dream one night shortly after he found himself stranded on the planet called Fools 6. But while the fact that the craft looked like nothing else in the Galaxy might have been a function of his slumbering vision, why it could move the way it did was the result of pure chance—or coincidence—even though there were many learned minds scattered among the stars that would argue that these two things did not exist.

In order to power his flying machine, Hunter had hooked up a series of what he thought were identical energy transfer devices taken from an ancient Empire ship he'd found wrecked over the hill from his dwelling on Fools 6. The crashed vessel turned out to be a Kaon Bombardment ship, a frightening military vessel that had the capability to freeze time itself over a battlefield, allowing its troops to slay their enemies, literally at leisure.

Hunter's seemingly random mating of the Kaon ship's Time Shifter components to the business end of his machine's power plant gave it the ability to travel very, very fast. So fast, in fact, there was no way to measure its velocity in terms of distance traveled. It was better to simply measure it in terms of time elapsed, usually from here to there in a thousandth of a second.

But Hunter's flying machine was both mysterious and unique. Though only the size of a standard Empire spacefighter, it had interstellar capability, and they did not. In fact, Hunter's craft could travel faster between star systems than a gigantic Empire Starcrasher battle cruiser, and they were able to do it at a speed of two light-years a minute.

He and the priest—his name was Pater Tomm—were looking for a lost planet.

It was called Tonk. It was located in what was once known as the Zorro-Wilco star system. Hunter and Pater Tomm had spent the last six weeks working their way across the midsection of the Five-Arm, the fifth of the Galaxy's multiple spiraling arms, trying to find a way to this place. It was not an easy thing to do. This part of the Five-Arm was on the edge of the Fringe itself, that being the halo of outlying stars that, in many places, marked the farthermost reaches of the Milky Way galaxy. The midsection of the Five-Arm was particularly dangerous space to travel through. Considered almost desolate when compared to the massive clusters of stars closer to the center of the Galaxy, there were still tens of millions of systems out here, they supported hundreds of millions of planets, and many of those planets had people on them. Lots of people meant lots of opportunity for disagreements and war, and Hunter and Pater Tomm had seen their share of both on this journey.

In many places, way out here, war was simply a way of life. The recent dustup on the tiny jungle moon had hardly been an isolated incident. In the six weeks since the end of the noble but ultimately disastrous war on Zazu-Zazu, Hunter and Pater Tomm had found themselves involved in no less than a dozen other conflicts simply because many sectors of the space they were traveling through also served as interplanetary combat zones.

Most of these wars had a clear good guy and bad guy, and when the cause seemed just and the conflict unavoidable, Hunter and Pater Tomm had chosen sides and fought with the good guys. They did this in return for navigation data or information that might bring them closer to the elusive stepping-stone of Tonk. These enlistments rarely lasted for more than a day. Once they'd signed on and Hunter was able to do his thing with his magnificent (some said enchanted) flying machine—well, the conflict was usually decided quickly thereafter, and always in the favor of their employers. And while Pater Tomm despised the notion that they were, in effect, serving as mercenaries, he knew this was a necessary evil if they wanted to find their way through this vast, troubled neighborhood of the Five-Arm and reach their first goal.

That Tonk was so damn hard to find was in itself very strange. It was once the most prominent planet in this part of space. At one time, Tonk had been a major spaceship rebuild-and-repair facility, boasting customers from thousands of light years around. Ship owners and government officials would wait up to a decade to have their massive ion-ballast space cruisers cored out, restored, and renovated on Tonk. At its peak, more than one hundred million people lived on the smallish planet, and every one of them was filthy rich. And how rich was that? At one point, the citizens had talked about reigniting Tonk's dying sun, a massive space engineering project. But alas, this proved too costly even for them. When the light from Tonk's sun eventually began to fade, just about everyone on the planet packed up and blasted off, heading for other, brighter places to live.

All that had been two thousand years ago. Tonk was so far off the beaten track now, it didn't even appear on any of the standard star charts, at least, none that Hunter and Pater Tomm had picked up in their six-week odyssey. It had simply become lost.

Finding Tonk was important, though. For it was here, Pater Tomm believed, a man lived who might know how they could get closer to their ultimate destination: the star system known as the Home Planets.

If it existed at all.

Shortly after leaving the jungle moon, they found their way to a desolate planet called Sigma-TKE.

It was second out from a dying white dwarf sun, the only puffed planet remaining in a small system of five. It was very out of the way, which was essential, because on top of everything else, Hunter was also a wanted man. He was AWOL from the Empire's military forces, and as an officer, the penalty for such a crime was banishment to some uncharted three-digit dimension, essentially a sentence worse than death.

But was anybody really looking for him? Had word of his desertion reached all the way back to Earth yet? He didn't know.

It took six weeks to traverse the Galaxy, and that's about how long he'd been gone. Maybe not quite yet, but he had to assume that somebody would be sent out to track him down eventually. Until then, he knew it was crucial to lowball his true identity, stay off the more beaten interstellar pathways, and concentrate on finding a way to the Home Planets, that place from where the Freedom Brigade was thought to have come. The place Hunter believed in every fiber of his being was calling him home.

He landed the flying machine on the remote highlands of Sigma-TKE and did a quick ground-level environmental check. The planet's puff was still adequate, though the surface of the place was entirely desert, meaning the air would be dry. Pater Tomm replicated some food and drink and lit a huge fire. Flames were good for the soul, the priest said, and Hunter could not disagree with him. For the first time in a long time, he set aside his crash helmet and loosened his flight suit. He felt the strain finally begin to lift from his shoulders.

They ate and drank and watched the wash of stars come out above their heads. This star system might have been isolated, but it was beautiful nevertheless. As they turned away from its pale sun, the night sky became filled with tiny bright white lights. These were moonlets, zillions of them, orbiting the desert planet, comprising a ring more readily found circling a gas giant. It made for a very elegant spectacle while they took their evening meal.

Once done, Pater Tomm pulled out the old star charts given to them by the rebels' intelligence officer. The priest refilled his wine cup and began to spread the parchments out on the flat, open ground. Leaning forward on dusty knees, electronic magnifying glass in one hand, his quadtrol in the other, he began poring over the maps almost as if they were ancient religious texts, which in some ways they were.

Some of the charts were intricately inscribed and provided high detail for those star systems once considered important. Others simply presented thousands of connected dots punched into an otherwise featureless map. Either way, they made little sense to Hunter. Even during his brief tenure as a military officer of the Fourth Empire, he could never understand the freaking things, and this collection was no different. While bearing a reputation for being isolated and sparse, this part of the mid–Fifth Arm actually looked damned crowded to him. Trying to wend one's way through the millions of star clusters and systems just on luck and pluck alone would take a few thousand years, even in a vessel as speedy as his own. Yet he couldn't imagine the ancient maps making that task any simpler, just the opposite, in fact.

Tomm, on the other hand, knew how to read the old star charts. He was what the ancients called a navigator. Hunter was not. So he sat back and tended the wine bottle, leaving the heavy thinking to the priest.

He knew it would be better that way.

They had just drained their fourth mug of wine when Pater Tomm suddenly came to life.

"Very interesting. . . ." Hunter heard him whisper.

"You've found something, Padre?"

"Alas, it is not our goal," Tomm said without looking up. "But I am familiar with some of the more notorious star systems nearby. Here is one known as Zorro-Beta. Tonk's star system used to be called Zorro-Wilco. . . . You see? They seem related, which means they may be close."

He flipped over to the next star chart, the twelfth of nearly one hundred parchments. At the same time, he held his cup out, hinting that Hunter should refill it. The pilot complied. Pater Tomm slurped his star juice noisily.

"This might take a while," he said. "You should get some sleep, don't you think?"

Hunter could only shrug in reply. He wasn't into sleeping, now or ever. Sleep was time wasted, or at least that's what he'd come to believe in the past few weeks. This was not some video game he was playing here. He was on a quest to find a system of planets that might not exist, at the same time possibly being pursued by the Empire, maybe with a price on his head. It didn't seem right to waste a single second out here falling asleep. He had to get to the Home Planets; he had to find out if they were real. He felt this deeply, almost painfully, way, way down in his psyche. Why? Because the soldiers he'd found on Zazu-Zazu were more like him than anyone he'd met since coming to this strange time and place. He had to find those people again, to find their home. To see if there were any more like him.

How could he possibly sleep with all that going on?

He glanced back at Tomm, studying the maps feverishly now.

Hunter had his excuse, but what was driving Pater Tomm on this quest? The priest had hooked up with the Freedom Brigade shortly after their arrival on Zazu-Zazu, providing them with spiritual comfort as they faced what would ultimately become their final battle. He had even gone so far as to journey to several Fringe systems seeking weapons for his adopted unit, frustrating sojourns as it turned out. But Tomm was there when the climactic battle began, and he'd seen the last of the Freedom Brigade disappear in the smoke of that battle. Later, he'd helped Hunter search among the dead, looking for one last soul who could point them in the right direction to the Home Planets.

They'd found that poor vessel, lying close to death on the battlefield. And he'd given them a few tantalizing clues before drawing his final breath. His last words were spent practically begging the priest to lead Hunter back to the Brigade's home system. Though he had little idea even where to start, Pater Tomm had agreed, and their journey had begun soon afterward. But was it simply the strength of that promise—the honor of his given word—that pushed him forward? Or was it the vocation that *every* soul in the Galaxy needed ministering, even those who dwelled in places that might not even exist?

Or was Tomm simply weary of traipsing from planet to planet, system to system, cluster to cluster, trying to single-handedly save the spirits of those many billions who inhabited the girdle of the Five-Arm?

Even after these six weeks, Hunter still didn't know. But the most likely answer, he finally decided, was probably a bit of all three.

He drained his wine and spread out a sheet of pressed gold. It was the material of choice for sleeping under the stars, and eventually he did decide to lie down upon it, if just to stretch his tired bones. The light display above him grew even more fantastic. He quickly realized that all of the moonlets were in separate but very close orbits; they were of varying sizes and shapes, as well. This meant that while some were moving across the sky at a relatively slow pace, others seemed to be streaking by. It looked like pandemonium, like the moonlets were but a heartbeat away from colliding with each other and ending the display with one massive pulverization. But then Hunter came to realize that this wasn't chaos, it was a dance. A dance between gravity and mass, choreographed long ago, millions of years perhaps. He took a deep breath and felt the dry air of the little desert world warm up his oxygen-saturated lungs. It was sad in a way. The moonlets' ballet was an amazing example of cosmic beauty, way out here, on a small forgotten planet, in a long-lost star system, with no one else to see it except him and Pater Tomm. . . .

He closed his eyes, just for a moment, and by habit tried to conjure up an image of Earth. It seemed like hundreds of years had passed since he'd been there. In fact, sometimes it seemed like he'd never been there at all. But the vision that came to him now was one of a shimmering diamond, reflecting the jewel-like quality of the mother planet. Revolving around that warm, yellow sun, the oceans, the ancient bridges, the floating cities. Everywhere buildings soaring, the star catchers lighting up the night. No wonder it all seemed like a dream. There was no place like it anywhere else. Nothing even came close.

Earth meant something else to him. Close to that part of his soul that had sent him on this strange quest, was the vision of the beautiful Xara, Princess of the Galaxy, and daughter of O'Nay, the Emperor himself. When he thought of Earth, he was really thinking of Xara. Her eyes. Her shape. Her hair. She, too, was a jewel, a living jewel from some fantastic diamond sun, a creature of startling beauty.

She had come into his life right after he'd won the famous Earth Race; at first it was to save him from the clutches of her rather dysfunctional family and later to help him take the first step in his search for someplace to call home. But faster than his flying machine could ever go, he had fallen for her and fallen hard. Space was curved, gravity could be a bitch, and he had been in love with Xara at first sight. These were the only three things Hunter was sure of these days. Everything else was really up for grabs.

He wondered what she was doing at that very moment. Was she asleep? Awake? Lying in the arms of another? Or was she staring up at the stars, just as he was doing? Might she be thinking about him, just as he was thinking about her? What were the chances of that?

He turned away from the moonlet parade and looked toward the thick band of stars that dominated the sky fifty degrees above the horizon. If he tried hard enough, would he be able to see right through the center of the Galaxy? Could he see beyond that brilliant clutter of a hundred billion stars, through its middle and clear to the other side? Because if he could, then somewhere way, way out there, was Earth.

And that's where Xara was.

"By God's good grace!"

Hunter was awake in a shot. He sat bolt upright, his blaster pistol in hand, pointing in all directions at once.

"What is it?" he yelled, only to be surprised that it was light again, and that the night had gone and had taken the moonlets' light show with it. His face felt slightly warm; a very dull sun was peeking up over the horizon.

So much for not falling asleep . . .

And now Pater Tomm was standing before him, cassock dirty, collar unlatched, a wine-stained grin reflecting the early-morning light. The priest didn't smile very often. When he did, it was usually for good reason.

"Favorable news, Padre?" Hunter asked him now.

"Bingo that, my brother," the priest replied, holding up what must have been the oldest star chart of them all. "For I have found it. I finally know how to get to Tonk."

3

Hunter had never been to an 8-Ball system before.

These were collections of planets stuck orbiting a nearly depleted star, one that was just a step away from becoming a full-fledged black dwarf. There was precious little light in an 8-Ball system. Sometimes the illumination coming from any gas-giant planets on hand was a hundred times brighter than that being thrown off by the system's dying, shrinking sun. This, and the fact that the star could go nova at any moment and obliterate everything for millions of miles around, made 8-Balls very strange places to call home. Who lived in an 8-Ball system? Cutthroats, murderers, and criminals, mostly. Or people on the run. Or people who simply hated other people. Whatever the reason, living the 8-Ball life was not for the weak of heart.

This one was appropriately nicknamed Dim Bulb 3. It held thirteen planets. Three were gas giants; the rest were rocks. When the ancient puffers reached this part of the Galaxy thousands of years before, they'd apparently bypassed the sickly sun and engineered two of the giants to revolve on roughly parallel orbits. The intention was to give a semblance of daylight to the solid planets floating nearby, but it had been a halfhearted affair, even back then. As a result, the dim light from the coupled gas giants provided only half of what would be considered normal sunlight. This meant a system with lots of shadows, lots of murk, lots of places to hide.

The fifth planet in this unsavory bunch was Tonk.

It was 238 light-years from Sigma-TKE to Dim Bulb 3. Hunter's flying machine covered the distance in just under two hours, using what he considered cruising speed: two light-years a minute, the same speed as an Empire Starcrasher at full throttle. While his speed could be unlimited—he really didn't know—he still had to consider the wear and tear on the rest of his craft. He figured if the empire ships held together at two light years a minute, there was a good chance his would too. Anything faster than that for extended periods of time tended to peel the paint off his rig.

They found Tonk right away and entered orbit around the gloomy little world. Its past glory long gone, Tonk was now a graveyard planet, a place where old spaceships came to die. Graveyard planets were the result of a strange space-faring custom. When an interstellar vessel came to the end of its useful life, there was really nothing else its owner could do but crash it into a planet or send it into a sun. Sending an old ship into a sun was considered very bad luck in just about every part of the Galaxy. On the Five-Arm it was almost never done. On the other hand, crashing dying ships onto a graveyard planet was a very strong tradition here. It was supposed to bring clusters of good luck. It also meant that the planet soon became a scrap heap for ion movers looking for cheap parts. These people were rarely model citizens, either.

So Hunter and Tomm were now orbiting a graveyard planet in an 8-Ball system; it really didn't get much more depressing than that. Hunter engaged his long-range acquisition systems and did a scan of Tonk's major hemispheres. The visuals began flowing back immediately. They said there were more than twenty-five thousand space wrecks on Tonk, most in advanced stages of atom decay. As the materials of an ion-ballast vessel slowly disintegrated, their molecules became so saturated with ultragamma radiation, a fine gray mist was produced. This fog tended to hang over everything. This was why Tonk was colored sickly gray. Gray air, gray skies, gray water running underground. Gray everywhere, dark and sooty, the color of nothing good.

And as if Tonk needed any further negative vibes, its puff was slowly leaking away, too. Several millennia of industrial fumes had defiled the original artificial atmosphere, and it had sprung many leaks over the last ten centuries. It was so bad now that when it rained, which was often, the precipitation came down not in water droplets but in dirty gray blobs.

Dirty gray blobs would not do the glossy finish of Hunter's sleek flying machine any good. Indeed, ultrafast spaceflight had given the strange, winged craft a glow of its own, one which he hoped to maintain.

But looking down on the poor excuse of a planet, Hunter's intuition hinted that messing up the buggy's finish might be the least of his problems here.

Oddly, it was on this dirty little speck that they hoped to find a man who could help them enormously on their quest.

His given name was the rather unwieldy Lezz Dezz-Klaaz, aka Son 99. But he was more famously known as the Great Klaaz. Klaaz was a fabled starship captain and interstellar hero. He'd roamed the Five-Arm for hundreds of years, lending his considerable talent for military strategy to the most noble causes. He'd led hundreds of campaigns, some of such breadth they involved defending entire star clusters against marauding armies of space pirates and vandals. He was recognized as a Marshal of Outer Space by the militaries of no less than three dozen planets. His image adorned the aluminum coins of seven star systems. His face appeared on the flags of several more.

Just barely out of the seminary, Tomm had served as chaplain for several of Klaaz's armies, and the two men had become close friends a couple centuries before. When his full-time fighting days finally ended, the Great Klaaz, always a man with stars in his eyes, bought into a very crazy notion: reviving Tonk to its former glory. The idea was to not only rebuild the planet's immense ion-revitalization bays, but to make Tonk the cultural, political, and military center of the mid–Five-Arm again—and try once more to reignite its sun. He joined a clutch of like-minded dreamers, but the task proved more difficult than sealing off a seventeen-star cluster from the Interstellar Huns. After just a few decades, the dreamers gave up and moved on—all except Klaaz.

The last Pater Tomm had heard, Klaaz was still trying to make Tonk work.

All by himself.

• • •

Tomm had heard the last known domicile of the Great Klaaz was said to be an ancient castle, made entirely of burned ice, located at one of Tonk's two arctic poles.

After two orbital circuits, Hunter's long-range acquisition scan finally located a huge structure sitting nearly on top of the planet's north pole. Even though a blizzard was in full blow across Tonk's high arctic region, this structure was so enormous that, once acquired, it registered hot and solid on Hunter's main scan screen.

"Good Lord, look at it!" Pater Tomm exclaimed, studying the image over Hunter's shoulder. "Have you ever seen such a thing as this?"

Hunter shook his head no. Never.

This was not just a castle. This was a fortress, with hundreds of spires and parapets and weapons mounts, an immense sparkling mountain of burned ice that soared nearly a half mile into the sky. The outer walls were more than a thousand feet high; they encompassed an area at least a couple miles square. Running like spokes from the dozen or so main gates, tubes built just above the surface led to clutches of smaller buildings next to the main structure. From one hundred miles up, they looked like tiny cities.

The place seemed fit for a hero of such stature as described by Pater Tomm. Hunter imagined there was a huge army in place behind these walls, with massive amounts of firepower on hand. Maintaining a well-armed fortress on the edge of nowhere—there was something Hunter could admire about that. He already regarded this man Klaaz with honor. It was a great warrior who was smart enough to know that one had to have muscle to back up his good fortune. Who knew the wealth of information such a man could provide for them? For the first time in this long, tiring trip, Hunter actually felt that they might be getting somewhere.

But then he ordered his LRAS to zoom in—just to get a better look at this magnificent monstrosity. It showed something entirely different from the view in orbit. From this perspective, it first appeared that the centuries had not been so kind to this ancient place. At least half of the spires of the main quarter were in the process of deterioration. Some of the fortress's outer walls were slowly crumbling away, too. Hunter telescoped his scan device even further; soon they were looking at an extreme close-up of the main structure. There was more evidence of decline here. Not only were many of the soaring spires in disrepair, the roofs of several attached buildings had caved in as well. In fact, there were hundreds of holes and craters pockmarking the entire building.

That's when a more startling truth became apparent: There was more than the harsh weather and time at work here. Hunter recognized battle damage when he saw it. This huge structure looked as if it had suffered thousands of massive weapons hits recently. More extensive damage could be seen around the compound's smaller buildings. Even through the dirty gray blizzard, smoke from recent explosions was clearly blowing in the wind.

Alarmed, Hunter called over his shoulder to Pater Tomm, "I know your friend is beloved in these parts. Any chance he made some enemies out here, too?"

"A few, maybe," was the priest's muted reply.

Hunter pulled back the LRAS and surveyed the area immediately surrounding the battered ice fort. What it registered hardly surprised him now. Two huge armies were encamped close by the fortress, one to the north, the other to the south. Though hidden by the storm, it was obvious both bivouacs were substantial in size. They boasted extensive barracks complexes, power-producing systems, and gigantic weapons arrays, including enormous Z-gun blasters.

The situation below suddenly became very clear: The ice fortress was under armed siege.

Tomm groaned as Hunter put the flying machine into a steep dive through the dirty atmosphere.

"God's children always manage to find each other's throats," the priest whispered, holding on for dear life as they plunged through the grimy clouds. "Even way out here."

The flying machine quickly descended to 500 feet and sped above the dirty surface, approaching the battered ice fort from the south. About one mile out from the fort's main wall, a sheet of blaster fire suddenly appeared just off the flying machine's nose; the barrage came not from the castle's defenses but from forward outposts belonging to one of the besieging armies.

Hunter simply pushed his power lever forward and did a lightning-quick bank to avoid the enemy fire. The maneuver worked to perfection but also managed to turn Pater Tomm onto his head. Just as quickly, Hunter pulled back on the power, banked hard right, then hard left, righting the elderly priest again. Another jink, another jag, and they were suddenly over the wall. One last dip, and an instant later the flying machine came screeching to a halt just inside the ice fort's main gate.

It was quickly surrounded by heavily armed troops.

Hunter couldn't believe it. True, he had approached the landing spot at high speed, and this tended to blur one's vision for a few moments, but he could have sworn the courtyard was empty before he set down upon it.

Yet now, scraping the frozen condensation from the inside of his canopy, he could see dozens, no hundreds—no thousands of armed soldiers forming concentric rings around his aircraft. It was snowing fiercely, and the wind was blowing hard, so Hunter could not get a good look at them. But each soldier appeared to be holding a gigantic blaster rifle with a massive ray gun as a side arm. They were dressed in harsh blue and white uniforms, ones that seemed hard and flexible at the same time, and their helmets were opaque glass globes, their features barely distinguishable beneath. Hunter had envisioned a massive army inside this place. At the moment, it seemed as if he'd been all too right.

He spoke over his shoulder to Tomm: "Well, at least your friend has plenty of company down here with him."

But again, Pater Tomm seemed to know better. "Maybe," he replied cautiously. "But then again, maybe not."

At that moment, Hunter saw the hundred or so soldiers standing just off the nose of his plane raise their blaster rifles at him. The soldiers standing off to the left and right did the same thing as well.

"These boys are getting serious, Padre. Maybe we should have called first?"

"Patience, my brother," Tomm said, tapping his shoulder. "Let's see what happens."

See what happens? The way Hunter figured it, they only had one option here: Depart the area in the blink of an eye. But Pater Tomm had other ideas. Suddenly, the priest began banging furiously on the inside canopy glass.

"Open it, my brother!" he was telling Hunter excitedly. "I'm convinced we have nothing to fear here!"

Hunter had to disagree. The hundred or so soldiers in front of him were taking dead aim at the flying machine. Other soldiers were now popping up along the battered walls, and they were aiming down at them as well. Hunter's aircraft was a bit magical, but it was not invulnerable. He tried to point all this out to Pater Tomm in as few words as he could.

But still the priest kept banging on the glass, insisting that Hunter let him out. So with a shrug, he did. He hit the canopy release button and the aircraft's hat lifted up with a whoosh.

All Hunter could see was snow and weapons muzzles, and he certainly didn't need an extra sense of perception to know those blasters were just seconds away from opening fire.

But Pater Tomm was undeterred. He literally climbed over the pilot's position, grappled his way out of the crowded cockpit, and stepped out onto the fuselage itself. Kicking down the access panels with his feet, he quickly reached the ground and disappeared into the gale. The snow was blowing so heavily, Hunter lost sight of him in an instant.

"Jessuzz, Padre!" he yelled. "Wait!"

But it was no good. He was gone.

That's when something very strange happened. There was a sudden explosion off to Hunter's right. He saw the flash of fire and the puff of smoke for only a second before they were blown away by the wind, but the rumble under his airplane had been severe. No sooner had this passed when another explosion rocked the courtyard, this one off to his left and closer to the ice castle itself.

Another explosion went off. This time he saw the ball of smoke and fire come right over the high wall, as if it had been lobbed from somewhere on the other side of the thousand-foot parapet. Another followed right behind it, and another after that. Hunter knew what these things were: depleted-ion artillery shells. Their fiery trails were unmistakable. One of the encircling armies was bombarding the fort.

Another barrage went over his head and impacted on the north wall of the frozen fortress. The noise was deafening; everything shuddered within. A moment later, another stream of blaster shells smashed into the western wall. Then another landed at the foot of the castle's second highest tower. It began swaying dangerously; it looked as if the 1,200-foot structure would come tumbling down at any moment.

More explosions. More fire. More smoke. But here was the strange thing: The hundreds of soldiers surrounding Hunter's aircraft had not moved a muscle. No dropping to the ground and covering up, no quick dispersal to seek shelter from the explosions. The soldiers just stood there, frozen in place, their rifles still pointing directly at his head.

Very odd . . .

Hunter knew he had to get moving. He wasn't about to leave Tomm behind in a place like this. So he punched the canopy up again and dove right from the cockpit to the snowy ground below. He landed hard, going in flat on his face, his mouth and nostrils instantly full of grimy snow. Still, he was able to roll out of the snowbank and pull a small ivory box from his pocket.

Pushing a small button on the top of the box, he activated a long, wide, green beam that quickly engulfed his flying machine. In less than a microsecond, the aircraft dissipated into an emerald mist, which then flowed back into the small box, dragging every atom contained in the flying machine along with it. The device was called a Twenty 'n Six. It allowed the user to infinitesimally condense solid objects and send them into the twenty-sixth dimension, (which was essentially contained within the small box), where they could be kept in relative safety.

Though instantly wet and cold, Hunter breathed a sigh of relief. At least his aircraft was out of harm's way.

Now, suddenly, Pater Tomm was at his side. More ion blasts came raining down on the courtyard.

"Do you know what's going on here, my brother?" the priest screamed in Hunter's ear.

Hunter began nodding frantically, pushing the priest down into the snow as another ion blast went off close by.

"These explosions are real . . . but the soldiers are fake!" he yelled back to the priest.

Even with a face full of slush, the padre managed a smile.

"You catch on very quickly my son," he yelled back. "Very quickly, indeed!"

They both scrambled to their feet and started running. There was a door about two hundred feet away from them; it led inside the ice fortress itself. They headed for it with all due haste. The explosions were still going off around them, and the soldiers were still firmly in place. But Hunter now was seeing that the debris and shrapnel being kicked up by the explosions was going right through the phalanx of frozen soldiers. In reality, this storm of high-speed, highly irradiated metals should have sliced right through the small legion, causing an ocean of blood and gore.

But that did not happen for one simple reason: These soldiers weren't soldiers at all. They were holograms. Projections. Fakes.

It took some more zigging and zagging, but finally the two men reached the relative safety of the huge door leading into the ice fort.

It was locked.

Tomm started pounding on the door. Another explosion went off close by. The door did not budge. More explosions, two of which were uncomfortably close. Tomm pounded louder, but again to no avail. Finally, Hunter drew out his blaster pistol and aimed it at the door's substantial lock. But before he could engage the trigger, Tomm reached up and pulled the barrel down.

"No, wait, my friend," he urged Hunter. "I'm sure they're just a little slow in answering the door."

Hunter started to protest, but then, sure enough, they saw the huge metal bolt running through the center of the lock begin to move slowly. Make that very slowly. It took what seemed like forever, but finally the lock sprang loose, and the door flew wide open. Hunter and Tomm tumbled inside.

No sooner did they regain their footing when another explosion went off close to where they'd been standing just seconds before. The huge door took most of the blast, but the concussion was enough to knock Hunter's crash helmet nearly halfway around his head. Temporarily blinded, he heard the huge door slam behind him.

He straightened his helmet to discover a dark figure was standing before them. They were in a vestibule of sorts, but it was nearly pitch black inside, so Hunter could only see an outline of this person. By the size of it though, he thought it had to be a child. But then a candle was lit, and by its light Hunter finally saw this person was actually a tiny, bent-over ancient-looking man wearing a garish red and yellow uniform, old, worn-down boots, a severely dented space helmet, and a frayed weapons belt, which held the most pathetically rusted sword imaginable.

Tomm immediately leaped forward and embraced the man. The old-timer did his best to return the gesture; he was actually trying to laugh with joy, but he had not yet caught enough of his breath to let out anything more than a gleeful wheeze. There was no doubt, though, that he was very happy to see Pater Tomm.

The priest turned back to Hunter and said, "Can you believe it? Here is the man himself! Answering his own door."

But Hunter was having a hard time processing this information.

"Do you mean?" he asked in a mumble. "That this is—"

"Yes!" Tomm shouted. "Behold the Great Klaaz!"

But this guy looked positively ancient. His beard was long enough to touch the frozen ground.

"Padre," Hunter replied. "Surely you must mean this is Klaaz's *grandfather*."

But Tomm waved his words away. "No, my brother," he said. "This is Klaaz himself!"

Hunter took another look at the very elderly, very broken-down soldier and uttered just one word: *"Damn."*

This is not what he had expected.

Klaaz was finally able to get some air into his frozen lungs. "Tomm, my brother! Are you really here? Or am I dead and just dreaming?"

"I am here old friend." Tomm replied.

Klaaz wrapped the priest in a weak bear hug.

"We have waited too long for this moment!" he croaked. "You are not only my confessor, you are one of the bravest soul seekers of our times!"

Pater Tomm shook his head. "It is *you* who are the hero, Klaaz! Entire star systems speak your name in their histories. . . ."

"I just did my job." Klaaz replied with a wink.

Pater Tomm opened his mouth to say something further, but a terrifying screech drowned him out. An ion shell had impacted right on the main door. The sudden green glow was a dead giveaway. That, and the ear-splitting noise.

"Quickly!" Klaaz said, although he began moving quite slowly. "We must get below!"

They made their way down a long, dark corridor that led deeper into the castle.

Hunter had never seen burned ice before; now it was all around him. Actually, they were blocks of ice saturated with gamma radiation, so much so they looked and felt like glass.

The walls of the castle were made of huge blocks of the stuff. Each one appeared as if it had a faint yellow flame glowing from within, the eternal, if diminished by-product of the massive gamma bombardment. Though the decay of the fort's interior made the glowing blocks of ice look more like gigantic, dirty diamonds, the place must have been stunning when first built many centuries ago.

They eventually reached a kind of subchamber about five hundred feet below ground level. There was a dull lamp hovering near the ceiling here, and it was noticeably warmer. The Great Klaaz stopped, needing to catch a breath.

Tomm needed a break as well. He produced a flask of slow-ship wine and offered it to Klaaz. The old man took it without a moment's hesitation and nearly drained the vessel dry.

"So, you old dog!" Tomm yelled at Klaaz, retrieving what was left of his wine supply. "All the stories I have heard about you were true!"

The old man smiled widely, displaying a mouthful of cracked and yellowed teeth. "You know better than to believe more than half of them, Padre," he said with another wheeze. It was strange. Hunter couldn't recall ever seeing anyone so old so happy.

Klaaz pried the flask from Tomm's hands and drank once again.

"After all these years, dear brother," he said to the priest, "you have arrived at a very interesting moment!"

"You do seem to be in a sort of bind here, my friend," Tomm agreed.

Klaaz wiped his mouth with his sleeve. "Obviously, a dire situation exists, Padre," he said. "The enemy beyond the walls number more than twenty thousand. They are a gang of the usual suspects: space pirates and no-goodnik mercs who seek something that does not belong to them."

"How long has this been going on, my brother?"

"Centuries—or so it seems," Klaaz said with a cough. "You saw my holo-army. Impressive, no?"

"I've not seen such trickery in two centuries," Tomm replied diplomatically, "and I suspect it was an ancient strategy even back then."

"It was and still is," Klaaz admitted. "But in case you have not noticed, there is a bit of desperation in the air we are breathing."

Above them the sound of more blaster barrages could be heard landing inside the fort's high walls.

"But you've been able to hold out, my brother," Tomm said. "You must have *some* kind of brilliant defense in place—"

Klaaz cackled loudly.

"I have six power-gravity fields surrounding this place," he said. "And they are really the only reason the Huns haven't stormed the gates already. Trouble is, all six fields are degrading very rapidly. I mean, your craft had no problem getting through, did it?"

The priest shook his head solemnly. Klaaz shrugged again. "Their integrity must be worse than I thought."

Tomm let his friend drain the flask.

"My old chum," he said. "Those twenty thousand soldiers outside your wall. Why are they here? What could they possibly want? You? This castle?"

"Not me or the castle, Padre," Klaaz replied. "But the people I am protecting here."

Tomm did a double take. "People? What people? You mean you aren't out here alone, my brother?"

The twinkle returned to Klaaz's eye.

"Alone?" he asked with a wink. "Hardly . . ."

They resumed walking down the long, descending hallway, Klaaz moving slowly in a kind of staggering gait. The lower tube was lit by simple proton-decay lanterns. They provided just enough light to reveal that the walls of the tunnel were adorned with faded ice paintings of Tonk's golden age. One depicted the planet as being the brightest body on the entire Five-Arm, literally the center of a small universe. Another illustrated a huge battle between thousands of spaceships of all shapes and sizes, with those from Tonk winning mightily, of course. Judging by the murky detail and the porous nature of the burned ice wall, Hunter guessed the paintings were done even before Tonk's heyday, and that was at least two thousand years ago, probably more.

They finally reached the end of the hallway to find themselves stepping onto a somewhat rickety balcony; its supports were as rusty as Klaaz's sword. The balcony looked out on an enormous chamber. Also made of burned ice, it was nearly an eighth of a mile wide with a ceiling at least five hundred feet high, and no doubt reaching the bottom layer of the courtyard itself.

Sitting in the middle of this chamber was a spacecraft. Or at least that's what Hunter thought it was. Actually, he'd never seen anything like it before. It was long and slender; its sharpened nose nearly touched the roof of the huge chamber. It had rows of portholes running down one side and was standing on three huge fins. A vast network of scaffolding surrounded it, and it was draped in power cables and tattered golden sheets. A bubble of knowledge rose up from the deep recesses of his past life and told Hunter that this was an ancient combustible-fuel rocket he was looking at, a passenger carrier built at least three thousand years before, more probably closer to four. The pictures back in the tunnel were almost recent by comparison.

Scattered around the bottom of this rocket were hundreds of tiny white bubble-top living compartments, shelters more readily found outside in a temperate battle zone, not within a frozen, dilapidated enclosure. But this was not an army encampment they were looking down on. The people below were not soldiers. They were young women. All of them beautiful, all of them dressed in the barest of clothes. Torn gowns and ripped shorts mostly, some were wearing tops, many not, as if they were stranded on some uncharted tropical world and not inside a crumbling ice fort on a very chilly dead-end planet.

Hunter saw Tomm's face blush at the first sight of all this, and even his own chest was suddenly growing warm. Two thousand beautiful women, hiding way out here? It didn't seem possible.

Was there any chance he might be dreaming this? Hunter wondered.

The women below were very quietly going about the daily routines of life. Talking, walking, sitting, eating. The balcony was about fifty feet above the living level, and those women who saw Klaaz looking out at them waved vigorously to him. Many blew kisses. The old soldier pretended to catch each one and then smack it on his own lips.

"Behold these poor women," he said among these antics. "They are the survivors of a small star system called Mutaman-Younguska. It is but a hundred ten light-years from here. Or it used to be, for the Huns that now encircle us destroyed the system five years ago, killing the few soldiers it had and blowing up all but a prison planet. Their advance forces have been pursuing these females ever since."

Pater Tomm could barely speak—a rare occasion indeed.

"But . . . how did they wind up here? With you?" he finally managed to ask.

"Their ship landed here a year or so ago," the old soldier replied. "They'd heard the Klaaz was still here on Tonk and hoped that I could help them. Trouble was, the space scum arrived not two weeks later."

He paused a moment; the smile left his face.

"A sad vision, isn't it?" he asked wistfully. "Imagine what they thought when they saw that I was just an old man, practically marooned here myself, with a fortress built by the ancients crumbling around me? Of course that's probably what you thought on your own arrival as well."

"These people came in that . . . spacecraft?" Pater Tomm asked his friend incredulously. "It seems older than this castle!"

"It might well be," Klaaz replied. "And there is a reason for that: Look at these women below. You will notice that they all possess great beauty. Mutaman-Younguska was well-known for this. Effects of a red sun, you see. Now, with all that beauty everywhere you looked, well, I guess building modern spacecraft just wasn't a priority."

"Yes. Why leave a planet so especially blessed?" Tomm blurted out, adding quickly: "Unless you had to . . ."

"Exactly, Father," Klaaz said. "You see, the Huns got hip to Mutaman-Younguska and decided they wanted these girls simply for pleasure. They are being driven by . . . what is the word for it?"

"Lust," Pater Tomm said. "It's as old as the hydrogen in the universe."

"Precisely," Klaaz said. "They are lustful. And they have not seen a real woman in decades, I suspect. That also fuels their passions. It's a bad combination, and these young women do not deserve such a fate. So here I am, trying my best to prevent it."

More girls waved. A ripple was going through the camp now, and more eyes went toward the balcony. This meant more air kisses sent Klaaz's way. He began the drill of catching them, when suddenly he stopped and realized that maybe not all of them were intended for him. It was at that moment that Klaaz's ancient eyes finally fell on Hunter. The old soldier screwed up his face in puzzlement. It was almost as if he was seeing the pilot for the first time.

"Excuse me, sir," he said. "Did I ever get your name?"

Tomm turned red again. He'd been impolite—unforgivable in some parts of the Galaxy.

"My apologies to you both," the priest said hastily. "This is my friend, Hawk Hunter. He is a pilot, as well as an explorer . . . of sorts."

Klaaz was unimpressed. "That uniform," he said directly to Hunter. "It's an odd one. Under whose flag do you fight?"

"No one at present, sir," Hunter quickly replied.

But that wasn't nearly enough of an explanation for the Great Klaaz. He studied Hunter's garb even closer, causing Hunter to shift nervously. The mostly black flight suit was different from what billions of other soldiers across the Five-Arm wore. First of all, it wasn't frayed or dirty, and it didn't look dull. It was lined with emerald thread, except for red collar stitching, and overall, its material quality was very high end. (And a bit *stylish,* to use the ancient word for it.) But it could also take a blaster shot from twenty feet away and not even register a dent. Even closer in, such a shot might not be fatal, or at least that's what Hunter had been told by the Empire quartermasters the day he'd been fitted for it. It bore red shoulder epaulets and the four gold stars on its collar, ornaments very foreign in this part of the Galaxy. A cape could be pulled out of its shoulder seam for use in bad weather. The crossed double-X symbol of the Empire's Expeditionary and Exploratory Forces adorned its chest. The overly large, lightning-bolt trimmed crash helmet only added to the oddity.

"I knew of such a uniform many years ago," Klaaz told him now, from the end of a feebly pointing finger. "The man who wore it claimed that he was lost and that he was an officer in some great empire that ruled most of the known Galaxy from a tiny planet clear on the other side."

Klaaz's eyes narrowed on Hunter. It was Pater Tomm who shifted uncomfortably now.

"I do not know the man of whom you speak," Hunter stuttered in reply.

He didn't want to go any further with this. While local interplanetary contact was routine out here, the immense Fourth

Empire was practically unknown on the Five-Arm. Much of the fifth spiral was considered yet-to-be-reclaimed territory by Imperial Earth, meaning no substantial contact had been made— yet. The stray visitor had been written and talked about down through the ages, but for the most part, many people on the Five-Arm thought life petered out somewhere near the boundary of their local super-cluster. Not unlike the Home Planets, if they'd ever heard of the Fourth Empire at all, it was through the telling of legends and myth.

This was one reason why Hunter had studiously avoided talking about the Empire with anyone he'd met out here. As an ex-officer in the Earth's advanced expeditionary forces, he knew the possible ramifications for a planet's population if they suddenly realized they were not alone in the Universe; that the Galaxy was totally inhabited and teeming with life. This was knowledge that had to be gradually absorbed. The sudden appearance of a stranger from outer space rarely sat well with a planet's collective psyche, especially one that didn't yet realize life existed beyond its own orbit. Panic, the collapse of religions and mores—when it happened, it usually wasn't very pretty. For all its faults, this was a matter still held with great concern by the Empire itself. First contact was something usually handled with great care.

In that regard, Hunter knew that any time he stepped on an isolated world out here, he was in fact an alien on that planet, with all the baggage that entailed. And of course, he did not want to call undue attention to himself, again just in case agents from that very real Empire had begun pursuing him. His trail was best left as cold as possible—reason three for keeping one's mouth shut. Though he had his suspicions, even Pater Tomm wasn't sure where Hunter was from. Not exactly, anyway. And that's the way Hunter wanted to keep it, at least for now. So his policy had been to keep his lips sealed shut and his eyes open.

Getting a new uniform someday would help, too.

Still, an uncomfortable moment hung in the air. It took Pater Tomm's quick interruption to break the spell.

"Brother Klaaz, you have a ship here. Why not simply pack up these beautiful unfortunates and blast off out of here?"

He indicated the very aged spacecraft.

"I mean, that craft is certainly old," Tomm went on. "But if it flies, then it is surely big enough for everyone to fit."

"Correct as usual, Padre," Klaaz sighed. "But you see, it's a question posed by an ancient discipline called Rocket Science. And it's a simple problem really: The ascent phase of that old stick is so slow, I just know we will be shot down in the first few seconds of flight. Alas, this has been my dilemma for months."

The old soldier paused for a long breath, then went on:

"My instincts tell me I must somehow counterattack the two armies that encircle my position . . . or at least distract them long enough for that old buster to take off and have a chance to make it into orbit. But how can I do that? I just don't know. Moreover, the combined gravity-field shield surrounding the fort would have to be lowered at least a few minutes before I attempt the very slow, vertical takeoff. If I do that, we would leave ourselves wide open to attack and, well . . ."

He let his words drift off and looked up at the ice-glass ceiling way over his head. His eyes had misted over. Hunter took a deep breath and stretched to his full height. Klaaz was not a fake; he was an authentic hero, a man who'd saved literally billions of people on the Five-Arm from the hands of various interstellar scum. And even now, after a handful of centuries, he was still trying to do the right thing. He had no massive space fleet at his disposal this time though, no endless legions of space soldiers ready to follow him into battle. This time he was alone, on one of the crappiest planets in the Milky Way, with crude projections of empty holo-soldiers as his army, and a slowly draining gravity shield as his last defense.

It was no way to exit such an illustrious career.

Pater Tomm caught Hunter studying the old soldier.

The priest leaned over and whispered to the pilot, "At the moment, Klaaz needs our help more than we need his."

Hunter just nodded. "I know."

He put his hand on Klaaz's shoulder.

"If you leave our brother Tomm to get your rocket ship ready," he told the old warrior. "I'm sure you and I can take care of the rest."

4

The larger of the two armies beseiging Klaaz's ice fort
was known as the Goth-Star BallBreakers.

Boasting more than ten thousand troops, the Goth-Stars held
most of the territory south of the battered fortress. They had
fielded an enormous arsenal of long-range Z-gun arrays, known
appropriately enough as Master Blasters. These fierce weapons
held up to ten laser-tube muzzles surrounded by dozens of
diamond-studded firing rings that lit up like so many halos
whenever the blaster mount was engaged. Weapons of this size
could deliver massive amounts of destructive power; just how
the fort's combined gravity shield had held up against them for
so long was indeed a mystery. True, because of the frigid air
above the isolated battlefield, it took each Master Blaster up to
an hour to recharge sufficiently before firing again. But still, the
siege had been going on for months.

The Goth-Stars were a quasi-mercenary army of space pirates.
They were presently in league with another pirate army, the
SpeedBall Saints, which was slowly battering the massive ice
castle from the opposite side. It would be a fifty-fifty split once
this long, drawn-out affair was over. This meant that the Goth-
Stars would acquire approximately one thousand beautiful
Mutaman-Younguska females to dispose of however they
pleased.

The Goth-Stars were holding a line about a mile south of the ice fort. They had not allowed any food or supplies to reach the beleaguered castle in months. That by these actions hundreds of frightened, innocent people were suffering inside the fort had little bearing on the Goths. In fact, many of them liked the notion of keeping their victims helpless, simply by their whim, making the inevitable invasion of the huge structure even more exciting. After all, preying on the weak and defenseless was what being a space pirate was all about.

Or so they thought.

The first real sign of trouble for the Goth-Stars came just as their front-line troops began reporting for evening chow.

Feeding thousands of hungry soldiers in arctic conditions was not an easy task. The power drain on the army's food replication units lasted for an hour or more sometimes, depending on just how hungry the horde was and how cold the weather might be outside. That's why most of the troops ate in shifts.

The top communications man for the Goth-Stars returned to his forward position after dinner to find his small corps of transmission operators looking perplexed. They were having trouble contacting their allies, the SpeedBall Saints. It was routine for the two armies to exchange targeting information before commencing the night's bombardment of the ice fort. A few stray blaster rounds could wreak havoc on a bivouacked army. This communication sought to eliminate any potential fuckups during the brief dark hours.

But try as they might, the Goth-Stars just couldn't get the Saints on the phone.

The comm officer checked their communicator readings; they all seemed to be in order. The problem was not on their end. The SpeedBalls were not as organized nor as disciplined as the Goths, so the glitch didn't come as a big surprise. Their main communicator screen could be down for a variety of reasons. Most likely the operator was drunk or asleep at the switch.

"Launch a probe," the Goth comm officer told his men. "Put a viz-screen bug inside it and buzz those jerks."

The underlings did as told. In seconds, a small rocket blasted off from the top of their comm shack and traveled twenty miles through the frigid wind and snow in just a few seconds. It was soon circling the main part of the SpeedBalls' base.

Or at least what used to be the SpeedBalls' base . . .

Because at the moment, it looked like nothing more than a string of big, black holes, slowly melting into the ice.

The comm officer stared at the viz screen; his jaw dropped to his chin.

"What the hell happened there?" he asked no one in particular. "Did those fools blow themselves up?"

Just as the comm officer turned to alert his superiors, another panel on his main communications screen started pulsating.

"What the hell is this?" one of his lowers remarked.

"Spill," the comm officer ordered him.

"It seems we have some kind of flying object, coming out of the west, with a trail originating not far from the Speedballs' position."

"A *flying* object?" the comm officer mouthed silently.

The man turned to him, his face a mask of confusion and concern. "Yes sir," he said. "It's going very fast, heading right for us."

Now this *was* odd. There were really only two kinds of flying objects in this part of the Fringe: the huge vessels that flew in space and smaller craft—space fighters, invasion shuttles, ships—which could fly inside an atmosphere, but never very fast.

Yet at that moment, something rather small yet very speedy was coming out of the black, frosty smoke that was once the location of their ally's main base. A similar object had been spotted fleeing the Goth's blaster units earlier in the day. But this time, the intent was unmistakably hostile.

A hostile threat from the air?

A strange thought came to the comm officer's mind. "Do we even *have* any weapons made to shoot down flying objects?" he asked.

The underlings looked at each other and did a group shrug.

The comm officer just shook his head. "I didn't think so," he said.

The Goth-Star front-line units occupied a mile-long, perfectly straight trench, carved out of the snow and ice about a mile south of the ice fort's front gate.

This trench was dotted with prefab combat dugouts, heated, self-sustaining units much more elaborate than anything found below Klaaz's dying fortress. Each of these units could house up to a hundred soldiers very comfortably. In between the snowball-like structures were the Master Blaster tubular arrays. Thirty-six in total, all of them were pointed at the ice fort, which dominated the horizon directly in front of them.

There was no such thing as a red alert for these front-line troops. They were responsible for little more than firing off their Master Blasters every hour or so and waiting for the eventual order to finally move on the ice fort *en masse*. They had no defensive weapons of any sort simply because they had no need for them. The weapons fire they'd faced coming from the ancient fortress had been inconsistent at best. It was the gravity shields that were keeping them out.

This lack of any true surface-to-air weaponry meant that when the object hurtling out of the west at them was first spotted, there was nothing any of the Goth-Star troops could do . . . except watch it approach.

It came barreling over the far horizon, a bright flash of red light, leaving a long trail of yellow sparks across the darkening sky.

The aircraft was of a very strange design. It did not look like a typical space fighter, the only other machine the Goth-Stars could compare it to. To their eyes, it looked more like a smaller version of a enormous battle cruiser, but even then, the resemblance was only fleeting.

The flying machine was rocketing along just fifty feet above the flat, frozen, snowy plain. The noise it was making was very bizarre in a world of silent propulsion devices; a sort of mechanical scream, it was deafening and extremely unnerving. The aircraft overflew the mile-long trench line once, wings tipped, as if it was looking for something. It appeared that two figures were riding inside the contraption, one sitting behind the other and looking out at them through a long, slender bubble-type glass top. After one long pass, the aircraft went into a violent, sweeping maneuver, boosting its power plants to ear-shattering speed and lining itself back up with the trench.

Then it started shooting.

This was a new experience for the Goth-Star soldiers. Attack from low-flying, high-speed aircraft was something few soldiers on the Five-Arm or anywhere else in the Galaxy had faced before. The flying machine's nose seemed to explode in bright orange flame. What they didn't know was that this was a blaster—a six-barrel, airborne blaster—a weapon never conceived before. This stunned some of the soldiers so much, they didn't think to turn their own personal weapons toward the oncoming aircraft.

A big mistake . . .

The flying machine swept in on them, its nose gun dispensing short but lethal bursts of ultragamma energy. The six continuous blasts made a frightening rippling noise as they rushed through the frigid air, heading for their targets. Suddenly, housing units began blowing up all along the front line. Then the comm shacks, the power units, even the mess halls and latrines.

Meanwhile, the flying machine was gyrating all over the sky, spinning, tumbling, zooming left and right in the blink of an eye. It was moving so fast and so wildly, the Goth-Stars wouldn't have been able to hit it, even if they were hip to the concept of antiaircraft fire, which they weren't.

About four-fifths of the way down the line, the flying machine went into an incredibly sharp 180-degree turn, causing such a massive screech from it power plants, many soldiers still alive along the trench line felt their eardrums explode in a gush of blood. The aircraft's nose stopped firing. It seemed to be looking for something again. Suddenly, it swooped low on one of the largest Master Blaster arrays, a twelve-tube assembly located just about halfway down the mile-long trench. With another horrifying screech, the aircraft's nose lit up again and delivered a flood of ultragamma fire to the base of the multitubed blaster. There was a huge explosion—all but silent in the cold, arctic air—as the power units within the weapon began coming apart and falling into some unknown, three-digit dimension. The resulting collision of so much matter and antimatter (though only a spoonful) set off an explosion of such force, the tiny planet of Tonk was actually wobbled on its axis for a moment. The ball of flame and radiation that followed disintegrated everything within a quarter mile: snow, soldiers, weapons, everything.

But it did not end there. A river of lethal energy cells gushing from the torn-apart blaster array began spilling into the trench and racing in both directions, flooding into other troop quarters located nearby. Each time one of the snowball-shaped bivouacs would go up, it would issue a resounding pop and then be engulfed by a sharp greenish blue secondary explosion. These only added to the conflagration. In seconds, those that could still see realized the weird flying machine had just made a perfect shot on the exact weapons array that would cause the most devastation along the Goth-Stars' line. The machine's pilots were doing what seemed impossible: They were destroying both their huge guns and killing large numbers of the Goth-Stars' best front-line troops all in one fell swoop.

Nor was the flying machine through. It continued to sweep along the trench line, blaster beams spitting out of its nose, hitting smaller but no less lethal gun arrays. This was the last thing seen by many of the front-line mercs: the strange aircraft, its nose aglow, hitting the blaster arrays, which in turn drowned anyone in the vicinity in a burning soup of pure, liquid energy.

Finally, the flying machine looped again and did one more pass before rocketing off to the east. All that remained of the Goth-Stars' position was a series of big black holes, melting their way down into the snow and ice field: dead, just like those back at the SpeedBalls' devastated base. A few soldiers in the rear area survived the catastrophic attack, though many had gone into an immediate state of shock at the suddenness of the lightning-quick strafing run.

How could this be happening? Who was flying this strange machine? And why were they pissed at us?

These were questions that few would ever get the answers to. But the handful of survivors agreed on one thing: that the strange flying machine that had left such a swath of destruction seemed to be painted in a strange combination of colors not seen on the Five-Arm or in many parts of the entire Galaxy in a very, *very* long time. The strange craft, they would later swear, had been painted in red, white, and blue.

In its wake it had left more than five thousand Goth-Star special forces troops dead or dying and just about all of their front line weaponry damaged or destroyed.

In all, the attack had lasted just twenty seconds.

It took both Hunter and Tomm nearly five minutes to peel Klaaz out of the flying machine's tiny backseat.

Hunter had taken the old soldier along on the bombing mission ostensibly as his target designator, and it was the Klaaz who helped spot the main Master Blaster array whose destruction was the major goal of the lightning-quick raid. But Hunter had an ulterior motive for bringing Klaaz with him, one more subtle than target spotting.

When they finally closed the book on the Great Klaaz's life, Hunter wanted history to show that the ancient warrior had a hand in getting the refugees off Tonk. He felt it important that the hero's image remain intact, right till the end, if only because some kid might someday hear about Klaaz and want to be just like him. And that would be a good thing, especially in such a lawless part of the sky. To Hunter's mind, it was the least he could do.

There was no doubt that Klaaz had experienced the ride of his life to boot, laughing wildly the whole way. But the mind-boggling speed had pinned the old warrior against the rear of the temporary jump seat Hunter had installed in the aircraft to accommodate Pater Tomm. The old guy was wedged in so tight, it took Hunter and Tomm several minutes just to get his safety straps unfastened.

Finally, they were able to lift the old soldier out of the aircraft, the extraction being done in the middle of yet another raging snowstorm, but tellingly without the hassle of any bad-guy blaster bombardment. Through it all, Klaaz was crowing loudly, describing in startlingly accurate detail the jumble of maneuvers Hunter had performed during the bombing mission.

They carried him down into the rocket chamber, where a hero's welcome was waiting for him. Regaining his strength as soon as the first wave of applause hit him, Klaaz walked the last few feet from the tunnel to the balcony by himself, raising his arms in feeble but determined triumph. Many among the throng of beautiful women screamed back at him in appreciation; others wept softly. Klaaz had come through; it had taken him a while, but he'd delivered them from their enemies, just as he had promised.

Hunter was wise enough to stay several steps back in the darkened tunnel, allowing Klaaz to greet the beautiful refugees solus. This was Klaaz's moment. An old hero hearing the cheers again—that was the important thing. Only once did Klaaz turn around and look back at Tomm and Hunter, and that was just to give them a very sly wink.

The celebration would have to be a brief one, though. A clock was ticking here. The refugees' ship was powered by combustible fuel, which it burned in several huge motors; the resulting thrust would slowly push them to orbit. It was an ancient method of achieving spaceflight—workable, but fraught with complications and a far cry from the current technology, where a vessel, big or small, could get to space with the mere push of a button.

While it was true that Hunter's mission had wiped out a lot of the besieging forces outside the ice fort, there were still thousands of enemy troops in the area. As soon as they got over the shock of what just happened to their comrades, they would surely renew the bombardment on the ice fortress and maybe even launch their long-anticipated attack at last.

In other words, if the beautiful exiles from Mutaman-Younguska were ever going to get off Tonk and head for a planet paradise Klaaz had already picked out for them, now was the time to go.

Tomm had overseen the last-minute preparations for the spaceship's departure, including drawing down the battered gravity shield. But as the priest now related to Hunter, the upcoming launch would not be any simple thing. If the fuel got too cold, it wouldn't ignite and would ruin much of the ship's internal piping. If the fuel became too warm, due to attempts to keep it from freezing, it could blow up and take most of the ice fort with it. In other words, once the old bird's fuel tanks were full, it had to leave right away.

The fueling cycle was just about complete, Tomm reported. The top of the huge chamber had already been cut away, and the snow was falling in through the big hole. The chamber was getting cold and losing its rickety life-system integrity very quickly.

The ship had to go now.

Klaaz knew this.

He wrapped his arm around Pater Tomm and said, "Please my brother, come with us. You and Mr. Hawk would be like kings when we reach our new world. I mean no offense, but once we are settled, there will be two thousand very grateful beauties who will want . . ."

Tomm's face turned red on cue. "They'll need only one king, my friend," he said, tactfully interrupting the old soldier. "And Hawk and I have very pressing business elsewhere."

Klaaz finally accepted this. "But perhaps you will visit our world someday soon, when your business is complete?"

Tomm shook hands with him. "You have my word."

"Very well," Klaaz said with a clap of his hands. "Suffice to say, you have both helped us immensely. And as you can see, I will be departing soon. So please, if I can't convince you to come with us, at least tell me why you came here in the first place."

Hunter and Tomm just looked at each other. Their quest had nearly been forgotten in all the excitement.

"It's a simple thing, really," the priest replied to Klaaz.

The old soldier winked slyly. "I like simple," he said.

Tomm lowered his voice. "We want to get to the Home Planets. Do you know anyone who might know where they are?"

Klaaz laughed. He thought it was a joke. But as soon as he realized that Tomm and Hunter were serious, the grin disappeared.

"There are many people in this part of the Five-Arm who would blow a hole in you for asking that question," he said darkly. "Indeed, many believe those two words can bring the worst kind of luck, should they hear them spring from another's lips."

"As a priest, I am immune to such superstitions," Tomm finally replied.

Klaaz thought about this, then his smile returned. "I forgot that you possess supernatural powers, Father."

He tightened their little circle. "But if you really want an answer to your question," he said in an excited whisper, "you must find a man named Zarex Red. Ever hear of him?"

Tomm and Hunter shook their heads no.

"He's an interesting sort," Klaaz said. "A bit of a rogue. An arms merchant of great wealth and expertise. But a grand explorer as well. It has been said that Zarex Red has been to more uncharted places on the Five-Arm than anyone else."

"Where can he be found?" Hunter asked.

"Well, that's the question, my friend," Klaaz replied. "For Zarex has also probably made more enemies on the Five-Arm than anyone else—even me. So he keeps his movements very secret. However, the last I heard, he was hiding out on a place called Bazooms. Like I said, he's made his share of enemies along the way of his travels. But the bad guys who have been seeking him lately are a very relentless sort: brutal, intelligent, well-equipped."

Tomm looked at the old soldier strangely.

"There are not many bad guys out there fitting such a description," the priest said.

"Only one that I know of, old friend," Klaaz said soberly.

"The Bad Moon Knights? Really?"

Klaaz nodded. "I heard Zarex was running guns to some of their enemies, and well, I guess they figured it was wiser to get rid of him than battling those he'd armed."

Hunter asked, "Who are the Bad Moon Knights?"

"No one really knows," Klaaz told him. "They are very mysterious sorts. Been around for a number of centuries now. They seem to be content these days with taking over key parts of the Five-Arm, most of them closer to the Ball, and doing so whether the people on those planets have ever been contacted or not. But the BMK are also most brutal in their methods. Besides launching huge campaigns, usually against very weakened and unsuspecting targets, they have a penchant for carrying out personal vendettas. Once they conquer a region of space, they immediately hunt down the teachers, the heroes, the poets—and yes, even explorers and the like. Along those lines, they've been trying to find my friend Zarex for years. But only a few of us know where he is."

"Will he mind us coming to look for him?" Hunter asked.

"He won't mind if he knows I sent you," Klaaz replied. "I used to be one of his best customers."

He smiled again, and the teeth didn't seem as cracked this time.

"Though the sight of a priest coming toward him might scare him more than a fleet of Bad Moon Knights," he said.

Pater Tomm bowed again.

"It will not be the first time I've instilled such fear," he said with a straight face.

The old rocket ship lifted off five minutes later.

It left slowly, with a huge ball of fire and smoke. The noise from the takeoff was deafening—so much so that the inner walls of the ice fort began to shake and crumble. The scaffold tower, which was essential to the rocket's liftoff, was blasted away in this sudden storm of flame. On the ground where the rocket ship had once stood, a deep pool of quickly melting ice was forming.

Hunter and Tomm were already airborne. They followed the

rocket ship up, escorting it through the lower stratosphere, all the while keeping an eye on both of the battered siege armies. They could see activity at both devastated army camps, but there was no hostile fire. The ship left unmolested. The space scum had had enough.

They accompanied the rocket into orbit, Hunter maintaining parallel formation as it finally reached escape velocity and popped into space. He waited while the rocket oriented itself, and then, with the blink of their navigation lights, it streaked off toward its new home, a world some fifty light-years away.

"They are in the good hands of the Great Klaaz," Pater Tomm said, watching the ancient vessel disappear into the stars. "And will remain as such—"

"Bingo that," Hunter replied.

5

Earth Time

It was raining again.

This seemed to happen way too much over Chesterwest, the small patch of inhabited forest just a few miles up the river from Big Bright City, the capital of Imperial Earth.

Though the climate engineers claimed they controlled the weather over this part of the world—indeed, they supposedly controlled the weather all around the planet—it never seemed to work out that way. Especially over Chesterwest. Why? No one was sure. One theory, and it was an old one, had to do with the forest itself. It was thick with extremely rare pine trees. No one knew if they grew better with more water or less, so the climate engineers opted for the former. And that's why it was always raining up here. Or so they said.

The enclave was reserved for dwellings of the most fortunate of the Very Fortunates, those people who weren't quite part of the extended Imperial Family but were damn close. Mostly, these people were rabid social climbers who had made the grade somehow. But there were a few legitimate human beings, including some military heroes, sprinkled among the population here as well.

There was a series of narrow dirt roads coursing through the forest at Chesterwest, mazelike paths that kept repeating back on themselves in intricate patterns. Few people who lived outside the enclave knew the secret of the roads, a design that ensured even further privacy for the privileged residents. On one of the more serpentine paths, there was a house built just a stone's throw from the top of a cliff, which looked out on the river below. The house was a modest affair, almost rustic when compared to some of the other homes in the area. With an over-grown garden out back and a tangle of wisteria covering the front, the ten-room dwelling was almost completely hidden from view.

The road running by this house was paved with soft dirt; it became very muddy any time it rained. Now, as the night grew longer, it began raining even harder. The wind had kicked up as well; it was coming right off the cliff, the direction of trouble. Thunder was rumbling again, and lightning was crackling high above the pines.

It was not a good night to be out.

Sitting by the light of many candles was the owner of the small cliff house, Petz Calandrx. He was a short, late–middle-aged man, nearly 223 years old. He had long white hair, a recent beard, and a slightly burned leathery face, the signature of a veteran Starfighter pilot. He'd been living in Chesterwest for many, many years.

Calandrx was an official Hero of the Empire, an accolade given but once a century. He was famous for two reasons. In his first century he was an acclaimed space pilot who took part in dozens of famous campaigns out on the Fringe. Then, return-ing home after an illustrious career, he won the Earth Race, the most prestigious aerial contest in the Galaxy. That made Cal-andrx super-duper famous, so much so, that by Imperial decree he was forbidden from ever flying in space again, lest he die in some accident and the Galaxy unnecessarily lose its hero. Cal-andrx was a victim of his own celebrity, and it killed him a little bit each day. He'd become so famous, he'd been forced to give up the thing he loved the most.

He spent most of his days reading now. Nearly every room in his house was filled with holographic recreations of what used to be called books. His favorites were rare texts from the Second Empire. Calandrx loved the classic rebel poets of that epoch; he was an authority on the military history of the era as well, what little of it there was. Calandrx had spent much of the last two decades poring over these texts, always by candlelight, looking for clues as to why the Second Empire, supposedly the greatest of the four, fell so quickly. Next to flying, this pursuit had become the passion of his life.

That's what he was doing this stormy night: reading the middle verses of the classic Second Empire poem, "The Last Battle for the Center of the Galaxy." He'd just completed the two hundred sixteenth stanza when a knock came on his door. It was a strange tapping. Uncertain, yet sharp, as if the person responsible had been dreading this moment for a long time and now that it was happening, some false forcefulness had set in.

Either that or it was that crazy robot who lived down the road, the one who was always trying to get Calandrx to drink oil with him.

Calandrx laid the book aside and walked over to the door. He glanced up at the small slit window above its top sill. People who flew in space these days, especially those in vessels powered by the Big Generator, returned to Earth emitting a faint greenish glow. This was the signature of traveling in Supertime. But there was no glow above his door now. Whoever was on the other side had been earthbound for a while.

Must be someone from the city, Calandrx thought. *Or that nutty robot.*

He opened the door to find a man wearing a long, black cape with a floppy black hat pulled down over his eyes. Calandrx could not see the man's face or his hands, usually not a good sign. But his immediate sense was that the man was not holding a gun. Outside, the thunder and lightning storm raged on.

"Are you lost, my brother?" Calandrx asked him.

"No, I am not," the man replied. "Though this is just the night for such a thing."

He lifted his hat a bit. "I come in peace," he said, finally displaying his hands to show he was not holding any weapons.

Calandrx was nearly two and a quarter centuries old; by now he could tell an honest man at first sight. This man was honest, or at least part of him was.

"Come in, my brother," Calandrx finally said.

The man gratefully stepped out of the rain.

That's when Calandrx took a deep sniff and realized the man was an imperial spy. The smell of water on his cape gave him away. It was an odor Calandrx was familiar with. Back when he was a space fighter pilot, he'd been in countless preattack meetings, and inevitably a spy would pop in, always coming out of the rain somewhere and usually bearing pressing news about the battle soon to commence. All imperial spies wore the same type of cape: thick, black *velveeta,* by the commonly used ancient word. This material had a very distinct, earthy smell, especially when wet. Therefore, so did the spies.

"And why is a spook here to see me?" Calandrx asked him; he was known for his direct approach.

The stranger seemed not surprised that Calandrx had pegged his occupation.

"I figured an old soldier like you would know who I was— or perhaps more accurately, *what* I was," he said. "The truth is, I am more a messenger than a spook this stormy night."

"And what message do you bear?"

The spy took a breath. "You are wanted down in the city— immediately."

Calandrx's eyes brightened at once. He didn't get down to Big Bright City much anymore. But when he did, it was usually for an occasion that was honoring him in some fashion—a dinner, a testimonial, an awards ceremony. This always meant good food, good wine, plenty of women, and more accolades than he could digest. It was not an unpleasant way to spend an evening.

But the spy could read his thoughts.

"This is not another fete for you," he told him frankly. "It does not appear that it will festive at all."

Calandrx stared back at him. This was a bit worrisome.

"Who is asking that I appear then? And why?"

The man shrugged. "A member of the Imperial Family has made the request. That's all I can say. And as you know, these things can not be refused."

Flash!

More than two billion people lived in Big Bright City.

The imperial capital of the Fourth Empire boasted millions of structures, including many superskyscrapers and spaceports, interlaced with miles of hovering roadways, air-car tubes, people movers, and canals. The sprawling city was so big, it took up nearly 10 percent of the hemisphere's northeast quadrant. Its total power consumption was equal to that of a large planet.

At ground level, the place was packed with housing units, military barracks, imperial offices, sports clubs, nightclubs, dance clubs, sex clubs, casinos, bars, arenas, weapons shops, and distilleries. There was some kind of flag or banner draped from almost every one of these establishments, proclaiming the greatness of the Fourth Empire. Thousands of monuments to the Emperor could be found all over the city, too, usually jammed in between the enormous, skyward-pointing power towers. And then there were the lights. They were everywhere. All colors, all shades and tones, burning brightly, day or night, creating a garish neon glow that practically guaranteed no one in Big Bright City ever went to sleep.

Not that anyone would want to.

Cruising above the immense metropolis was the floating city known as Special Number One.

It looked like a huge castle in the sky: high walls, hundreds of ornate buildings, spacious courtyards, a labyrinth of streets and back alleys, it was ten square miles in all. There were multiple spires rising from the clutter of these palatial buildings; each tower glowed with a different iridescent color. Long, sloping passageways crisscrossed these spires like lattice work. In the tallest, there were ornamental zaser beams so bright, they could be seen clear beyond the solar system.

Special Number One was where the Imperial Family lived. And even though it was past midnight, the floating city was about to get very busy.

A signal had just been flashed to the small army of security forces stationed on the floating city: the Emperor was on the move; get to your positions. Within seconds, every roof, street, intersection, gate, and tower was lined with heavily armed Imperial troops. So many of these soldiers were materializing from their barracks that the combined shimmer of greenish electricity—always seen during a transport—gave the flying city an unusual emerald glow.

The alert had been sparked by a very simple thing: a light at the top of the Imperial Palace had switched from white to red. This meant that O'Nay, the Supreme Ruler of the Galaxy, was changing locations. He was considered a god to many, an omnipotent being who reigned over 80 percent of the Milky Way, an empire encompassing billions of star systems and trillions of planets. His realm was so vast and far-flung, no one was really sure just how many people were under his rule. Hundreds of trillions certainly. Probably more.

As such, O'Nay was much too important to move from one location to another without a great ceremony. These elaborate exercises involved hundreds of additional soldiers, officially known as Holy Palace Guards. Like the security troops around them, these soldiers were at the ready day and night, just in case O'Nay wanted to move.

As far as anyone could tell, O'Nay spent most of his waking hours at the top of the tower built above the gigantic Imperial Palace. This tower was five hundred feet high and was considered a very sacred place. There was a small room at the top, a very simple affair, as described by the few mere mortals who had seen the inside of it. It lacked even the most basic comforts, reportedly containing but a single wooden chair. It was here that the Emperor would sit for hours on end, gazing out the room's only window, thinking his deep thoughts.

He did come down occasionally, though, and that's when things could get buzzing on Special Number One. The assembled soldiers watched now as an eerie glow began descending the stairs from the tower. This was the odd greenish yellow haze that always marked the space immediately in front of and immediately behind the Emperor. In centuries past, it would have been called an aura. These days, it was known as the Holy Light.

It took more than ten minutes for the Emperor and his coterie of special Tower Guards to reach the bottom level of the Imperial Palace. The massive front door finally opened, and O'Nay was spotted within. At the first sight of him, music started up. Lots of it. The sudden blare of synthesized trumpet sounds, thick with pomp and circumstance, quickly filled the grand concourse. Then hundreds of small, white, mechanical flying things were released into the air. They fluttered across the grand walkway, then turned upward into the night sky, where they quickly disappeared forever.

A battalion of House Guards formed up in front of O'Nay now. Their helmets and ceremonial weapons gleamed with nearly the same intensity as the zaser beams atop the floating city's tallest spires. Even in Big Bright below, a sort of hush descended, as word was flashed that O'Nay was coming down from his tower.

As always, O'Nay himself seemed oblivious to all that was happening around him. He looked like a god: tall, sturdy, a full white beard and very long white hair that fell past his shoulders.

He was wearing his usual long, flowing, emerald gown and had his gold green miter planted firmly on his head. In the center of this cone-shaped hat was the distorted image of a green three-leafed plant. This was the ancient symbol of the Specials, as the extended imperial family was known. It was one of the few things that had survived the three previous empires and the centuries of Dark Ages in between.

O'Nay looked out on the grand concourse and slowly raised his hand. The music became louder. It was here that he was turned over to the Concourse Guards, soldiers even more massive than his imposing Tower Guards. Quickly surrounded by four phalanxes containing one hundred soldiers each, the Emperor began crossing the esplanade, gliding along as usual about three feet above the ground, his troops marching in unison on all sides of him.

Once at the curb, O'Nay was met by another ceremonial army, the Holy Street Guards. With much weapons-slapping and boot clicking, they joined the head of the procession and led it through the empty, pristine streets of Special Number One. They eventually reached the plaza of the nearby Gold House, a building nearly as massive as the palace itself. Here still another contingent of ceremonial troops, the Plaza Guards, joined the ranks. The Emperor floated along with them, maintaining the same detached air as with the other marching units. Gliding across the plaza, he moved very smoothly within his emerald glow.

The Plaza Guards had the easiest mission of the night. They had to lead the burgeoning parade a mere hundred feet, the distance from the street curb to the front of the Gold House. Here, the Eternal O'Nay would be turned over to the Gold House Guards.

There was an orgy of lights flashing and saber rattling as this changing of the flags was made. The company of Plaza Guards then turned on their heels and marched off the hundred feet in reverse, stopping only when they reached the curb, where they lined up alongside their comrades and snapped to attention. All eyes were on the Emperor now as he glided not to the massive front door of the Gold House but to a smaller, less ornate one located off to the side. This room was known around the floating city as O'Nay's "favorite comfortable place."

He went through this door alone, shutting it tightly behind

him. The thousands of troops remained at attention and waited. These things never took very long. Sure enough, not thirty seconds later, the door opened, and O'Nay glided out again.

Mission accomplished.

Now the whole ceremonial process had to be reversed. O'Nay was surrounded by the Gold House Guards, who turned him over to the Plaza Guards, who gave him over to the Holy Street Guards, who marched him back up to the Imperial Palace, where the Concourse Guards delivered him back to the Tower Guards. Through it all, the music continued to play and more and more white, furry, flying things were sent aloft.

Only after O'Nay disappeared back into the palace did the pageantry die down. His glow was seen ascending the stairs back to the top of the tower, to the small meditation room, which by all reports did not contain a "favorite comfortable place" for O'Nay. Finally, the glow reached its apex, and the single light at the top of the tower blinked back to white again.

That's when the music finally stopped, and any remaining flying things were returned to their holding area. All around the floating city, soldiers and guards were ordered at ease. Things went back to normal as well down in Big Bright City. O'Nay was back in his tower, and all was right with the Universe.

Back at the Gold House, the two soldiers posted closest to the small room that had been O'Nay's destination eased themselves into standing regular guard duty again.

After a while, one looked at the other and shrugged.

"My guess, it was just a tinkle," he said.

Farther down the floating city's main street, all the way to the bright southern edge of Special Number One, there was an extremely futuristic building known as Blue Rock.

This was the main operations center for the Space Forces, the largest of the Empire's trinity of military services. The job of the SF was to project the Empire's policies to the far reaches of the Galaxy. Comprised of the Navy, the Army, and Air Service, the Space Forces were the Emperor's front-line troops, nearly twenty billion in all, with millions of spacecraft under flag to get them where they wanted to go. The SF was also the Empire's senior service; its roots went back more than a thousand years, a history that had somehow survived the last two

Dark Ages. As such, its members liked to think of it as the most professional of the Empire's military units.

On this night, the SF building was lit up as always, each of its many levels glowing brightly. A full duty shift was inside, more than fifty thousand people. They were all working nonstop, lording over millions of superfast communications bubbles, the cells from which the reports of the nonstop comings and goings of the vast space service gurgled up.

At the exact opposite end of Special Number One, hanging off the floating city's northern tip, was another very futuristic building. It was built entirely of black superglass, and unlike the brightness of SF's Blue Rock, it was rarely seen emitting any light at all.

This was the operations center for the second service of the Empire's triad, the Inner Defense Forces. More readily known as the Solar Guards, they were about half as big as the Space Forces and were responsible for security within the Pluto Cloud, as the boundary of the Earth's solar system was known.

Or at least that's how it was supposed to be.

Truth was, the Solar Guards could be found in just about every corner of the Galaxy, while many vessels of the Space Forces fleet spent their time on assignments closer to Earth, where most of the Empire's major repair and training facilities were located. This disparity was one of the great ironies of the Empire, and it had been like this for longer than anyone could remember.

To say the two services did not get along was a ridiculous understatement. Their top officers never communicated with each other. They used different types of weapons and flew different types of starships. They had different orders of rank and even different style uniforms. The Space Forces wore blue with yellow trim; the Solar Guards wore black with red. Their missions were nothing alike. The Solar Guards were like an army of policemen. They cruised the Galaxy, working on countless investigations, some of them legitimate (like tracking down tax outlaws and criminal armies), but many not. As a result, the Solar Guards conducted their own wars and the Space Forces conducted theirs. The two services had never fought side by side against a common enemy.

The Solar Guards had been established just three hundred years before—or so they claimed. And while they boasted fewer men in arms than the Space Forces, their troops were considered more specialized, better trained, and more ruthless. They were also much closer to the inner workings of the Imperial Palace, the ultimate seat of power. While the Space Forces were never shy in making their views clear to the Emperor, by tradition they usually did so through normal channels of protocol. The Solar Guards, on the other hand, excelled in getting the Emperor's ear via back channels and well-practiced intrigues.

A difference in philosophy fueled the main conflict between the services. The SG believed the Empire's best path to success was to reclaim as many of the Galaxy's planets as possible, as quickly as possible, and bring them into the Empire's fold. The Space Forces were dedicated to the same goal but believed the way to accomplish this was to go after the troublesome planets first—those inhabited by pirates, criminals, and other interstellar lowlifes—and bring the more peaceful, law-abiding planets back in gradually.

So, it was not a question of expansion; that was everybody's objective. It was how quickly that expansion should be carried out.

The Solar Guards ops building was almost always covered in shadow. Even now, in the dead of night, no lights illuminated its main entrance. Barely two dozen people were on duty inside, and none was working very hard. Unlike their SF rivals, SG commanders rarely reported in on a regular basis—not officially, anyway. Anything of any importance they always sent in deeply coded layers of biosecrecy, the so-called "brain-proof" cryptics that very few people could read, least of all the building's night shift. So while any bubble noise being transmitted to this place during the night was probably coming from the darker places in the Galaxy, the handful of communications beams received were simply stored away to be read by others in the morning.

Unlike the SF building, though, the Solar Guards had built a bunker below their ops center. It went down thirteen levels. In one section of the lowest level was a room restricted to everyone but a select few at the top of the Solar Guards' hierarchy.

In this room there was an ultrasecret communications beam selector, one that was always set to the same atomic band. This apparatus worked even less frequently than those in the upper

levels of this shadowy place. But a message had come in
through it this night.

It would make sense only to someone who understood exactly
who was on the other end of the communicator.

"Post-Fringe Five Mission, Day 3," the encoded message bubbles read. "Nothing new to report. . . ."

The Expeditionary and Exploratory Forces, known more simply
as the X-Forces, was the third service of the Empire's trinity.

It had about one-tenth the number of troops as the SF; way
less than half that of the Solar Guards. The X-Forces' mandate
was to fly to the Outer Fringe—meaning all arms of the galactic
spiral—and identify those planets lost since the last Dark Age
and even beyond. In many ways, they were the scouts before
the cavalry. Any planets they did not reclaim themselves were
left for the Space Forces. The X-Force's starships carried highly
trained troops but also professional humanitarians, scientists,
physicians, and representatives of the Empire's diplomatic
corps. Very often the first time the people of a reclaimed world
saw the Empire's banner it was painted on the side of an X-
Forces vessel. While the SF and SG battled each other for in-
fluence both on Earth and throughout the Galaxy, the X-Forces
went about their far-flung jobs somewhat quietly.

As such, they had absolutely no political power anywhere in
the Empire and least of all on the Imperial floating city.

In fact, they didn't even have a building up there.

All of the buildings immediately surrounding the Imperial Palace were brick-by-brick reconstructions of ancient dwellings
found on Earth thousands of years before.

There were twelve of them in all, their interiors full of intricately carved oak, one of the rarest commodities in the Galaxy.
These buildings had very few windows and many were made
of stained glass. Though elegant, this made the buildings unnaturally dark inside. Full of shadows and dimly lit hallways,
they were also honeycombed with secret passageways, and, it
was rumored, dungeons.

These were the Holy Houses, the places where the Specials
resided. And it was into a room on the top floor of one of them
that Petz Calandrx suddenly popped in.

He hadn't traveled so fast in years. One moment he was

standing in his foyer talking to the spy; the next, he was here, in this dark place, his head throbbing with pain, his skin still emitting a greenish glow. He checked to make sure all of his vital parts had survived the transport process. They had, thank God. Then he studied his new surroundings. No windows, no furniture, not even a chair. He knew he was inside a Holy House though; the room's exquisite woodwork gave it away.

But *where* was he exactly? Which house? Whose room? These things he didn't know.

This had all happened so suddenly he'd not been given the opportunity to even change his clothes. Whatever member of the Imperial Family had summoned him, Calandrx would be greeting them in his smoking jacket and slippers!

And what shape had he left his house in? Had he extinguished his reading candles before answering the fateful knock? He couldn't remember—not that it mattered. He was sure the spy was rummaging through his things at that very moment, doing what spies do. He just hoped the man would blow out all the candles before he left.

Calandrx suddenly felt a bit claustrophobic. This room was very small by imperial standards. Why was he here? Who was he supposed to see? The Emperor? Hardly . . . O'Nay would not have gone through the trouble of sending a spy for him. He could have simply willed it into the wind, and Calandrx would have been standing before him instantly. The Emperor's wacky son was a more likely suspect. The kid was a royal fuckup, known as much for his inability to handle slow-ship wine as the disrespectful way he treated real women, a rarity throughout the Empire. He also loved Starfighters and in the past had approached Calandrx to talk tactics. But Calandrx had always put him off, having little desire to spend even a minute in the presence of such an idiot. Could this be the Prince's method of revenge?

No, sending a spy did not seem like junior's style. A battalion of Earth Guards maybe. But not a spy.

This really left only the Empress, who was just as nutty as her son and well-known for her love of intrigue. Calandrx felt a chill go through him. What would the Empress want with him? He had nothing to hide. Or did he?

True, he was a man of honor and scruples, but that did not mean he hadn't slipped on occasion. Everyone had a bit of the rascal in him, especially these days. He began worrying that perhaps one of his latest adventures might be coming back to haunt him.

Suddenly there was a flash, and just like that, there were two more people in the room with him.

They almost looked like twins. Both were stout but powerful men of middle age, with shiny bald heads and huge, drooping mustaches. Battle scars were prominent on their hands and faces. Their uniforms were black with gold collar badges. The double crosses of the X-Forces were emblazoned on their chests.

The strange thing was, Calandrx knew them both. In fact, he was good friends with them. Their names were Erx and Berx. They were senior officers of the X-Forces and well-known in many parts of the Galaxy.

And they were as surprised to see him as he was to see them.

"Calandrx, our brother!" Erx cried. "They scooped you up, too?"

"Yes—in my nightclothes yet . . ."

"By a spy?" Berx asked. "With no explanation?"

"The same," Calandrx replied. "That only deepens the mystery as to why we have been called here."

Erx and Berx shook off the last of the green luminescence surrounding them, then began examining the room. They quickly took note of the woodwork, the shadows.

"Is this really a Holy House that we've been delivered to?" Erx asked, going over a wood carving like a detective.

"It is indeed," Calandrx said.

"Whose is it, brother?" Berx asked him. "Have you noodled that out yet?"

"My guess is the Empress," Calandrx whispered. "And to no good end, I fear."

"You see nothing positive in this, brother?" Berx asked him worriedly.

Calandrx shook his head. "I am no longer an expert in palace machinations. I just know they don't send out spies to summon people like us for any small reason."

The three men looked at each other. There had been one episode of mischief among them lately. Could that be why they were here?

"Where did you pop in from?" Calandrx asked them worriedly.

"We've been in the secret court of inquiry for the past six weeks!" Berx exclaimed; he was usually the more excitable of the two.

"Still?" Calandrx asked them. "That's way too long."

Erx and Berx nodded glumly. The secret inquiry was looking into what happened during the battle of Zazu-Zazu. The tiny moon at the end of the Five-Arm had come very close to being destroyed by a very mysterious military force using weapons never seen in the Galaxy before. The battle was finally won by the moon's inhabitants after, ironically enough, the Solar Guards came to their rescue. But the mysterious enemy departed in a very strange spaceship, again, not of a type ever seen in the Galaxy.

These were very disturbing events for the people at the top of the Empire. A number of bizarre episodes had been reported in various places around the Galaxy in the months leading up to Zazu-Zazu, but none so strange as the tiny war on the tiny moon so far out on the Fringe, you would fall off the edge if you went any farther.

But the rub was this: The central character in all this had not been Calandrx or Erx or Berx, but Hawk Hunter. In fact, it was Erx and Berx who first found Hunter on the desolate planet of Fools 6, not quite a year before. That Erx and Berx were the last ones to see him before he went AWOL made them very suspicious in the eyes of the Empire's top inquisitors. That's why the investigation into *l'affaire* Zazu-Zazu had been ongoing for so long.

And Calandrx's involvement? He'd been instrumental earlier, by getting Hunter a spot in the most recent Earth Race, which the pilot won superbly, making Calandrx a pile of money. But the triumph also led to Hunter being commissioned by the X-Forces and sent into deep space, where he disappeared.

"They keep asking us the same questions over and over," Erx was telling Calandrx now. "First, the interrogators from the Space Forces, then the Solar Guards, then the X-Forces. Once they seemed finished with us, they just start it all over again. We told them everything we know—"

"But at some point it must end," Calandrx said. "Right?"

Both men shrugged on cue. "Surely. But when it does, so what?" Erx said. "What will we have to do then?"

Calandrx played upbeat. "You will go back to your duties, of course."

But both men were immediately crestfallen.

"That will be impossible, brother," Erx said. "Obviously you have not heard the latest news on our predicament?"

Calandrx shook his head no.

"They have barred us from flying in space," Berx replied, barely able to say the words. "No matter what happens in the inquiry, we've been grounded . . . permanently."

Calandrx felt his heart sink. This was a blow he'd experienced himself some years ago. Grounded: It was a fate worse than death for most.

"But that's ridiculous!" Calandrx roared. "With all your years of service? With all your battle decorations? With all you've given for the Emperor?" His voice was very loud—not a good thing, considering his current location. But he didn't care.

"For what reason are you banished?" he asked them.

Both men just shrugged.

"We've seen too much? We know too much?" Erx replied. "Take your pick."

On those words, the door suddenly opened, and two enormous Earth Guards walked in. They didn't speak; they rarely did. Instead, they simply indicated it was time to go. The three men gloomily trooped out.

They were led down a long corridor, dark and brooding, with many locked, unmarked, ornately carved wooden doors on either side. There was no doubt about it now; they were in a building very close to the Imperial Palace. Calandrx took a sniff. He detected the unmistakable scent of Venusian perfume in the air. Not a good sign . . . O'Nay, the Empress and their son were all known to use the fragrance.

They finally reached a huge black door located at the far end of the hallway. The air was especially thick with perfume here. One guard opened the door to reveal a room vast even by imperial standards. An entire forest of precious maple must have gone into the woodwork; the floor was dull with ancient metallic rugs. A huge fireplace dominated one side of the room. Several giant logs, precious oak, were roaring within.

The guards nudged them inside and quickly shut the door behind them. The first thing that went through Calandrx's mind was: *This doesn't look like a torture chamber.*

But when the Empress was involved, who knew?

That's when they looked to their right and saw, by the light of the fire, a diminutive figure dressed in white, sitting on a couch.

All three men sighed with relief. This was not O'Nay, nor the Empress, nor the mindless Prince. It was, in fact, the fourth member of the Imperial Family, the sweet and beautiful Xara, Princess of the Galaxy.

She looked up at them, and all three went to one knee immediately. Erx and Berx had never met the Princess formally before, and they'd certainly never seen her this up close. As a friend of her father's, Calandrx had spoken to Xara many times, but that was back when she was a little girl. Of course, all three had seen her from a distance over the years, but until that moment, never did they realize just how beautiful she was.

To say she was just a smaller version of her mother was doing her an injustice. Though the Empress was regarded as a true galactic beauty, Xara was even more radiant, more angelic, more heavenly, and quite a bit younger. She was not yet twenty, of slight build, her hair luxuriously blond. It was hanging loose over her shoulders now, a real treat, as she rarely appeared in public without it being tied back somehow. She was wearing a simple, form-fitting white smock with a sash tied loosely just above her abdomen. She was barefoot.

"Uncle Petz," she said with a sad smile. "It has been too long."

"The years have been worth the wait as I now see how beautifully you've grown," Calandrx told her.

She blushed and motioned them closer. The three men rose and slowly moved toward the couch. Calandrx introduced Erx and Berx, but the two men could barely speak.

"I have heard about your exploits," Xara told the two explorers. "Our citizens are better for your service."

Both men bowed deeply.

"You honor us, my lady," Erx managed to croak.

The fire crackled as another log materialized from nowhere and was added to the small blaze. An awkward moment came and went.

Finally, Calandrx said, "My lady, excuse us, but we are a bit surprised that it was *you* who called us here."

She pushed some hair back from her face.

"I understand," she said. "And I'm the last one to indulge in such cloak-and-dagger stuff. But I'm afraid it was necessary. No one must know of our meeting like this."

"And they will not," Calandrx assured her. Erx and Berx bowed in agreement as well.

Again, the fire crackled.

"So, we are here then, my lady," Calandrx said. "How can we help you?"

Xara wiped her eyes. For the first time, Calandrx realized that she had been crying.

"You are Hawk Hunter's closest friends," she began with trembling lips. "He told me so himself. That's why I must ask you. Have you heard from him . . . anything at all?"

She looked at them, a faint glimmer of hope in her teary eyes. But Calandrx glanced at the others, and they were shaking their heads no.

"We're sorry, my lady," the old pilot told her. "We have not."

Xara's hand went to her mouth. "Do you know where he is?"

Again, all three men just shook their heads.

Erx spoke up. "If only we did. We miss our brother Hunter, his company and his spirit."

Xara turned away for a moment. The words sounded too much like a eulogy to her.

"It's been so long since he was last heard from. . . ." she whispered. "He left us so suddenly. And there are things he should know. . . ."

Finally, she began to cry in earnest.

Calandrx glanced at the others and did an eye roll. At the same time, though, his heart became a bit heavier. He'd gone through this sort of thing—a couple centuries ago. They all had. And it was understandable. Hunter was a good guy. Handsome, honorable, mysterious. Was there anything else a teenage girl could want?

So the mystery was solved. They'd been called here not for some dark reason but to comfort a teenage girl who had lost her first love. It was not the type of work Calandrx, Erx, and Berx were known for, but they were hugely relieved. They could have been summoned to the Imperial Palace for many things a lot worse than performing a mission of adolescent comfort.

Erx and Berx gave Calandrx the high sign now. The meaning was clear. It would be up to "Uncle Petz" to do the actual hand-holding. The pilot shrugged, then sat down next to Xara on the couch. And indeed, he took her hand in his. It felt incredibly soft.

"May I ask you all a question?" she resumed with a sniff.

All three men solemnly nodded yes.

"Do you believe the notion that the farther we go out into the Galaxy, the more we will learn about the empires that have passed?"

All three nodded, Calandrx with authority. "*I* certainly do, my lady," he said.

"Why do you believe so?" she asked.

Calandrx shrugged—a bit impolite maybe. "Because it is true, my lady. The farther we look out there, the more we look back into time. The more we look, the more we find evidence of the three previous empires. Scant evidence, but evidence, nonetheless. With each planet that's reclaimed, we see the handiwork of our predecessors, their footprints in the dirt, their fingerprints on civilizations, some of whom haven't the slightest idea what went on in their history before. And neither do we, really. That's why it's so important."

"But that's the problem, isn't it?" she asked with a sniff. "That as a race, in this time, this place in history, we are so obsessed with our past?"

She addressed Calandrx directly. "I know that in addition to being a great warrior, Petz, you read the poets from the previous ages."

Calandrx did a slight bow. "Reading and understanding are two different things, my lady—"

"No need to be modest, Uncle," she said. "Just tell me: What do the poets say about this? Is our obsession with the ancients healthy? Is it just in our human nature to want to know? Or are we just like the adopted child, never resting until all is known—good or bad—about the past?"

Calandrx just stared back at her for a long moment. He couldn't help it. He was more than mildly astonished that such a question would come from the lips of an Imperial Family member, a clan not exactly known for intellectual prowess.

"Dear Princess, I believe the answer to your question lies somewhere in between," he said finally. "True, we may be obsessed, but it's still important to know."

She dabbed her eyes again.

"I agree," she said. "And that means that I single-handedly signed Hunter's death warrant."

There was a real gush of tears now as Calandrx, Erx, and Berx exchanged worried glances. What was she talking about?

More eye dabbing. "What I have to tell you cannot leave this room," she said, trying to rescue some mascara that was running down her cheek.

"We promise," Calandrx said, squeezing her hand tighter.

"I am the one responsible for Hawk being lost," she suddenly blurted out. "After he and I met, and he told me the few clues he had as to where he might have come from—before being found on that ridiculously desolate planet—I uncovered an emblem on an ancient spacecraft that was found many years ago deep in the ice up on Mars. It was the same design as the flag that Hunter always carries with him. . . . You've seen his ancient piece of cloth?"

All three men nodded. "The flag is a series of white and red stripes, with a field of stars set in blue," Calandrx said.

"Yes, and so was this emblem that I showed to him," Xara went on. "And I told him something else as well—something that is such an Imperial secret, I'm not sure my father even knows."

She took a deep breath.

"Our scientists many years ago were able to interpret a slight burn mark that is evident on this spacecraft in the ice," she said. "They determined that it is the result of a very long-range scanning device which, if understood properly, would lead a person to a place called the 'lighthouse.' It was a beacon of sorts, calling all those once familiar with that flag to come home. . . . *That's* where I think Hunter went. To find his lost home . . ."

She looked at them, more tears about to cascade from her eyes.

"Don't you see?" she said. "I'm the one who urged him to take the X-Forces' commission so he could go to deep space. *I* gave him the means by which he is now a fugitive. Now, if they catch him, he will be worse than dead—and it will be all my fault."

The three men stayed frozen in place. All three knew pieces of the story Xara had just told them, though they hadn't been aware just how involved she was in the beginning of Hunter's quest.

"You did what you thought was a noble act," Calandrx finally told her. "Every person must know his past. You were just helping a lost soul find his home. It was an honorable thing to do."

"Besides, Hunter is very clever," Erx said. "Should someone catch up to him and return him for trial, he would very smartly argue his case. The worst sentence is not a foregone conclusion. Others have beaten it before."

"But you don't understand." Xara began sobbing again. "Those that are now in pursuit of him—their goal is not to bring him back for being AWOL. They are worried what he might uncover if he finds what he is looking for—and they will kill him before he does."

Now dead silence fell on the room. The Empire killing one of its own officers? Even the darkest elements of the imperial military were never accused of that.

They were all quiet for a very long time. The fire was roaring, but they barely felt its heat.

Finally Xara said, "There is really only one thing that can be done to help Hunter."

"Please my lady," Calandrx said. "Just tell us, and we will do it."

She looked at all three of them. At that moment, they would have jumped over the moon for her.

Well, almost . . .

"You must find him," she finally said to them.

All three were stunned.

Find Hunter? How?

Calandrx looked at the others. They appeared as shocked as he. Suddenly, this had changed from imperial hand-holding to . . . well, to what exactly?

They had no idea where Hunter was. And they knew there was a good chance Hunter didn't know where he was himself! He was most likely in some part of the Galaxy not under control of the Fourth Empire. And how does one exactly go about looking for a person out in the vast fringes of space? Especially one who probably doesn't want to be found?

But all three men were soldiers, and this was their Princess. They were supposed to do anything she asked, simply for the honor of it.

"But I'm afraid that this is a mission of desperation that I am sending you on," she said. "One fraught with danger for you as well."

"What do you mean, my lady?" Calandrx asked her.

"I've heard whisperings," she confessed. "And the things I hear are rather frightening. The foundation of the Empire itself may be at stake here. And that is not good for us, nor is it good for Hunter."

The three men weren't sure what she meant.

"You will not be the only ones looking for him," she explained again. "In fact, others have already gotten a head start."

She paused and wiped her eyes again.

"I can provide you with a fast ship," she finally resumed. "And safe passage through any sector of the reclaimed Galaxy. I can arrange for the best star charts. The best intelligence."

Suddenly it seemed as if the big room got a bit brighter, as if the Earth had just wobbled a bit on its axis. Calandrx began to say something but stopped. Erx and Berx bit their tongues as well.

A long pause.

"Just find him first . . . please." Xara told them.

The men bowed deeply. Rascals three.

"We will, my lady," Calandrx said, hiding a smile. "Or die trying . . ."

6

Hunter slipped the flying machine into orbit around the small planet, then reached back into his cockpit and shook Pater Tomm awake.

"Are we there yet?" the priest asked sleepily.

"If Klaaz's directions were right, this should be the place," Hunter replied.

The planet below was called Bazooms. It orbited a yellow star known simply as BDG, short for Big Dan's Girl. The star system was located roughly below the elbow of the Five-Arm, in an isolated sector of the fifth spiral known as the Twist.

They'd reached BDG about three hours after leaving the dirty snowball of Tonk. Once inside the system, it was not hard to locate the planet in question. BDG was a rather boring collection of uninhabited rocks orbiting a dull sun. Only Bazooms showed evidence of past life.

An ancient image called up on Hunter's quadtrol showed the planet once shimmered with the bright glow of circus colors: red, green, and yellow. Its atmosphere was once cobalt blue. Thousands of ultrabright beacons, not unlike the powerful zasers of Earth, had flashed crazily in all directions, their beams reaching beyond the edges of the star system.

At one time, Bazooms was a place to be. Essentially an orbiting brothel, the planet was once a very high-end resort where only the richest and most fortunate citizens could stay and play.

All that had changed a few dozen centuries before—or at least that's what Hunter's hand-held quadtrol was saying. It predicted that Bazooms would be as dull and dark as everything else floating around the moribund system. The wash of time and events had passed this place by. Its current status was listed as "unknown."

A good place if someone wanted to hide out.

It took some digging during the first hour of the flight, but Tomm had managed to scan his own quadtrol's distant memory bubbles for information on Zarex Red.

And the Klaaz had been right again. Zarex Red was no ordinary arms runner. True, at one time, he'd provided weapons to literally thousands of warring parties all over the middle regions of the vast Five-Arm. In fact, about a hundred years before, Zarex Red had no less than sixteen planets stockpiled with his war-making merchandise. So many people wanted in on the dealing, his home-base solar system had been prone to space-traffic jams around its innermost orbits. War had been big business on the Five-Arm for centuries. At the peak of his career, Zarex was probably one of the biggest dealers on the entire Fringe.

But after he'd made his fortune, Zarex Red gave up his edgy life as an arms merchant and became, of all things, a deep-space explorer. Using his profits to finance numerous expeditions, he had visited the farthermost reaches of the outer Five-Arm, way out beyond the Last Star Fields, even beyond the Final Stream. The memory bubbles in Tomm's quadtrol claimed, insisted even, that Zarex had journeyed farther out on the Five-Arm than anyone else had ever dared.

Tomm's quadtrol also confirmed that Zarex Red was last reported to be living on Bazooms, "retired from all positions."

Now viewed from a lower orbit, the remains on Bazooms looked to be everything its name and reputation had implied. It was a small world, just a couple thousand miles or so in circumference, with rocky highlands north and south of a tropic equator. The two large landmasses were covered with hundreds of fantastically old structures. Palaces, resorts, casinos, sky-scraping hotels, not decayed, just abandoned. Cities once bathed in garish lights now unlit and dark. Thousands of artificial lakes, rivers, and lagoons, and one entire sea, dried up. Just about every square inch of level terrain had been taken up at one time with a hedonistic establishment of some kind. But now the planet appeared to be dead. Desolate. One big ghost town.

Yet, switching over to his long-range scanner, Hunter saw the barest glimmer of light coming from a spot on the larger of the two landmasses, just north of the equator. It came over as a patch of color in the otherwise gray background. There was a bit of life still left down there.

Or so it seemed.

Hunter set the flying machine's auto-scan on high, and after a few passes he got a closer blink on the life signs below. Nestled into the side of a high peak about two hundred miles north of the planet's equator was another palace of sorts, built with seven spires and a large artificial lake in the middle. Hunter booted his azimuth and was soon in a low orbit just ninety-five miles above this place. According to the scanner, only one life-form was left on Bazooms. All alone, right below them.

Hunter suggested Tomm strap down in his cramped jump seat; at the same time he ran a few environmental checks on the planet's climatic conditions. Unlike so many planets way out here, Bazooms's puff status was stable. The surface temperature was seventy-two degrees, the atmosphere itself was holding at a constant 92 percent. This meant the weather was fine and the air was good.

But Hunter's instruments revealed an atmospheric oddity as well. Like every other planet and moon in the Galaxy, Bazooms's atmosphere was the essential mix of nitrogen and oxygen. But Hunter had also detected a trace of the gas nitrous oxide—laughing gas. In fact, back in the planet's heyday, there had been two facilities, one at each pole, pumping N_2O into the atmosphere on a constant basis. Hunter had to laugh at this. Apparently, the people who ran this place felt that if the perfect weather, the landscape, and the palatial resorts weren't enough to please you, maybe the spiked atmosphere would.

Breathe deep and go with the flow, Hunter thought now. *Not bad advice . . .*

They finally burned in through the atmosphere, setting down on a flat piece of ground located right outside the main gates of the resort. But something was strange here. There was only supposed to be one person living down on the surface—Hunter's scanning devices had told him so. Yet they could hear the sound of many voices coming from the other side of the resort's wall. People talking, laughing, pealing with delight. The sound of water cascading, glasses clinking, the staccato popping of many slow-ship wine bottles coming to life. Music blaring—it was the unmistakable din of a 'cloud party in full blast.

"Either my scans are skewed," Hunter said to Tomm once they'd climbed out of the flying machine. "Or a couple hundred people in there just woke up from the dead."

Tomm just shrugged. "Sometimes things aren't always as they appear," he said.

There was another thing: The high-walled resort appeared much grander up close. From this perspective, just a hundred feet from the main gate, the seven towers spiraling above the resort seemed to reach into orbit themselves. The valley below them was shimmering in an amazing shade of green. The sky was an absolute crystal blue. Or was it?

Pater Tomm took in a deep breath and smiled. So did Hunter. Suddenly the place looked even better.

"Must be the air," the priest said with a laugh.

Hunter secured the flying machine inside his Twenty 'n Six and they walked through the main gate of the resort.

The place was buzzing with activity, contrary to what the scans had implied. There was a swimming pool the size of a small ocean just inside the gate. It was surrounded by a bevy of bathing beauties that seemed to stretch as far as the eye could see. Hunter and Tomm walked past the pool, not eliciting as much as a curious smirk from any within the curvaceous collective. Up the grand steps, they entered the expansive lobby of the resort's main tower. Like the pool, the lobby was jammed with hundreds of beautiful, young, scantily clad women.

There was a huge floating desk in the middle of this hall; it seemed to be the center of this little universe. Six gorgeous women in white tunic uniforms were sitting behind it. Unlike the girls at the pool, they seemed aware that two oddly dressed strangers were suddenly among them. They eyed Hunter's unique Empire uniform first, then the priest's cassock and collar.

"Are you two lost?" one of the females asked.

Hunter began to say something when Tomm nudged him aside. "Let me handle this," he said.

The priest studied each girl for a moment, then stood before a rather stunning blonde. Without a word, he reached across the desk and with the back of his hand, lightly stroked the skin above the girl's breasts. He let his fingers travel up to the nape of her neck, finally resting them on her cheek. The girl did not move; she did not object. She just sat there and smiled.

"Exquisite work," Tomm whispered. "If only . . ."

He turned back to Hunter, who was clearly puzzled.

"Isn't that called 'copping a feel,' Padre?" Hunter asked him.

Tomm just shrugged and turned back to the six girls. "We're looking for someone named Zarex Red."

All six females laughed at once. "Sorry," one finally said. "He doesn't take visitors."

"So he is here then?" Tomm asked.

"He is," another replied. "But he is a very busy man. We have instructions not to allow anyone to—"

"You can counter those instructions," Tomm told the girl firmly. "Beam us up to his room right now—and that's an order."

Without a moment's hesitation, she smiled and pushed a button.

Flash!

The next thing Hunter knew, he and Tomm had popped into the entranceway of an enormous three-tiered penthouse.

It took him a moment to realize they were atop the resort's tallest spire. The room looked like a miniature palace. The main rooms were all circular and lined with windows throughout. Even the floor was made out of glass, creating the illusion that everything up here was just floating on air. No matter which way one turned, the view was awesome.

They took a few tentative steps inside. The interior of the main room was as impressive as the view. There was lots of crystal. Lots of diamonds. And lots of girls. Some reclined on the dozens of couches strewn about the penthouse. Others sat on pillows on the floor. Still others simply floated around aimlessly, with little more to do than look beautiful.

"I'll give him one thing," Hunter said, surveying the big room. "This guy knows how to hide out."

Tomm just shrugged. "Remember, though, all might not be as it appears."

"Yeah," Hunter replied. "You keep saying that."

At the far end of the main room, a large veranda protruded mightily from the side of the tower. There was a floating couch located on this balcony, and it was surrounded by another dozen girls so gorgeous, they made all the beauties inside pale a bit in comparison, if that was possible.

The balcony girls were in various stages of undress. Their undivided attention was being directed at the figure lying on the couch. Several girls were stroking his head, others his back, his chest, his legs. Still others were hovering around his nether regions.

Eyes barely slits, catching some rays from the system's spunky sun, it was Zarex Red himself.

He was a large individual, muscular, brutish-looking, at least from this angle. He was probably 160 years old or so, no more than 170 certainly. Unlike the shaved-head-and-goatee look that was the rage throughout most of the Galaxy these days, Zarex had a head of wild and woolly dark red hair that reached past his shoulders. His face was clean shaven. He was wearing a standard space uniform that had been strategically ripped around the shoulders to emphasize his rock-hard biceps.

He was oblivious of the two visitors. Between the legion of preening angels and the concerted effort at getting tanned, Zarex's mind seemed to be taxed to its limit. Hunter and Tomm just sort of shrugged and stepped out onto the balcony. Though they appeared to be nearly a half mile above the planet's surface, only a mild breeze was blowing past them. The view was incredible.

Just like the girls inside the penthouse itself—indeed, just about every female they'd met so far—these new beauties flatly ignored them. In fact, they didn't even seem to be aware of their existence. Each was totally devoted to the job of comforting Zarex.

Finally, with no little drama, Tomm cleared his throat.

Zarex finally came to life, but just barely. He opened one of his eyes and took a look up at the priest.

"My God," he whispered. "I'm either dead or I'm dreaming. I mean . . . why would I imagine a priest suddenly standing on my balcony?"

"Because he is real," Tomm told him. "Unlike many other things around here."

Zarex still did not move a muscle, except the ones in his left eyelid and lips. "Maybe you're a ghost . . ." he mused. "One that will go away as soon as I take my next sip of wine. . . ."

"Drink then to the honor of the Great Klaaz," Tomm told him right back. "He's the one who sent us to see you."

Both of Zarex's eyes managed to open now.

"My friend Klaaz sent a priest for me?" he asked with a gasp. "I'd say that is a scarier prospect than being visited by a ghost."

Tomm looked about the balcony; so did Hunter. To his eyes, it was a cluster of naked and near-naked breasts, some slightly moist, some gleaming in the sun. Still, the beauties seemed oblivious to everything except Zarex.

"You might find yourself dead or somewhere worse, should you ever have a power outage up here," Tomm told him in a very priestly tone.

This comment finally brought a change in Zarex. He raised himself from the couch and got to his feet. He was an even more massive individual than Hunter had first thought.

"Forgive me, Father," Zarex said with a slight bow. "I've been here so long, I've obviously forgotten my manners."

Tomm made a very quick crossing motion with his right hand, ending it with a hard slap upside Zarex's head. The man winced.

"Klaaz suspected you might be losing the battle to temptation," Pater Tomm said. "He was right, as always."

"I prefer to think of it as fighting the good fight, Padre," Zarex replied, rubbing his afflicted cheek.

Tomm just sniffed. "It's self-abuse," he said, not entirely priestly now. "To the highest degree . . ."

Hunter was barely paying attention to this odd conversation; his eyes were still saturated with all the gleaming, tanned, jiggling breasts. Tomm looked back at him, saw the state he was in, and threatened to slap his head, too.

He turned back to Zarex and said, "I pray you to reveal your little secret . . . before my friend here explodes."

Zarex frowned and reluctantly snapped his fingers.

Suddenly, all the girls disappeared.

Hunter was stunned—for about two seconds.

Then it hit him.

"Holo-girls?" he mumbled.

Zarex nodded sadly. "The best . . ."

Of course, Hunter thought. *Now it all makes sense.*

He had met only one holo-girl in the flesh, so to speak. Or at least he didn't think he'd encountered any more; there was no way to really tell. That was the problem. Holo-girls were holographic projections of the most superior kind. They looked, felt, and acted as if they were human. And they were always perfect—*always.* Or at least the more expensive models were. They came packaged inside a small container not unlike a Twenty 'n Six box, just slightly more egg-shaped. Push the button, your holo-girl was there. Face, shape, hair, voice. *Perfect . . .* and ready to do anything.

Don't like blue eyes? Push the button, they turn to brown. Don't like blondes, another push, she's a redhead or a brunette or a raven-haired beauty. Another push, her breasts begin to grow. And grow. And grow. When it seems her top is about to burst, push again, and her breasts begin to shrink, almost until they become nonexistent. Push again, a tight top becomes a simple white blouse. Push. Skintight pants became a skintight skirt. Push. The boots disappear, revealing a beautiful set of bare legs and feet.

Push . . . Push . . . Push . . .

But that was not all. The top-of-the-line holo-girls had the ability to take their suitors into the thirty-fourth dimension, a place programmed to provide endless scenarios usually involving paradise settings—all projected, of course. The top holo-girls had large memory banks, meaning the suitor could go into the Big Three-Four for days, weeks, even months, however long one could stand it. Then, with another push of the button, he would return to his starting point before his friends had taken another sip of their drinks. No time had passed at all. Invariably, the traveler would ask, "What I miss?"

But now, as the last of Zarex's holo-girls began blinking out all over the resort, a sense of gloom descended upon the penthouse. Suddenly, things weren't as bright, the colors not as vivid. The diamonds and crystal had lost their gleam.

It was apparent what was really going on.

The girls in the tower. The girls in the lobby. The girls lounging around the pool. They were all fakes. Zarex *was* alone here.

A long moment passed as the tidal wave of despair washed

through the room. Now it really did seem like they were on a barren planet in a no-good star system with a guy who was simply hiding out. Hunter took a deep breath. It did no good. The gloom remained.

Zarex sighed and collected the few dozen holo-eggs and stored them away in a small carrying case, his only discernible luggage.

Then he turned to his visitors.

"Well, you've succeeded in banishing my one and only real vice," he said dryly. "Can I at least offer you a drink before you go?"

Without waiting for an answer, he led them over to an enormous bar, which was floating above what looked like a miniature self-contained sea, complete with rows of tiny waves and whitecaps. There were more than a hundred varieties of slow-ship wine on display above this really wet bar. Zarex reached across the tiny sea and selected a bright red bottle from the hovering rack. He poured out three healthy shots.

They held their glasses aloft.

"For fallen friends," all three intoned.

They downed their drinks in one noisy, simultaneous shot. Hunter let the sweetly pungent liquid flow down his throat. Instantly, he felt his feet lift a bit off the ground again.

Good stuff.

Zarex poured out three more shots. He seemed to relax a little.

"So you are friends of the Great Klaaz?" he asked with a booming voice. "Few names could break my spell."

"A friend of his is hopefully a friend of ours," Pater Tomm said with a polite bow.

They toasted again, this time silently. If possible, the second shot of slow-ship tasted better than the first. Hunter studied their host for a moment. For someone so huge and wild-looking, Zarex did have a dashing air about him. There was more than a hint of intelligence in his face, a bit of larceny in his steely eyes. The bubbles claimed Zarex had single-handedly charted thousands of isolated star systems and probably hundreds of thousands of planets as well. Though he didn't look the part, when he wasn't doing his weapons-selling gig, Zarex was one hell of an explorer.

He also knew his star juice.

"So, Father," he said, pouring out three more shots. "Are you also here to tell me the Great Klaaz is well?"

"Klaaz is well, and therefore so are our lives," Tomm replied properly. Then the priest nodded toward Hunter. "But actually, my friend and I have been shooting the Five-Arm for many weeks now, looking for a certain passage. . . ."

Zarex's eyebrows rose with amusement. "And you took a wrong turn at the last nebula?" he asked.

Tomm shook his head. "No, we simply need directions. To a place, that . . . How shall I say it? Is off the beaten track."

Zarex laughed. "My specialty, once . . ."

The priest lowered his voice. "We want to find the Home Planets."

Zarex's smile disappeared.

"The Home Planets?" he asked with mock ignorance. "Well, then you've been on a fool's mission, Padre. They don't exist."

Tomm sampled his third drink. "I should remind you that it is very bad luck to lie to a priest."

Zarex took this admonition to heart somewhat, but he did not change his tack.

"The Home Planets are things of myth and legend, Father," he said. "Stories to be told to children at bedtime."

Zarex took a sip of his drink; they all did.

"Besides," he continued, "why do you think *I* know how to get to them?"

"Because of your reputation," Pater Tomm replied simply. "That, and the fact that Klaaz told me you would."

Zarex looked down at the holy man and then shot back the rest of his drink. His defenses were crumbling.

He turned toward Hunter. "Your uniform, my friend, where does it come from? I'm not familiar with it."

"It belongs to my former employers," Hunter replied.

Zarex studied it a bit more closely. "A deserter, eh?"

Tomm began to say something, but Hunter raised his hand and cut him off. There was no need to avoid the truth here.

"That's exactly what I am," Hunter said. "And in my own defense, I believe I left for honorable reasons."

"That's what they all say," Zarex replied with a smirk.

He poured out three more drinks.

"And what would your business be in the Home Planets?" Zarex asked him pointedly. "If they exist, that is—"

Tomm slammed his glass on the bar hard enough to cut Zarex off in midsentence.

"We don't need that line again, brother," the priest said sternly. "We *know* they still exist."

Zarex looked down at the priest. "Really? And how, may I ask?"

"Because we saw their fighters in action," Hunter revealed. "On a world in the Dead Gulch System called Zazu-Zazu."

Zarex stopped pouring another drink in midflow. He was clearly shocked by this news.

"You *saw* them? When?"

"Six weeks past now," Pater Tomm said.

"Six weeks?" Zarex exclaimed. "My God, if you had said six years—or even sixty—I would have been surprised. But so recently? I mean, I really thought they'd all be gone by now. When I last heard of them, their ranks were nearly depleted, even then . . ."

Zarex resumed filling their glasses. He shook his head.

"The Dead Gulch System, you say? Way out there? What the hell were they doing so far from home?"

"They were there because it was a holy place for them," Tomm said. "A place that was very important to their history, their mythology. Their whole everything. They were protecting the people who had acted as caretakers for the place. I know this because I traveled there with them. I hooked up with them at a staging planet two systems over. They needed a chaplain, I was available. They were just very tight-lipped about their planet of origin at the time."

"But what happened to them then?" Zarex asked. "Surely these fighters could have told you the way home."

"They're all gone," Hunter told him quietly. "Killed in battle."

Silence in the room.

"Every last one of them?" Zarex asked in a whisper. "Are you sure?"

Hunter nodded. "We were there. We saw it."

Zarex just shook his head again. He had to take a moment to collect himself. It was obvious the news had hit an emotional chord within him.

"Poor bastards," he said finally with a tip of his glass. "Sorry for the language, Father . . . but if that really was the last of them, well, I'm afraid that's not a good thing for any of us. Our existence needs more people like them, not less."

Pater Tomm took this as his cue. "So the Home Planets *do* exist," he said. "You know it, we know it. Now, their soldiers are gone, but those they left behind might still remain. It is these people we want to find."

Zarex contemplated them both. "Again, may I ask why?"

"I think I might have family among them," Hunter replied. "That's the simple answer, anyway."

Tomm drained his drink. "So, is it time to get down to brass tacks?" he asked Zarex.

"I'm listening, Padre," the explorer replied.

Tomm retrieved a bag of aluminum coins from his pocket. It was their payment for a mercenary job they'd done shortly after leaving Zazu-Zazu. He held it out at arm's length, barely up to Zarex's chest.

"We like our privacy, too," the priest told him. "So just tell us how to get there, and we leave this bag behind as insurance that the secret dies with us."

Zarex eyed the bag, was tempted mightily, but then shook his head. "This goes beyond gratuities, father."

The priest patted him on the arm. "We mean these people no harm, brother. They want to stay hidden; we understand that. It's only dialogue that we seek."

"It's not as simple as that," Zarex said. "It's a very long journey just to get to the first step. And after that, it gets worse. Nearly impossible, in fact."

He poured them all another shot of wine.

"Believe me, I've had more than my share of such treacherous journeys, and frankly, my friends, they are not good for either heart or soul."

He drained his drink and capped the bottle. "So, I am sorry," he said. "But there's nothing I can do for you. Please give my regards to Klaaz when you see him again."

Suddenly, Hunter grabbed him by the wrist. "Don't move," he warned the explorer.

Even Tomm was shocked by this sudden departure of good form.

"Please, brother," he cautioned Hunter. "There are other ways to—"

But Hunter wasn't listening to him. His eyes were looking all

the way to the left, and his ears were perked up. It was as if he
was trying to hear something from very far away.

Zarex tried to untangle his arm, but Hunter was too strong
for him.

"Listen," Hunter told them urgently. "We have to get out of
here . . . *immediately.*"

Zarex and Pater Tomm just stared back at him.

"What did you just say?" the priest asked him.

"I said we have to get out of this tower *right now!*"

But Zarex wouldn't budge. "What's got into you, man?" he
roared at Hunter.

"Trust me," Hunter said, head still cocked skyward. "Something very bad is coming this way."

Pater Tomm needed no prodding; he was already convinced.

"Mr. Hunter has a way about these things," the priest said to
Zarex. "We must go right now!"

Zarex did not argue any further. He gathered most of his holo-
eggs and . . .

Flash!

They popped out a moment later, standing behind a huge
boulder about a half mile from the resort's main gate. Zarex and
Tomm were looking highly distressed and staring at Hunter, as
if to ask him: *Why?*

They would know the answer in just a few seconds.

The missile had entered the BDG star system just three minutes
before, and only an instant before Hunter's elevated senses detected it. As soon as he felt it, though, there was never any doubt
where the missile was headed. How could he detect a missile
from so far away with just his instincts? He didn't know. As
Pater Tomm said, he just had a way with these things.

It came out of the blue sky with an ungodly roar, heading
right at the resort's highest tower. The missile was a LR/
SDBM—a long-range space-deployed bombardment missile. It
was an almost antique weapon closer in to the Ball, but still a
formidable piece of hardware out here on the Fringe.

Two hundred feet long, with a squat fuselage and a triangular,
almost arrowlike warhead on its tip, it was a weapon used centuries before to conduct massive bombardment of entire planets;
indeed, a barrage of these missiles, hitting key strategic areas in
unrelenting attack, could deplete a planet's global defenses in a

matter of hours, softening it up for invasion from space.

But the real beauty of the LR/SDBM was its tactical capability. The missile could be programmed to seek out one particular spaceship or even one particular individual and then be set loose in space for days, months, years, even centuries, searching for its prey and reviving to active mode once it had been acquired.

Therefore it could take out whole populations in some cases—or just one man.

It was apparent that in this case, the missile had been looking for just one man.

It hit the largest tower an instant later, impacting on the top floor, which had been occupied just minutes before by Zarex and his electronic entourage. The resulting explosion was so spectacular, it set off a minor quake beneath their feet. The three of them stared in astonishment as the tall tower was vaporized, and the remains of the missile plunged deep into the mountain behind the resort, driving an enormous hole into the layers of solid rock.

It took nearly a minute for all the echoes of the blast to finally fade away. Through it all, Zarex was speechless.

"It must be the Bad Moon Knights again," he finally mumbled. "I mean, it *has* to be them. Every once in a while they take a shot at me—over some past disagreements. But an LS/SDBM? That's a bit much."

Zarex turned back to Hunter and Pater Tomm. Things had changed.

"Well, it now appears that I owe you my life, and I need a new place to relocate," he said. "So, I'll point you in the right direction of the Home Planets, provided just one thing . . ."

"What's that?" Tomm asked. "Our bag of money?"

"No," Zarex said. "I want to come with you on the journey. Me and a friend of mine . . ."

"One of those holo-girls, you mean?"

"Hardly, Father," Zarex replied.

He reached into his case and took out not a holo-egg but a Twenty 'n Six box. After checking out the surrounding terrain, he activated the intradimensional device. The usual cloud of green mist appeared, and after a flash of light, they found a huge robot standing in front of them. It was at least ten feet tall.

"He's not only my best 'bot," Zarex told Hunter and Tomm,

"but he's my bodyguard as well. I have found him extremely useful in the past. I would like him out of his box and at my side for the entire journey ahead. He might even come in handy for what is before us."

Hunter studied the robot standing just a few feet away. He was a clanker, that is, a robot who had two arms, two legs, one head, and a body in the shape of an average man, but who made no pretense of looking like a human being, as some other more upscale robots did.

This clanker's ID was 33418. Bright gold in color, he had an eerily blank face, a small speaker for a mouth, and a thick red visor that served as his visual system. He looked old and slow, and if the gun-shy explorer wanted him out 24/7, someone who would take up a lot of space, especially in flight.

"I'm not sure about this," Hunter started to say. "We can use your help where we are going, but—"

"He is an excellent pilot," Zarex said of the robot.

Hunter shrugged. "But my space craft is unique; I'm afraid I am the only one who can figure its controls."

"Well, he is also an outstanding navigator."

Hunter motioned to Pater Tomm. "The padre is one of the best. I would hate to see both their talents wasted by an over-lapping of duties."

"But he's also a mechanic, a translator of odd tongues . . ."

Hunter just shook his head. "I can fix my own aircraft, and Pater Tomm speaks in many tongues."

But Zarex was determined. "At the *very least*, let me give you a demonstration," he said.

Finally, Hunter relented.

Zarex flashed a brief smile of victory, then snapped his fingers. A tiny control panel materialized out of nowhere. It was wobbly on arrival. Zarex touched the main bus, and the rest of the control panel lit up. Another panel touched, and the robot suddenly blinked to life. His arms tensed, the visor covering his mechanical eyes narrowed a bit. A soft whirring could be heard coming from its chest.

"Behold, my friends," Zarex said, pressing the first of the control panel's trio of red lights.

A small storm of sparks erupted beneath the robot's big metal feet. There was a loud bang and a mighty puff of smoke. Then, suddenly, the robot lifted off the ground and shot straight up at eye-blistering speed, deep into the very blue sky. The robot quickly reached a height of nearly two thousand feet, then very slowly turned over. Arms now tucked into his sides, his jaw sticking straight out, he began a dive so fast and so steep, he cracked the sound barrier, registering a boom that reverberated off the nearby mountains. The robot zoomed right past them, banked hard left, then leveled out about four feet above the ground. An instant later, he pulled up again and did a kind of power loop over the remains of the recently destroyed resort, very noisy, very smoky, but also very, very quickly. The robot was moving extremely fast, yet was taking turns and cutting angles with incredible finesse.

Zarex pushed the second red button and in a flash, the robot looped again, came screaming down at them, pulling up at the last possible instant before coming to a stop in the exact position and on the exact same spot he'd left just seconds before. Zarex pushed the third red button. Suddenly, the robot's head turned and his eye visor lifted up, revealing a deeply glowing red lens beneath. An incredibly bright beam of purple red light burst from the lens, traveled across the valley, over the resort's shattered wall to another rugged mountain range beyond, a distance of at least five miles, where it exploded just below the top of the highest peak.

Hunter looked at Tomm, then at the robot, and then at Tomm again. Their jaws were hanging open. They were simply astonished.

"On second thought," Hunter said to Zarex. "Let's take him."

7

Despite the great distances involved and the profusion
of uncharted or lost planets in between, there was a strong tradition of oral myth among the peoples of the Five-Arm.

Almost all of the epics passed down through the centuries
involved wars fought along the Fringe or up and down the Five-
Arm itself. The greatest myths always involved the classic duel
between hero and villain. Sometimes the conflict was between
two planets, sometimes between entire star clusters, or even
clusters of star clusters. But no matter how big or how small,
the moral of the story, always hiding right below the surface,
was that even in conflict, honor wins out. Not only do the good
guys always triumph, they are always magnanimous in victory
and quick when it came time to forgive their foe.

This was an odd song to sing in this fragment of space, where
at any given moment as many as a million wars might be in
progress. The absolutely forgiving nature of the mythical warriors was a universal mystery; such a code of honor certainly
didn't exist on any grand scale in real life here. Those scholars
who chose to ponder such things always came to the same conclusion: that the idea of people treating each other with honor
was a notion that had been practiced sometime back through the
ages, and was now ingrained, if obviously repressed, in every
soul on the Five-Arm. This was proof, the great minds said, that
sometime during a history now long past, things had been better

for the human condition. Respect and dignity must have prevailed.

By far, the most oft-told story, the classic myth of honor, was the legend of the Great Michael. It always began with a small planet in a small, very isolated star system. As the story went, this planet, sometimes called Myx, was a world that had been fought over for centuries by two rival planets, usually called the Whites and the Grays. Myx was said to be thick with jewels, aluminum, the so-called good stuff, and both planets claimed it belonged to them. In the legend, the Whites were always the nobler of the two planets; they simply wanted to mine Myx just enough to keep their people fed, healthy, and happy. The Grays, on the other hand, wanted to rape the planet, using the money to buy weapons so they could overcome smaller, defenseless planets nearby and create an empire for themselves.

So many wars had been fought over Myx, eventually all the good stuff had been blasted away. Yet the wars continued simply because the animosity between the two rivals was so strong, the cycle could not be broken. Even though they were literally fighting over nothing, even though the aggressive Grays always lost, the conflicts went on. Millions would die, a temporary peace would ensue, only to end when the Grays attacked the Whites again a generation later.

Then the Great Michael—sometimes called Michael the Angel—arrived on the scene. He was King of the Whites, and after fighting one extremely brutal war, he declared he had a solution to the never-ending wheel of violence. Instead of training a new army for the inevitable next war against the Grays, Michael built an army of robots instead. They looked like humans, walked, talked, fought, and died like humans. But there were no beating hearts involved, and when the robots bled, it was liquefied hydraulic gas; it just looked like blood.

The robots were programmed for a maximum degree of aggressiveness. They were also given a degree of self-replication. (Robots had been building other robots for thousands of years across the Galaxy.) When the next war erupted, the Whites sent their kick-ass robots to battle, won big, and invaded the Gray planet to boot. That's when the Great Michael forgave his enemy, and then, in a bit of intrigue, left behind the secret for building the realistic combat robots. The Grays got the point. When the two planets went at it again, the Grays sent an army of robots, too, and after a century or so of combat, the war finally ended in a draw. By that time, both sides were loathe to commit any live soldiers to the morass, and a cycle of preserving life took hold.

But the story didn't end there. In almost every retelling of the myth, it was said the robots were *still* fighting on Myx, untold centuries later. Or more accurately, they periodically rose up from the wreckage of the war-torn planet and fought each other again and again and again, with undiminished ferocity, until all were destroyed and fell back into heaps of wreckage, to sleep until it was time to rise again. The robots served as ethereal reminders of the folly of war. Mechanical souls who came back from the dead, unstoppable in their mission, to fight over and over, victims of their own futility.

Robots as ghosts? It was a novel invention. But the myth had been retold many times in many variations among those ten million planets whose civilizations were aware of each other in the denser regions of the Five-Arm. It was supposed to serve as an enlightened morality play, something to remind the listener that peace among the stars was not a total impossibility.

But what people didn't know was that Myx was a real place, and that the planet could indeed be found very far out and very far away from the rest of the Five-Arm, and that it was a magical place as well, though not for reasons that were immediately apparent.

But where was it exactly? Only a handful of people in the entire Galaxy knew.

It just so happened that Zarex Red was one of them—or at least he thought he knew how to get here.

But as he told Hunter and Tomm, if they really wanted to find the Home Planets, they would have to find Myx first.

The voyage took almost a week.

The ghostly star system that held the mythical planet of Myx was almost fifteen thousand light-years away from Bazooms. Plus it was a trip that could not be done in a straight line. Space wasn't like that, not this far out on the Fringe. If the Fifth Arm was shaped like a slightly crooked arm, Bazooms was located just above the elbow. Tonk was just below. The moon of Zazu-Zazu, where Hunter first met Tomm and found the Freedom Brigade, was out on the tip of the outermost finger.

Myx was way out beyond the wrist, off the beaten track by nearly five hundred light-years. Zarex was fairly certain he could recall how to get there, but only by flying to a succession of isolated star systems, each one farther away from the other. Thus the trip featured long periods of streaking through absolutely empty space—or as absolutely empty as space could be.

The departure from Bazooms had not been immediate. Just as he had done when Pater Tomm joined him on the quest, Hunter made modifications to his flying machine in order to bring Zarex and his robot along. Wielding an electron torch like a painter wields a brush, Hunter elongated the flying machine's fuselage by six feet. Then he sculpted a flight compartment in this new space, one big enough to accommodate both Zarex's massive frame as well as his robot, 33418.

Hunter had also widened the plane's frame for two seats, two bunks, and more legroom. He added a superglass bubble on top to allow his friends to see where they were all going. Hunter programmed these changes into his electron torch's unlimited memory strings. This meant that with the mere push of a button and a steady hand, the aircraft could quickly revert back to its previous configuration.

They passed the six days of travel playing a game of chance Zarex had learned years before called Sh'exx. It involved a set of six dice played on a three-dimensional floating matrix. Randomly scattered within the matrix were a dozen tiny, temporary wormholes through which a player could lose his marker and as a result, his bet. As the location of the wormholes was always changing and always random, this was the ultimate game of chance. And of good timing. Just one day into the trip, Pater Tomm had lost all the money he had to his name to Zarex. By the third day, the priest had won it all back and had relieved Zarex of most of his aluminum chips as well. By the sixth day, Tomm was broke again. Zarex allowed 33418 to hold all his winnings.

Hunter spent most of the time driving the ship and taking in the sights along the way: blue stars, green stars, dead stars, and stars about to be born. They passed over, under, and through massive clouds of space dust, usually colored brilliant red or yellow, or sometimes, pure, angelic white.

One of the odd things about Hunter's flying machine and the way it quickly moved from one part of the Galaxy to another was that despite the incredible velocity, one could see other spaceships—both flying in Supertime and at the slower high warp ion speeds—as if they were going by them in slow motion. The laws of physics said that this was actually the opposite of what should be happening, and indeed, the same was not true for pilots of Empire Starcrashers. They went so fast, they could see only vessels that were also traveling like them, in Supertime. But Hunter had given up long ago trying to figure out why his craft acted the way it did. Sometimes he thought it might be better that he didn't know.

He kept a running count of other spacecraft he spotted during the journey, knowing that they could not see him. In six days, he counted just two dozen spacecraft, all of different sizes, all built in different variations of the triangular shape that permeated the Galaxy.

Each spaceship he saw was powered by ion-ballast engines and was not flying in Supertime, the mysterious extra dimensional star highway used exclusively by ships of the Fourth Empire. This was important information for Hunter. Should any member of the Empire's military cross paths with him out here, they would be duty bound to place him in chains and return him, if not to Earth, then to the closest imperial military post. This was something Hunter wanted to avoid at all costs, of course, so he was constantly on the lookout for ships of the Empire.

He saw none, though.

The one thing he had going in his favor was the near-total isolation of the part of the Galaxy he was flying in. The Five-Arm was considered isolated even by those people who lived there. Indeed, it was considered by many to be the last frontier of the Galaxy, the fringe beyond the fringe. Again, very few people out on the Five-Arm even knew of the existence of the Fourth Empire, or life on Earth, or even about Earth itself. For a ship as powerful as a massive Empire Starcrasher to suddenly arrive above their unsuspecting planet—well, of such things worldwide panics are made.

So Hunter knew if he did see an Empire ship cruising around out here, it would be a very unusual thing. That's why he kept his eyes open at all times.

They finally spotted Myx on the morning of the seventh day.

It was a strange-looking place, the only world circling a yellow blue star, which itself was the only star for light-years around. They were so far off the usual starways, it could be argued that this tiny system was not part of the Five-Arm at all. Its location also begged another question: If this was indeed the real Myx, where did the Whites and Grays come from?

Hunter drained off 99.999999018 percent of his speed and maneuvered the flying machine in toward the planet. A thick murk was rising into the atmosphere, nearly into orbit itself. The place looked shrouded in clouds, but in reality it was smoke. That was something else Zarex told them during the trip: Most of Myx was actually on fire.

"There are probably just a handful of people who know about this planet," Zarex said now, looking down at the absolutely weird world. "Of that handful, only a few are as crazy as me to fly all the way out here."

Tomm could only agree. "And I thought Zazu-Zazu was a lost rock," he said.

Hunter swooped beneath smoky cloud cover, leveled off at five hundred feet, and commenced his aerial recon. There really wasn't a lot of variation on the planet's surface, however. No matter what part of Myx they passed over, the scene was that of utter devastation. Entire cities, forests, valleys, mountains, all laid to waste. The wreckage of many giant weapons was also in evidence, including hundreds of ancient-looking multitubed blaster rays. They also sighted many large military installations; all of them blasted to bits. In many cases they were dotted with hundreds of solidified piles of white dust: incinerated soldiers that never even made it to the battlefield.

And everywhere were the robots.

From the highest mountains to the deepest valleys, in the heaviest debris of the cities and along the thousands of miles of front lines, there was the wreckage of millions of battle robots. It made the planet Tonk, which was strewn with thousands of junked ships, look like a tropical paradise by comparison.

It didn't take more than a few extremely low circumnavigations of the planet for the story to come together. This was hardly the battered but noble place described in the heroic myths. This was a dirty little planet, awash in destruction, centuries-old blood, and liquefied hydraulic gas. During his brief stint in the Empire's X-Forces, Hunter had seen many battle-scarred worlds, uncharted places that looked so uninviting, his recommendation back to Earth was simple: "Avoid until necessary."

Still, he'd seen nothing that compared to this.

And there was more: To make a very treacherous place even worse, the entire planet was sown with mines, trip wires, and other exotic booby traps. Hunter's sensors indicated millions of these devices in place, from pole to pole, east to west, all over the vast battlefield. One wrong move down there, a sneeze, a burp, a dropped quadtrol, could set off every implanted weapon within a half-mile radius of the act, causing a massive chain reaction that was more than enough to perforate the offending party until they were nothing more than a zillion little pieces of subatomic dust.

Put it all together—the remote location, the haunting myth, the layers of dangerous junk below—and Myx was probably the last place anyone would want to land. Throw in the millions of skeletons, well-preserved and bleached by cosmic rays, rivers that literally ran in the color of blood, the near-poisonous atmosphere and, for good measure, several pyramids that had been built eons ago—well, the result was probably the most inhospitable planet in the Galaxy.

Yet Zarex had been there once before and lived to tell the tale. He'd delivered a weapons load to the planet seventy years before, in the heyday of his arms-dealing career. At the time, his buyer was unknown to him, and the contract, for several thousand used blaster rifles, had been given to him after passing through more than a dozen separate hands.

He didn't stay around long enough to unravel the real secret of Myx. Per his buyer's instructions, he'd brought the arms cache down to a prearranged coordinate packaged in a Twenty 'n Six. Zarex waited not even a minute when the cache disappeared and his payment materialized. He left quickly after that, completing the strangest deal he'd ever done.

It was only later, while running blasters to one side in the brutal Bunker-Sabrini System civil war, that he learned exactly who his client that day was. One Rebel planet in the Bunker-S was holding out until reinforcements could fly in from the next system over. Royalist forces battered the planet for months, until the cavalry finally arrived and chased them away. When the victorious forces beamed down to the planet, they found all of its valiant defenders dead. One contingent had been made up of mercs who, it had been whispered, were from "way, way out." On hearing this, Zarex visited the battleground, saw the bodies, and examined their combat weapons. They were from the load he'd dropped off on Myx just months before.

His buyer had been a battalion of the Freedom Brigade.

"But how can such a wretched place have a connection to the Home Planets?" Tomm asked Zarex, now that he'd had a good look at the place again.

"It's a hard question, with a hard answer, Padre," the explorer replied. "Perhaps whoever inhabits the Home Planets—if, in fact, they still exist—knows that this place is the most cursed rock on the Five-Arm, if not the whole Galaxy.

"Add in the whole mythological jumble about the place. At the very least, the person who put that juicy legend together wanted people to believe this planet was holy, scary, unlucky— all at once. Just further incentive to stay away should anyone happen to come upon it. In my mind, that all makes a perfect place to do supersecret things"

Tomm could barely look down at the planet now.

"Amen to that," he said.

Zero Degree Zero. That was the coordinate on Myx that Zarex had beamed down to that day many years ago.

This was a point, located in the western hemisphere, where legend said, the Whites and the Grays had maintained their longest front line, a twenty-five-mile stretch of territory that cut through a deep valley about midway across the planet's largest landmass.

It was no surprise that the ZDZ looked even more devastated than the rest of the planet, if that was possible. Bomb craters everywhere, wide swaths of blaster residue torn into the landscape. The region was extra thick with exotic booby traps. On the entire planet, this seemed to be the absolute worst place for anyone to want to land.

Yet this is where Zarex told them to go.

After circling the coordinate several times, Hunter's keen eye found a spot where he could set the flying machine down without disturbing any of the trip wires. This LZ was actually the highest elevation found in the vicinity of Zero Degree Zero. Not a hill, but the remains of mountain that had been caught in a massive cross fire of blasters ages ago, shearing off its summit.

Hunter landed close to the edge of the flattened-out peak and immediately checked the atmosphere with his environmental management systems. How the planet's puff was still intact was yet another mystery, but his gear said the air was still breathable, though barely so.

This didn't make what they saw outside any more appealing. The wreckage, the echoes of the carnage, the dreary overcast. The pyramids off in the distance. The vibe here was not good.

"Whose idea was this again?" Hunter asked as he gazed out at the endless miles of wreckage.

Both Pater Tomm and Zarex answered on cue, *"Yours . . ."*

Hunter just shook his head. "Oh, yeah, I keep forgetting."

He popped the canopy and gingerly climbed out of the flying machine. There was an eerie wind blowing across the ZDZ. It sounded like many voices crying at once. And no matter where Hunter looked, he saw nothing but destruction. Fires still burning, devastated buildings, and tens of thousands of silhouettes of white soot. The ground, when you could see it between the robots, was stained mightily with blood.

Tomm, Zarex, and 33418 climbed down from the cockpit, and Hunter immediately put the flying machine into his Twenty 'n Six.

"Not exactly what I pictured from the fairy tale," Pater Tomm whispered, moving his hand from his forehead to his chest and then giving a tap to each shoulder.

They stood there, the four of them, for a very long time, not talking, letting it all sink in. The all-encompassing destruction under the blur of the dull blue sun became oddly fascinating after a while.

Hell . . . That was the word that kept popping into Hunter's mind. If there really was a Hell somewhere, it had to look a lot like this.

They set up a small camp. Tomm produced some ancient fire, Zarex commanded 33418 to go on full-passive scan. The robot's head began swiveling back and forth. Even Hunter had to admit he felt better with the ten-foot mechanical man standing watch over them. This place was giving them all the creeps.

But no sooner had 33418 been activated when the usual hum coming from its chest suddenly skyrocketed in pitch. The clanker walked to the edge of the precipice and stared down into the trench-filled valley. A beam shot out of his helmet visor and began actively scanning the battlefield below. Suddenly the robot pitched forward—it was almost as if he was throwing himself into the maw. But then the power jets in his boots ignited, and he was airborne a moment later. The three humans watched, mystified, as the clanker flew to the deepest, foggiest part of the valley, eventually diving down and disappearing into the murk. He reappeared a moment later, shooting straight up for about one thousand feet, then curving over and coming in for a perfect landing not far from where he'd taken off.

He was carrying with him the remains of two battle robots. He dropped the wreckage at Zarex's feet.

"I think he's trying to tell you something," Hunter said.

"Or educate us," Pater Tomm added.

Zarex tugged at his woolly mane. "I should tell you I'm not the best when it comes to communicating with him," he admitted. "He understands our basic language, but he's so old, I think he was programmed in a more ancient version."

"Go ahead anyway," Hunter urged Zarex. "Encourage him."

Zarex shrugged and then said to the robot, "Ah, OK . . . *Proceed.* . . ."

The clanker did not move.

"Ah, *carry on?*" Zarex tried again.

Still nothing.

"Try this," Hunter said. *"Engage.* . . ."

The robot moved, but ever so slightly and only for an instant.

"Try it again, Hawk," Zarex told him.

Hunter cleared his throat and said even louder, *"Engage!"*

That did the trick. Twin beams suddenly erupted out of the clanker's visor, hitting the dead robots at his feet. Almost instantly, the two piles of wreckage began to move. Twin hums of electricity filled the air. Incredibly, the mechanical corpses were beginning to stir.

Pater Tomm's eyes went extra wide. "We might want to take a step back for this," he said.

All three did, and right before their eyes, the two robots began rebuilding themselves. First it was just a clink here, a clank there. Then an arm stretched out. Then a leg started coming together. The process began to speed up, and before they knew it, the two snarling, snorting robots had regained their full height, which was just a tad shorter than 33418 itself.

"So it is true!" Pater Tomm said with a gasp. "They *can* come back to life!"

Hunter and Zarex were just as startled as the priest.

"I've never . . . I mean I really didn't think . . ." Zarex began stuttering.

The battle robots stood about eight feet tall, looking fierce in their metal faces, their huge clamperlike hands, powerful torsos, and ridiculously muscular legs. They had a variety of weapons strapped to their belts and many more sprouting from their huge wrists and forearms. Further diluting the legend, neither robot was white or gray. In fact, one was deep black, the other dirty green.

In perfect synchronous movement, both robots coiled back, and after an instant or two of contemplation, lunged at each other with snarling ferocity. The humans quickly retreated even farther as the mechanical soldiers commenced to tear each other apart again. Few weapons came into play in the brief but brutal battle. It was simply massive force versus massive force. The robots pounded away at each other, creating huge dents and searing rips in their metallic fabric. And sure enough, they fought each other to an absolute draw. In less than thirty seconds, both robots had been reduced to piles of junk again.

"Wow!" Pater Tomm whispered, as 33418 gently pushed both piles of rubble over the cliff, sending them tumbling back into the deep valley again. "That certainly *was* educational."

"It surely was," Zarex said. "I just learned that I don't want to be here when the five million *other* tin cans on this rock decide to rise from the dead again."

"I'm with you there," Hunter said, visualizing the entire planet in the throes of a relentless mechanical struggle. It was not something to be caught in the middle of. "But now what?"

"Well, that's the problem," Zarex said, scanning the smoky sky above them. "Now, we just have to wait. If the people who know how to get to the Home Planets from here want anything to do with us, they'll have to let us know."

Pater Tomm needed no convincing. He collapsed to the seat of his pants, as if all the energy had suddenly been sucked out of him. Zarex, too, found the most comfortable rock to sit down on. Hunter was at the point of exhaustion as well. The long trip added to so much uncertainty didn't help the condition. What lay now in the future? It had taken them so long and so much effort just to get to this place, it seemed like such a dead end now that they'd finally arrived.

Could they really find their way to the Home Planets from here? At the moment, it seemed very unlikely.

Hunter finally sat down and rubbed his weary eyes. The wind blew again, and it sounded like another thousand voices screaming in agony. The robot stayed rigid, his head again sweeping back and forth, constantly scanning. But definitely slower. The hum coming from his insides had taken on a mournful note.

Pater Tomm looked at the sullen group gathered around the fire and just shook his head. "What a merry band are we," he sighed.

The night came quickly.

Setting in the west, the dull blue sun cast the weirdest shadows as it died away. Purple, aqua, hints of bloodred flooded across the wreckage-strewn plains. Then came complete darkness. There were no moons to glow and precious little starshine here. Once all light was gone, the wind began to absolutely howl. Now it sounded like *tens* of thousands of people screaming in pain. There were even more horrific cries rising up from the valley below, more chilling than the wind. Low-pitched, mechanical, guttural, like some gigantic clanker trying to catch his breath. Every once in a while, a bone-rattling electronic moan would float up from the ancient killing fields, causing the humans to stir. Hunter found himself constantly feeling for the handle of his blaster pistol. Zarex had a massive ray-gun rifle resting on his knees. Pater Tomm sat between them and tended the fire. The robot simply kept scanning.

Hunter tried to pass the time, as always, by staring up at the heavens, but the night sky here was uncomfortably devoid of stars. In almost every direction he looked, he saw only the blackness of space with just a few pinpricks of light shining through. If they needed any further proof just how far out they were, this was certainly it.

The only wash of stars at all was off to due south, looking back into the Five-Arm. Hunter tried to play his game again, tried to see right past this thin band of light, hoping if he squinted hard enough, maybe he'd be able to see right through the center of the Galaxy and beyond.

To where Earth lay.

To where Xara was.

But it didn't work too well this time. Her face came to him as always. And her near perpetual smile. But her hair—what color was it again? More brown, than blond? Or the other way around? And her eyes—they were blue, right? Or were they green? Hunter shook his head sadly, his gaze still fixed on the lonely patch of starlight to the south. The truth was, Xara's image barely registered in his memory. Even now, her face began to fade. He fought a silent battle to retain it, but it was no good. She was just too far away.

The hours dragged on. The howling below became more intense, the sky even scarier in its near emptiness.

After a while, Zarex slowly eased his way closer to where Tomm was sitting.

"May I have a private conversation with you, Father?" Zarex asked once the wind had died down a little.

"Do you mean a confession, my son?" Tomm replied, his tone clearly indicating that he would rather forgo such a thing.

Zarex almost laughed. "We'd be here an eternity for that, Padre."

"I feel we might be here that long, anyway," Tomm replied.

Zarex nodded in Hunter's direction. The fighter pilot was fast asleep. Or so it seemed.

"Who *is* he, Father?" Zarex asked. "Do you know?"

Tomm looked over at Hunter.

"I'm not exactly sure," he replied carefully. "He is a different sort, that much I will grant you. But a likable chap. And an honorable one as well."

"He seems that way, which is no little relief," Zarex said. "But how can we be sure?"

"For several reasons," Tomm answered. "His compulsion to find the Home Planets is genuine . . . of this much I am certain. And the Freedom Brigade were honorable men. This I know from the few months I spent with them—though at the time they were all very reticent to discuss where they came from exactly, which I now realize was understandable. Finally, I just stopped asking."

"But where is the connection then, Father?"

"It's simple: the men I knew from the Freedom Brigade were all very much like Mr. Hunter over there. They were different from anyone else I'd ever met out here—and so is he. And he keeps some things close to the vest, just as they did. Makes me think that he actually *is* connected to them somehow and that this calling-home stuff might be real. He's on a quest—a soul-quest of sorts. I just think it's my priestly duty to help him."

Zarex paused for a moment. A strange green light went streaking over their heads. Finally he asked, "Another question Padre: Do you believe in all this Empire nonsense?"

Tomm shrugged. It was not the first time he'd been asked the question.

"I'm not sure," he replied. "I mean, an immense galactic empire, out there, somewhere? It seems we would've run into some of these people by now if it was true. But then again, maybe we have, and we just don't know it. These Empire types are supposedly very talented at concealing themselves, and the legends say they are very careful in selecting which planets they choose to reveal themselves to. Either way, they are covered insofar as keeping their presence among us mute, until it is our time to know, that is."

"Yes, but couldn't that simply be a convenient deception, proof that it's all a fabrication?" Zarex asked. "I mean, if we've never met them, does that mean they aren't really there? That's the only either/or in the equation."

"Then it's probably an unknowable thing," Tomm replied. It was his favorite saying. "But why did you ask me that in the first place, my son?"

Zarex shrugged and again nodded toward the sleeping pilot. "Because I, too, think Hunter's quest is legitimate. He also saved my life, thus I am bound to help him."

"And?"

"And I think it is odd that Mr. Hunter seems so much like these mythical people from the Home Planets yet . . . I believe that if there really *was* a big empire out there, slowly but surely making its way toward us, Mr. Hunter would be just the type of person to be the first off the ship, to greet us. A benign invader. The combination really becomes a very mysterious thing."

Tomm nodded in agreement. He knew Hunter well, yet then again, knew very little about him.

"I saw some very strange things happen during the war on Zazu-Zazu," Tomm confessed. "And I will tell you that Mr.

Hunter certainly has some unusual acquaintances, with some very unusual weaponry, not the least of which is that flying machine of his."

He paused. "But is he from this mythical Empire we keep hearing about?" he asked in a whisper. "Maybe that's an unknowable thing as well."

It was just a few minutes past midnight when 33418 suddenly stopped scanning again.

The sound of his electronics changed so abruptly, Hunter woke up immediately, blaster pistol in hand, ready for anything. Other things had changed on the mountaintop. The wind had ceased howling. The air had become thick and pungent. And the restless spirits of the mechanical soldiers below had become quiet as well.

Too quiet? Hunter thought.

Tomm and Zarex were quickly awake, too. They'd also detected the new hum coming from the clanker. The robot was now frozen in place, looking off to the west.

"Is this what happens when he's spotted something?" Pater Tomm asked Zarex.

The big explorer just shrugged. "I'm never really sure what he's up to." He's a good bodyguard, but beyond that, who knows?"

The humming grew louder. Then the robot lifted his arm and pointed to the west. They all looked in that direction, but it was very dark, and the smoke made it difficult to see very far. But then, through the murk and gloom, Hunter spotted something way off in the distance flying above the war-torn fields.

Tomm and Zarex saw it, too. It was a single, glowing orb.

"What is this?" the priest asked Zarex worriedly. "I thought everything out there was supposed to be dead."

"On this place, you can never know," Zarex replied.

No sooner were those words out of the explorer's mouth when the object was suddenly right on them. It looked like a ball of light at first but just a few feet away from the edge of the cliff, it morphed into the image of a horribly disfigured woman. Eyes, blood red and bulging; a nose crooked and long and covered with growths. Teeth black and dripping, long hair trailing like a tangle of slime. The skin was a sickly corpse gray.

And it was coming right at Hunter. He saw its mouth open

to gigantic proportions, its teeth turning into a mouthful of tiny daggers. He quickly dove to his right. Had he waited a second longer, this thing would have bitten his head right off. Instead, the apparition rocketed right over him, dragging a trail of foul-smelling smoke behind it.

"Is this the person you made your blaster deal with?" Hunter yelled over to Zarex.

"Hardly!" the explorer replied to the grim joke.

They watched as the apparition turned over and dove on them once again. This time Zarex was its target. Two bony hands with razorlike fingernails suddenly appeared out in front of it. Hunter could see the gleam coming off the pointed tips—they were that sharp.

Zarex waited until the last moment, then dove away as well. The banshee was just inches away from perforating him when he fell to the ground and rolled to the left, a powerful blast from his rifle going right through the demon. The apparition let out a horrible screech and turned once again. This time, Pater Tomm was in its sights.

The hands now became gigantic pincers intent on carrying the diminutive priest away. But Pater Tomm was quicker than he looked—an occupational necessity. He let the apparition swoop down on him, and at the very last second, stepped aside and let it streak past him just as Hunter and Zarex had done. But as the banshee went by, Tomm unleashed a small billy club he'd taken from his back pocket and cracked it over the demon's hindquarters.

The resulting howl echoed right around the planet. Hunter was forced to drop his blaster pistol and put his hands to his ears—still he could not keep the blood-curdling screech out of his head. The apparition flew straight up into the dark, smoky sky. But then, with the finesse of a Starfighter pilot, it looped over and performed a wide-out, high-velocity arc. About half-way down, there was another bright flash. The demon had morphed into something else.

This new form came to an abrupt halt right in front of them. The transformation couldn't have been more dramatic. Gone were the ugly features, the razor nails, the hairdo of snot. In its place was a stunningly beautiful woman, dressed all in white. She was floating, or more accurately, things were floating around her. There was a thin haze covering what they could see of her body, almost like a gathering of miniature clouds. And behind her was not the murky sky of Myx but the sky of someplace else entirely. It was deep blue, with a bright sun shining. And stars were sparkling in this sky, even though it was obviously daytime, wherever it was.

Hunter had never seen anything like this. The Galaxy was filled with strange things, yet every one of them related back to the universal laws of physics somehow.

But this . . . this was something entirely different.

"By the very stars!" Zarex exclaimed. "It's a poof . . ."

"I'm almost afraid to ask this," Hunter said. "But what is a poof?"

"A spirit, sometimes holy, sometimes not," Pater Tomm replied. "No one is sure where they hail from. They are supposed to come first in the form of a demon, then transform. The question always is: Which form is the right one? Demon or cherub?"

Throughout this, the angel stared at them, face expressionless, everything floating around her. And they stared right back.

"Well, you're the expert," Tomm said to Zarex. "Tell her why we are here."

The explorer gulped once, then stepped forward.

"Forgive us this intrusion," he said slowly, trying to remain calm. "But we came here with a purpose."

The apparition didn't reply. Its expression didn't change a bit.

Zarex pointed to Hunter. "My friend here wants to go to the Home Planets."

Still nothing.

"He feels he might be one who is being 'called back' . . .

The spirit took its eyes off Zarex and glanced at Hunter.

"Show her," Zarex told Hunter.

Hunter withdrew the piece of cloth he always kept in his upper left breast pocket. The angel's eyes went wide at the sight of the red, white, and blue flag. Suddenly there was another flash. It was so bright, all three humans were thrown to the ground. When they looked up again, the apparition had morphed once more. This time, the shape was hovering just a few inches above the ground in front of them. It was dressed in a brightly colored outfit. Red, yellow, and green striped jacket, bright purple and yellow pants, a strange hat, with two peaks and bells hanging from them.

A jester? Hunter thought.

A delicate hand pushed back the low-slung fool's cap, revealing the face of a very attractive young girl. Blonde. Sweet.

"Why do you feel you are one who's being called back?" she asked Hunter in a high-pitched melodious voice.

Hunter shook his head. "I really don't know. I have this thing inside me that's saying I must find the Home Planets—and, I think, one in particular. I just feel I *must* get there, somehow—"

"So, you have this compulsion and that flag?"

"Is that enough?" Hunter asked in reply.

She smiled. "It's more than enough. But what of your companions here?"

Hunter looked at Tomm, Zarex, and the robot.

"They helped me get here; they helped me find you," he replied. "I want them to come with me."

The girl laughed. "Well, at this point they have no choice. They've seen me, they've seen this way station. They now know the secret of this place."

Zarex and Tomm seemed relieved.

"I've got nothing else pressing," Zarex deadpanned. "And I've been known to visit a strange world or two in my lifetime."

Tomm also managed a smile. "A chance to journey to a place that isn't supposed to exist?" he said drolly. "How can I pass that up?"

Even 33418 made a squeaking noise. He had nowhere else he could go either.

"I guess it's the lot of us then," Hunter told the girl.

Tomm looked up at her. "Now these Home Planets," he said. "They are close by? Right?"

The girl laughed again. "Look around. Does anything seem close by to you?"

With that, she snapped her fingers, and a bright golden ball suddenly appeared in front of her. She studied it for a moment, then said, "You will have to go immediately. Our time is growing short here—"

"Wait a moment!" Zarex said. "You *have* to tell us *how* we are going . . ."

She shook her head no.

Zarex pressed her. "But what will our means of transport be?"

Again, she shook her head. "I can't say. Those are the rules."

The three humans looked at each other. "Well, how long will our journey take?" Tomm asked her.

The girl just smiled and then winked. It was clear no answer was forthcoming.

She passed her hand over the ball, and suddenly all four were reduced into a Twenty 'n Six box that had appeared in her other hand. The girl manipulated the globe again. The Twenty 'n Six box turned into a smooth, pearl-colored stone. She examined the stone for a moment, then turned to the northwest, toward a piece of the night sky that was particularly devoid of stars. Or at least any that were "close by."

Then she held her hand up to her mouth and blew on the stone.

There was yet another bright flash, and suddenly the stone rocketed away at great speed. Traveling at a velocity that rivaled even that of Hunter's flying machine, the stone was out of the planet's atmosphere, out of its orbit, and out of the star system completely, all in the blink of an eye.

PART TWO

Ashley's Dream

8

Lisa Lee was lost, and she didn't know why.

Either her map was too old or they had changed the highway signs in this part of Illinois recently. She'd been driving for hours and yet didn't seem to be getting any closer to her destination. None of the landmarks were as they should have been, and it didn't help that her watch had stopped running early in the trip. As a result, she had no idea what time it was.

This was not good. This trip was her first solo assignment as an FBI agent. She'd been nervous since the git-go. She was out of the FBI field office in Chicago, and up until a week before had always worked with a partner. Now, finally, she had a case of her own. She'd waited for this day ever since graduating from the academy sixteen months ago. And what happens? She winds up lost!

Her only consolation was that her survival kit was holding out. She had three Cokes remaining from a six-pack. Her large bag of Fritos was only half gone. She had ten cigarettes left. Not bad for nearly a full day of driving. She opened a Coke now, downed a handful of Fritos, and lit a cigarette, all in the same motion. She checked her gas gauge. Her vintage Pontiac Firebird was notoriously bad on fuel. Stepping on the gas pedal was like flushing a toilet. But she had had this ideal notion that the long drive down from Chicago would actually be good for the car's engine. Muscle cars needed a long drive every once in a while to blow the carbon out of the motor—or at least that's what her brother told her the day he gave it to her, as a present, for getting her special agent's badge.

However, a muscle car was not the best vehicle to get lost in; when the gas gauge started plunging, it was only a matter of time before you either had to find a filling station or wound up at the side of the road. She prayed this would not happen. Being late for her first assignment would be bad enough; running out of gas and getting stranded would be dreadful.

She was trying to find a town called Betaville. It was in the southwestern part of the state, forty-four miles off Interstate 55. She had taken the exit the AAA traveler's guide had recommended and had proceeded west on State Highway 67A. But twenty miles into this, she'd come upon a detour, which brought her to a Temporary Route 467B. She was forced to travel on this empty, straight-as-an-arrow highway for nearly an hour before returning to Route 67A.

So the question was: Had she passed Betaville already? Had the detour swung her too far north to see the town? She didn't know. She'd been due at the police station at noon; it was now getting dark. The highway seemed unending, no towns, no signs, no gas stations. She dragged heavily on her cigarette and then nervously checked her lipstick in the mirror.

It seemed like she'd been driving for days.

It was just around the time she saw the top of the moon peeking over the eastern horizon that her fuel gauge needle hit empty.

It was now nearly five o'clock by her estimate, and she could have made it to Betaville and halfway back to Chicago by this time. Her cell phone had been on Roam, which in this part of Illinois simply meant the chances of actually making a phone call were little and none. A very creepy sensation washed over her. She tugged at her skirt, it was too short to begin with and now, after such a long ride, it had really become very uncomfortable. Her pumps were beginning to make her feet ache, too. Not a good outfit to be stranded in.

The Firebird finally began running out of gas just as she was approaching the top of a fairly steep hill. She drained the last of her Coke, took one final drag of her cigarette, and then started urging the car along, for just a few feet more, just to the top of the hill, where, on the faintest hope, she might be able to roll down the other side and into a gas station.

The car began sputtering badly with about twenty feet to go before the crest of the hill. Lisa gripped the wheel tighter, pushed the accelerator all the way down to the floorboard, and swore loudly. Somehow this and the few drops of gas left in her lines was enough to just make the top of the rise.

But then the car died for good.

Well, this is just great.

She was late, she was lost, she was out of gas, and her cell phone was not in range. The nose of the car was pointing to the pinnacle of the hill. It was getting dark.

She screamed twice, then fixed her hair, and lit a cigarette. There were only seven Marlboro 100s left. Rationing would soon have to begin. She dragged on this one heavily and thought back to those days, not so long ago, when she actually thought of herself as a lucky person. Lucky to be smart enough to make it through the Academy. Lucky to be pretty enough to actually corral a good field office. Lucky to be persistent enough to get a case of her own in nearly record time.

She looked at the full moon, rising quickly now above the field to her left. The face seemed to be laughing at her. A brisk wind blew by. She crushed out the cigarette and really tried very hard not to cry.

Then she climbed out of the car, walked the last few feet to the top of the hill, and discovered that she'd been lucky one more time.

Because on the other side of the hill, not a quarter mile down the road, was the town of Betaville.

Lisa arrived at the small police station just as the clock in the town square was striking six.

She'd managed to roll the Pontiac down the hill, and the first place she came to was a gas station, where she promptly filled up. She also bought a fresh pack of smokes and a spare Coke from the vending machine. The ladies' room was surprisingly clean, enough for her to check her look, freshen her makeup, and slap the wrinkles from her skirt and jacket. She'd taken her contacts out and put her glasses on, as she thought this made her look a bit more astute.

She took the parking spot next to the chief's Jeep and calmly walked into the red-brick station. The desk sergeant knew who she was right away. He said something about some people expecting her all afternoon, but added that he knew the FBI was busy, and could be excused for being late every once in a while. She turned down his offer of a cup of coffee and wordlessly followed him through a pair of swinging doors and down the bright, white hallway beyond.

They eventually reached a door marked Conference Room. Next to it was a door marked Janitor—Private. This second sign was actually a bit of misdirection, to keep secret what kind of room actually lay beyond the first. Lisa's escort opened the janitor's door and let her in. Inside was a tiny room with a glass panel installed on one wall; it looked into the room next door. Two State Police investigators were peering through this two-way mirror. They stood up as Lisa entered. She acknowledged their chivalry with little more than a nod.

She took a seat next to them, retrieved her notebook, and peered through the two-way herself. Two uniformed Betaville cops were interrogating three suspects in the next room. The men were sitting in metal folding chairs; the cops were leaning on a desk in front of them. Both cops had laptops open nearby.

Lisa scanned the three suspects and then let out a groan. *Here we go again*, she thought, *just a foot away from the loony bin*. It was her own fault though. The big reason she'd been able to convince her superiors to let her out so soon on her own was a special forte she'd carved out for herself and her partner, back when she had one. It was simple talent really: Lisa would take on any case no one else in the Chicago office wanted, i.e., the far-out stuff that never went anywhere except into a mountain of paperwork. Many times these cases involved your assorted psychos, vampires, mad bombers, and cannibal wanna-bes. It drove her partner nuts and hastened his early departure, again part of her plan. But the problem was, now she was stuck with the wacko cases alone.

In this instance, the Betaville police had arrested the three suspects the night before, after they'd been caught trespassing on a farm just outside of town. Minutes prior to their first being spotted, there had been a huge explosion on the farm's north forty, one that shook every building in Betaville and even a few as far away as Plato, some twenty miles to the west. The owner of the farm quickly alerted the police about the explosion, and they found the three wandering aimlessly through an alfalfa field, their clothes and hair still smoldering from the blast. Careless use of explosives was the other pending charge.

But why did the Betaville police call in the FBI? For one thing, the Bureau was always notified whenever there was an incident where large numbers of explosives were involved. But there was also her oddball factor as well: The suspects, Lisa had been told, were "three guys in Halloween costumes."

They were also claiming to be from outer space.

"OK, let's go back to the beginning. Do you know where you are?"

The three suspects shrugged in unison.

"Haven't we been over that already?" one asked.

"It's important that we hear it again," the cop said, winking at Lisa through the two-way.

She had already begun to scribble notes. The three suspects were wearing what appeared to be Halloween costumes. The first guy was dressed like a superhero, complete with a black one-piece suit, wacky boots, a cape, and a double-X logo emblazoned on his chest. The second guy was wearing a perfectly ripped, tight-fitting muscular uniform that would put any pro wrestler's wardrobe to shame. The third guy, he being the oldest, was dressed in a long cassock and a white collar. The Betaville cops had already dubbed him "The Priest from Outer Space."

Lisa scanned the trio's arrest report. They had tested negative for drugs and alcohol—or at least nothing showed up on the local cops' sobriety devices. And though they looked ridiculous, the three men seemed coherent and intelligent. They were also extremely curious about their surroundings, studying in minute detail the ashtrays on the table in front of them, the slowly rotating ceiling fan above, the extremely dirty cups the Betaville cops were using to drink their hot, black, foul-smelling coffee.

"We don't know where we are," the diminutive guy in the priest costume finally said. "We thought we did, but now we're not so sure."

"OK," the second cop said. "How did you get here then?"

"But we've told you that at least a half dozen times," the guy in the ripped shirt with all the muscles said. "How many more times are you going to want to hear it?"

"At least once more," the first cop said, trying to suppress a grin.

All three suspects groaned, again in unison. The big guy and the one in the superhero costume wearily looked over at the priest. He'd done most of the talking, one of the state cops told Lisa. Almost as if he was their spokesman. She made a special note of this in her book.

The little man began their story again. He started off by explaining how he and the guy in the caped costume were actually interplanetary travelers. They'd hooked up with a group of soldiers who roamed outer space looking for honorable battles to fight; they were called the Freedom Brigade and were quite heroic. Many of these soldiers eventually died, though, in a war on a moon at the end of the galaxy called Zazu-Zazu. They'd traveled to this Zazu-Zazu place because somewhere on the tiny satellite there was once a beacon that swept the entire universe, looking to bring all of their lost brothers back home again—here, to *this* planet. The guy in the cape learned about the beacon and thought he was one of those being called back. So when he and the priest found one last dying trooper on the battlefield of Zazu-Zazu and were given the barest directions by him, they set out to find the Home Planets, the place the beacon was calling everyone back to. Along the way, they had battled a huge death star, space pirates, had met princesses, and discovered a long lost world covered with ghostly robots. That came after the muscle man had joined their quest.

Lisa had scribbled about half of this down in her notebook before she gave up. It was just too funny to go on. The state cops could barely contain their amusement. Pretty soon, all three of them were laughing out loud.

"I drove all the way down here and got lost for this?" Lisa groaned. The state cops laughed even harder.

"We've been here for five hours," one of them told her. "And it gets better every time!"

Lisa finally composed herself and pushed a button on the wall nearby. This opened a link with one of the interrogating cops in the other room, via a hidden earplug.

"Ask the guy with the muscles this question: "Is there a chance that you might be hallucinating this?"

The interrogator did as told. Surprisingly, the man nodded in the affirmative.

"Ask him to explain why," Lisa told the questioners.

The muscle man complied. He stated that everything on this planet looked so bizarre to him, he felt like he might be inside a "bender dream."

And what was that?

"The result of ingesting too much slow-ship wine.

"Or maybe I'm actually on a transdimensional holo-trip," the muscle man went on. "That's an excursion that comes with activation of one of the top-of-the-line holo-girls, like an Echo-623 or even a 773. Haven't you people ever heard of these things? Such mind trips can last up to a month—though not in real time. They usually take you to a deserted island somewhere in the thirty-fourth dimension, where there is no need for any bodily functions except to breathe, sleep, and have sex, sex, *sex.*"

The state cops were howling by now. Lisa felt her face go flush at the man's insistent repetition of the word *sex.* How the two Betaville cops were managing to keep straight faces, she would never know.

"Did you say you suspect this might be a 'holo-trip,' is that the right term?" one of them asked the muscle man.

"A transdimensional holo-trip, yes," was the reply.

"Well, how do you know that isn't what's going on here then?" the interrogator asked.

The muscle man just shrugged. "Because if this is a holo-trip," he said sadly, "where are all the girls?"

"Good answer!" one of the state cops said. They began laughing again, and so did Lisa.

"Ask the other one what he thinks of all this . . ." she was just barely able to whisper to the interrogating cops without cracking up again. "The guy in the superhero costume."

Of the three, he was obviously the most reluctant to talk.

"It just seems like a very odd place," finally came his reply. "On one hand, this town seems very primitive to us. It really does. The buildings, the streets, the vehicles. The way you are all dressed. But, at the same time, everything here looks new to me, or by some frame of reference, *modern.* As I told you before, I've been to a number of uncharted planets. The people on many of these worlds have no idea that a vast empire rules most of the Galaxy. Some weren't even aware that there were inhabited planets within their own solar systems or in the star systems close by. On all these planets though, the pace of civilization has been more or less constant. No one was living in caves and running around unclothed.

"But this place is different. It seems as if you have progressed to a certain time frame—and then stopped. People are obviously living, walking, talking, and going about their lives here, but it is almost as if someone had blasted you with a Time Shifter centuries ago—and never bothered to turn the activation switch off. The result being that all progress had ceased at exactly that point or at least slowed down in a very drastic way."

A pause. More laughter from the other room.

Then the priest from outer space said, "Either that, or you people just like it this way."

The interrogation went on for another ten minutes.

It almost became even more amusing, with the priest again doing most of the talking. The suspects' claims were so outlandish, even the craziest tabloid would have taken a pass on their story. Yet Lisa had noticed something. While providing no small entertainment for those on hand, the three men were not really saying anything specific about how they happened to arrive on the outskirts of Betaville or about the huge explosion on the farm nearby. It was almost as if they were intentionally deflecting those questions by going on and on about being from outer space.

So, Lisa made a notation in her book: "Shared psychotic persistence," and for a moment, she wondered if she might have just coined a new term for the lexicon of criminal psychology. All wackos began ranting after a while. Sure, some would start off rationally enough, even persuasively. But usually after ten minutes or so, the cracks in their head would start to show, and many would devolve into foaming, maniacal wrecks whose pronouncements became more outlandish with every breath.

But not these guys. They had a wacky story—and they were sticking to it. In other words, they were persistent in their shared psychosis.

Finally, the state cops had had enough. They drained their coffee cups and started gathering their things together.

"I'm not sure how the Feds want to tag this one," one told Lisa. "But unless we find pieces of a UFO or evidence of a small nuclear device out there, this one gets the loony wrap from us."

Lisa was inclined to agree with them. But she was here for the night anyway, and dealing with these kooks might provide her an education for future cases. Besides, she needed *something* to bulk up her first-ever solo report.

"I'm going to do a quick twenty twenty-two sheet on them," she told the state cops. "I'll send you a copy. And thanks for your help."

The two policemen put on their jackets and hats, handed Lisa their business cards, and left. Lisa threw both cards into the waste basket, then activated the microphone to the interrogation room.

"Do you have a spare room I can borrow?" she asked the man with the earplug. "I want to talk to these guys alone."

Ten minutes later, Lisa and the three strange men were sitting in a large hall on the third floor of the Betaville police station.

It was close to nine o'clock by this time, and having quickly made some overnight accommodations, Lisa was now intent on asking the three perps a few questions for her criminal assessment file—the famous 2022 sheet. After this, she would turn the case back over to the local cops. There was no need for a federal investigation here. Mentally challenged vagrants carrying a few sticks of dynamite—it didn't go much beyond that. She would leave it to the locals to figure out how the trio got the explosives and why they chose to blow a hole in the ground while dressed in Halloween costumes. Her guess was the men would get ninety days, either in the local jail for trespassing and destruction of property, or more likely, under observation at the state mental facility in Palmyra.

The hall was an old basketball court that had been cut in two by a brick wall. It held the town's only voting machine, a small army of old target-practice dummies, and a mountain of boxes containing the police station's Christmas decorations. While one of the Betaville cops insisted that he stay just outside the door while Lisa talked to the suspects, he also didn't bat an eye when she offered to buy the coffees all round. He took her money and was off like a shot.

There was a long table in the center of the hall; it was surrounded by many old wooden chairs. This is where Lisa had the three men sit, up at one end, facing away from the door. She took a seat directly across from them.

She thought twice about unhooking her service revolver; these guys were harmless enough, but her academy training had emphasized the wisdom of having a gun ready at all times. So she unclipped it from her jacket holster and placed it on the table with a thud. The three men stared at it for several long, intense moments. Had Lisa not known better, she would have thought the trio had never seen a handgun before.

She looked up at them, smiled, and then got her tape recorder ready. The three men sat rigid in their creaky wooden chairs. Their eyes were off her revolver now and zoned right in on her. It was strange how they did everything in unison sometimes. She smiled again, and so did they, and suddenly, a very warm feeling came over her; it was almost like a glowing sensation. She reached into her briefcase to get a pen and caught a glimpse of herself in her makeup mirror. She was astonished at how attractive she looked. Her blondish hair was tousled and her makeup was fading fast. Yet the face staring back at her was the prettiest she'd seen it in a very long time. What a strange feeling.

It was almost as if . . .

She shook away these thoughts, pushed the tape recorder on, and began.

"Well, I've heard a lot about you three," she said. "And—"

"How?" the priest interrupted her.

"How what?"

"How did you hear about us?"

Lisa was stumped for a moment. She couldn't very well tell them that she'd been sitting behind the two-way mirror.

"News travels fast around here," she said instead.

The men just looked at each other, digesting this bit of information. Then all three nodded slowly, as if they'd just been given some bit of universal truth.

Lisa explained that she was an FBI agent and wanted to get a bit of background on them for her files. The questions would be nonintrusive and off-the-record; however, if they so desired, an attorney could be present.

"What's an attorney?" the muscle man asked her.

Lisa just stared back at him for a moment.

"An attorney," she repeated for him. "You know, a lawyer?"

"What's a lawyer?" the priest asked.

Lisa looked up from her sheet and took off her glasses. Were the three kooks goofing on her? Would they dare? She was an FBI agent, the last person they should be dicking around with. *What were these guys up to?* It was hard to tell. They looked too old to be in college, so she could dismiss a fraternity prank. And they *were* good actors; they were wearing their costumes like it was their everyday attire. But it also seemed as if they really *didn't* know what an attorney was.

"I'll take that as a no," she said, making an indication on the 2022. "So then, is it OK if we all have a talk?"

The priest replied, "If that's what is needed here, certainly . . . but I must tell you, we are all about talked out."

Lisa unbuttoned the top clasp in her blouse, then untied her hair and ran her fingers through it. The warm feeling remained.

"So let me see if I have your names right," she said consulting her notes. "You are Mr. Hunter . . . you are Mr. Zarex. And you are Father Tomm?"

All three nodded.

"And you claim that you are from outer space, correct?"

Again, they nodded.

"And, did you get here in, what? A spaceship?"

"We are not really sure," the priest answered. "As we told the officers downstairs, one moment we were on a planet very far from here; the next, well, we were *here.*"

"Just like that, huh?" she asked with a smile.

The priest snapped his fingers. "Just like that . . ."

Lisa scribbled something on her sheet.

"So what about the explosion then?" she asked them. "Judging by the burn marks on your clothes, it's obvious you were very close to it when it went off."

"Close to it?" the priest replied with some amusement. "My child, we were right in the *middle* of it."

She smiled at him, but in a crooked sort of way. "Really?"

"I'm a priest," he replied. "It would be very bad luck for me to lie to you."

Lisa unconsciously undid yet another button on her blouse.

"So, what you're saying is when you landed here, *that's* what caused the explosion?"

The priest nodded. "Somehow the poof shot us right across the Galaxy, at an incredible speed. When we landed here, well, our arrival was heralded by a blast of no small proportions. Probably had something to do with a slight fracture in the time-space thing, that's my theory, anyway. But it certainly came as a great shock to us."

Lisa began playing with her hair. *What the heck was a poof?* She was almost afraid to ask him. Plus, the priest was almost a little too smooth for her, and he'd done most of the talking already. She turned to the guy in the superhero costume.

"All right, it's your turn," she said to him. "Tell me your version of everything that's happened since you arrived here. And I mean *everything*."

Hunter almost laughed in the pretty girl's face.

Everything? What did she want to know exactly? How they had made a very hard, very undignified landing on some very hard ground.

Or maybe he could tell her about the certain unpleasant smell that surrounded him after he'd popped in, and how his eyes had been nearly sealed shut by soot and mud, and how it took him a second or two to draw in a real breath? Or how he saw the tiny red stars dancing around him, shrinking into infinitly as his jump became final. How these stars—yes, they *were* real—stung his face and hands as they slowly faded from view. Or how he sneezed and felt his whole body shake in response, confirmation that all of his vital organs had arrived intact?

So she wanted to hear everything? Obviously she couldn't handle *everything*. What made her any different from the two guys they'd just spent the last five hours talking to? The people here had a strange way of interpreting the truth—a tendency to twist it to fit their own beliefs. If she didn't believe that they were visitors from outer space, how then was she going to believe *everything* he could tell her?

This had been a big mistake. Hunter had convinced himself of this by now. And it was all of his doing. Over the billions of miles traveled, never once had the thought occurred to him that the people here *wouldn't* know about Zazu-Zazu, the Freedom Brigade, the Home Planets, and the long, strange journey needed to reach this place—assuming this was the right place. But it was apparent soon after the Betaville cops showed up in the smoldering alfalfa field that they didn't have the slightest idea what he or Tomm or Zarex were talking about. The problem was, by that time, some very crazy-sounding stuff had spilled out of their big mouths, and once gone, it was impossible to get back. It was also very clear by the reaction of the cops that this planet wasn't aware of spaceflight or that anything or anyone existed beyond its own atmosphere. Not a good sign, considering what Hunter and company had come here to do.

They were cuffed, put into a squad car, and driven to the jail. It was at that point the three silently agreed Pater Tomm would do most of the talking from then on, at least until they could figure a way out of this mess. And the padre was good at spinning. Once they were brought to the interrogation room, he was able to avoid giving the cops any more information by simply repeating over and over the bare essentials of what they had so foolishly blurted out to them already. By never deviating from this speech, they'd hoped to eventually wear down the Betaville cops, to the point of disinterest. Or at least that was the plan.

But that was where they'd made their second mistake. The three of them had naively assumed that once they'd talked themselves blue to the police, they'd be allowed to go free. But that certainly didn't seem to be the case now. The Betaville authorities clearly thought they were crazy, and they were not about to let them run loose in the streets. Instead, they were going to be processed, poked, and questioned. *Investigated.* For days, months, even years.

There was no time for any of that.

So instead of answering the pretty girl's question, Hunter posed to her one of his own.

"Would it really be so unusual?" he asked her suddenly. "I mean, would you be *that* shocked if it turned out that we were telling you the truth?"

She almost laughed, at the same time pulling the top of her blouse together.

"You mean that you were somehow transported here, from outer space?"

All three men nodded.

"Have you ever heard of *anything* like this before?" Hunter asked her.

She paused a moment.

"Well, it's an interesting question coming from you," she said finally. "I mean, sure, I've read stories. Mostly in the tabloids. People visited by beings from outer space. Or being carried away in their ships. Or just disappearing and never coming back."

"And you just don't think any of that is possible?"

She rolled her eyes. "No one does," she said.

"But why not?" Hunter pressed her. "It's a big universe out there."

She looked out the nearby window. The stars were shining brightly beyond.

"Big? It sure is," she replied, pointing toward the night sky. "But it also looks very, very empty from down here."

"But that all depends on how you look at it," Hunter told her. "From our perspective maybe it looks very busy, very full."

She laughed again. "Yeah, that's rich, pal. But OK, even if someone was able to somehow get off this planet, which no one has ever even tried, the distance to get anywhere else is prohibitively great, isn't it?"

She checked her notes. "Of course, the guys downstairs said you claimed you can travel more than a light-year a second. Boy, that's fast."

"And again, you think that's impossible?"

She looked right back at him. "Yes sir, I do."

Hunter paused for a moment. This wasn't going anywhere, and they were running out of time. The Betaville cop would be back with her refreshments soon, and that would just make a difficult situation even worse.

So he worded his next question very carefully.

"Let's say we were able to convince you that we are telling you the truth . . . and that we came here from outer space because we had this overwhelming need to. Or at least I did. What would you do then?"

She laughed, then reached into her handbag and came out with her car keys.

"I would tell you to take my car and just drive right around the planet, baby—see this lonely little place that had drawn you over billions of miles—and then I'd write a book about you, and we'd all become millionaires."

Hunter was surprised by her answer.

"Really?" he asked her.

"Really," she replied.

Hunter thought about this for a moment then looked over at

Zarex and Pater Tomm. That was good enough for them.

"Padre?" Hunter said to Tomm. "After you . . ."

The priest did a slight bow. "May I get something in my pocket?" he asked Lisa. "Not a weapon, I assure you."

"I'm a sucker for a good laugh," she said. "Be my guest."

Tomm reached into his pocket and withdrew an electron torch, the handy tool just about everyone in the Galaxy carried. He turned it on, then carved a square out of the air in front of him. The molecules instantly bonded into a pane of superglass, about two feet by two feet, glistening, yet pliable. Tomm grabbed the pane out of the air, and then began pushing it in from its corners, quickly forming a perfect, if overly large superglass diamond. Then he blew on it gently, causing the molecules to disperse and making it disappear.

They all looked at Lisa. She was staring back at them, mouth open, but skeptical around her eyes.

"A trick . . ." she managed to mumble. "A good one, but . . ."

Tomm looked at Hunter. More was needed. The pilot took a small white box from his pocket and activated the button on top. There was a sudden flash and then a burst of green smoke. When it dissipated, his flying machine was standing in the middle of the big room, its tail fin crushing some of the Christmas boxes.

Lisa dropped her glasses; they hit the table, then the floor, shattering into a thousand little pieces. Her jaw fell open. She turned pale. She tried to say something, but no words would come out. In fact, she had a hard time catching her breath. She managed to stand up, though, and stumble forward, approaching the spacecraft gingerly. She reached out and touched it, making sure that she wasn't in a dream.

Then she began shaking her head. "No . . . this . . . this can't be real. . . ."

They took her at her word; they couldn't help it, that's the way they were. So Zarex snapped his fingers, there was another burst of green smoke, and suddenly the clanker 33418 was standing before them, all ten feet of him. Metallic muscles, arm weapons, death-ray visor. The works.

Lisa looked up at him, and the robot made an unusual whirring sound.

That's when she fainted dead away.

She hit the floor with a bang, taking out one of the old rickety chairs with her.

"Oh great!" Zarex moaned. *"Now* what do we do with her?"

Not a minute later, they were bounding down the stairs of the police station, trying to make the least amount of noise possible, but tripping and slamming into things in the dark, nevertheless.

They reached the bottom floor and found themselves in a pitch-black hallway. Above them, they could hear many footsteps running down the stairs, coming their way. Hunter began groping around the wall and somehow found the rear door to the building. He hit the bar and the door sprang free. It also set off the building's security alarm.

There were only two cars in the parking lot. One had police writing all over it; the other was very sleek-looking in an odd kind of way, white with fiery decals on the front and a winglike contraption on the back. It was Lisa's Firebird. Zarex climbed in behind the wheel of the car; he'd fished the keys out of Lisa's jacket pocket soon after she collapsed. As Hunter and Tomm piled into the backseat, Zarex tried to figure out exactly how to insert the keys into the ignition. It took a few moments, but finally the key went into the slot.

Nothing happened.

Zarex pulled the key out and put it back in again.

Still nothing . . .

"What infernal machine is this?" he roared. "Surely these things tap into its power supply!"

Lights were blinking on all over the police station now. And the alarm was ringing even louder.

"Manipulate the key, brother!" Tomm yelled to Zarex.

That's when Zarex realized the key had to be not only inserted into the ignition but turned as well. As soon as he did this, the car's engine roared to life. Hunter reached forward and pulled the control stick down to the initial D, and off they went.

Wheels screeching, tires burning rubber, they peeled out onto the street in front of the police station, knocking over a line of trash cans in the process. Zarex didn't know how to drive; he was having trouble just keeping the wheel straight while pushing the accelerator to the floor. The result was a high-speed, careening journey down Main Street, sideswiping several parked cars and running two red lights. They were making so much noise, store alarms were popping on as soon as they roared past. Zarex took a sharp corner at the intersection of Elm and Main, creaming a park bench and taking down a no parking sign as well. Finally, they swerved onto Route 67A and took off toward the west. Though it had not been as subtle as they would have liked, they had not met any other vehicles since thundering out of the police station parking lot, and none were in pursuit.

Zarex managed to keep the car fairly straight on the road now and was intent on making the needle, which indicated their speed, climb to the far end of its limit, which was 160 miles per hour.

Only once he'd achieved this speed did Hunter and Tomm finally sit back and relax for a moment.

"We're safe now," Tomm said with a sigh of relief.

They drove for about twenty miles.

It was almost midnight. Traveling through the particularly isolated part of southwestern Illinois, they saw no other cars on the little-used highway nor any structures except for a few scattered barns and sheds. There were immense fields of alfalfa and wheat on either side of the straight, flat road. The winds rippled across these fields in such a way, they made the stalks move like waves on an ocean. Just above the roadway itself, a thick but shallow mist had gathered. Rain clouds hung low overhead. This was called inclement weather, Tomm reminded them. A rarity in most places, and in some parts of the Galaxy, it didn't exist at all.

Zarex had finally gotten the hang of operating the Firebird. Just keep the wheel steady and the pedal to the floor; it was really as simple as that. Yet the car did not ride very smooth at its maximum speed; this surprised them, as did the motor, which seemed a hundred times noisier than the power generator on any spacecraft they'd been in.

While putting distance between them and Betaville was an immediate priority, there was something even more urgent pressing on their minds. Their violent landing on this planet had come just after dawn, so they'd yet to glimpse this world's night sky. And that was the problem. They had told the Betaville cops the truth about one thing: They had no idea where they were. Not a clue. All that day, during their interrogation, they had yearned for night to fall just so they could see the stars and get a reading on their galactic location. Now it was dark again, and the rain clouds were finally beginning to break up ahead of them. So even though the police might be coming over the next hill in high pursuit, the three fellow travelers knew they had to stop and study the sky the first chance they got.

Spotting a fairly high hill ahead, Zarex pulled to the side of the road and killed the engine. All they could hear now was the wind. Suddenly, it was howling. They climbed out of the car and found the clouds above them were moving away very quickly. Strangely, it was getting very bright out. They climbed a wire fence, then forded a small stream before reaching the base of the hill. Scrambling up to the summit, they found the clouds were blowing away in every direction now, magically revealing the night sky for the first time.

"Am I seeing things?" Zarex was the first to gasp, shielding his eyes from the glare. "Or does this before us seem alien and unreal?"

That it did. Unlike the black-magic planet of Myx, the sky here was absolutely filled with stars. From horizon to horizon to horizon, there seemed to be nothing but stars. More stars than black space in between. More stars than it would seem possible, especially in the middle of the sky, where there were so many clustered together, they seemed to create one gigantic orb of light.

They had never seen anything like this.

"My God," Tomm breathed. "Where can we be?"

The three travelers had no idea. But it was important that they find out. Before being arrested, they'd given their personal items to Pater Tomm, hoping the police would not frisk someone who looked like a priest, which they did not. This was how they had been able to retain their various quadtrols and Twenty 'n Six boxes. Zarex pulled out his quadtrol now and scanned the vast, star-studded sky above them. He looked at the initial readings and let out a long, astonished groan.

"No wonder no one in the Five-Arm knew where this place was," he said finally. "It's because we're not *on* the Five-Arm anymore."

Hunter and Tomm didn't like the sound of that.

"If not the Five-Arm, then where are we, brother?" Tomm asked him anxiously.

Zarex pushed some more buttons; again it took a few moments for the calculations to bounce back to him.

"Goodness," he breathed. "Can this be accurate?"

He turned the quadtrol around so they could both see.

"If this is correct," he said. "We're not on any arm at all."

Hunter and Tomm just stared back at him. *Not on any arm?*

"Nor are we inward, near the Ball," Zarex continued. "We are at neither place."

"Is that possible?" Hunter asked.

Zarex just shrugged. "Certainly every known star in the Galaxy is located either on the arms or in the Ball, or very close by. Yet, if my quadtrol is to be believed, we are at neither point in space."

He paused and looked up again. "In all my years, I've never seen a sky such as this."

But why did the sky look so thick with stars? Hunter was the first to spit out a theory. Because the Galaxy was flat and spiral, they were used to looking through one of the arms toward the center. Could it be that they were actually somewhere looking down onto the Milky Way, so the stars were not spread before them on a straight plane, but instead literally filled up the sky?

"An interesting conjecture," Zarex said. "Except top or bottom, there aren't any systems anywhere near the area we would have to be. It is supposed to be totally empty space; the gap between us and the other galaxies—"

"But dear God, it's the only explanation!" Tomm cried. "As crazy as it may seem."

This was all becoming very unsettling for Zarex. As a lifelong star shooter, it was a bit frightening not knowing exactly where he was. Even in his longest explorations, he'd always left from a familiar starting point, knowing he could always return to the same.

But not this time.

"Oh Lord," the giant explorer moaned now as it all began to sink in. "We *are* looking down at the whole thing. Or up as the case may be. That flood in the center must be the Ball, the streams on its edge the beginnings of the arms. But we must be thousands upon thousands of light-years removed from the swirl to have such a view!"

He shook once, from head to toe, then whispered, "Brothers, this is truly an unnatural place for us to be."

But the flood of stars was not the only unusual thing going

on over their heads. Rising off to the east, breaking through the last of the clouds, was the strange planet's only moon. It seemed overly large, very close and familiar somehow. Bright white, with many craters in evidence, it was traveling so fast across the very starry sky, they could actually see its movement.

And still, that was not the strangest thing above them. Strangest of all was the string of heavenly bodies that stretched across the sky, roughly east to west, like a necklace of gigantic white gems. It was hard to tell just what these things were, or how far out from the planet. From their size and brightness, they seemed almost close to orbit. Yet the way they were aligned across the entire sky indicated they were much farther out.

Zarex began madly pushing the buttons on his quadtrol now. This was getting too crazy. He had to know where he was. But his device started going haywire. It made a very strange noise, and then it shut down altogether. All three men let out a gasp. A quadtrol going bust? They'd never heard of such a thing before.

Both Hunter and Tomm quickly retrieved their own quadtrols, but the effect was the same. Their devices took a few readings, delivered the unprecedented news that they couldn't fix their own location, then began beeping and whirring until fizzling out for good.

The three travelers stood mute in amazement. Then reality came flooding in. They still didn't know where they were . . . and without any quadtrols, they were like ships on the ocean without a compass. They really *were* lost.

Hunter swore under his breath. Damn, this was not going well at all. It wasn't just that they didn't know where they were. It was the planet itself. It just didn't look the part for this great adventure. What had he imagined their ultimate destination to be? A world inhabited entirely by valiant soldiers like the Freedom Brigade mercs? No, not quite. But certainly, he'd expected some kind of advanced civilization, maybe even *ultra*-advanced. A place that was impressive and exotic. An entire planet that looked like Big Bright City. *That* had been his fantasy. Buildings, air machines, towers, floating cities, and billions of people, waiting with open arms for him and others who had been called back home.

But this definitely did not seem like home. Surely his psyche would be flashing all kinds of signals, that yes! He'd finally made it to the end of what was supposed to be an impossible journey. But none of this was happening inside him now. Just the opposite, in fact.

But did this mean they'd ended up on the wrong planet? It was obvious the people here had never been contacted, either by locals from planets nearby or by anyone else. They were totally ignorant of other life in space. How could the Freedom Brigade come from such a place then? Had Hunter and his friends been tricked? Had the poof steered them off course on purpose? Or had she miscalculated somehow?

Or could there be some other explanation entirely?

Was this the place he was supposed to be?

Looking up at the very strange sky now, Hunter knew there was only one way to find out.

They would have to take Agent Lisa's advice.

9

It was fourth down and inches to go.

There were six seconds remaining on the clock. The score was twenty-fourteen. A touchdown here would give Mayfield High a tie. The extra point would win the game.

Tension gripped the stadium. The boisterous crowd had become eerily quiet. Two thousand people, collectively holding their breath. Even the vendors were paying attention. Along the home sideline, some of the Mayfield cheerleaders were crying. This was the biggest game of the year. The opposing team, the hated Smalltown High, had been their rival for like, ages.

Those cheerleaders not crying were either praying or trying to induce others in the crowd to pray. All except one, Ashley Woods. She was the squad leader, and this was a moment of big responsibility for her. Yet she was not thinking about the game, the crowd, or her squad. She was thinking about a dream she had had the night before.

She was walking down a long, straight road somewhere near her home. She met a very cute guy walking in the other direction. He didn't scare her. She talked to him for a while. They had a few beers. They kissed. Then, they did it. . . .

It!

They . . . did . . . it.

She'd never had a dream like that in her life.

She was blond and beautiful, the prettiest cheerleader on the squad, thus her elevated status. But she was not stuck up, not a clothes freak, not a druggie, not a smoker. Not an angel, either, but close. Some things tempted her. Mostly she thought of herself as a normal seventeen-year-old kid. She loved old movies. She loved Saturday morning cartoons. She loved dancing.

And she liked boys. A lot. She didn't have a boyfriend, and never really had one. Not a serious one, anyway. She had kissed a few, though. And done a few other things. Not much, but some.

But dreaming . . . about *doing it*?

Never . . .

The referee's whistle knocked her out of the trance.

She looked to the end zone just as the ball was being hiked. What happened next came like slow motion. The last six seconds begin ticking away. The quarterback—Billy Rogers, class hunk—gets the ball and drops back to pass but everybody is covered. Billy starts scrambling. Two seconds tick away. Billy is running for his life, half the Smalltown squad is chasing him. Two seconds to go. At the very last instant, Billy changes direction and heads for the end zone. He makes a great leap, twists in midair—and is stopped, dead, by one, two, three opposing players. Slammed to the turf, eleven Smalltown players pile on top of him.

He is still a half a foot away from the goal line. The last two seconds tick away. The horn sounds.

The game was over.

Ashley went back to thinking about her dream.

The other girls on the Mayfield cheering squad took the loss very hard. Even a half hour after the game was over, they were too distraught to do anything but cry some more and then eat.

So it was up to Ashley to pick up the squad's equipment— pom-poms mostly. But by the time she'd finished policing their area and gathered her own things together, she found herself alone in the stadium. All the fans were gone. The cheer squad bus, which was supposed to drop them all off at their homes, had left as well. Even the janitors were gone.

"Must be my lucky day," she thought.

Then she slung her gym bag over her shoulder and began the mile and a half walk to town and home.

It was a warm fall day, and after a while, she didn't mind the walk at all. Thoughts bounced between her pretty little ears as she sauntered down the barely paved road, looking everywhere but straight in front of her. There were at least ten parties she could go to tonight. Some with booze. Some with pot. Some with both. Some with none. All might be *tres* boring. She considered just staying home and renting a scary movie. If she went out, what would she wear? She was so sick of her jeans these days, but a skirt might not work, as all the parties would be outside, and it was starting to get cold these nights. So if it was her jeans then, which shoes? Which top? Would she need a jacket? Did she have enough money to chip in for beer? What if . . .

Suddenly she stopped in her tracks. There was a shadow on the road in front her, not her own. She looked up to see a guy standing practically in front of her. He was smiling. He was older. He was handsome. He also looked very, very different. And very lost.

Ashley did not feel nervous at all. She was out in the middle of nowhere—well, at least a mile from town. And this guy had literally popped up like magic. But she was okay, and she knew it.

"Well, hello," she said, her fingers suddenly twisting her long blond hair.

"Well, hello . . ." he replied. "I'm sorry if I startled you."

"I thought *I* was the one who startled *you*," she said sweetly.

He was wearing a very cool outfit. All black with the double-X logo of *Sorcerer's Dick* on his chest. They were Ashley's favorite band. Cool boots. Cool haircut. It had a military look to it. And so did the guy, in a way.

He spoke again. He had a slight accent. "I'm having trouble with my vehicle."

"Well, I'm not a mechanic," she replied. "Unless you think I look like one?"

"Not in the least," he said with a smile. *Great smile.*

She began babbling: "Is your car broken down? Do you know what's wrong with it? A flat tire? The battery?"

The guy just shrugged.

"I'm not sure," he said. "I don't know much about how they work."

He was a real hunk, she decided. Movie star handsome. She told herself to stop playing with her hair.

"Where is it?" she asked.

He turned and pointed farther down the road. A white Firebird was pulled off onto the shoulder, nearly hidden by cornstalks.

She just shrugged and said: "I don't know much about cars, either. But I'll take a look at it."

They walked down the road in silence. Ashley began twisting her hair again. When they reached the car, the guy got inside and twisted the key, but nothing happened. The engine sputtered and then just died away.

Ashley looked at the guy.

"Did you run out of gas?" she asked him.

He looked back at her, pure incomprehension on his face.

"Did I run out of what?" he asked.

Hunter pushed the car the last mile into town. Ashley steered—or she tried to. It was hard to do with the motor not running.

He discovered that a gas station was a place where they put a hose in a hole at the back of your car and pumped that hole full of liquid fuel and then, apparently, sent you on your way.

They also had food at the gas station. Concoctions the likes of which Hunter had never seen. While Ashley was doing the pumping, he looked through the window at one of the station's replication devices. But it seemed to be merely heating the food as opposed to creating it.

His tank full, Ashley signaled that he should follow her into the station's store. Hunter froze for a moment though. He'd been on the road for nearly a day now; He, Tomm and Zarex had decided to split up early that morning and voted that Hunter take the car. Their plan was to keep a low profile and do a discrete recon of the planet. Hunter had avoided interacting with anyone until now. Though he'd ditched his cape and helmet, he was still wearing his combat suit with the double X across the chest. This didn't seem so out of place here, though. At least not so far.

He finally did step into the store. His eyes were nearly blinded by the onslaught of bright colors. The place was stuffed with items of food and drink, and everything seemed packaged in the loudest, more garish hues possible. Hunter took down one of the packages hanging from a thin line that stretched across the top of the store. He opened it to find two long, yellowish confections inside. Spongy texture. Extremely sweet, creamlike material in the middle. He took a bite.

It was delicious!

Ashley was standing next to a large counter, smiling weirdly at him. Very strange music was blaring from somewhere, and she was tapping her two-tone shoe to its beat. There was a large guy behind the counter. He had dirty hands and a dirty face. He was leering at Ashley out of the corner of his eye.

"Well?" Ashley said to Hunter. "Time to pay . . ."

Pay?

"For what?" he asked her.

"For what you just ate—and for the gas."

Hunter was confused. This was food and fuel.

"You mean you have to *pay* for this stuff?" he asked.

Ashley's home looked unlike anything Hunter had ever seen. Most dwellings in the Galaxy, both within the Fourth Empire and out, were based on a simple block design, with few windows, and constructed entirely of random reconfigured atoms put together by electron torches.

But this dwelling was different. It was irregular, its roof was angled with a peak. A long funnel made of red stone shot up through the roof; wisps of smoke were rising out of it. The house was surrounded by a white fence, made of short, pointed wooden spikes that would have a hard time keeping out even the weakest intruder. There were trees planted between the front of this gate and the dwellings' main entrance, and a short, green plant growth covered the ground in between the trees.

The dwelling itself had many, many windows. Each one had a small box hanging beneath it filled with multicolored vegetation. There were houses of nearly the exact same design on either side of this one. In fact, the entire road on both sides was covered with them. Some were hard to see because of the trees, though.

Ashley never once hesitated. She opened the front door with a key and invited him in.

"My parents are away," she said as a means of explanation.

Hunter stepped through the front door. In most places in the Galaxy, the interior of the home was made up of one main room with a few smaller ones around the periphery. In this place though, there were many rooms, all of them relatively the same size.

The room to his right had a table at its center with six wooden chairs around it. There were plates and glasses and cutlery set up, even though there was no meal in sight. She led him to a room at the rear of the dwelling. It was filled with instruments of cooking: pots, more utensils, glass storage bins stuffed with grains and other unidentifiable foods. An assembly of silver pipes made up the unnecessarily elaborate device for transporting water into the house. This room also held a table and chairs and a large white box that seemed cold and was giving off a whirring sound.

She told him to sit at the table, then took off her sweater and put her hair back in a ponytail. She retrieved two glasses from a compartment hanging over the water-retrieval device, then went to the big white box and opened its door. A wisp of cold air filled the room briefly as she took out a large brown glass container and screwed off a cap from its top.

"You're thirsty, I assume?" she asked him.

She poured out an amber liquid without waiting for a reply. He watched with some amazement as the liquid began to bubble and foam over the lip of his glass.

She filled her glass, drained it, filled it again, licked her lips, and looked across the table at him. He was still examining his glass closely; he had not yet attempted to taste it.

"Take a sip," she urged him.

Hunter raised his glass and gave the liquid inside a quick sniff. The aroma came back pungent but not totally alien to him.

He just shrugged. How bad could it be?

With that, he took a healthy drink. An instant later, he was spitting the liquid noisily back into the glass. Ashley laughed so hard, she almost fell off her chair.

Hunter thought he'd been poisoned. The liquid was the worst tasting thing that had ever passed his lips.

"What is this stuff?" he asked.

Ashley poured him another huge glass.

"Man, where are you from?" she said. "It's *beer*."

They went up the stairs to Ashley's personal room.

The walls were covered with pictures of boys her age posing with musical instruments and sporting paraphernalia.

Ashley sat on the edge of her bed and took off her shoes and socks. "I hated beer the first time I tasted it, too," she said to him. "But you can get used to it after a while, don't you think?"

A device on Ashley's desk began ringing. Ashley picked up the ancient communicator and, retreating to the far corner of the room, began a quick, hushed conversation. Hunter could hear every word. Ashley was telling the person on the other end how she met him, how they got gas, what went on inside the gas station and how he had just spit up beer.

"But he is *so not* a freakazoid," she whispered. "Wait till you see him."

There was a short silence, then Hunter heard Ashley say, "OK, in an hour. And don't be a bitch, promise?"

Then she returned the device to its place and said to him, "Want to go to a party?"

The golf course was two miles east of Ashley's house.

It was getting dark by this time, and the moon and all those stars and the necklace of heavenly bodies began brightening all over the deep blue sky.

Hunter let Ashley drive; he wanted to study the sky through the open sun roof, in faint hope that he might recognize something shining way up there, something that might give him a clue as to where he was.

But no such clue could be found.

They reached the golf course, parked the car, and walked across a huge fairway. Ashley was wearing a short white skirt, a white blouse, and white sneakers. She looked gorgeous. Hunter tried his best to walk quickly beside her, his eyes still gazing at the stars. Ashley was talking to him, explaining that this was where all the kids came to do the party thing and avoid the authorities. They reached a small clump of trees located in the middle of the vast fairway. Other kids were already there. Some had blankets and tents and were obviously planning to stay overnight. Ashley met a guy who sold her six bottles of beer. Then they walked out of the clump of trees, over another fairway, to a nearly perfect circle of short green grass beyond.

Two girls were waiting for them there. Ashley introduced him as her friend. The girls showed Ashley a bottle of clear liquid they had secured. It was called vodka. Ashley explained to Hunter that they liked this location because it was far out on the fairway, and they could see the cops coming from any direction.

Hunter studied the perfectly manicured grass within the circle. There was a tiny, shallow hole in the middle with a flag sticking out of it. He sat down next to the hole and studied the stars further. Ashley conversed with the two other girls. One approached him and asked if he wanted a drink of vodka. Hunter agreed and took a slug from the bottle. From the moment it touched his tongue, he thought he was going to die. It tasted like a combination of liquid fire and bilgewater. Truly awful. Far worse than beer.

"I can't believe anyone would want to drink that stuff," he told the girl with a cough.

She smiled and took a swig herself. "That's what they all say at first," she told him.

At that moment, there came a small racket over his shoulder. Hunter turned to see three guys walking up to the green. They were obviously drunk and belligerent. One went up to Ashley's other friend and began a loud conversation with her about a broken date. The girl was trying to ignore him, but then the guy began screaming so loudly, the other girl started screaming at him to quiet down or the cops might hear him.

"It's good advice," Hunter called over to the bigmouth, not taking his eyes off the stars.

The next thing Hunter knew, the three guys were standing around his head, looking down at him. This was Reggie, Moose, and Weed. Reggie was the one with the big mouth.

"What are you?" he asked Hunter. "A wise guy?"

Hunter thought about that for a moment, then got to his feet and brushed himself off. He was roughly the same size as Reggie, even though the guy was obviously younger than him by at least a dozen years.

Hunter asked him, "Am I a what?"

"A wise guy," Reggie roared back. "An asshole, pal. What's the matter? They don't speak like this wherever you come from?"

Hunter shook his head no. "No, they don't. Can you explain it to me?"

"Explain it to you? You *are* stupid then."

"I won't be, if you explain it to me."

"Oh, yeah? Well, maybe I don't know either. How can I explain it to you if I don't know either?"

Hunter just shrugged. "Well, then I guess that would make you just as stupid as me."

This confused Reggie. He looked to Moose and Weed; they were no help of course.

Reggie turned back to Hunter. He swigged his beer and switched tactics. "I just bet your car sucks, man."

"It does, when it runs out of gas," Hunter replied.

Reggie went right in his face. *"Now whad the fook do you mean by that? I already asked you. You being a wise guy? You being a wiseass?"*

Hunter just laughed at him. He couldn't help it; it was funny. A 0.1783622-second bolt from his blaster pistol could reduce Reggie to a pile of ash. Half that would render him a babbling idiot for the rest of his life, maybe a slight improvement. But clocking Reggie wouldn't be in line with Hunter's low-key policy. He had to amuse this fellow somehow.

"Maybe it's *your* car that sucks," he told Reggie with a grin.

Reggie's friends immediately went, "Ooooooo . . ."

Even the three girls gasped. Obviously, Reggie was sensitive to what people said about his car.

Again, he went nose to nose with Hunter.

"Are you saying my car sucks? *Is that what you're saying?* Let me tell you something, you freak. My dad and I built that car. Hear me? *Me and my dad.* We built the engine. We built the frame. We built the chassis. *Me and my dad.* Get it?"

"You do a lot of stuff with your dad?"

Reggie's neck vein nearly popped. He was so furious he could barely speak.

Moose and the other guy closed in around Hunter. Were they threatening him? He couldn't tell. At this point, one of the girls started crying.

"Well?" Hunter said to the beet-red Reggie.

"Well—the fuck—what?"

"Well, show me your car," Hunter told him. "If it's so fooking special, show it to me."

Reggie hung there, like in suspended animation, for about ten seconds. With one fist cocked, he was using the other to slowly crush his beer can.

"OK, wiseass," he said finally. "I'll show you my *fucking car.*"

With that, Reggie ran off, across the fairway and into the woods from whence he came. Before anyone could say a word, there was a screech and the sound of rubber skidding on mud.

Suddenly another roar, this of a car engine. Then from the woods to the south, wheels turning madly, headlights wildly lighting up the night, came Reggie, driving his precious auto at high speed across the formerly pristine fairway.

There now were a few seconds when those standing on the green weren't sure whether Reggie intended to stop or mow them all down. Even Moose and Weed looked like they were ready to bail out should their overly sensitive friend forget they were standing there, close to his intended victims.

But Reggie did stop. He stood on the brakes, and the car fishtailed wildly on the knoll leading up to the green, tearing up huge chunks of dirt and sod in the process.

"Oh God," one of the girls moaned. "The cops will kill us!"

Reggie jumped from the car even before it had stopped moving. He was again right up in Hunter's face.

"There's my car asshole. See it? *See it?*"

"How can I not see it? It's right there."

"Yeah. Yeah it is. . . . So you like it, you freak?"

Hunter stepped to one side and studied the car. It was very basic. A metal body. Four wheels coated in rubber. Two seats in the front, a smaller single seat in the back.

"It looks like every other car I've ever seen," Hunter replied truthfully.

This was not the answer Reggie was expecting. Moose and Weed threw away their beer cans, ready now to fight. Reggie's face was as red as the finish on his car.

But at that moment, one of the girls—the one with the vodka bottle—laughed out loud. "Like any other car! Man, that's rich!"

No sooner were the words out of her mouth than Reggie spun around and violently slapped her across the face.

Whack!

Hunter's eyes nearly fell out of his head. He couldn't believe what he'd just seen. Reggie had actually *hit* the girl. Hunter was shocked. Never, ever, from the time he'd woken up on Fools 6 to his travels throughout the Galaxy had he seen a man strike a woman. In his world, such an act was beyond comprehension.

But then, just as quickly, the shock subsided, and anger flooded in. Reggie needed two friends to back him up but had no problem hitting a girl? That was not right. Low-profile or not, Hunter decided Reggie needed an education on something.

He reached over, grabbed Reggie by the collar of his football jacket, and spun him around, all in one fluid motion. Reggie tried to say something, but Hunter had his collar twisted so tight under his throat, Reggie could no longer speak. His face was becoming a darker shade of crimson with every moment.

Hunter yanked him even closer, so that Reggie's inflamed ear was now up against Hunter's lips.

"Now, Reggie, it's time for me to show you *my* car." Hunter told him.

He dropped Reggie to the putting green, then took the Twenty 'n Six box out of his pocket. He pushed the button; there was a small puff of green mist and a flash. And suddenly, his flying machine was there.

Moose threw up. All over the front of his football jacket, his pants, and his new sneakers. Weed was paralyzed with fear. The girls were, too.

Hunter retrieved Reggie from the seat of his pants and dragged him up the access ladder to the cockpit. "Here's my car, Reggie. See it? *See it?*"

Reggie tried to mumble something but found it impossible.

"Suddenly not much to say, Reggie?" Hunter taunted him.

Reggie was legless. All he could do was point at the suddenly materialized aircraft and babble.

"I think it's time you and I went for a little ride, Reggie."

With that, Hunter dropped him into the rear of the cockpit, then climbed in himself.

Hunter closed the canopy, lifted the wheels, then set his velocity handle on less than 1 percent of his basically unlimited power. The flying machine disappeared in a flash . . . and was back a thousandth of a second later. In that time, however, Hunter had completed a dozen high-speed circuits of the tiny planet, pole to pole, much of the flight made inverted.

To those still standing on the golf green, it seemed as if the aircraft had been gone for just the blink of an eye, no more. But Reggie's condition testified that it had not been a pleasant interlude. His face was plastered against the side of the bubble canopy, held in place there by his own gurgling saliva. Hunter popped the bubble top, reached in back and lifted Reggie up by his jacket collar, and dropped him to the ground below.

Then Hunter looked down at Reggie's two buddies, Moose and Weed.

"Who's next?" he asked them.

At that moment, the others started to react to what had just happened. And finally their feet began communicating again with their brain. The fight-or-flight impulse took over, and Moose and Weed lit out as if an entire enemy football team was chasing them. Somehow, Reggie got to his feet. But he vomited heavily, then tripped and fell into his own vomit. He got up again and staggered away. The girls took off as well—or at least two of them did.

One did not.

It was Ashley.

Hunter looked down at her; he couldn't tell if she was in a state of shock or not. But even with her jaw dropped open and her hair a bit out of place, she looked beautiful.

"I think . . . I'm still asleep," she began to mumble. "I think I'm still at home in bed, and it is this morning, and I'm dreaming all this."

"I know that feeling," Hunter told her.

She took two steps toward the flying machine. "What . . . what is this thing?"

Hunter started to say something, then stopped, then started again, then stopped again. How do you explain something that he didn't completely understand himself?

"I can't tell you," he finally replied. "But I can *show* you. . . ."

Ashley's eyes lit up. "Show me? How?"

Hunter lowered the access ladder.

"Want to go for a ride?" he asked.

Mayfield Police Officer Charles Eaton was working on his second cup of coffee of the night when the call came in.

There was a disturbance *above* the municipal golf course.

Or so his dispatcher was trying to tell him.

"Repeat, base?"

"Report of a disturbance above the town links," came the reply. "Could be a fire in the trees, over near the thirteenth fairway."

Eaton carefully poured his coffee back into his thermos and started his patrol car. He knew the thirteenth hole very well. A par-five, 575-yard killer with big woods off to the left. He'd spent a lot of time looking for his stray shots among those pines. But how could the trees catch on fire?

Eaton's present position was closer to the north side of the links. The whole golf course was part of his patrol area this night; the place routinely saw some extracurricular activity after any Mayfield football game, win or lose. Usually, a blast from the siren scattered any kids drinking out on the course. But fire meant vandalism. That meant Eaton would have to walk in and check it out.

He put his car in gear and rolled about two hundred feet to the ninth tee turnoff. He could park the car here, and walk in.

"Base . . . sixteen here . . . nineteen thirty-three hours. You'd better call the firehouse, tell them to get someone out here. I'm going forty-two from the car."

Eaton gathered his portable radio, his nightstick, and his flashlight and stepped out of the car.

His radio crackled again. This time Betty, the night shift dispatcher, had a bit of panic in her voice.

"Sixteen, we now have a report of something on fire and . . . *flying* over the links."

Flying? Eaton thought.

He was about to ask Betty for a repeat when he saw it. Right above the trees. A machine of some kind. Red, white, and blue. And yes, it was flying. And yes, it seemed to be aflame, with a low roar emanating from its midsection.

He dropped the light, the radio, and his nightstick, all at once. He went to his knees and tried to pick them up. But his hands were shaking too much.

"Base? *Base? Are you there?*"

He looked down to see he was talking into his flashlight.

When he looked up again, the machine was right over his head.

It hovered there, just for a moment. The thing had wings, two big ones, two little ones. Its nose was sharp, pointed. It was now making a very strange growling noise. And it was surrounded by a greenish glow.

Officer Eaton blinked again, and the machine was gone.

Soaring . . .

Off the ground, the golf course rushing beneath. Over more trees, over the last three holes, over the pond, over the high school, over the middle of town itself.

No feeling. Not really. They were standing still, and everything else below them was moving. The ground, moving, beneath.

Faster now. Very fast. Off in the distance, the lights of a big city. Chicago? Could that be?

Yes! Over the tall buildings, over the five bridges, over the lakefront. Now over the lake.

Another big city. Ships on the cold waters below. *Another* city. Then long stretches of highways. Going east, everything moving beneath. The moon was so close, she felt like she could reach out and touch its face.

This was real, but not real. Ashley was awake, but she knew she must be asleep. Her eyes were open, yet when she pinched herself, she could not feel any pain. She could still talk, but when the words came out, she could not hear them.

Was that New York ahead of them? *New York City!* Was it possible?

Suddenly they were flying through a canyon of buildings. Manhattan. The rivers. The lights. The bridges. A huge green statue of a woman holding a torch high over her head. A turn to the left, then a long curve back over the city. Going west now. Faster and faster. Over fields and dales and forests and many long, wide rivers. Houses, small towns, and miles and miles of growing things... and then suddenly, Ashley was walking on the road near the stadium again. And Hunter is there. Then they are in the gas station, then her kitchen, then her bedroom. Her rug turns into a wave of gold. And Hunter is smiling at her. His machine is gone, but she feels like she is still flying. He takes her by the hands and gently kisses her cheek. They are standing in a great hall, with hundreds, no, *thousands* of people around them. And Hunter is wearing a completely different outfit. This one was deep blue, and there were no *X*s across his chest, but many ribbons and medals and gold stars instead. And she is dressed in a long, white gown, with immensely curled hair and a string of diamonds plunging from her neck.

"I hope I can explain this to you someday," he says to her.

She looks back into Hunter's eyes and suddenly understands something.

"Oh my God . . ." she whispers. *"It's you. . . ."*

He smiles wearily. "Yes, it is . . ."

Another flash.

The gold weave turned into the finely manicured grass of the thirteenth green.

They were suddenly back at the golf course, looking up at the stars.

"Are you OK?" Hunter asked her.

But Ashley couldn't hear him. All she could think about was her dream the night before. *That strange dream.* She met this guy, they got along, they kissed, and . . .

Suddenly she grabbed Hunter by the sleeve and began dragging him across the fairway.

"I have to bring you someplace," she said. "And I mean, *right now. . . .*"

They ran this time.

Across the north end of the golf course, right by a gang of confused cops and firefighters, through the center of Mayfield to Pike's Hill. Ashley didn't talk the whole way, and she never let go of his sleeve. They climbed the hill swiftly. At the top was a patch of soft, high grass and a view that stretched for miles. Below them was the town, the lake, the river. The high school. Above them, all those stars.

She knelt on the grass and pulled him down with her.

"That thing you do," she said, still out of breath. "Turning things back on themselves? Or whatever it is! Can you do it whenever you want?"

Hunter smiled. "Sure can. . . ."

She leaned over and kissed him hard on the lips.

"Then do it again," she said, squeezing him very tight. *"Please . . ."*

The sun came up, and Ashley made it home before her parents.

Hunter stayed at top of the hill, lying on the same patch of grass, watching the sunrise and listening to his heart beat. It had been quite a night. And it hadn't been *all* fun and games. They'd talked. He'd asked about life here—and what a strange place the planet was turning out to be. They had cars here but no airplanes; microscopes but no telescopes. Lots of cops but no armed forces. They had no enemies except themselves. This world was one world, not a bunch of nations thrown together.

They'd looked at the brilliant night sky. Hunter was still amazed by it, but it was old hat for her. She told him that no one had ever bothered to name anything up there because there was so much stuff, where would one begin? And the heavenly bodies? No one knew what they were. And why did the moon fly around the planet at such an unnatural speed? Again, no one knew, and no one really seemed to care.

It was odd. There were brilliant people here: doctors, scientists, academic types. But apparently no one had ever had the urge to climb on a wing and try to fly it or to blast off into space and get a better look at what was happening out there. The people here had no idea what their planet looked like from outer space. But then again, neither did Hunter. During his two quick flights around the planet, he'd maintained a very low altitude and a relatively high speed. He'd yet to get the God's-eye view.

Maybe next time, he remembered thinking.

So they'd talked and talked and talked, and when it was time for her to go, Ashley realized she'd passed the night without her once asking him how all these things he was able to do could be real. It was not like her she said, but she'd simply accepted them. And she promised not to say a word about them to anyone. And she said she would like to do them all again. Soon.

The last thing Hunter had said to her was, "Can you meet me up here again tonight?"

And she'd smiled and said, "You bet."

That's why he was still on top of the hill. He didn't want to go anywhere else. He would stay here, hold his position, so there would be no chance that he would miss her when she came again.

Of course, he wished he'd thought to ask her what time she would return. Later or early? Did night start as soon as the sun began to go down? Or when it finally set? Or when the moon and all those stars came out again? Midnight or dusk?

He didn't know.

But, no problem. He'd just stay put and be sure that when she came, either early or late, he would be here, waiting for her.

So he just lay back on the same patch of grass and watched the sun slowly glide across the blue sky. He thought of how he got here, and wherever here was, and how now maybe he wasn't so sure he was on the wrong planet after all.

Then the sun began to set, and he sat up and watched the path at the bottom of the hill. Then the sun disappeared, and all those stars came out, and the heavenly bodies and then the moon streaked across the sky.

The night grew colder. The stars burned his face. And then the sun came up again.

And though Hunter had stayed awake all night waiting, Ashley never showed up.

10

Tony "Tony Burps" Balbini was the diner king of Jersey City.

He owned three of them: one by the tracks, one by the whorehouse, and one right off the Route 202 exit. The diners had originally been built to serve as fronts for the rackets, numbers running mostly. But the food side of it came along better than anyone had hoped. Now all the businesses were running in the black.

Tony Burps did everything in XL. He drove an extra-large Cadillac, he carried an extra-large gun, he wore extra-large, or sometimes even extra-extra-large-size clothes. Every one of his employees hated him but did everything they could to stay on his good side, this after he once spread some nasty rumors about a missing busboy and a particular Monday's meatloaf special.

Usually, at first sight of his Caddy flying into the parking lot, his employees would scatter to the far corners of the diner and just hope they could survive the random, intimidating encounters. Tony went through employees like some people went through cigarettes, but that was just part of the diner game. Dishwashers were the worst. They were usually just thieves in disguise. If one lasted more than two weeks, Tony became suspicious, earlier even if one showed any signs of initiative or any other wacky behavior.

That's what had brought Tony Burps to the Route 202 Diner

this rainy evening. He'd hired a new dishwasher less than a week before, and his spies were telling him the guy had not left since. He'd been taking every shift for nearly four days, allowing the other kitchen help to burn a rare day off their miserly sick time.

Even though Tony had hired the man he could barely recall what he looked like now. He just remembered this guy was big—real big. As big and tall as Tony was big and fat. His brief work record was something of a quandary for Tony. Working for nearly one hundred hours straight was great for the diner's overall operation, as there had been no backup at the sinks since the man was hired. But Tony was also paying for this spirited enterprise—at nearly five bucks an hour.

He was there today to investigate.

He barged through the front door, grunted in the general direction of some of the stool regulars, then cornered Marshall, his head counterman.

"That guy go home yet?" he asked Marshall.

The diminutive black man in the neatly pressed shirt and tie just shook his head.

"He's still back there, boss," he reported. "He ain't even broken a sweat yet. But I'll tell you, whenever he decides to work his magic, the dishes have never been so clean."

Tony did not like the sound of that.

He pulled out his employee/living book and began flipping through the last few pages.

"What's his name again? Clorox?"

"Zarex," Marshall gently corrected him. "I think he's sitting out back, having a smoke."

Tony brushed by him and pushed his way into the kitchen. The place was a mess. The dishes were piled sky high in the sink, there were dirty pots and pans everywhere. Tony took one look at the night cook. The man stood frozen for a few seconds before going back to his task of making a stack of silver dollar pancakes.

Tony stepped through the filthy cleaning area and kicked the back door open. The junkyard, a putrid canal, and the highway lay beyond. Sitting on a crate next to the trash barrels was his latest dishwasher.

"What's a matta wit' you?" Tony asked him. "You got a headache? Did you break a nail?"

Zarex looked up at him, took a long, sweet puff of his Marlboro, and blew the smoke right into Tony's extra-large face.

"I'm on break," he said, looking back out over the dirty canal. God, how he loved staring at it and the busy roadway beyond.

"It looks like you've been on break all day," Tony said, thumbing back toward the dirty kitchen. "I mean, when I hired you, Mr. Xerox, I wasn't doing it just to provide you with a place to hang out. If that's what you kids still call it. I mean, you're here to work, too."

Zarex sent another plume of smoke Tony's way. There was a screech of brakes on the highway nearby. A fascinating sound.

"I've done nothing but work since coming here," he told Tony. "Why? Have you heard complaints?"

"Yeah," Tony roared back. "A big one. Like the fooking kitchen area looks like a fooking mess. Like it's all dirty dishes and crappy pots. This ain't charm school, bozo. You're supposed to be cleaning all that stuff."

Zarex took one last drag of his cigarette, stubbed the lit end out on the palm of his hand, then stood up. Tony nearly stumbled backward. This guy was much bigger than he remembered him. He stepped aside while Zarex calmly put his apron back on and stepped back inside the kitchen. Tony saw a quick flash of light, followed by a puff of greenish smoke. Not two seconds later, Zarex stepped back outside, sat back down on his crate, and relit his Marlboro.

Tony backed away from him, stepped into the kitchen, and nearly peed himself.

The place was absolutely clean. No, clean was not the right word. Sparkling. That was it. All the dishes were now washed and stacked, all the pans were scrubbed and hanging in the proper stations.

Tony's jaw dropped through his three chins. The cowering night cook walked back to the cleaning area with a dirty pot covered with spaghetti sauce.

"He's been doing this since coming here, boss," the cook said with a quivering voice. "Place gets messy. He waits till no one is looking and—phfft! It's all clean again. I mean, don't get me wrong; every cook loves a clean kitchen. But, if you ask me, I think it's kinda spooky, what he's been doing."

But Tony was barely listening to the man.

"Mind your own business," he finally said to the cook, taking the dirty pot and throwing it into the pristine sink. "Get back to work."

The cook scrambled away; Tony gingerly stepped back outside. He looked down at Zarex, who was drawing on his stubby cigarette like it was his last breath.

There was a long, awkward silence. Tony looked at Zarex; Zarex looked at Tony. He'd been to thousands of planets in his lifetime, but Zarex knew the real root of discovery came not from a world's rocks and clay but from its inhabitants. Everything the explorer had to know about this part of this planet he would learn right here, in this place, at this moment.

"Did you have something else to say?" he finally asked Tony, breaking the spell.

Tony just stared back at him for a few beats, then said, "Yeah, you missed a pot."

Several hundred miles to the southwest, Pater Tomm was standing in the shadows of a huge cathedral, watching a police car roll by.

He was in a city called Washington, D.C. It seemed to be the political center of this little world, but it was virtually empty of people, and anyone he did see walking around was doing so very slowly. He'd caught a ride on an empty railroad car to get here, he and a number of other hobos. When they arrived at the station, more hobos jumped on the train than jumped off. Tomm was convinced this meant something, but he didn't know what.

He'd walked the city and saw little he'd describe as spectacular. Many of the structures were built of the same red brick that was featured on other houses strictly as a heat-release device. There were plenty of cars, too. In fact, they were parked everywhere: along the curbs, in people's yards, even on their front lawns. Yet Tomm could have walked down the middle of any number of main streets without fear of getting clipped by one of the four-wheeled monsters. There were plenty of cars around; there just weren't that many people driving them.

He found the cathedral the afternoon of the second day. His heart leapt when he first spotted it. The cross on its steeple was nearly an exact copy of the one he always wore around his neck, proportionately speaking, of course. To his mind, this could only mean one thing. While for whatever reason this planet had missed out on a lot of the cool stuff available throughout the Galaxy, this one thing, religion, had somehow made it here.

It was for moments like these that Pater Tomm lived. So he sat in the park across the street from the grand church, nursing the free coffee he'd received from the nearby homeless center, intent on studying the people who went in and out of the place.

He'd sat like that for several hours. The strange thing was, no one approached the place; no one came out. As soon as it grew dark, he'd stolen into these shadows where he waited now, as the police car idled past. The two cops had been eating something, and this only reminded Tomm that it had been ages and billions of miles since his last good meal.

But first things first.

Once he was sure that the authorities were gone, he picked the lock on the back door of the church and let himself in.

But any excitement he'd felt in his heart drained right out of him as he took a long look around the inside of the cathedral. The altar was incredibly elaborate with much gold and silver in evidence. Finely carved wooden benches and a magnificent pulpit only added to the aura. Beautiful frescoes on the walls and ceiling. Marble for the altar rails and floor. A beautiful piece of architecture.

But then there was the dust. It was everywhere. Not just a scattering; it was nearly a half inch thick on some of the pews, and it was as hard as stone on some parts of the floor. Hymn books lay decayed and rotting. He picked one up, and it just fell away, its fibers only adding more to the dust.

Tomm sank into one of the pews and looked up at the altar. There was only one explanation.

No one had prayed in here in many, many years.

11

The name of the highway was Route 66.

Hunter had been driving it for the past four days, finding it shortly after leaving Mayfield—and Ashley—behind.

Route 66 was more or less a straight highway, going west. It was well maintained, clean, pothole free, lined with trees or multicolored desert brush in many places. It also featured numerous dips and bumps. He'd literally sailed through the air after hitting a few of them. The Firebird had a little wing attached to its rear end; perhaps its function was to stabilize the car whenever it left the ground. He didn't know. Either way, it made for exciting driving.

He'd passed many strange things along the way. A huge barn with a rounded top. A leaning water tower intentionally built to look like it was falling over. Near a place called Amarillo, a line of Cadillacs buried halfway into the ground. Near a place called Tucumcari, a motel shaped like a gigantic mushroom. In Arizona, a huge canyon, spectacular, and older than anything Hunter had seen so far on this tiny planet.

He loved going fast. The road was smooth, no one was in front on him, no one was behind. Flying several light-years a second was a gas, too, but this was different. This was moving in a different way. Cars had begun to fascinate him. A machine that traveled on rubber wheels, used them not just for taxiing like those on his flying machine, but for actually going some-where.

What a concept!

The open highway. The fresh air. Pedal to the metal. It all made incredible sense to him now. Driving at precisely 160 miles an hour, roof down, one hand on the wheel, the other wrapped around a bottle of Seagram's . . .

Yes, *this* was freedom.

The night before, he'd pulled off Route 66 near the big city of Tulsa and made a bunch of new friends in a bar down by the river. It was there that he'd traded a music-producing device found under the dashboard of the car for some currency and six bottles of Seagram's whiskey. His new friends drove motorcy-cles, and some were nearly as huge and hairy as Zarex. Hunter had spilled his guts to them about Ashley, and they took pity on him. They told him not to dwell on her. It just wasn't worth it. But he missed her. Missed her, even though he didn't really know her. Many times he wished that she'd come to the hill that night. Many times he had wished that she was here with him right now. Would she have thought of any of this as having fun? He'd never know.

Everyone gets their heart broken by a blonde eventually, his new friends had told him.

He'd just had his.

He drove all night after Tulsa, all the next day and into the next night. Past miles of controlled vegetation, then grassy fields, then the desert, then over some enormous mountains where he'd seen snow, even though it was obviously not quite winter. Then came more desert, more mountains, then many, many hills.

During this stretch, he'd stopped several times for fuel. He was adept at interacting with the citizenry now. Everyone seemed friendly enough. His overgrown hair and erupting beard passed for high fashion at some of the stops along the way. Dealing with the coinage was different than the aluminum chips used throughout Galaxy though. The exchange of money out among the stars was far more low key. You needed something, you gave someone a few chips, and whatever you wanted was yours to keep. Here, on this little world, people seemed a bit more interested in getting the currency and a little less concerned that what you were getting was of the highest quality for the price.

A strange little quirk.

So was he on the wrong planet?

After almost a week and more than a few face-to-face encounters with the natives, the truth was, he still didn't know.

That didn't mean he disliked the place. To the contrary. He was getting to like it very much. But not for the reasons he would have suspected.

The people here really didn't know very much, beyond the basics of life, anyway. And they weren't very curious, either. Even though they sat in what had to be one of the most spectacular locations in the Galaxy, no one seemed to have any pressing desire to learn anything more about the great star roads beyond. Or even what was happening just beyond their own atmosphere.

But after four days on the road and just as many bottles of Seagram's, Hunter had come to the conclusion that there was freedom in all that, too. Ideas were what weighed you down. The less you had to carry around with you, the less the burden became. *That* was freedom. Or a type of it, anyway. And while it was not something that, given a choice, many people he knew would want, here on this planet, it was almost seductive. For someone who felt like he had too many ideas stuffed inside his head, living on a world like this might just be the ideal thing to do. With such people, Hunter could relate.

Or maybe there was another explanation. Maybe he was just stuck inside some long, elaborate dream. Or maybe he was in the middle of a mind-bender, after drinking too much slow-ship wine. And lucky for him, there *were* girls in his reveries.

Or maybe he'd just come home and still didn't know it.

Deep thoughts—or at least they seemed that way now as he left Flagstaff behind and began his ascent over the Sierra Nevadas.

Open another bottle, he told himself.

Over the mountains was a place called California.

He reached the ocean early the next morning.

To get there, he'd driven down off a descending series of

hills. At some points, the stars overhead seemed so bright, they lit his way even more than the car's headlights.

About an hour before dawn, he entered the city of Los Angeles. It seemed like a very nutty place: jammed with people, cars clogging roads and bridges, surprising at such an early hour. The city was remarkably clean, though—*sparkling* almost. Every street was lined with magnificently grand trees, all bearing long palmlike fronds, and many of the sidewalks seemed made of gold.

Beyond the city, he found the sea. It was bright blue, with high waves crashing against miles of pristine beaches. He discovered a place to park up a beach road that led to a cliff that overlooked one stretch of beach. Again, the natural tendency for him or any starman was to seek the highest point around. The cliff looked out over a place called Santa Monica Beach. Even though it was still a bit chilly, the beach was quickly filling up with thousands of scantily clad girls.

Hunter was there when the sun came up. Sitting on the hood of the car, the last of his Seagram's bottles in hand, he saw out on the clearing horizon, just barely within sight, something very surprising.

It was the skyline of a huge city.

And it looked familiar.

Now how could this be? The only big cities he'd seen so far were miles behind him. Then it hit him: When he'd taken Ashley on the joy ride, they'd passed over a place called New York City. It was a huge metropolis that at the time reminded Hunter of Big Bright City back on Earth. This place had hundreds of high buildings; they had flown between them. There was also a huge green statue of a woman holding a torch high over her head in a bay near the jungle of skyscrapers.

Hunter strained his eyes now, and sure enough, he could see this statue way off in the distance, nearly hidden by the ocean mist and the picket line of tall buildings.

Could this be right, though? He closed his eyes and saw the canyons of New York City roll as if he and Ashley had just flown between them. But all that had happened *back there*. He looked east, over the hills to the cloud-filled sky, as if just over those mountains was where Ashley lived and just beyond that was the grand city of New York.

Now he turned back toward the water, and to the vision on

the horizon. And then he started laughing. The statue of the woman with the torch was in the harbor of New York City, and he knew New York City was on the east coast of the planet's only landmass. Yet, here he was, looking at it across this expanse of water.

How could that be? There was really only one explanation; it seemed crazy, but at the same time, he knew it made sense. This hadn't been as much a recon mission as it had been a circumnavigation. Because if that *was* New York City he was looking at just across the sea, then he'd not only crossed over a major part of this country, he'd nearly driven right around the planet.

Hunter spent the day parked up on the cliff, nursing his last bottle, looking down on all those girls, the expanse of blue water before him, and of course at the distant light reflecting from New York City. The sea became very busy with boats and other seagoing craft. During the warmest part of the day, Hunter took off his shirt and remained stretched out on the hood of the car, simply watching the never-ending parade of people and things go by.

He fell asleep a few times, woke to turn more toward the sun, swig from his bottle, adjust his shirt as a headrest. Night came again, and the lights of New York shone even brighter. All those strange stars appeared overhead again with the necklace of heavenly bodies lighting up the sky here just as it had over Mayfield.

Though he tried many times to resist it, Ashley was never very far from his mind. Again, strange in that he didn't know her very well. His night with her was just a blur to him, as he was sure it was to her. The way they met, their joyride, the night spent on the hill. It was the nature of these things that they all seemed hazy to him now, just a splinter of time, lasting a single heartbeat or just one deep breath, but not much longer than that. But it had left him with an aura of sorts. A buzz, of good feeling, unrelated to the Seagram's. Or so he hoped.

Yes, he missed her. How much? Well, almost as much as . . . as . . . ?

Hunter suddenly sat up.

That girl back there. *Way back there*. On Earth. The daughter of O'Nay. The Princess of the Galaxy? What was her name again?

Xara.

Of course, *Xara . . .*

He laughed nervously, then took another swig from the Seagram's bottle.

That was a funny moment. He'd almost forgotten Xara's name.

It was just a second later when he detected the distinct feeling of cold steel resting on the back of his neck.

He turned slowly to see an enormous gun barrel pointing right at his nose. Another was aimed at his temple. Two cops were staring at him from behind the triggers. They were wearing blue uniforms, funny hats, and dark glasses.

"Don't make any sudden moves, partner," one of them said.

"No problem, partner," Hunter quickly replied.

They told him to climb off the car, then pushed him facedown on the hood where he was frisked up and down his body.

"We've been looking for you for quite a while," one cop said.

"Really?" Hunter asked drunkenly. "What for?"

Both cops laughed.

"What for?" One mocked him. "What the hell do you think?"

The two policemen took out a pair of shackles and began to put them on Hunter's hands when suddenly, another vehicle roared up the steep beach road. It was larger than the car the two policemen had arrived in. It was all black with many windows, which were also tinted black.

Six men jumped out of this vehicle. They were all dressed the same: in blue suits, white shirts, and blue ties. Each man was also wearing sunglasses. They rushed over to where Hunter and the two cops stood, immediately removed the cuffs from Hunter's wrists, placed him in a pair of their own, then started to lead him away to their vehicle.

That's when one of the two cops said, "Wait a minute. Who the hell are you guys? This is our collar. We've been looking for this mook for a long time."

One of the suits just pushed the policeman out of the way and helped shove Hunter into the back of his vehicle.

"So have we," he growled at the cop. "He's crossed state lines, so that makes it a federal crime."

But the policemen continued to protest.

"State lines?" one said. "We're busting him for loitering. For carrying an open container in the car. And for public drunkenness. What do you guys want him for?"

The guys in the suits all laughed.

"Well, we got him for auto theft," one said. "*And* suspicion of murder."

PART THREE

Moon 39 vs The Love Rockets

12

A welcome calm had settled over the tiny jungle moon in the past few weeks.

The people who had previously fought the now-vanquished battle star from the depths of their underground space fighter base now walked about their world's surface without worry. No more concern about being discovered by the enemy. No more need to contemplate last-ditch battles.

They were free, thanks to two strangers.

Just what had happened in their underground base that day not so long ago, when the strangers came through looking for directions and wound up saving their skins—well, no one had quite explained it yet. Maybe it was something that would never be explained adequately. Angels from heaven was the current prevailing theory.

But whoever the heroes were, the people—taking the lead from their grateful Princess—had erected a shrine of sorts on the spot inside the underground cavern where the strangers had so suddenly appeared in that hour of dire need, to save the day.

This shrine now featured a plaque of pure diamond-cast elevated slightly above the taxiway. Flowers, incense burners, and private notes of thanks were clustered around it now. The underground base wasn't used very much anymore. But just to lend a solemnity to the place and preserve the memory of the two mysterious men, the Princess had assigned two guards to watch over the site, day and night.

It was just after sunset-midnight, that being the complete setting of both the tiny moon's mother planet and its sun, when the vision appeared.

There was at first a bright flash that lit up the huge underground chamber. Then, as the two astonished guards watched, mouths agape, three men suddenly appeared in their midst.

They came from nowhere—literally. They were holding hand-sized devices that seemed to be taking readings from the floor and the space around the plaque. They were oblivious of anyone watching them.

The three interlopers were dressed very oddly. Two wore heavy black spacesuits and no helmets. They had shaved heads but very long, pointed mustaches. The third man was quite elderly and was dressed in a bubble-top spacesuit that was ancient a thousand years ago.

The three men were in the middle of a hushed conversation.

"My readings indicate that they were here before they went on to the moon in the Sigma-TKE system," the man in the bubble top said, shouting through a tiny door near his mouth.

"As do mine," one of the other men said. "The gamma decay here is tremendous, but the readings were stronger on Sigma-TKE."

"This then was their eighteenth touchdown after Zazu Zazu," the third man said. "We can just double back from Sigma and pick up the stronger gamma decay trail from there."

Finally, one of the guards stepped forward and rattled his ceremonial weapon. Only then did the three men look up and realize they were not alone.

They all stared at each other for a long moment. Then the three men each bowed slightly.

One said, "Sorry. Our apologies to you . . ."

Then they blinked out.

The Planet Erox 357

Their names were Jixxy and Minxi, and they had climbed the mountain every night for the past two weeks.

They were from the Mutaman-Younguska star system, a place known for its beautiful women, and Jixxy and Minxi were all that and more. They had been transplanted here recently after successfully escaping the planet Tonk, along with hundreds of their sisters.

Their savior, the Great Klaaz, had selected their adopted planet very well. Erox 357 was a paradise, temperate, sparsely populated, with plenty of natural food and easily built shelter. All of the refugees from Mutaman-Younguska were happy with their new home, and this meant the Great Klaaz was very happy.

But it was not all fun and games here—mostly, but not all. As soon as they were settled, Klaaz suggested it would be wise that they all meditate on the stars every chance they got. The reason? To get a better perspective on how they'd arrived here. He suggested they look back toward the red-halo nebula, the place that now marked where the destroyed system of Mutaman-Younguska used to be. Another evening body they should contemplate was right across the sky from them: the nearby star system that contained the planet Tonk, shining like a blue ball in the warm night sky. It was important that they never forget these places from whence they came, Klaaz had told them. That's what Jixxy and Minxi were doing this night: remembering the past.

They had brought their candles and their incense plant, and at the first sight of Tonk, they lit the first leaf. The soothing aroma covered the mountaintop. When the red-halo nebula came into view, they lit the second one.

Then they broke open a bottle of slow-ship wine and lay down together to ponder the sky.

And suddenly, both felt hands tightening around their necks.

Where the gang of spacemen came from, the two girls would never really know.

All they were sure of was, one minute they were kissing, the next they were surrounded by five heavily armed star troopers, two of which had blinked in with their hands already around their necks.

The spacemen smelled heavily of slow-ship, and though they were trying to talk to each other, each was slurring his words so badly, they couldn't be understood.

Jixxy and Minxi could not cry out; the men were holding their throats too tightly. And even if they had been able to scream, they were a long distance away from their settlement. No one would hear them.

They struggled, though, and when they did, the two men assaulting them eased up a little. Then the spacemen began babbling and somehow started to make sense.

"Where are they?" one managed to growl.

"Where are *who?*" both girls screamed back at once.

"Your guardian angels. The spacemen who helped you escape from Tonk."

Both girls fell mum. They had barely seen the two men who had assisted Klaaz in getting them off the snowball planet. Klaaz said that the two men had requested anonymity, and he'd respected their wishes, just so history would not be cluttered when it came time to report the heroic masterstroke escape.

"They're gone . . . long gone!" Jixxy managed to scream now. But the guy with his hands around her neck only tightened them further.

"She is telling the truth!" Minxi gurgled. "We never really saw them. They helped us and then took off. . . ."

"We must know where they went, and we do not have time to fool with you," yet another drunken soldier growled.

Jixxy's assailant began squeezing the air out of her. "If you do not tell," he said, emphasizing each syllable with an even tighter squeeze, "then you will die in a manner even more painful than the one we have planned for you."

"And if not you two," the fifth soldier mumbled. "Then another two. Or three. Or four . . ."

Both girls began to panic now. These monsters could kill them here and then find more of their sisters and do the same, yet they really did not know the information the air devils so desperately sought.

So they fought back again, this time even harder. This seemed to convince the attackers that the girls didn't know anything. They were wasting their time.

The leader of the assailants gave a quick nod to the two soldiers holding the girls down. It was their death sentence. The final act had to be done. With a whoop from all the assailants, the two men began squeezing the life out of both girls while the other soldiers helped hold Jixxy and Minxi.

"Hurry up about it," the nervous squad leader said. "You never know—"

That's as far as he got. For when the man tried to say the next word, no sound came out. He looked down at his chest and realized he had a gaping hole going right through him. He toppled over instantly, dead before he hit the ground.

Then the two men who were holding the girls down were suddenly headless. The would-be executioners looked up and saw twin beams of blaster light coming right at them. In a flash, both were decapitated. They fell in a heap on top of the two terrified girls.

It took a few moments for Jixxy and Minxi to realize they'd been saved. They pushed the bodies off of themselves, scrambled to their knees, and hugged each other very tightly. Then the tears came. Only then did they look up to see the person who had rescued them standing nearby.

It was the Great Klaaz himself, twin ray guns in hand, their barrels still emitting some greenish blaster gas.

While he was obviously relieved to see the two girls were still alive—and it was only an instinct that had brought him to this place at exactly the right time—his very wrinkled brow was especially deep with worry now.

He helped the girls to their feet and comforted them as they cried on his shoulders. The bodies of the five dead raiders disappeared in a blink, called back to their ship, no doubt. But Klaaz spotted something on the ground nearby, a piece of uniform ripped in the initial struggle.

Klaaz picked it up to find a button was attached to the thin piece of fabric. There was lettering imprinted on the button. Two words that Klaaz did not completely understand: *Solar Guards*.

He studied the emblem for a few moments, then looked up into the night. Somewhere, up there, the ship these cretins had beamed down from was lurking or perhaps already leaving orbit. But that was not all the cosmos was telling Klaaz at this moment. Something else was being whispered in his ear

"My friends . . ." he mumbled now as the girls hugged him even tighter. "My friends are in trouble."

Above the Planet Myx

There first came a crack of lightning above the now-deserted peak known as Zero Degree Zero.

The bolt quickly turned into a swirl of sparks and a strange blue mist above the hilltop. Then came a sound akin to thunder. An instant later, a spaceship popped into view: a very strange spaceship.

Every space-going vessel traveling the Galaxy was shaped like a triangle. From the smallest interplanetary cargo humper to the massive, miles-long space cruisers flown by the Fourth Empire, the same basic tricornered design prevailed.

But this craft was not shaped like a triangle. It was shaped like a saucer.

Hovering over the hill for a few moments, it whirred slightly, occasionally emitting a high-pitched sound. Then a bolt of blue light shot out of its bottom and scanned the hill briefly before moving down to the valley of devastation below. In its glare, the enormous blaster craters, the miles of booby traps, the wreckage of a million robots. The rivers that ran like blood.

This went on for several minutes; the saucer's occupants were obviously looking for something or someone. But then the bolt of blue light disappeared, and the high-pitched sound went away. The saucer began spinning madly once again. There was another crack of lightning and another roll of thunder.

Then the saucer-shaped craft blinked once and was gone.

13

There were twelve drunks inside the Metro-D.C. Police's 3rd Precinct lockup.

This was an overflowing crowd for the ten-by-fifteen cell, the result of a warm fall Friday night and the anticipation of the big Redskins-Raiders game that Sunday. Usually, with a crowd of inebriates this large, the cell floor was awash in vomit and other body fluids, providing a stink of despair as each man waited to get bailed out.

But something different was happening here tonight.

There was a thirteenth man being held. He was not drunk, though at the moment he was dying for a cup of coffee, a beverage he'd become addicted to by simply smelling it a couple of times. Nor was he in his late twenties or early thirties like the rest of the prisoners. In fact, he was much, much older.

It was Pater Tomm. Charged with demonstrating without a permit, proselytizing without a license, and creating a public nuisance, he'd been in the cell for nearly twenty-four hours, sharing the place with a constantly changing cast of characters, but never as many as now.

The police had arrested Tomm outside the national cathedral early the day before. He'd been carrying on a spontaneous one-man protest, complete with a crude sign that read: *Why Doesn't Anyone Worship Anymore?* on one side and *Repent! The End May Be Near* on the other. This was his way of displaying outrage at the nonuse of the huge, ornate national cathedral he'd found so dusty and vacant. He, too, was awaiting arraignment.

Tomm had never met a crowd he didn't like. As the holding pen began filling up, he'd started talking religion to the assembled drunks. At first, his fellow prisoners ignored him. Then they threatened him. Then they challenged him. But by midnight, they were in awe of him as he spun tales about the majesties of Creation that he'd seen all across the universe. Tomm had preached so much, he soon ran out of stories to tell. No matter. He simply began repeating the ones he'd already told, and his fellow prisoners never seemed to notice.

But there was a catch to all this. His new flock was paying such rapt attention to him not so much because of what he was saying but how he was saying it: literally hovering one foot off the ground.

Some of the twelve were convinced this was a trick; some thought they were in the DTs and hallucinating. Some simply could not believe their eyes. But Tomm had shown his little bit of levitating skills to get the attention of these men, to instill in them the necessity of getting one's butt to church on a regular basis and committing some time to prayer before it was too late. It was the same message Tomm had preached up and down the Five-Arm for two centuries with mixed results. But just because he was in another place didn't mean he stopped being a man of the cloth. In reality, there was nothing else he could be.

He'd been sermonizing like this for about two hours when two guards entered the hallway outside the holding pen. At the first sound of their keys clinking in the door, Tomm crashed to the floor, scattering his disciples and banging both knees. He quickly bounced back up to his feet though, performing a long, dramatic bow as his startled cell mates showered him with ragged applause.

"Which one of you is Peters, Thomas . . . ?" one of the guards called into the tank. "You're being moved."

The drunks all looked at each other and did a kind of group shrug. Then they glanced over at Tomm, who was examining his scraped knees.

"Peters, Thomas?" he finally replied. "I guess that would be me."

• • •

Tomm was put in a car with two D.C. police officers and driven across town to a nondescript building on the other side of Washington.

He was brought in through a side entrance and led to a freight elevator. Two men in blue suits and dark glasses were waiting here. They took custody of him and without a word ushered him onto the elevator and up to the thirteenth floor.

He was escorted down a long, dark hallway to a room whose door was marked No Entry. One of the men knocked three times. The door opened, and Tomm was nudged inside. The room was small, dark, with a single lightbulb hanging from the ceiling. There was a table right next to the door with five chairs around it.

Sitting in one, casually smoking a cigarette, was Zarex.

Tomm barely recognized him. Gone was the explorer's grandly ragged space costume. He was now dressed in baggy checkered pants, size twenty sneakers, a T-shirt, and a baseball cap turned backward. He was smoking the very end of an unfiltered cigarette. His eyes brightened when Tomm walked in.

"Padre! You are well!"

"Only by God's grace," Tomm replied. "But yes, I am."

The men in suits removed Tomm's handcuffs and placed him in a chair one over from Zarex. The two spacemen shook hands quickly as their handlers retreated to the far corner of the room.

"And I am so glad to see you, my brother," Tomm whispered to Zarex.

"As I am you, Padre," Zarex replied, "though I fear the game is up as related to our keeping a low profile on this world. Frankly, I may have made too much of a stir."

Tomm patted him twice on his forearm. "We all make mistakes," he said.

The huge explorer took a deep drag of his near-depleted cigarette, then stiffly waved the cloud of smoke away.

"I'm afraid I found this whole place rather intoxicating, Padre," he said with a bit of concern. "I fell prey to temptation, though I'm not sure why."

"Yes," Tomm agreed. "*Intoxicating* is the exact word."

Zarex finally crushed out the cigarette and let the last plume of smoke fill the room.

"Why did they arrest you, Padre?"

The priest just shrugged. He was loathe to tell Zarex that he, too, had broken their agreement to stay low key while studying the planet.

"It was less an arrest than a difference in philosophy," he finally said. "I discovered grave neglect here on behalf of the people of this city and tried to right the wrong. The authorities disagreed with me. But they will see the light one day. And you, brother. Why were you taken into custody?"

"I beat up my boss," Zarex replied simply.

Tomm looked at him for a long moment, then just shrugged. "Well, I'm sure he had it coming," he said.

Three more knocks came at the door. One of the suits opened it, and a third prisoner was brought in.

It was Hunter.

His colleagues were not that surprised to see him. Their fortunes were now fully reversed. Hunter, too, looked different. His hair was wild, his beard grown in. He was also sporting a tan. They exchanged quick embraces, and then Hunter was put into a seat next to the priest and the explorer. The guys in suits locked the door and sat down across from them. The light hanging from the ceiling had an adjustable shade on it. One of the suits twisted it so the glare of the single lightbulb was shining directly into the space travelers' eyes.

At that point, it became clear to Hunter that these weren't the Betaville cops they were dealing with here—and this certainly wasn't the Betaville police station. He'd been taken here directly after his apprehension in California, having crossed the western sea in a high-speed police boat, pulling in at Baltimore and then rushed to this location. He knew the two men in suits were FBI agents; his handlers had told him so. This place was one of the Bureau's most secret interrogation cells.

Finally, one of the agents spoke.

"You three have been charged with a number of local crimes," he began. "But that is not why you're here. You're here on a federal warrant. And we can make this very simple. In fact, we just want to ask you one thing."

The three space travelers just stared back at him. "OK," Hunter finally said.

Where is she?" the agent asked.

Hunter looked at Tomm and Zarex, who both shrugged.

"Where is who?"

"Don't get cute!" the second agent erupted. "You three are going to jail for a very long time, anyway. It might go a little easier on you if you tell us where the body is."

The three space travelers were completely bewildered.

"You think we *killed* someone?" Zarex asked incredulously.

"My God . . . tell us who," Tomm pleaded with them.

The agent angrily pulled a photograph from his shirt pocket and threw it on the table in front of them.

"Her . . ."

The spacemen looked at the photo, looked at each other, then started to laugh. This infuriated the FBI agents. One nearly came across the table at them. Tomm reared back, ready to hit him. Zarex began to growl.

Finally, Hunter calmed everybody down.

"May I get something in my pocket?" he asked the agents.

In a flash, both agents pulled out enormous hand guns and pointed them directly at Hunter's temple. "Get whatever you have to get, punk," one agent told him.

Hunter reached into his knee pocket and pulled out three small boxes. He laid them on the table in front of him. He pointed to the yellowish box and looked at Tomm and Zarex. Both men nodded solemnly.

Hunter pushed the small button on top of the box, and a stream of greenish mist came pouring out. It collected next to Hunter's chair, swirling and sparkling; then there was a bright flash. When the glare dissipated, in its place was standing Agent Lisa Lee.

The FBI agents' mouths dropped to the floor. Lisa was frozen in the exact same position as when they had put her into the Twenty 'n Six back in Betaville: Back on her feet, her left hand was reaching out in front of her, just as she was offering her car keys to Hunter, her other hand was up to her mouth, as if she was suppressing a scream.

She came to life a second later. Her eyes darted about the room. Finally, she took her hand from her mouth and pointed at the door.

That's when the scream came.

Not a second later, the door exploded in a storm of smoke and splinters. A small army of black-uniformed men rushed into the room. They were carrying enormous rifles with gun sights that emitted high-intensity light. This served to blind everyone.

Three of the armed men surrounded the FBI agents and with firm hands, kept them sitting in place. Another held Lisa back. Three others ran around to where Hunter, Tomm, and Zarex were sitting, picked them up out of their seats, and pushed them through the shattered door. All this happened in about five seconds, barely enough time for Hunter to grab the three small boxes.

"You know where to send the bill," one of the armed men said to the FBI agents on departing.

The spacemen were hustled down a long set of stairways. At every landing, there was another man in a black uniform, holding a rifle. They reached the basement of the building and were thrown into the back of a black, windowless panel van. The doors were locked behind them, then the van screeched away, going up the delivery ramp and careening out onto the empty street.

Hanging on as tightly as they could, Hunter, Pater Tomm, and Zarex just looked at each other tight-lipped. They were not sure whether to laugh or cry. This certainly was a strange turn of events, but they were getting used to such things by now.

Finally, Zarex broke the spell.

He said to Hunter, "Excuse me brother, you don't have a cigarette on you, do you?"

The van traveled for nearly an hour, never slowing down and frequently tossing them about the blacked-out interior. The noise of tires screeching and a very loud engine made conversation nearly impossible.

Finally, the vehicle squealed to a stop, and they were pulled from the back. They were at the entrance to a tunnel that led directly into a huge mountain. There was a guardhouse surrounded by several layers of electrified fencing. Six soldiers in black uniforms stepped from the guardhouse and escorted them through the entrance. It was about three in the morning by this time, a dark and windy night. The sign next to the guardhouse read Weather Mountain Research Facility.

Once through the main gate, they were put into a smaller van and driven into the tunnel. After several minutes of plunging deeper into the mountain, the van stopped in a small parking area near a set of elevators. The spacemen were taken out, put on one of the elevators, and then began a very long journey not up, but down, deep into the belly of the mountain.

When the elevator finally stopped, they stepped out into a large chamber. It had a very low ceiling but was expansive, with strings of blue lights running everywhere. One wall was dominated by a visual screen. At the moment, it was filled with nothing more than rows of ever-changing numbers.

There was a narrow oval table in the center of the room. Seven men were sitting along one side of it. They were all rather elderly for this planet. Each man wore longish gray hair, and several had long, gray beards as well. Their faces were wrinkled unlike any Hunter had seen since coming to this world. The seven men were all dressed casually, mostly in denim, and each was wearing a large red ID badge attached to a chain around his neck.

There were only three letters visible on these badges: CIA.

These men weren't brimming with antagonism as the FBI agents had been.

They politely asked the spacemen to sit down, and coffee was passed their way. Tomm slurped down two cups before anyone else could be served. Zarex silently accepted a cigarette; he was soon lit up and puffing away. Hunter was half hoping someone would turn up with a bottle of Seagram's.

There were no formal introductions. They were a top-secret government intelligence group, the man sitting in the center chair told them, and he was their spokesman. He looked slightly younger than the others, was clean-shaven, his skin red and robust, a wry look around his eyes. His name was Gordon.

"Unlike our dull-witted cousins over at FBI," he began, "we know who you boys are. We know you're not from this planet. We know you landed here about a week ago. We know you split up shortly after arrival. We know you all spent time in various parts of the country."

The three spacemen were surprised by this news but didn't say a word. This was their third trip to an interrogation room in less than a week. They knew by now that it was best to keep their mouths shut.

"And how do we know all this about you?" the CIA man asked.

He pulled a sheaf of papers from a folder. They were newspaper clips. He held one up. It was from the *Newark Ledger.* Its headline read, "Mystery Man Arrested for Diner Assault—

Defendant Said to Possess 'Strange Powers.' " He flipped to another. It was from the *Washington Post*. It read, " 'Priest' Said to Be Performing Miracles Outside National Cathedral."

Then he held up the entire front page of a third newspaper, the *Chicago Tribune*. In huge black letters, the headline read, "UFO Spotted Over Mayfield." A story below was headlined, "Chicago, Erie, New York Also Report Saucers."

Gordon leaned back in his seat. "Now, gentlemen, if your mission here was to quietly infiltrate us, I have to tell you, you failed miserably. I mean, you did all right getting out of Betaville. But after that, well . . ."

He returned the newsclips to his case. The three spacemen sank lower into their seats.

"It's OK, though," Gordon continued. "It actually worked out better this way. Once we got a whiff of what happened in Betaville, we knew we had to find you. We thought it would take weeks, months, years. But you broke so many laws and made so much of a racket, we were able to apprehend you all rather quickly."

Hunter was just staring at his thumbs now. By splitting up, he, Tomm, and Zarex had thought it would be easier moving around the tiny planet, as they wouldn't attract as much attention.

Obviously, they should have considered a Plan B.

The CIA man went on, "I mean, auto theft? Assault and battery? Demonstrating without a permit? Suspicion of *murder?* That's not exactly leaving a cold trail, is it?"

The man seated next to Gordon passed him a scribbled note.

"Right—and let's not forget the missing two seconds," Gordon said. "Several days ago, two, near-simultaneous blackouts occurred across our national power grid. They seemed to be just glitches at first, and backup systems tripped in, so for the most part, the average citizen did not notice anything had gone wrong.

"But then we began getting reports that during these two events, other things besides the power flow had been affected. Our atomic clocks lost time. Some broadcast systems went down. To make a long story short, everything on this planet just . . . well, *stopped* for those two seconds last Saturday night. To be precise, one event around 8:32, the next just two minutes later, at 8:34 or so. We assume you three were somehow responsible for this, too?"

Zarex shrugged; so did Tomm. This was none of their doing. They looked over at Hunter. He was staring at the floor. Those were the exact times of his flights with Reggie and then Ashley. There had to be a connection. But why would operating his flying machine disrupt things on this planet? He didn't have a clue.

"Any thoughts on any of this, gentlemen?" Gordon asked them.

The spacemen remained mute.

"All right then," the CIA man said. "I understand your reluctance to talk. But let me tell you this: We have no intention of cutting you up just to see what makes you tick. As those dopes at the FBI might be inclined to do. We have no intention to examine you in any way. The truth is, we've been expecting you. And the fact that we can understand each other and converse seems to indicate a connection here. Now, of course, we have many questions we'd like to ask. And I'm sure there is much you can tell us."

The three spacemen looked at each other in glum agreement. There was no doubt about that.

"But we don't even have to get into those areas, either," Gordon said. "In fact, all we would like to know is the answer to one primary question, something that might solidify that we are all on the same page."

Still, they would not say a word. Gordon took off his glasses.

"Look, you've obviously come from a great distance away," he said. "And there must be some reason you landed here."

The three visitors stirred, but just a little.

"We *may* even be working toward the same goal," Gordon told them. "Maybe looking for the answer to the same question."

Hunter finally broke the silence.

"What question might that be?" he asked.

Ten minutes later, the seven CIA officers, the three spacemen, and a squad of armed guards had arrived in yet another chamber, this one even deeper inside the mountain.

This chamber served to house a huge vault. Its oval door was enormous and thick. The vault itself was built into solid rock, with blast protectors all around and huge springs beneath its floor to cushion any unlikely blow. More than a dozen soldiers were guarding the door. Even though the seven CIA men were obviously high up on the security chain, they still had to show their IDs and do voice, fingerprint, and retina scans in order to make it past the rock-jawed, unsmiling guards.

The interior of the vault was nearly as big as the agents' blue-lit conference room upstairs. A narrow, soundproof door closed behind them once they'd entered; the interior of the vault became very dim. Subdued lighting along its ceiling gave everything a greenish glow. Suddenly, the vault looked like the inside of a church.

One wall was made up of about three dozen small doors. Each was made of highly polished brass; each had a number engraved on it.

Gordon finally spoke.

"This is a matter of such grave importance to us," he began, "that we have no choice but to be open with you. That said, you must be aware that what I am about to tell you is the most closely guarded secret on this planet. It is a secret that is known only by the people inside this room. The secret is actually hundreds if not thousands of years old and has been passed down, from generation to generation, by organizations like us—along with the artifacts kept in this room, which support it.

"Some of the secret's caretakers over the centuries have been religious sects. Others were governmental agencies such as us. The secret has passed through the hands of writers, poets, mystics. But whenever it is passed on, usually from dying lips, it is always with the vow that it be held between no more than a dozen people at any one time. Indeed it *must* be kept from the public at all costs, at least until all of its aspects can be confirmed and the population is made ready to absorb it. We seven are this generations' 'enlightened ones,' you might say. Like those before us, we are not only the secret's keepers, we must also attempt to interpret it. Verify it. Understand just exactly what it means. In fact, this is just about all we do. The burden of the secret's proof rests with us."

Gordon paused and took a deep breath.

"The secret is this: We have evidence that we, the people of this planet, really don't belong here. That sometime back in our history, our ancestors were brought to this world from somewhere else."

He let these words hang in the air for a moment.

"We have uncovered a number of clues," he went on. "Some of them suggest a massive migration of sorts, somewhere in our distant past. The clues to all this are contained in this vault. Most of the evidence was found hidden away in the deepest mountains on this planet, at the bottom of mine shafts or in natural caverns miles under the ground. Some items were found inside rock itself. All of them are so deteriorated, even our best carbon dating cannot establish a firm time frame. We estimate that most are at least three thousand years old. Some possibly as old as five thousand years. But that is not the most intriguing thing about this evidence."

Gordon stopped, looked at the space travelers for a moment, and then said, "The intriguing thing is that we've determined most of the objects in this room are not of this world. They originated someplace else."

He opened one of the doors and rolled out a long drawer. It held a solid glass case. Within were several dozen collections of individual pages carefully bound together in spines. All were so old, they were in the last stages of disintegration.

"You are familiar with the concept of books?" Gordon asked the spacemen.

They nodded as one. "More or less," Tomm mumbled: "They are ancient things; we know that."

"Well, these before you are of an educational sort," Gordon said. "It is very difficult to handle them, as you can see, and we can't make out very many of the words or understand those words that we can see. But some of the photographs are still intact, and by interpreting bits and pieces from them, we found that they depict an existence similar to the one we live here, yet one that obviously took place somewhere else, thousands of years ago. Several of these books talk about culture. Others contain maps. Still others have broad texts on geography. They show a world like ours, yet very different."

He picked up one of the books. It looked like it was about to turn to dust.

"We've been able to do analysis on the molecular structures in these materials," Gordon said. "Pages, covers, the ink, and so on. We have concluded, without a doubt, that they are not like anything found on this planet. In fact, in many cases, they are exact *opposites* in atomic composition. They look the same, act the same, do the same things, but they are not the same. I'm not sure if you are familiar with the concept of left-handed sugar, but if you are, imagine such a thing, just on a much larger scale. We can show you the data if you want, but for now, take our word for it: Most of this stuff didn't originate on this planet."

He lowered his voice a bit.

"Now there is another thing I should tell you: The extent of our own recorded history goes back just two hundred forty-seven years. That's it. No one is sure what happened before that. But it seems that some kind of disaster befell this planet back then and completely wiped out everything. And I emphasize the word *completely*. Nothing from that part of our history has ever been found. Not a scrap. Can you see the irony, gentlemen? We have in our possession artifacts that are thousands of years old, yet we have none from as recently as three hundred years ago. Whatever hit our planet, hit hard. Whatever few survivors there were, we are their children. Our civilization bounced right back, relatively speaking, but there are many years that are simply blank. What's more, we have found geological evidence that indicates this planet suffered similar catastrophes down through the ages. Near-total extinction events that leave absolutely nothing behind, unless its been hidden well underground."

He swept his hand around him. "So you can see, for us, the ancient things in this room—and the mysteries they hold—are even more puzzling.

He pointed to one large volume. "More evidence: This we call the Book of the Dead. It is an ancient collection of names; possibly of people who were shipped here and died soon afterward. There are hundreds of these names, but here's the rub: Many are the same surnames we use here today."

He indicated another volume. It was so old it smelled like dirt.

"This book seems to show us how this long-ago government was run. How the political structure worked. How the people came to rule. Coincidentally—or not—it is just about the same form of government we have now."

Another ancient book. Its cover had long ago faded away.

"This is apparently a recounting of a love story between adolescents. Or a silly interpretation of one." Another book, dirty and slim. "This might contain ancient recipes for beer, vodka, whiskey." Another blackened book. "This tells the reader how to grow things, like tobacco, wheat, and coffee beans."

Gordon returned the books to their case.

"Careful interpretation of these volumes, as well as other things, is what led us to our conclusion. They are about us, yet again, they are not about us. They didn't originate here, so neither did we. And not only are their materials unlike anything manufactured here, we can't seem to duplicate them, either. We've tried. Yet the pictures within seem to speak of a life that is very familiar to us. Things like bustling cities, vast agriculture, financial dealings, art, music, sports—our culture itself. But it's all from somewhere else. We believe these things were hidden thousands of years ago in hopes they would survive the periodic catastrophes, be found, and interpreted. But either by design or fate, these books bring up more questions than they answer. The deciphering process has been going on for more than two centuries. It continues, very slowly, to this day."

Hunter, Tomm, and Zarex were fascinated by all this, but only to a point. Certainly it was a big deal for a civilization that was so backward it didn't even know about flight to discover that thousands of years before, they'd been moved from one planet to another. But for the three spacemen, such a thing was ho-hum. Throughout the Galaxy, populations had been evacuated from planets before, such as when a collision was imminent between two star systems or clusters, or if a planet's puff had run out. Then there were the nefarious types who conquered worlds and delivered their inhabitants into slavery. Where the three of them had come from, while unusual, moving one people from here to there was certainly not unheard of.

So Hunter asked himself, *What does this have to do with me?*

It was almost as if Gordon had heard him. "Obviously, you are from a more advanced situation than us," Gordon said. "And the truth is, before you three came, we weren't even sure if there were any other planets out there in the entire universe. Never mind people. But we do have a connection. And I think once you see what we mean, you'll agree with us."

He then unlocked the next door and rolled out a drawer.

It contained another glass case, but inside this one was a piece of tattered cloth about five feet long and three feet wide. It consisted of just three colors: red, white, and blue. Hunter nearly fell over. He recognized this thing right away. It was a flag: red, white, and blue, the same design as the one he always carried in his pocket.

"Is there any chance that this looks familiar to you?" Gordon asked.

Hunter took his flag out and compared it to the frayed banner inside the glass case.

It was a perfect match.

Stunned silence in the chamber now. Tomm and Zarex were just as baffled as he. Where the flag in the glass case was barely more than bits and pieces of cloth, Hunter's flag was intact, almost brand-new by comparison.

Gordon looked at Hunter. "May I ask where you got that flag?"

It was a good question. Hunter had found the flag neatly folded in his left-hand pocket the day he suddenly woke up on the desolate planet of Fools 6. The flag and his name tag, which identified him as Hunter, Hawk, were the only two real clues he had about his true identity. But he rarely told anyone about the origin of the flag; even Tomm and Zarex had no idea how he'd come by it. And he wasn't about to tell Gordon—at least not right now.

So he replied to Gordon, "If I ever find out, you will be among the first to know, I promise."

Gordon thought about that a moment and smiled. "I hope to hold you to that," he said.

Then he pulled out another drawer. It held another glass case, and inside were two dozen more red, white, and blue flags. Several were as small as the one Hunter carried in his pocket. Others were larger, but not by much. Some were as tattered as the one they'd been shown first; others were in the last stages of decay. They all appeared to be thousands of years old.

Hunter just couldn't believe what he was seeing. He'd only encountered the red, white, and blue emblem once before on the mysterious spacecraft found beneath the ice on Mars. Before that, he'd thought the flag he kept in his pocket was the only one of its kind in the universe. To see so many now, right in front of his eyes, was a shock.

"You found these?" Hunter asked Gordon in astonishment. "Hidden below the ground?"

"We did," Gordon replied. "And the fact that you are carrying one in such good shape . . . and the fact that you are, well, not from here. I . . . well, I guess I really don't know *what* it all means."

Hunter was unable to take his eyes off the tattered flags.

"Neither do I," he replied.

"Notice this one," Gordon said pointing to a flag that seemed to be made of polymers rather than cloth. It had been stamped with the strange design of a circle with a line passing through it. Several other remnants were scarred with similar markings.

"We believe that symbol indicates the object was forbidden or banned at one time," Gordon explained.

Hunter spoke up. "But clearly this is the flag of this . . . other place. Why would it be banned?"

"Just one of many things we don't know," Gordon replied. "But this, and the Book of the Dead, seems to indicate that our forefathers came here not by their own decision."

Hunter finally took his eyes off the flags and looked up at Gordon.

"This place, where you think you came from thousands of years ago. Any idea what it might have been called?"

"We are not one hundred percent sure," Gordon replied. "But the consensus over the years has it the place was called America."

America!

It was amazing how the word hit Hunter between the eyes first. Then it went down to his throat. And finally, it got him right in the heart.

America . . . Yes, he'd heard this word before. He couldn't remember when, and it was certainly before he'd found himself on Fools 6, but it was in his consciousness somewhere, locked away in the memory banks, trying to get out.

America . . .

He closed his eyes and said it, over and over again.

America . . .

The flag in his pocket. The colors on his aircraft. The same red, white, and blue. They were all swirling in his head now.

America . . .

The ancient spacecraft back on Mars. The lighthouse on Zazu-Zazu. Calling him back.

America . . .

His quest across the Five Arm. To Tonk. Bazooms. Myx. The star road home to . . .

My God, he thought. *America? Is that where I'm from?*

He began to choke up but then stopped. True, the people here seemed more like him than anyone else in the Galaxy. But something was telling him the puzzle was not yet complete. He was still a couple of steps away.

Was he from *this* planet and somehow he'd become stranded on Fools 6 just a year ago? No, he knew immediately that all this was much bigger than that. He was not just from another place, he was obviously from another time as well.

So, could he be from this planet but from a different time in its history?

No, that didn't seem right, either. . . .

So, what was left?

Could he be from somewhere *this* place was named for?

He actually thought he heard a bell go off in his head.

"Do you think this planet might be a *replica* of someplace else?" Hunter asked.

Gordon brightened. The other CIA men did, too.

"That's *exactly* what we want to find out," the CIA chief replied.

They walked about halfway down the length of the vault, where Gordon pulled out another drawer.

"While checking out those UFO sightings last week, we received several reports describing what the unidentified object looked like," Gordon said to Hunter. "Thinking it was probably you, we're very anxious for you to take a look at this."

This glass case contained another collection of papers, again bound together along one side with a spine. There were many words on these pages—almost like a newspaper—but the print was so faint, it was impossible to make them out. One page, though, was partially sealed within a thin plastic sleeve. Inside was a faded, deteriorated photograph. It was so old, the image was barely discernible.

But it was clear enough for Hunter to see one thing: It was a picture of his flying machine. Or something very close to it. Sharp nose, two wings in front, two smaller ones in back, another sticking up out of the tail. It was in flight, fire spilling out of its rear end. And right there on the underside of its wing was a painted-on version of the same red, white, and blue flag.

"Is this a machine like one that you possess?" Gordon asked.

"Let's just say it looks familiar," Hunter replied. "Any idea how old this picture is?"

Gordon shrugged. "Just a guess? At least five thousand years old. I mean, especially that example; it was old when it got here to this world. And like everything else, we can't figure out what it's printed on. It's not indigenous to this planet, though, we are sure of that."

Now this was nutty, Hunter thought. Here was an image, thousands of years old, depicting almost an exact duplicate—at least on the outside—of the aircraft he'd built himself from what he'd always assumed was some kind of lost memory.

There were words beneath the photograph, badly faded text that was barely discernible.

"Any idea what it says?" Hunter asked them.

"Now, *that* we've worked on for years," Gordon replied. "And as far as we can tell, it says something like 'Thunderbird over Las Vegas.' "

Gordon looked at the three spacemen.

"We know what thunder is," he said. "And Las Vegas is a city out in the western part of our country. But we were wondering: Do you guys happen to know what a *bird* is?"

The three spacemen shrugged.

"Not a clue," Tomm said.

They closed that drawer and opened another, this one containing more collections of individual pages attached by spines. Again, most of these documents were ancient and deteriorated. But some were not quite as old.

"Here lies documentation of another very strange piece of this puzzle," Gordon said. "It was discovered about one hundred fifty years ago that at certain times throughout our known history, there have been, on occasion, mass disappearances of people. Individuals. Sometimes families. Two or three hundred at a shot, over a two- or three-day span, and then nothing for years. These are the files on the missing. Most of them, anyway. Many witnesses nearby reported strange aerial lights just before these people vanished. The last incident was about thirty years ago. That's when some people supposedly went willingly. Waited on mountaintops for days before finally being picked up. Strange thing too: Many of those who've vanished over the years were policemen."

Hunter looked at Tomm and Zarex. It was a short leap from policeman to soldier. Could this be evidence of the Freedom Brigades?

"Maybe you can enlighten us on that sometime," Gordon suggested. "Because now we have the most intriguing item of all."

They walked to the very end of the vault. There was a door here marked #666. It was different from the rest in that it had additional security devices attached to its door handle. Gordon passed an ID card across this small scanner, and a succession of clicks was the result. Another agent stepped forward and did the same thing. More clicks. One by one, the rest of the CIA men flashed their IDs before the electronic eye. Finally, after the seventh man, the door unlatched and very slowly swung open.

Inside was a drawer that held a box approximately six feet long and four feet around. It was not made of glass. The spacemen recoiled for a moment. It looked like a coffin.

But as Gordon rolled the drawer out, it became clear that the long, slender box was actually a capsule of some kind, made of recarbonated sodium iron, also known as cobalt steel. It was sealed at its midpoint by a complicated-looking lock. A bulky, confusing control panel nearly took up one entire side of the dark box just below this lock. Every light on this panel was blinking, though weakly. There were even a few switches on the control panel. Switches hadn't been in use anywhere in the Galaxy for more than 2,500 years.

"This was found buried inside the deepest mountain on this planet, a top secret location out in our southwest called Groom Lake," Gordon explained. "It was discovered sealed inside a layer of hardened limestone in the sub-subbasement of a structure that had survived all of our periodic catastrophes. We know it's old, or it *looks* old, but the technology it contains is obviously highly advanced, at least for us. Finding a way to open it has so far eluded us. We believe it is a container of some kind, but we have no idea what is inside. I'm almost embarrassed to tell you that over the past fifty years, we've had dozens of scientists take a look at this thing, once they'd passed a hundred or so security checks, that is. They weren't told anything about it or where it came from. We just wanted to know how to open it. But not one of these learned men could figure out a way of breaking that seal without destroying whatever is inside."

He looked at the three space travelers. "Any ideas, gentlemen?"

Zarex studied the control panel but shrugged. It made no sense to him. Hunter also took a pass at it, with the same result.

Finally, Pater Tomm nudged the others aside, took his handy blackjack from his back pocket, and slammed it down on the lock. It sprang open immediately.

The CIA men were shocked. Hunter and Zarex just shook their heads.

"Well done, Padre," Hunter murmured.

Inside the box was a large spherical capsule, about a foot long and the same again around. It shimmered with a shade of bluish emerald. The CIA men had never seen anything like it. But to the three space travelers, it was quite familiar.

"Could that possibly be what I think it is?" Zarex asked with a gasp.

It was a holo-girl capsule. The shape, the color, the shimmering green. They were all the same. But this one had to be at least ten times larger than the handheld ones the space travelers were familiar with.

Hunter turned to Zarex. "One of yours?" he asked.

Zarex huffed and studied this object's control panel for a moment. This he was schooled in. He very casually pushed a succession of light panels. Suddenly, a beam shot out of the side of the capsule. Everyone took a step back. There was a blinding flash, and then a cloud of deatomizing smoke. A holographic projection began to take shape. The image flickered, appeared solid, then flickered again. When it finally stabilized, they found a rather large female standing before them. She was holding an enormous gun.

The CIA men were shocked, bewildered. That this amazon could so suddenly appear like this—they'd simply never seen anything like it before. It was more like a horror movie for them. A being from the distant past/future, unlocked from a magic box, proceeds to demolecularize them all?

"It's all right," Tomm comforted them. "Some of us see these things all the time."

But the truth was, this was unlike any holo-girl the spacemen had ever encountered. She was much bigger, much more muscular, much *rougher*-looking than the models currently in use throughout the Galaxy. And she wasn't exactly built for speed. She was more along the lines of Zarex's body type. It took the spacemen a few moments to realize that what they were looking at was not a holo-girl at all, at least not the erotic, sexually pleasing ones they knew.

Rather, this female projection was a soldier, clearly made not for sex but for war. Her uniform was bulky; her weapon was huge and ancient-looking. Her combat belt, boots, and helmet all looked like relics of days gone by, most especially the jet pack on her back, a cumbersome two-tube assembly that gave the wearer a certain amount of airborne capability but hadn't been seen in the Milky Way in two millennia at least.

She was staring back at them, a slightly mystified look on her face, eyes darting back and forth, accessing her data banks. She scanned the CIA men first, in their denim and western boots, then the space travelers. She raised her huge rifle in a cautious stance. Everyone froze. Could a holograph's weapon shoot real stuff? No one knew. A tense moment went through the room. Then, as so often happened when no one else knew what to do, Pater Tomm stepped forward.

"You are among friends here," he gently told the skittish projection. "There is no need to harm anyone, because no one is going to harm you."

"Where am I?" she asked them, her voice garbled, mechanical.

Tomm did his best to explain the surroundings to her. She checked a device on her wrist.

"This is the 73rd century!"

Tomm nodded. "By some accounts, it is."

This was news to the CIA agents.

"What year are you from?" Tomm asked her.

The holo-spy replied, "My original program date was in the year 3777. That was 3,500 years ago!"

She paused, gathering her thoughts. Old circuits were coming to life. "I have been programmed to tell you my background before disclosing my mission here. . . ."

She explained that she was a combat-intelligence operative. Her job was to infiltrate enemy installations prior to battle and gather information on them. In essence, she was a spy.

"Does this mean that the holo-girls of today evolved from spy technology centuries ago?" Zarex asked Hunter in a whisper.

"It must be," Hunter whispered back. "They could have created the first holographs to look and feel and talk and walk like a real human being, in an effort to make them blend in. What better spy could there be?"

Tomm was nodding, but with disgust. "And then for man to design one model that could be used for more carnal activities; well it's a concept that really doesn't involve that much of a leap in imagination, does it?"

The projection went down a long list of her abilities: above-normal strength, X-ray vision, instant recall. Of course, everything she saw and heard was recorded on the primitive version of a viz disk. And judging by the size of her muscles, though not designed primarily for combat, she would have had little trouble defending herself.

"Why are you here?" Tomm asked her finally. "Do you know?"

"I was sent here in advance of a combat mission on this planet," she said, eyes again darting back and forth. "I was programmed by a civilization that was allied with your ancestors around the year 3778. Our goal was to help free you, the people of this planet—"

"Free us?" several asked at once.

The holo-girl could see the confusion on the assembled faces. They didn't know what she was talking about.

"Yes, free you? Help you? To break you out of here?"

More confused looks.

"You *do* know you're incarcerated here?" she asked with some uncertainty.

Everyone in the vault shook their heads no.

"We think our ancestors may have been brought here from someplace else," Gordon managed to say, "But—"

"So you *don't know* that you're in a prison camp here?"

"Prison camp?" several of the CIA men gasped at once.

"This planet. This whole system," she said. "It's a prison . . . and you are still here. Even after all this time. You are still inmates."

The CIA men all tried to say something but couldn't. Even

the space travelers were at a loss. How could an entire star system be a prison camp?

The holo-spy read their faces and just shook her head.

"I suggest you take me someplace where you can all sit down," she said. "This might take awhile."

14

Twenty-four Hours Later

The black panel van flew through the gates of the White House, waved on by the small army of uniformed secret service agents assembled there.

It was three in the morning. The streets of Washington, D.C., were deserted as usual. Nevertheless, acting under the orders of the CIA, the D.C. police had blocked off all streets within a ten-block radius of the Executive Mansion. Several highways had been sealed as well. In all, the van's ride in from Weather Mountain had taken less than a half hour.

The van pulled around the back of the White House and stopped at the servants' entrance. It was here that the Secret Service's video surveillance cameras could be shut down without anyone noticing. The three passengers were hustled out of the van, each wearing a long, hooded cape. They were followed by Gordon and two of the seven elderly CIA agents.

The spacemen were brought into the White House kitchen and halted there. They were surrounded by yet another breed of well-dressed government agent, the Secret Service's presidential protection team. These guys all wore gray suits. They ran metal detectors over the three travelers and frisked them as well, but they could not find anything. That was another good thing about the Twenty 'n Six boxes. They could be set for intradimensional recovery.

This meant they just weren't there, until the owner reached for them.

The president was awakened and told that some unexpected visitors had arrived and that the CIA was insisting that he meet them—right now.

With some complaint, the Chief Executive rose and got dressed: just slacks, sneakers, and a sweatshirt bearing the presidential seal. He made his way down from the living quarters to the Oval Office with a minimum of fuss. The mention of CIA director Gordon's name gave the President the only clue as to what this might be about.

He'd been briefed in the past week on what the CIA had dubbed "the Betaville Three." Unknown persons having arrived by unknown means from somewhere unknown. The President hadn't taken that much notice. He'd been told this kind of stuff—top-secret paranormal crap—usually came up about twice in a four-year term. It was something he had to deal with, but his predecessors had told him it always turned out to be just that: crap.

In other words, the President had been briefed on the Betaville Three, but that didn't mean he believed.

His plan was to bound into the Oval Office, quietly agitated, his way of showing displeasure about the ungodly hour.

But when he came through the door and caught his first look at the three visitors, now without their hoods, standing in the middle of the office, he stopped in his tracks.

Hunter was back to his full X-Forces regalia: cape, boots, helmet, the works. Zarex had recalled his star duds from the twenty-sixth; they were cleaned and pressed and, if anything, seemed even smaller on him. Tomm had also managed to scare up a new cassock. This one was jet black, with a built-in shiny white collar, smartly pleated cuffs, and slightly flared shoulders. It was a hard concept to grasp, but for once the diminutive padre actually looked, well . . . *religious*. In an interstellar kind of way.

The President just stared at them for a moment, then shut his mouth and continued on to the safety of his desk. He sat down, at the same time silently counting the number of armed Secret Service men crowded into the room. There were thirteen in all.

Not a good number, he thought.

He took his glasses out, put them on the end of his nose, and then looked up at Gordon.

"OK, Steve, this better be good."

Gordon was a man who rarely looked flustered or nervous, but he was a bit shaky at the moment.

"Mr. President, something very grave has come up," he said. "I believe you must be briefed on it immediately."

The President looked at the three visitors.

"Does the CIA want Halloween moved up a couple weeks?" No one laughed.

Gordon started again. "In the past twenty-four hours, we have made a series of rather startling discoveries. The first one is that these three gentlemen here are not from this planet."

Gordon stopped there for a moment. The President rarely showed emotion; it was his best political trait. He barely blinked when Gordon dropped the ET bombshell. Gordon plowed on.

"These gentlemen have been able to work a piece of unknown technology that had stymied us for years. And what I'm afraid I must report to you, sir, as a result of this, we have some information that is rather frightening to contemplate."

The President finally blinked. He knew Gordon fairly well. The CIA man was not one to speak foolishly.

"Mr. President, if what we have learned today proves to be true by any stretch of the imagination, then the people of this planet, as well as people who might be living on other planets in this solar system, have been the victims of a great injustice. An injustice of enormous, *monumental* proportions."

The President didn't move. "I wasn't aware that there were any *other* worlds out there," he said dryly. "I learned in grade school that our planet was the only one—"

"Sir, that is the prevalent opinion only because no one has ever bothered to invent something that could actually look for other things up there," Gordon said sharply. Then, curiously, he added, "Much beyond the moon, that is."

The remark went right over the President's head, so Gordon just kept on talking.

"Mr. President, as crazy as it sounds, there is a chance that we are prisoners in our own solar system. We are living in a concentration camp of sorts. We were sent here, thousands of years ago, by persons unknown. We have been kept here, and intentionally delayed in our cultural development, by these same jail keepers."

The President cleared his throat. *Gordon is looking a little pale these days*, he thought. *He is one of our oldest civil servants. Maybe old Gordo has finally flipped his wig.*

"Well, this is all very interesting stuff, Steve," the President finally replied, "but do you have any . . . ah, *proof*?"

Gordon saw the disbelief in the President's eyes, disbelief tinged with pity. Time for his secret weapon.

He looked over at Zarex, who simply snapped his fingers. Before any of the Secret Service men could react, the large holo-capsule was sitting on the President's desk. Zarex leaned over and punched the capsule's ancient controls. Two seconds later, the female holo-spy was standing in the center of the room.

A couple of the Secret Service men dropped their guns, stunned at the apparition. The President looked very startled, to say the least.

"Gordon, is this some kind of—"

But the President never finished his sentence. The holo-girl interrupted him.

"This is no joke," she told the President sternly, as Gordon had asked her to do. "What is happening here is real. Hard to believe, maybe, but real. You must come to grips with it."

The President's face went from pale to beet red.

"Is this *our* technology?" he demanded of Gordon.

The CIA man shook his head no. "This technology is actually from the very distant past. And a complicated one at that. We've spent the entire day trying to understand each other. Her extent of this knowledge is somewhat limited. But please, sir, listen to what she has to say."

The President shifted uncomfortably in his seat. This was not quite the sort of paranormal crap he'd been expecting.

"All right," he finally croaked. "By all means, go ahead."

The holo-girl snapped her fingers, and a three-dimensional map of outer space appeared in the air in front of her—another startling moment for the President and his security men. The map showed a star system with a yellow sun and many planets orbiting it, virtually along the same orbital plane.

"Your planet, all the planets in this system, even the star itself, are all part of an enormous prison," the holo-spy began. "This system was engineered thousands of years ago and towed way out here in what was, and still is, considered unknown space. Your decedents were transported here against their will, and space guards were hired to keep them from escaping. They did this by intentionally slowing down the rate by which your society would develop. The people who programmed me believed that every planet in this system was encompassed in a time bubble. Time bubbles do not stop time completely, but they do slow it down drastically. This would explain why you are less advanced than just about every other place in the Galaxy. However . . ."

She paused for a moment, eyes darting back and forth, obviously accessing other memory circuits.

". . . . even though you are probably being held back by this constraint, there have been times in your history when you have reached a certain pinnacle of advancement. When that happens, the people who imprisoned you here send their hired guards to wipe you out. They turn your civilization over as if it never happened, leaving very few survivors. Then you start life all over again."

The President's face was ashen by this time. His security team looked the same way.

"Why are you in prison?" she went on. "I don't know. I was not programmed with that information. Why didn't this oppressive civilization just kill you off eons ago? Again, I am not programmed to know. I do know they never wanted you to know why you are here or even that you were in a prison at all."

She paused. The President began fumbling for words.

"Do they come without warning?" he finally asked her. "These periodic apocalypses?"

The holo-spy's eyes began darting back and forth again. Accessing . . .

"One event triggers it," she said. "I am not programmed to know beyond that. It is a milestone, a technology advance of some kind. If anyone in this system manages to pass it, your doomsday is cued to strike. Automatically."

"But who is behind this?" the President demanded to know. "Who imposed such things on us?"

It was the most important question of all.

But the holo-spy just shook her head.

"I'm sorry I'm not programmed with more information on the

subject. My memory circuits can't even tell me how *I* got here. My last activation was at a classified briefing regarding a combat-imminent situation within this system. I was told I'd be going into action on this planet. This could indicate that a battle *was* fought here several thousand years ago. An attempt to break you out. A futile one, for sure, though. Had it been successful, your civilization would have progressed to the point where you would have left this place a long time ago."

Silence descended on the Oval Office. If what the holograph was saying proved accurate, then the planet's culture, already a bit weird, would be turned completely on its head. But could this really be? Had the people of this planet been prisoners for more than three thousand years? Kept here by some unknown power, all without ever realizing it? Even worse, had someone not had the foresight, three millennia before, to carefully hide the artifacts that the CIA and others before them had uncovered, would all of this have been unknown to them forever?

It was a bit hard to swallow.

Finally, the President addressed the holo-spy directly.

"Are you asking me to believe that all this time someone has been watching us from . . . *out there*? Keeping us penned within an invisible jail? Anchored to this planet? For thousands of years? How would that be possible?"

The holo-girl began accessing again. Then she put her finger across the 3-D map and drew a series of circles above the planets that stretched to infinity. The meaning was clear. These were the mysterious heavenly bodies.

"That's what these things are for," she said simply.

Everyone shifted uncomfortably. The President looked up at Gordon.

"Do you know how to shut that thing off?" he asked. Gordon nodded to Zarex, who then leaned over and hit the control panel's deact panel. The holo-girl disappeared in a flash.

The room fell dead silent. The wind was suddenly howling outside. Rain was on its way.

"How much of this do you believe, Steve?" the President asked Gordon directly.

The CIA man replied, "By her own admission, she is a spy. It is an essential business of spies to spread lies. Believe me, I know. And it seems impossible to know where she came from, much beyond what she told us. So, she could be programmed to tell lies as easily as she could be to tell the truth. Even she wouldn't know the difference. But here's the problem: Her information is so grave, so dire, we must take even a suggestion of it seriously. Plus, it *does* fill in a lot of empty spaces in our past. And, according to our three new friends here, such shifting around of planets and stars is quite common. Everywhere else but here."

The President took off his glasses and rubbed his tired eyes.

"OK, Steve, I'll ask you this just one time: Do you really want me to believe such outrageous claims by a bunch of people dressed like *comic book characters*?"

Gordon did not hesitate.

"Yes sir," he said. "I do."

The President threw his glasses on the desk and ran a hand through his thinning, uncombed hair. He was extremely agitated now, for real.

"Well," he finally said. "Is there any way we can confirm any of this? Some way to check it out? See if any of it is true?"

That's when Hunter stepped forward and spoke for the first time.

"Excuse me, sir," he said. "But I believe there is."

15

The place was called Andrews Field.

It was in a fairly isolated area just outside Washington, D.C., once a huge working farm, now abandoned. Hunter had been out here for two hours now, working on the flying machine with his electron torch. The idea he'd put forth to the President was simple: Let him leave the planet in his aircraft and investigate whether the holo-girl was telling the truth.

Weary and confused, the President agreed. His only caveat was that Hunter take off from a location that was isolated from public view. The last thing they needed now was more UFO stories in the newspapers. So Andrews Field was found and quickly cordoned off by armed CIA agents. That had been around four A.M.

It was now almost six. Hunter had watched the stars blink out above the field, and then the storm clouds started to gather. A convenient downpour would further mask his ascent, which was just minutes away. Though the woods were crawling with CIA agents, for the most part they left him alone to work. He'd reduced his cockpit back to its original proportions, before he'd taken to carrying Tomm, Zarex, and 33418 around with him. This enabled him to shave three feet off the fuselage and shorten his wingtips as well. He'd be battling winds and a lot of rain once he got aloft, "inclement weather," as Tomm had called it. The sleeker his plane's aerodynamic profile, the better. He'd also fabricated an oxygen tank and a breathing system, and, for the first time, there was a safety harness attached to his seat.

Hunter was taking these precautions because he was not intending to launch in his normal split-second fashion.

Why? Because of the "missing two seconds."

He had a theory as to why he'd caused time to stop twice that night back in Mayfield. Though it came to him after hearing the holo-girl's claims the second time around, the spark actually went back to his early days in the X-Forces. The key weapon in the Fourth Empire's vast inventory was the Time Shifter technology employed by the Kaon Bombardment ships. Once in orbit, they had the ability to literally freeze time on the battlefield below, allowing Empire troops to touch down and make quick work of their foes. During his short stint as an X-Forces officer, Hunter had heard someone mention that Time Shifters worked by encompassing their target inside a kind of bubble in which all time stopped. Be it a city or an enemy stronghold or even an entire planet. Once the enemy was vanquished, the bubble was dissolved, and time went back to normal.

The science of shifting was a closely held secret, possessed by the Fourth Empire alone. Hunter was now wondering if this technology and what the holo-spy called time bubbles were distantly related, similar somehow. Could a time bubble be an ancient form of time shifting, something left in place, rather than being dissipated once a battle was won? If so, would everything inside the bubble remain more or less frozen in time? Is that *really* what happened here on this tiny planet? According to the holo-spy, it was.

All this led to a second question: What if a long-standing time bubble was disturbed in any way? How? By operating another time-shifting device *within* it. That's the other thing Hunter recalled someone mentioning to him. That shifting time inside time that's already been shifted was not a prudent thing to do. The person had said, "It can screw up a lot of things in a lot of different ways."

Trouble was, the propulsion unit for Hunter's flying machine was based on time-shifter technology. He didn't know how it worked exactly; no one did. But its critical components had come from a Kaon Bombardment ship he'd found crashed on Fools 6. The wreck proved to be a treasure trove of time-shifter secrets.

He knew the way his aircraft moved was partly an illusion: It only appeared to be going incredibly fast in ultradrive. In reality, it was shifting through time. But was this enough to affect a time bubble?

That's what he suspected. When he activated his flying machine those two times back in Mayfield, it might have caused a ripple across the time bubble. In those two seconds, the entire planet froze, and therein lay the problem: If the two little hops had produced such an effect here, what would have happened had he booted up to full power? What if the ripples had suddenly become a tidal wave? One that lasted an hour or two? Would he have popped the time bubble completely? Would that have thrown this planet back to where it was ages ago? What happens when an entire planet reverts back several thousand years in just a second or two? When there are suddenly rivers where no rivers had been, high ocean waves instead of beachfront property. No electricity, no power, no roads, no bridges. The potential for widespread devastation would seem very high.

So what did all this mean? Especially for the upcoming flight? Safe to say, taking off would be a little more complicated than just revving his machine up to near full volume, disappearing in a microsecond. He would have to be very careful with his velocity. He'd used just the barest fraction of his aircraft's ultradrive power during the two Mayfield flights. He couldn't even come close to those speeds again, at least until he reached orbit and presumably escaped the invisible membrane of the time bubble. This meant that for the upcoming mission he would have to take off and ascend slowly, building to a maximum speed less than that of his Mayfield trips.

The fastest he'd gone on that night was fifteen miles a second—with all those seconds of both trips actually reduced to about 1/1000th of a second, the miniscule time-frame in which his flying machine operated whenever he engaged his power systems. If he cut that number in half, and only rose to the max gradually, things should be all right. And here he was lucky. In the real world, half fifteen miles a second was about 18,000 miles an hour, or seven miles a second.

That was almost the exact velocity he needed to break free of this planet.

• • •

Dawn came, and so did the rain. Hunter was ready for takeoff.

Hunter took a deep breath from his oxygen mask—a bulky necessity for this unusual ascent—and did one last check of his flight instruments. Everything was reading green.

This was going to be different right from the start; that much was evident now. Usually, he needed just an infinitesimal amount of roll-off to get his machine off the ground. But because of the two-second problem, even the takeoff would have to be done in a more conventional manner: rolling down the long field, building up speed, and getting some lift under his wings. Flight should soon follow.

He positioned the flying machine at the far end of the field. One more deep breath, helmet visor down. He glanced to either side of him. Small groups of CIA agents were watching him from the woods. He looked at the long, grassy airstrip in front of him; two miles away was a large grove of trees. He gripped his control tighter. Did he really know how to do this?

The last modification he'd made had been to his throttle bar. He'd stretched a piece of very low-tech electrical tape across the mechanism's gear channel. This would block the throttle from moving forward more than a half inch, the speed he'd determined would be safe enough to use, until he got to orbit at least. Then he could finally let it rip.

The rain was splattering on his canopy now. One of the CIA men in the woods was sending him a hand signal. The immediate area was clear of civilians. Time to go. Hunter pulled his safety harness tight, took one last gulp of oxygen, and then edged the throttle ahead about the width of a hair. *Bam!* He was thrown back against his seat with such force his helmet strap broke. The flying machine went zooming down the field at a violent, heavy speed. Those trees two miles away were on him in an instant. Only by pure instinct did Hunter yank back on his control stick and jerk the flying machine into the air, clipping off the tops of several pines in the process.

He banked hard left to avoid even more trees; in retrospect, he should have gone right. That would have put him out over the water in just a few seconds. Instead, he found himself streaking right above a highway that was crowded with morning commuters heading into D.C. The aircraft was traveling at nearly two miles a second, much faster than he'd anticipated, but there really wasn't anything he could do about it. That was its lowest speed.

Hunter finally adjusted full right and tried once again to ease back the speed, but it was impossible. So he simply yanked his control stick again and pulled on the nose of the aircraft until he was pointing straight up.

That's when the voice inside asked a very simple question: Had he done this before?

Had he, in his distant past, strapped on a machine like this and pointed its nose skyward, ascending so lightly as if in a dream? The sensations washing through him as he shot up through the rain clouds, into the blue morning sky—they seemed so familiar. This was not like flying at two light-years a second. Moving at that speed wasn't flying at all. It was just that: moving. From here to there, through time and hence the illusion of great speed. But it was not flying.

Flying was when the atmosphere had an effect on what your aerial machine could and could not do. Flying was wind. Flying was heat. Flying was metal and cold air crashing into each other, head-on, and turning that metal sizzling hot. Flying was actually a battle against the resistance of flight. With power and skill and daring and a touch of insanity—from that mix, somehow winning the war.

Hunter felt his hand grip the control stick even tighter as he passed through thirty-thousand feet. He began breathing deeply from the oxygen mask. The high g-forces—never a factor in ultradrive—had him pinned against his seat. The sun was burning his face, around his eyes, along his cheekbones, on the bottom of his forehead. Not like the burn one got from flying too fast for too long in space. That was a glow, stuck under the skin. This was the burn of a star, close by, one that looked awfully big from this perspective. Still, its warmth felt good on his face.

Yes, Hunter had done this before. The way the electricity was rushing out of his body, through the steering control, through the control panel, out to each square millimeter of the aircraft's frame and back again, this was a feeling. *The* feeling. It was not about what was pushing him through the air but rather that he was actually doing it, seemingly against all odds. Against the law of gravity.

And that's when two words popped into his head. Just two words, but he knew right away what they meant, and suddenly he had the first real memory of what he might have been before he found himself on Fools 6 that dark night. Just two words, yet they'd managed to make an impossible leap over several thousand years from who and what he was before to now, this moment. All because this ascent into these sun-drenched, clear blue skies was something he'd done so many times before, it would have been impossible for his psyche to keep the secret down any longer.

Two words: *Fighter pilot.*
That's what I used to be. . . .

The spell was broken right after his aircraft passed through seventy thousand feet.

He twisted the plane on its tail and looked over his shoulder. The funny little world was quickly dropping away from him.

Very soon now, his flying machine would have to become a spacecraft again. This was where it might get hairy. He removed the strip of electrical tape and eased the throttle up a notch. Again, he was slammed back against his seat. Just a touch, and he was suddenly going seventy-five hundred miles per hour.

Another touch, he was at nine thousand miles per hour.

Another, eleven thousand, then thirteen.

Hunter suddenly crossed his fingers. Another kiss of the throttle. Another deep breath. He was now going fifteen thousand miles per hour . . . straight up.

His machine was shaking violently now. Yes, he knew every bolt and seam in the aircraft, and at the moment, he imagined each and every one of them was coming undone. He'd come a long way just to break apart trying to get off this tiny little world. Is that the way it would be?

He held on, fingers still crossed, aircraft still shaking. Speed at seventeen thousand five hundred.

Then came a bright flash, and everything . . . just . . . slowed . . . down.

He was in orbit.

So far, so good.

He quickly killed the throttle and drifted up to an altitude of 110 miles. Then he turned his craft over.

The flying machine had been knocked around a lot lately.

Bouncing back and forth between dimensions wasn't the best of situations for a complex piece of machinery. Sometimes what blinked into the twenty-sixth dimension wasn't always exactly what blinked back out. But plainly, his craft had survived the ordeal of his unconventional ascent. All the nuts and bolts were still together, and everything was still reading green.

Even better, puncturing the time bubble had apparently been effortless as well. Hunter had seen no indications that he'd physically broken through anything once he'd left the atmosphere. This seemed like a big relief, like one less thing to worry about.

He went completely upside down now, feet pointing toward all those stars. Below him, the little planet was turning very peacefully. This was Hunter's first glimpse of it from any great height. It surprised him how small it really was. Just one large landmass, the one he'd driven across not so long ago, surrounded by all that blue, sparkling water. He felt his heart thump twice. There hadn't been a dull moment since coming to this place, yet he'd enjoyed his time on the surface so far. Pretty girls. Cool cars. The open road. The Seagram's. From here, the planet didn't look like a place harboring so many dark secrets.

From here, it looked like an oasis in this vast, empty piece of space. Something warm in the endless, cold blackness. Despite all the drama, he liked it down there.

Planet America . . .

It was the next best thing to home.

But now it was on to the mission.

He turned the flying machine around and put the nose pointing up. Hanging at about the two o'clock position was this desolate system's rather wacky moon.

It was about one-fifth the size of the planet below, and Hunter guessed it was about sixty thousand miles out. He flicked his throttle, and an instant later was a thousand feet above the satellite's north pole. The glare from its white, powdery surface was so bright, Hunter had to lower his helmet visor again. The moon had a heavily cratered face and bore a striking resemblance to *the* Moon, Earth's sacred *luna*. But Hunter knew right away this satellite was a fake. It wasn't a natural body; it was manufactured. How could he be so sure? Because there was a visible wobble to its motion as it roared through space; it was also traveling at an unnaturally high speed. Both were clear indications of space engineering.

But strangest of all, the moon was not exactly orbiting the tiny planet of America. It just appeared that way.

Hunter steered around to the dark side of the moon, astonished at how fast the satellite was moving. Once in the moon's shadow, less the satellite's intense glare, he had a clearer view of the local solar neighborhood, and it turned out to be a very crowded place. This system did have more planets, just as the holo-spy had claimed. There were at least two dozen of them, and those were just the ones he could see. They were all different colors and sporting different types of terrain. But strangest of all, they were all floating in the same orbital plane.

Hunter began chasing the swiftly moving moon now, his sensors telling him that the satellite was actually locked into a pre-programmed path that brought it into orbit not just around Planet America, but around the other planets in the system as well. It would rise and fall on one planet, then dash along to the next planet in line, go into orbit, provide a moonrise and set for it, then move off again to the next planet and the next. His scanners confirmed the moon would complete this circuit of planets once every twenty-four hours. This meant it could be observed by every planet in the same way, just at different but predictable times, similar to the way that *the* Moon was observed from Earth. Again, an amazing if puzzling example of celestial manipulation.

Though Hunter knew time was of the essence, he couldn't resist doing a very quick recon of the system's other nearby planets. The next one over from America was snow-covered, not unlike Tonk. The next appeared to be half jungle, half desert. Next came a temperate, mountainous world. Then one that was green and blue like America, but instead of having a sea, it had one huge river running right through it. Conversely, the next planet in line was nearly all water, with a huge island stuck in the middle of its southern hemisphere.

The sixth planet over was the one that most resembled America. It, too, had an irregular landmass that stretched around its circumference, though north to south. It had lots of mountains, lots of rivers, and two smaller islands hanging off the northwestern portion of the mainland.

Hunter was able to fly close enough to these planets to confirm that they, too, held life. There were cities and roadways and small towns and villages scattered all over the half-dozen worlds, even the polar one.

And the line of planets did not stop there. Based on the distances between these immediate bodies, quick calculations told him there might be as many as thirty-six planets revolving around the tiny star. All of them appeared to be orbiting just far enough away from the next so as not to be seen, big and bright, in the night sky, another startling feat of space engineering.

Hunter suppressed the urge to zigzag his way right around the inner system. Time was too important now. But he was able to look over the fantastic celestial display with a small measure of satisfaction.

Undoubtedly, these were the Home Planets.

I finally found them, he thought.

Another nudge of the throttle, and he was streaking toward the outer edge of the solar system, to where the so-called heavenly bodies lay.

Located about 700,000 miles out from the Home Planets, Hunter discovered on approach that these bodies were huge, at least five times larger than the planets orbiting closer in to the tiny yellow sun. Like the Home Planets, they all traveled along the same orbital plane, just farther out from the sun. This configuration made a ring that surrounded the inner ring of planets, not unlike a fence around a prison. Once again, the whole thing just screamed of massive space engineering, a gigantic project even by present day's standards. In fact, Hunter wondered if even the Fourth Empire would have the tools to take on such an endeavor today. Yet the Home Planets' system was at least three thousand five hundred years old.

He pulled back on the throttle and was quickly orbiting one of the heavenly bodies. The first thing he noticed was that body didn't look heavenly at all.

It was essentially just another fake moon. It had no topography to speak of, no terrain, mountains, or water. It was a big white globe wrapped in with what Hunter assumed was the ancient version of terranium, the artificial-yet-living fauna which covered many engineered planets, including Earth itself. Nothing was growing down on this surface, though. It was covered with craters. Hundreds of them pockmarked the powdery, life-less surface.

What had happened here? This moon was built, no doubt, with grand ideas in mind. But it was dead.

No puff. No life.

Interesting . . .

Hunter decided to call this Moon 01.

His intention was to go right around the ring of sentinels. If everything went right, Moon 01 was where he would wind up at the end of the journey.

He kicked into ultradrive again and was soon passing close to the next moon in line, several million miles away. What he found here was more of the same. Both his eyes and his scanners told him that this was another huge, artificial world, built for some reason but apparently never occupied. Like the first one, it was hanging lifeless in space. And it was the same for the next eleven moons. There were mirror images of themselves, every one. Lifeless, deserted.

Then he came to Moon 13, and here he found another sur-prise. This satellite hadn't even been completed. The upper half of its northern hemisphere was missing. The massive networks of girders and floating pilings could clearly be seen beneath the thick fake crust. Hunter went down low and hovered above its surface for a moment, just long enough to see the great jagged edge and look down into the maw of gigantic support beams. Hundreds of ancient tools were lying about the powdery surface. A trail of them led up to the precipice itself.

They appeared as if they'd been dropped there suddenly and never touched again.

Hunter continued the ultraquick tour, coming upon more than two dozen sentinel moons that were less than complete. Indeed, some barely had their superstructures built.

As he passed by the empty moons with routine quickness now, the idea that these sentinels were manned by monsters, somehow gazing down on the Home Planets, ready to rain down all sorts of destruction, had proved to be a false one so far. The heavenly bodies seemed to be little more than a massive facade. Was that what the original builders had intended all along? To fabricate a bunch of empty moons and a bluff? Or had some-thing happened in the distant past that had forced the abandonment of the sentinels? Or had they ever been occupied in the first place?

Then he came to Moon 39.

The first clue that something was different about this satellite appeared when his very-long-range environmental scans bounced back saying the place had a 99.99 percent puff. None of the previous sentinels had boasted any atmospheres at all. Yet his gear was telling him Moon 39 had breathable air, clouds, weather—and possibly, a whole lot more.

Hunter slipped into a very high orbit around the artificial satellite, jigging his throttle so he didn't stay in the same place too long. He didn't need his long-range scanners to see what was happening below him. The moon was definitely occupied. It had a gigantic military base located on its equator on the side facing the sun. This installation appeared large enough to house hundreds of thousands of personnel. The barracks alone stretched for miles in every direction. The base also had many spaceport facilities, at least a hundred launch platforms, with what appeared to be working spaceships in their bays. Two gigantic control towers provided the center of this enormous installation. Its airspace was thick with sky cars, combat patrol craft, even a few battle cruiser–class vessels lumbering about.

Hunter felt his heart drop to his boots. Any dreams that maybe the sentinels were just a hoax had now gone up in smoke. Just as the holo-spy had claimed, there *was* someone out here. A *lot* of someones. This base went on forever; some offshoots nearly wrapped themselves right around the artificial moon. Hunter asked his scanner to estimate how many soldiers the planet was holding. The answer came back: "one million, probably more." And just from what Hunter had seen, they had enough spacelift to pick them up and deliver them somewhere, if the need for that ever arose.

"Damn," Hunter whispered to himself. Home Planets *was* a solar prison.

And these were its prison guards.

So now what?

Hunter had the fleeting notion to attack the place. Lay waste to it just as he'd done back on Tonk. But right away, his instincts told him this was a very bad idea. First of all, it was biting off more than he could chew. This base was thousands of times larger than the enemy installations on Tonk. It would take him days of endless strafing just to try to get it all, something that whoever was below probably wouldn't sit still for. Plus he didn't know if any other moons down the line were occupied, or if these guys had any backup forces somewhere close by.

Besides, torching this place, even if he could do it, would not answer two really important questions: Who were these guys, and what did they really have to do with the imprisonment of Planet America?

No, this flight had not been intended as a combat mission; its aim was to recon and gather intelligence, and Hunter knew it was wise to just stick to the plan.

His job now was to get a closer look.

He'd put his time-advancing spy technique to the ultimate test only once before.

Back on Zazu-Zazu, while the final battle was taking place on the walls of the city of Qez, Hunter had flown superquick out to the enemy's huge battle tank, a monstrosity known as a xarcus. He'd traveled so fast between two points, he literally got ahead of himself in regular time. Operating within this twilight zone, he'd been able to land on the xarcus, penetrate its hull, and move around inside, seeing all, while not being seen.

It sounded fantastic and cool, but actually it wasn't. Walking around invisible in any enemy's camp was not a pleasant experience. The seeming impossibility of it all created a strong measure of doubt that it was even happening. This gave everything a sort of distorted, dreamlike quality, not a plus, considering the situation. There was further stomach tightening because of the feeling that at any moment, the natural law he was breaking would somehow whip itself back to shape and make him pay. By making him visible.

So the time-busting vanishing act was not something to be taken lightly. But Hunter knew it had to be done.

All he needed was a running start.

He whipped around the moon exactly one hundred times, throttle opened up to full ultraspeed overdrive, building up the momentum needed to get ahead of himself.

Once he'd become advanced in time, he floated in for a soft landing next to a small power station. The site was about a quarter mile from the hub of the vast military base and not far from the soaring twin towers that looked down upon it all.

Now he just waited. The inner base was mobbed with space

soldiers and officers, some walking, some marching, some streaking by overhead in sky cars. Hunter sat perfectly still for what seemed to him to be more than a minute, watching as these troops passed by on all sides of him. From all indications, they could not see him. He finally popped the canopy, collected his blaster rifle and his ray gun, then jumped to the ground. Two soldiers passed right through his body, the final proof that he was invisible. His time-cheating technique had worked again.

The soldiers around him were wearing basic black combat uniforms, not unlike Hunter's own, but with tiny ornamental fins sprouting from each shoulder and a set of winglike projections on the back. The uniforms looked oddly out of date.

The personal weapons these troops were carrying with them seemed elderly, too. They looked like ray guns issued to the Fourth Empire's units several hundred years before. This did not mean they were any less deadly, though. Same for the literally thousands of battlefield weapons in evidence around the sprawling base. These included an incredible number of Master Blasters, smaller death-tube arrays, and even some antique sonic guns. All this made the pop guns employed by the bad guys back on Tonk look puny by comparison. And it was a lot of stuff for such an isolated place far beyond the edge of the Galaxy.

Hunter folded his flying machine into a Twenty 'n Six and began walking. His ray gun was up and ready, only because it made him feel better. Could he actually fire his weapon effectively while operating inside the one-step-ahead situation? He didn't know. Though he'd exchanged gunfire inside the xarcus with some mysterious enemy troops, looking back on it, he believed that gun battle might have been fought in a different time or dimension entirely. His theory now was that yes, he *could* probably fire the handgun, but the deadly ray it emitted would most likely show up an hour or two later. He kept the gun up in front of him anyway.

He passed through the crowded administrative and control areas of the base, seeing lots but learning little about this powerful garrison army. Their uniforms bore no markings, and there were no flags or banners about. Obviously, the huge army was, in a sense, working undercover. He wandered through its transport yards, taking note of the hundreds of troop shuttles, gleaming under the weak yellow sun. These were not the Bugs he'd traveled in during his first trip on an Empire ship. Those little scooters could barely carry a hundred soldiers for a distance never exceeding the trip down from orbit. Though they looked dated as well, these shuttles could accommodate at least a thousand men each and were big enough to take them clear across a good-sized solar system. There was no doubt that these vessels could reach any of the Home Planets quickly and deliver an enormous space army to their surface, ready for battle.

Or was *invasion force* a better term?

He walked the length of the congested space launch farm. There were twelve gigantic docking ports here that could handle big ships, and hundreds of smaller pads where patrol craft and sky cars were maintained. At the end of this mile-long stretch of tarmac was a long, tubular building emitting a barely visible yet clearly sparkling stream of greenish mist. This was an ion-ballast works. While the much quicker technology of Supertime was used exclusively by Empire spacecraft, the vast majority of flying things in the Galaxy were powered by ion-ballast–fueled engines. This facility was big enough to provide plentiful energy for ion spacecraft of all sizes.

It was most interesting that every one of the large spacecraft bays was holding a vessel in stasis. Twelve bays, twelve ships. That probably meant there were no sizable spacecraft out patrolling in the star system somewhere. In fact, except for the small atmospheric craft and sky cars, it seemed to Hunter that much of this hardware had been sitting here, planet bound, for a long, long time.

Like a phantom, he moved around the base for the equivalent of a half hour, counting weapons, noting ammunition bunkers, estimating troop strength. He was gathering a lot of intelligence, some of it valuable, but Hunter was not yet satisfied. He'd confirmed that yes, the holo-spy was right, there was an enormous army out here, apparently poised to strike anywhere, at any time. But he still needed to know two important things: Who were these guys, and why were they out here? He couldn't leave until he found out.

He managed to locate the base's intelligence building. It was the structure with the highest number of communications bubblers on its roof. He passed through the main entrance with no problem and was soon standing in the central control room of the place. There were at least two hundred technicians at work here, monitoring various scanning arrays. At the center of the room there stood a large black box with a red light attached to its top and an enormous Klaxon protruding from its midsection.

Hunter approached the black box and, after studying its bare controls and eavesdropping on its attendant gang of techs, discovered that the monolith was actually a very simple warning device, one that would erupt whenever a certain kind of event was detected. A bank of thirty-six screens nearby told a further tale. This array of monitors was zoomed in on the Home Planets, one screen devoted to each of the three dozen worlds.

But what kind of event were they looking for?

Hunter studied the screen showing Planet America. It was just a static image of the green and blue ball, spinning through space. The attending devices didn't appear to be monitoring the planet's overall puff or working any kind of time bubble maintenance. Instead, the numbers running down the screen itself were labeled in various atmospheric measurements, such as air pressure, temperature, wind speed, and so on. The monitors seemed built to detect minute changes inside the atmospheres below.

One of a long line of light panel controllers was marked with an icon that Hunter interpreted to be the system's simulation test. Without really thinking about it, he gave this button a push. Instantly, the live shot of Planet America turned into a lifelike graphic of the tiny world. The words: "Event Detection" began flashing on the screen. A tiny flash of bright light began rising from the landmass below. It grew brighter and brighter, a long smoky tail flowing from behind. The atmospheric readings running down the side of the screen—they, too, were part of the simulation—were going crazy. Several more warning flashes appeared. One said: "Event in Progress." Then the bright pinprick of light reached "orbit" around the graphic of the planet, and that's when the gigantic black box erupted with flashing red lights and skull-fracturing sound.

Hunter immediately cupped his ears and averted his eyes from the strobing light, but of course no one else in the room could see or hear any of it. In their reality, the simulated warning device hadn't gone off yet. And it probably wouldn't for at least another hour or so.

Hunter quickly released the sim panel button and the box stopped flashing and bleating. Everything went back to normal.

It took a few moments for Hunter to get his senses back.

It had been painful to his cranium, but snooping in the right place had solved one mystery. These thirty-six arrays were looking for only one thing: evidence that any of the planets below was about to achieve spaceflight. If a successful launch was detected, the buzzer would blare and the blinding red light would flash until eyes hurt and ears began to bleed.

So this was actually a tripwire station, the means by which the mysterious celestial guards kept track of their unwitting prisoners below. There was beauty in the simplicity of this. How best do you keep prisoners in the prison? You monitor each planet around the clock, looking for the one sign that would indicate that the planet's inhabitants had reached the point of trying to get off, unintentionally trying to break out of jail. Then, presumably, *boom*! That's when the hammer came down.

Was this an explanation for the periodic disasters that had befallen Planet America every few centuries? The same apocalypses the holo-spy had warned them about? Was it simply part of the makeup of the people back there to try to escape their confines, unwittingly bringing catastrophe down on themselves? Could it be the same on the other planets as well?

Hunter was beginning to think so.

But why hadn't this gaggle of detectors spotted him leaving Planet America's atmosphere? Was it because his craft emitted things that these monitors could not detect?

He thought this as well.

Time to move on. He decided to find the most sensitive area of the entire intelligence complex, a place where all the top secrets would be stored. He eventually came upon a large vault, ironically on the top floor of the multistoried building. There were a dozen techs and several armed guards inside this secure room; the vault itself was open. Hunter simply walked inside.

The vault was eerily similar to the one under Weather Mountain. Lots of numbered doors containing pull-out drawers. But instead of holding artifacts, these drawers contained suspended droplets of liquid ether. One drop contained ten-to-the-twentieth-power bits of information. The drops were files; you put them on your tongue, and suddenly you knew their contents. Amazing technology, yet it was more than a thousand years old.

Hunter knew he didn't have much time left. The dreamy nature of this invisible exercise made it almost impossible to tell how many virtual minutes had gone by since the start of it. Nor was he sure just how far in the future one hundred times around this moon would put him. Certainly no more than two hours or so. By his estimate then, he only had about another twenty minutes or so left on the ground before he had to think about getting out. So instead of going through all the liquid files, he began a search for the one drawer that appeared to be holding the most secret information of all. He found just such a drawer at the rear of the vault. Its door was painted white with bright red stripes crossing through it. A holo-sign indicated only the top echelon of the base's command structure had access to the contents. A neutron lock kept the door sealed tight.

Hunter bore through the subatomic clasp with ease; all he had to do was disengage the quarks from the larks with the aid of his electron torch. His hunch about this drawer paid off. Inside he found not a miniocean of brain drops but a set of mind rings. One was marked "Mission Background, Day One. Guard Duty. Year 3237."

It was just what he was looking for.

Without hesitation, Hunter took off his helmet and jammed the mind ring onto his head.

Flash!

He was suddenly standing in a crowded spaceport. Everywhere he looked, he could see gigantic rocket towers spiraling overhead. And people. Everywhere. Millions of them.

He looked down at his clothes. He was wearing a bright green battle suit with thick epaulets on the shoulders and a long, flowing cape. He had a helmet under one arm, an ancient style atomic rifle under the other. He was a soldier. He looked around and for almost as far as he could see, there were soldiers wearing the exact same uniform as he.

And the strange thing was, Hunter knew where he was. The gigantic spaceport, the monstrous launch towers and galleys. The electric city across the river to the west. He was on Earth, at the Eff-Kay Jack spaceport. The lighted metropolis spread across the horizon was Big Bright City, the capital of Earth—but as it looked almost four thousand years before.

What was going on here? Hunter joined one stream of soldiers who were walking toward one of the gigantic launch gantries. The spacecraft attached to this tower was at least two thousand feet high. It was also very bulbous, with a blunt, pointed nose and tiny fins on its rear. At this moment, they seemed to be the only thing supporting the rocket's massive weight.

This rocket was painted bright green, as were all the others in the gigantic forest of spaceships. There were loading ramps sticking out of the bottom of this rocket, twelve in all, ringing the spaceship like spokes. There were literally thousands of people climbing these gangways, all of them civilians. They were being herded onto the gigantic spaceship by soldiers wearing the same caped uniforms.

He stayed attached to the loose column of soldiers. They marched about a half mile down the spaceport's tarmac before turning in to the launch area of the next green spaceship in line. Like with all the vessels he could see, people were being marched onto this spacecraft as well. Hunter's detachment of soldiers wound up relieving another unit that had been manning the entrance to one of these crowded gangways. The soldiers were pushing along anyone not moving fast enough up the narrow ramp. Hunter nudged his way to the front of the line and eventually found himself not fifty feet away from the entrance to the gangway.

Nearby, he saw hundreds of people—men, women, seniors, kids—being deposited in a huge receiving area by sinister-looking shuttle craft flitting in and out. After a quick security bath, these people were being pushed toward the ramp and eventually into the ship itself. Some were carrying baggage. Very few were wearing very much more than the clothes on their back.

Above the entrance to the gangway was a sign that was engraved with characters, many of which were too small for Hunter to see. But at the top of the poster, he thought he recognized six words: "By Order of the Second Empire . . ." Stationed next to the sign was an ancient deatomizing device. Within its chambers were bits and pieces of burnt cloth, the remnants of lackadaisical pulverization. Each bit of this cloth was either red, white, or blue. Each had once been a piece of a flag.

Hunter just froze on the spot. It all became so clear now. Even though the mind ring had probably originated as an orientation tool for up-and-coming prison guards, it had told him just about everything he needed to know on this subject.

These were the people of America being deported from Earth

more than 3,900 years ago. They looked beleaguered, bitter, angry, lost. Hunter didn't have to go any further into the mind ring to know where the big green ships went once they'd blasted off for space. And he didn't have to inspect the ashes of the deatomizing machine to know its job was to destroy the Americans' flags. This was a forced deportation. The Americans were being shipped out of their own country.

Hunter found an anger building so deep inside him he thought it would affect this little mind trip he was on. All he knew was he had to get the mind ring off his head now and return to whence he came. But just as he was reaching up to remove his headgear, a person passing by in a group heading toward the gangplank caught his attention: blond, blue eyes, cheeks that were pink because she smiled so much. . . . It was Ashley.

She was dressed differently, and she wasn't smiling at all now, but Hunter was sure it was her.

But how could this be? She lived on what Planet America would become, four thousand years later. How could she be here, in the memory of this mind ring?

He tried to push his way through to her and succeeded in reaching the entrance to the gangway at the same time she did.

Their eyes met. Hers went very wide. Then came an astonished smile.

"Hawk?" she said. "Is that really you?"

"It's really me," he replied.

But just as he was about to reach for her, he found himself staring at an enormous blue screen instead. It stretched in every direction as far as he could see; its top literally went right up into the clouds.

Hunter thought his heart would stop beating right then and there. As part of the Earth Race, he'd had to penetrate several blue screens not unlike this one, and behind each he found a reality that was far stranger than anything he'd experienced since waking up on Fools 6. The mysterious blue screens were part of the obstacle course that made up a large portion of the Earth Race.

So what the hell is one of them doing here?

He put his hands up against it . . . and felt himself falling. He lost his balance, passed right through the screen, and hit his head on something very hard far below.

Flash!

• • •

When he opened his eyes again, he was lying on the floor of the intelligence vault on Moon 39. The mind ring was spinning across the floor away from him.

There were several techs staring into the vault now, quizzical looks on their faces. Hunter did not move. He was hoping they'd been alerted only by the sound of the mind ring hitting the floor, something that hadn't really happened yet.

Once they seemed satisfied that nothing was amiss inside the vault, the techs returned to their posts. Hunter slowly got to his feet, tried to shake the stars from his eyes, then put the mind ring back in its compartment, closed the door, and left.

He'd come within one inch of touching Ashley's face.

He staggered back out on the parade grounds and tried to get his bearings.

He knew he had to get going. On one level, the recon had been an outstanding success. Hunter was now very familiar with all the visible aspects of this army's capabilities. So he knew what they were: a quick-reaction space force, equipped with passable arms and a lot of transport. And he knew why they were here: as prison guards, just as the holo-spy had indicated.

The trouble was, he still didn't know *who* they were. He'd seen no flags or banners identifying the space corps by name nor any ship markings or weapons stamps stating exactly who they were. Again it was obvious the massive army was working undercover.

But it was important that Hunter ID them. For this he stole into one of the barracks nearby. An army was an army, no matter how well equipped, no matter how distant the garrison. With around-the-clock shifts, the legitimately ailing and the simply malingering, at any given time, about 20 percent of any force was usually asleep.

Hunter found the barracks he'd selected dotted with sleeping soldiers. He walked down the space between the hovering bunks looking for someone who appeared to be above the rank of space grunt. Finally, he came upon a cluster of floating beds that were larger, more comfortable, and more stable than the rest of the bunks. *Officer country*, Hunter thought correctly.

He idled up to one officer's personal effects box hovering right beside his bed. Slowly, carefully, Hunter waved its security halo away and reached down into the guy's stuff. He quickly came out with a subatomic knife. It was sealed inside a plastic air case and looked more like a ceremonial piece than a combat instrument.

Just what he was looking for.

He quickly stuffed the knife into his boot and backed out of the barracks. He found another somewhat remote piece of flat ground and summoned his flying machine from the Twenty 'n Six.

He climbed in and engaged his power systems. Only once he was sure that he would be able to get off the artificial moon did he take the knife out of his boot and remove it from its sheath.

He was looking for some kind of trademark or inscription on the blade. This army was expert in keeping a low profile as to who it really was. But sometimes officers slipped up and carried an instrument with markings from the actual unit.

And that was the case here; Hunter had picked the right pocket. There was an inscription across the blade that answered one question but also opened up about a million others.

The inscription was just three words, but Hunter felt his stomach twist itself a bit tighter when he read them. Who was the undercover army, waiting way out here for one false move by the people on the Home Planets?

Some unknown ancient order, nearly four thousand years old, the same age as the star system prison?

No.

The army of prison guards was actually none other than a large detachment of the Bad Moon Knights.

16

Hunter very carefully punched back into orbit around Planet America and started the long plunge down.

He'd checked out the rest of the sentinel moons; they were just as lifeless as the ones he'd found before coming to Moon 39. Now he was anxious to get back on the ground and tell the others all that he'd discovered.

But as soon as he had cleared the top layers of America's atmosphere and gotten below the clouds, he was confronted with a startling sight: The planet was on fire. He could see hundreds of smoke plumes rising into the air all across the continent. On that part of the planet turned away from the sun, there were no lights, no signs of life below. Using his very rudimentary communications device, Hunter tried to raise someone at Andrews Field.

There was no reply.

He touched down in the rain a few minutes later, passing over many fires and collapsed roadways on his approach to Andrews Field.

He rolled to the end of the makeshift runway and was relieved to see Zarex and Pater Tomm waiting for him. Gordon was on hand as well, along with a squad of CIA agents (all of whom were talking on their cell phones) and a small convoy of black vans. But some of the agents looked as if they'd just gone through a war. They were sporting bandages on various parts of their bodies. Gordon himself was dabbing a head wound with a piece of gauze.

Hunter jumped from his plane and ran over to the group of walking wounded.

"What happened down here?" he asked them.

"Only a vision of doomsday," Tomm replied quickly. "Or about thirteen minutes of it, anyway."

"It was like the whole planet did a jig," Zarex confirmed. "Everything just started rocking and rolling, and it wouldn't stop. I've been through a lot in the past two hundred years, but that might have been the longest thirteen minutes of my life."

Gordon had it all written down in a hastily scrawled report, which was now getting smeared in the rain.

"The power blackouts came first," he told Hunter. "Two short ones, about a minute apart. Then a few more, longer in duration. Then it seemed like the whole planet just started to shake. Up and down, back and forth. We were lying flat on the ground, yet at times I swear I was upside down."

The others nodded in painful agreement.

"And it lasted such a long time," Gordon continued, dabbing his head wound. "Once it finally stopped, the reports of damage started coming in a minute later, and they haven't stopped since."

He handed Hunter the written report. "It was just the damnedest thing, and it seemed to happen just a few seconds after you left."

Hunter just stood there, stunned, not quite believing what he was hearing. Could he be responsible for this? He quickly read the report. The bad stuff began happening just about a half minute after he'd reached orbit. There was one blackout followed quickly by several others. And these outages did not just happen in the vicinity of Andrews Field. They had rippled right across the continent.

The real shaking began about two minutes later and did not stop for thirteen long minutes. Again, the effect was felt right across the country. Not a quake, rather a gigantic disruption that, in Gordon's written words, felt "as if a giant's hand had picked us up and just started shaking." The worst of it came in the last three minutes.

Hunter began matching up the times of these events with his own activity. The first series of blackouts coincided with his initial engagement of ultradrive in space. The planet started shaking just as he'd begun his tour of the half-dozen Home Planets and continued when he'd zoomed out to where the sentinel moons lay. Then the *real* disruption began at the precise moment he'd gone into his time-busting spy mode, which, in real time down here must have taken about thirteen minutes. The trembling continued until the moment he kicked out of full ultraoverdrive and returned to America's orbit.

The numbers didn't lie. His takeoff had been okay. But every time he'd pushed his throttle into ultraspeed, the people back on Planet America had paid the price. Yet this didn't make any sense. Why would what he did out there affect what was happening back here, inside the planet's time bubble?

The ink on Gordon's report began running off the wet pages. Hunter was now soaked to the bone. Bad things happen when the ground shakes. Fires break out. Water mains crack. Electrical wires fall. How many had been killed? How many injured? It was almost too terrible for him to contemplate.

And most important, *why* did it happen?

Hunter and the others were whisked back to Weather Mountain.

For security reasons, they were put in three separate vans and driven by three different routes back to the CIA facility. Hunter surprised himself by falling asleep during his ride back. One moment they were pulling out of a muddy road near Andrews, the next, the van was flying through the front gate at Weather Mountain. The unexpected sleep had done him a favor. It had relieved him of thinking about the devastation he had just caused—at least for a little while.

He was brought to the CIA "blue room" as they had taken to calling the huge conference room with all the blue lights. Two of Gordon's aides gave him a plate of hot food, which he wolfed down without even knowing what it was. When they inquired if he wanted coffee or a smoke, he asked for a bottle of Seagram's. After a hushed conversation, they brought him a glass of it instead.

He then asked for permission to speak to his two colleagues alone. More discussion. Gordon was contacted in the first aid room, where he was getting his head wound attended to. He told his aides to grant Hunter's wish. It made no difference. The blue room was thick with eavesdropping devices, anyway.

Tomm and Zarex were brought in, and a pot of coffee and a pack of Marlboros appeared soon after. Then the aides left them alone in the cavernous conference room. They sat huddled at the far end of the oval table, Tomm with his coffee, Zarex with his smokes, Hunter with his drink.

"Brothers, I felt we three should talk first," Hunter told them. "With what I have to report from my mission, I'm not sure our hosts can absorb it all at once."

"Bingo that," both men replied.

Hunter sipped his drink.

"But before we get into it," he went on, "I have something else I must reveal to you."

Tomm and Zarex looked back at him strangely. His voice was dead serious.

"I've been keeping something from you, brothers," Hunter began. "A deep secret that is crumbling just as fast as all the other secrets around us. I feel it is time for me to come clean."

He took a deep breath.

"Brothers, the Fourth Empire exists," he told them bluntly. "I know because I was once an officer in its exploratory corps."

Tomm and Zarex just stared back at him. Essentially, Hunter was telling them that one of the greatest myths of the Five-Arm—indeed of the entire Fringe itself—was in fact true. That a huge empire controlled most of the Milky Way and was expanding its realm by gobbling up more planets with each passing day. Tomm and Zarex had speculated about this before, of course, and about Hunter's mysterious nature as well. But never had they expected him to just come out and tell them.

"Are you sure about this, my son?" Tomm asked him. "And that you just didn't hit your head on reentry?"

Hunter smiled. "Sometimes, Padre, I wish that *was* the case."

He explained that he'd been reluctant to tell them of his origins before, because knowledge of the vast Fourth Empire had to be absorbed gradually, just as the people on this planet had to absorb that fact that the three of them had come from someplace else. But now that they knew, there was no sense holding anything back. So Hunter told them about the Fourth Empire itself. About Time Shifters and Kaon Bombardment ships, and how he wasn't exactly sure why his flying machine moved the way it did. He described the omnipotent power of the Big Generator and the fleets of Empire Starcrashers that traveled in the mysterious dimension called Supertime, and were many times faster than ion-ballast starships. He told them about his amnesiac origins, his home on Fools 6, his time as an Empire officer, his less-than-coincidental arrival on Zazu-Zazu.

When it was over, Hunter felt like a huge burden had been lifted from his shoulders.

His two colleagues were quiet for a long time. Then Zarex reached across the table and shook his hand, nearly crushing Hunter's fingers in the process.

"Thank you, brother, for telling me," the muscle man said. "It makes my life so much more interesting to know that the *entire* galactic swirl is ringing with life."

Tomm leaned over as well, but instead of shaking Hunter's hand, he slapped his cheek none too lightly but in a priestly sort of way.

"I knew it all along, of course," he told Hunter dryly. "But thank you for confirming my suspicions."

Hunter took another drink of his Seagram's. He had about a half glass left and was already aching for more.

"So tell us, brother," Zarex urged him. "We can't take the suspense. What did you see up there?"

Hunter just shook his head. "What I found up there is the reason that I revealed to you what I know about the Fourth Empire. The empire is controlled from a planet called Earth. I've been there. It's out on the One-Arm, and a more magical and intriguing place does not exist. But I found evidence, up there, that the original peoples of Earth were taken off their planet and brought here. To the Home Planets. It's the missing clue to all the artifacts the CIA has found. It also means whoever was controlling Earth four thousand years ago created this place out here, and they are still maintaining it.

Tomm and Zarex were visibly shocked.

"Are you saying," Tomm asked him, "that this place, this mighty Earth, center of a huge empire, actually belongs to—"

"The people here," Hunter finished the sentence for him. "Here, and on the other planets I found up there."

Hunter quickly told them about his mission: Finding the Home Planets, weirdly uniform in their orbital proclivities. The heavily engineered local moon. The string of empty sentinels. Then his discovery of Moon 39 and what he'd found while on the ground, especially his viewing of the space launch event

detector and the experience inside the mind ring—all except
Ashley. And the mysterious blue screen.

"The holo-spy spoke too well," he concluded. "This system
is a prison. What she didn't know was, it was built to imprison
the people who rightfully own the Earth. And there is an entire
space corps sitting out there, guarding it."

"But who are these guards?" Tomm asked. "What is their
business in this?"

"That's another thing," Hunter replied. "Equally disturbing.
It leads to a strange question."

"Spill, please," Zarex said.

"Brothers, earlier in our journey, you had spoken of the Bad
Moon Knights," Hunter said. "How long have they been operating on the Fringe, do you think?"

Both Tomm and Zarex shrugged.

"My dealings with them go back a hundred eighty years,"
Zarex said. "I'm guessing they've been around at least twice as
long. Do you agree, Padre?"

"Three times as long probably," Tomm said. He turned back
to Hunter. "Why do you ask, brother?"

Hunter pulled the space knife from his boot pocket and
showed it to his friends.

"The Bad Moon Knights?" Tomm said, examining the blade's
holo-inscription. "But where did you come upon this?"

Hunter pointed his finger skyward. "Up there," he said. "On
Moon 39. The prison garrison is made up of Bad Moon
Knights—about a million of them."

Zarex's face almost drained of color. "You mean they followed me all the way out here?"

Hunter shook his head. "Fear not, brother. I think they're up
to bigger things this time."

Hunter told them how the BMK equipment on Moon 39,
while highly polished and undeniably lethal, was also very, very
old. At least by six or seven hundred years. As were the soldiers'
uniforms, their base layout. Everything about them screamed
mid-6500s.

"That's very odd," Zarex said, settling back down. "As one
who has dealt with people trying to resist these savages, I can
tell you the BMK is usually very well equipped. Even their
protégés have the latest weapons."

"They were known at their beginnings to take on the worst

jobs of the Galaxy," Tomm said. "Hence their reputation for sheer brutality. They were also not very expensive in their younger days. They were in it for the cheap thrills, and they weren't too fussy about what merc contract to take. Now they're the biggest outlaw army on the Five-Arm—and probably other places as well."

"Interesting," Zarex said, through a cloud of smoke. "Someone must have hired them to do this job and then stuck them way out here. But who? The villain in your mind ring trip— this Second Empire—are we to assume that it was a predecessor to the one in power now?"

"In some shape or form," Hunter replied. "But my brothers, the Second Empire fell on Earth thousands of years ago. And we know the BMK has not been around for *that* long."

"Someone must have renewed the contract," Tomm said, "and brought the BMK in. But when?"

"And we have an even further problem," Hunter said. "These disruptions that occurred while I was away. I'm sure I was the cause of them, though I'm not sure I know why. My aircraft is based on Time Shifter technology. And I know that shifting time inside something whose time has already been shifted is not a smart thing to do. That's what happened with the missing two seconds Gordon spoke about. That's why I insisted on such an unusual takeoff. But even though I left this planet—and presumably pierced the time bubble—operating my machine still caused these disruptions. Ones much greater than simply losing two seconds of time."

Zarex just shook his head.

"This whole time-space thing confuses me," he confessed. "Time Shifters. Frozen time. Time bubbles. I just don't understand it."

"Not many people do," Hunter said. "But I think I have a theory about what happened."

"Tell us," Tomm urged him.

Hunter took a healthy slug of his drink now. "Could it be that not just the Home Planets are encased in time bubbles, but the whole system itself?"

Tomm and Zarex considered this for a moment. "Including the sentinel moons?" the priest asked.

"Yes, exactly," Hunter replied. "It's really the only thing that makes sense. I flew two times down here while we were on the lam. That resulted in two seconds of lost time, reversed time, frozen time, whatever you want to call it. But those flights were short, and I didn't come anywhere near full ultraoverdrive."

"Go on," Tomm urged him.

"But what if the entire system was locked in a time bubble? And anytime I go into overdrive, I disrupt it. Back here, out there. Everywhere. It's the only explanation. It also could explain why those BMK troops out there look like throwbacks to the last millennia."

"My God," Tomm whispered. "We know the people down here are stuck in a piece of near-frozen time. But could it be that those dopes up on Moon 39 are, too? And is it possible that they don't know it either?"

Hunter shook his head. "Could it be that they took a contract for this, what? Some nine hundred years ago? And have been living up there ever since, causing havoc when needed, but at the same time unaware that so much time has gone by?"

"It's certainly a clever ploy if you are paying them by the hour," Zarex said.

"But even still," Hunter said. "We know they haven't been out there for the entire four thousand years of this. Someone hired them, and took advantage of them, within this last thousand years. Perhaps just as they'd taken advantage of other earlier armies. That to me means this whole thing is an ongoing enterprise. The BMK are just the lackeys. Whoever wanted to keep the people of this place, America, and all the other planets behind bars is still out there. Or at least they were a thousand years ago."

Hunter needed his drink refilled. He felt like his head was about to pop.

"But, whatever their situation," he began again. "There is one thing we can be sure of. The BMK is just sitting out there, waiting for something to do. And now we know what spurs them into action: spaceflight. So if there is only one way we can help our hosts here, it will be by warning them off any ideas of space travel, lest catastrophe hit this place yet another time."

"Yes, an important point," Tomm said after a long pause. "But a question for you, brother Hunter—possibly unimportant in light of everything else. But I'm a curious man and I've never asked you before: Where did you go in those first two flights after we had split up?"

"Yes, brother," Zarex added. "Why did you feel it was so important that you take to the air, especially since at that time, we had agreed to keep a low profile?"

Hunter felt his heart twist a little more inside his chest.

"Well," he began uneasily, "there was this girl, and—"

But before he could say another word, the doors to the conference room flew open and Gordon hurried in. He was followed by the other six senior agents. They all looked very worried.

"Please don't ask us how," Gordon told them. "But we've heard everything you've been saying. And I'm afraid we have some very disturbing news."

They all gathered in front of the huge screen that dominated one of the blue room's walls.

Gordon pushed a button, and the screen came to life. Suddenly they were looking at a location somewhere out in the American Southwest desert. It seemed to be a base of some sort, extremely isolated and surrounded on all sides by high mountains. It was early morning out there, not yet sunrise. Still in the waning darkness, an unmistakable silhouette could be seen: a rocket standing attached to a launch platform.

Hunter groaned. This vehicle looked older than the tub of bolts he'd seen lift off from Tonk. It was also bigger, fatter, and had the same blunt nose and four fins to stand on. Steam was venting from several places along its fuselage. Technicians could be seen moving like ghosts around the launch pad.

"Next to your presence here, this is one of the best kept secrets on the planet," Gordon told them. "Not even our Vice President knows about it. It's a black program we've been working on for almost fifty years now. It was due for launch within days."

"You mean that thing is operational?" Hunter asked.

Gordon nodded. "We'd hoped for an orbital flight. But there was also a secret option for a lunar mission."

This was not good. If the rocket was allowed to launch, it could trigger an invasion of the Planet America. One that the tiny world couldn't possibly resist for very long.

"You simply can't launch that vehicle," Hunter said finally. "It would have catastrophic consequences."

"I don't need further convincing of that," Gordon said. "After what happened earlier today, I'd just as soon go along with whatever you guys have to say. But, correct me if I'm wrong: If we have been constantly striving for spaceflight, only to be smitten down every time it's in our grasp, wouldn't this also be true for the rest of the planets in this system?"

The spacemen looked on the CIA man with newborn respect. Even though he'd obviously listened in on their private conversation, he was picking up on this new game pretty well.

"Other planets might be close to the level of development you've reached again here," Hunter said. "For all we know, your cultures might all be on a similar track, just as your planets all follow the same orbital plane. There's a chance that one of the other planets is on the verge of spaceflight, just days away as well. Maybe more than one. They aren't aware of all this. They are wide open to being slaughtered."

"We can't stand by and allow such a thing to happen," Tomm added. "No matter what planet it might happen on. We know a terrible secret. As honorable men, we are duty bound to not stay quiet about it."

"But what are you saying exactly?" Gordon asked.

Hunter stared at the big screen for a long time, then told Gordon, "He's saying it's time to meet your neighbors."

17

It took all of forty-eight hours.

The plan was simple. Do a little scanning, a little spying. Identify the *numero uno* leader of each Home Planet, then make contact with them quietly, subtlely. Lay out the Moon 39 situation, show them the evidence, and let them come to the only logical conclusion.

Then came the hard part. Telling them they now had to take a ride to another planet. Some went willingly. Some with great enthusiasm. Some did not. A microburst from any standard ray gun provided enough punch to stun its victim temporarily. For those who went feetfirst, a terrifying interplanetary trip followed.

Hunter had done all the work. He'd traveled to each planet, did the snooping, made the contact. And he did it all at speeds way below full ultraoverdrive and with conventional takeoffs and landings. He caused several massive power blackouts, nevertheless. The public was allowed to believe these were aftereffects of the frightening events earlier in the week. What exactly had happened that day the world shook? Shifts in the planet's crust was the official government line. The best scientists were studying the problem. The President was monitoring the situation personally.

• • •

It was now noon on the third day.

Thirty-five guests were seated around the oval table in the CIA's subterranean blue room. Sitting in silence, staring at each other, not quite believing that they were actually there, they were leaders of the Home Planets. They all had at least one thing in common: Until very recently, they had awakened every morning with the unwavering belief that their planet was the only world in the star system, the Galaxy, the Universe. That such a tightly held belief was now hopelessly obsolete had come as a great shock. It takes a while for the psyche to finally give itself over to a new reality. That's why no one in the room was talking.

Still, these thirty-five people could not get away from the fact that they were all related to each other. Some were white, some black, some brown, yellow, tan, olive. Their dress was as varied as their names, their titles, their hairdos. Yet they all looked the same. They moved the same. They thought the same things. And though they were reticent now, there had been enough murmuring for them to realize they had something else in common: They all spoke the same language. The universal tongue of the Galaxy. The mother tongue of Earth.

So they *were* connected.

And they were more than neighbors.

They were family.

Gordon ran the meeting.

Hunter, Tomm, and Zarex sat to his left, the six other CIA chiefs sat to his right. The room was ringed with uniformed CIA guards, but all weapons were kept out of sight. The big wall screen was showing a huge graphic of Moon 39 taken from Hunter's always-on viz flight recorder. It looked dark and sinister.

To begin the meeting, Gordon took a cue from the space travelers. He raised his right hand, palm out, thumb extended. The universal sign of peace in the Galaxy.

"Welcome, friends," he said. "It is my job to tell you why you are all here."

They already knew most of the story, but Gordon went through it again anyway. The discovery of Moon 39. The secrets found locked away in the mountains of the American Southwest.

The evidence pointing to Earth's original population being imprisoned here for nearly four thousand years. The faces around the table registered the same emotions all over again: disbelief, denial, anxiety, anger.

When Gordon finished, he simply held his arms out in front of him and said, "I think you'll agree some discussion would be helpful at this point."

That opened the floodgates. Nearly all of the representatives began talking at once. Most had just one question in mind.

"How could the entire population of a planet be sentenced to prison?" someone finally got out. "What crime could possibly call for such a sentence?"

Gordon looked over at Hunter, who was taking a long sip from his whiskey glass. He knew this question was coming.

"You are not criminals," Hunter began. "I don't believe you're in prison because of anything your ancestors did wrong. You're in prison because the people who did this wanted you out of the way. *Way* out of the way. Why? To take over the Earth and thus, an empire. It sounds grandiose, but it's the only explanation. I've told each one of you about my experience in the mind ring. In my opinion, as soon as all those rockets left Earth, that's when the *Second* Empire began. So they are the ones responsible for this. . . ."

Another sip of Seagram's. He swirled the ice cubes around in his glass for a moment.

"Where I came from, the historians will tell you that the First Empire most likely colonized every planet and star system in the Galaxy. Some consider it the greatest of the four empires, even though they know next to nothing about it, nor the other two as well. But one thing is for certain: The First Empire must have been made up of *all* of the peoples of Earth. That means *you* are the remnants of the First Empire. And that means the Galaxy was taken away from you. It means Earth was taken away from you. You were shipped way the hell out here, where no one would ever think to look for you. They built this monstrosity of a star system and then fixed it so your evolutions would crawl along with the speed of a glacier, while the rest of the Galaxy was moving faster than the speed of light. That's very sinister, gentlemen. It's cruel and unusual punishment. And it has to be changed—"

The representative from Planet Germany asked, "You've confirmed that we are locked inside a very elaborate concentration camp—and we have been for centuries. You say there are a million soldiers out there with weapons that will make our heads spin. My friend, how exactly can we change any of that?"

Gordon took over. "The first thing we do is come to an agreement on one major point," he said. "Just for self-preservation alone, no planet can attempt to reach space until the whole situation can be properly assessed. We suggest that when you return home, you tell the facts to your people and warn them that from this moment on, frankly, nothing will ever be the same again. That's really why we brought you here. We uncovered the secret, and we had to tell you. Through our three friends here we had the means to contact you, unorthodox and undetectable as it was. I think everyone in this room would have done the same thing if they were in our position."

There was some discussion, mostly about how best to reveal the facts to the peoples of their individual planets. Each of their worlds had suffered cataclysmic events in their histories, yet none of them had ever figured out why. Now they knew, and as it turned out, nearly two dozen of them had space-launch programs nearing completion. Money, time, and resources had been spent in these endeavors. But in the end, the space-ban agreement just made sense. It really was for everyone's own good.

Eventually, there were handshakes all around, even some embraces. Nothing was ever written down. No language ever formalized. There wasn't even a show of hands for a vote. They just *agreed* with each other. Though the people in the room didn't know it, that was the moment the United Planets was born.

And it was in the next moment that their first crisis arrived.

One representative spoke up. He'd sat stone silent throughout the historic meeting. Even now, his voice was barely above a whisper.

"I believe we might have a problem," he said. "There is a cabal of industrialists on my planet that has been secretly working on an orbital spacecraft for two decades. They call it the Love Rocket. These industrialists are not under my government's control; frankly, they are too big for that. The last I heard, they were ready to launch this spacecraft at any time. Possibly any minute . . ."

Every eye in the room was suddenly burning a hole through this guy. No one wanted to hear this. Seeing one of the Home Planets utterly destroyed would be bad enough. But the unspoken fear was that while one world was getting pulverized by Moon 39, the invaders might somehow get wind that the other planets were hip to what was going on, setting them up for invasion, too.

"Well, surely you can talk them out of it," Gordon told the man now. "Just present them with the evidence and—"

But the man just shook his head. "Even if I could get back to my world in time, I have to tell you that the chances of them heeding my warnings are nil. Even your friends here would find them like a brick wall. These are vainly obstinate men I'm talking about. To them it's all about ego. They wield much more power than my government does, and at this point they would probably try to overthrow us rather than be told they cannot launch. This is arrogance to the nth degree. I realize that. But this space program of theirs is a pure power play. Plus their launch site is so secret, even we have no idea where it is. Trying to find it will take weeks, months even. By that time, they will know we are looking for them, and they'll launch it anyway. I'd almost have to say they will be impossible to stop—"

"The fools!" Pater Tomm suddenly bellowed angrily. "What the hell planet are you from?"

The man just shook his head slowly.

"Planet France," he replied.

18

Moon 39

The noise made by the Event Detection Alarm was so loud, it woke Zenx Xirstix out of a deep sleep.

Xirstix was the supreme commander of the Bad Moon Knights' detachment on Moon 39. His luxurious billet was located more than a half mile from the intelligence center near the hub of the huge military base. Yet lying there in bed, eyes closed, still half asleep, Xirstix could hear the alarm screaming full throat. It was an unexpected way to begin the day. It was a sound he'd been waiting to hear for a long time, yet for some reason, now that it was actually happening, he didn't want to believe it was true.

Xirstix was the highest-ranking officer at the BMK outpost. He was a Star Marshal with seven galactic clusters, a brilliant military officer just 188 years old at last count. He was proud to be serving on the top-secret if very isolated post. It was great for his career advancement. Being in the BMK was all about guts and glory. As commander of more than one million men, Xirstix was in his element. He would be well paid for his services, and at any minute he and his men could be called on to start a blood frenzy on one of the Home Planets. What more could he ask for?

Again by his count, he'd been on Moon 39 for ninety-one years. His successor had been there three times as long and had stomped two of the Home Planets. (He'd died on Moon 39 of old age.) Under Xirstix's command, he'd incessantly schooled his troops on the three necessities of being a BMK space merc: smarts, efficiency, and total ruthlessness. True, they were way out there, beyond the outer limits of the Galaxy, in a place so isolated, he hadn't heard from any of his superiors since the last time the garrison was paid, nearly thirty years ago. But isolation was no reason for soldiers to go slack. To the contrary, he worked them so hard, they were among the finest units in the entire Black Moon Knights organization, a force of mercenaries that numbered some one hundred thirty million strong. Or at least that's what his superiors had told him three decades ago.

At first, Xirstix thought that he was still asleep and dreaming that he heard the Event Detection Alarm go off. He frequently dreamed such things, along with visions of the carnage his corps could cause on the unsuspecting planet below. Or maybe it was another false alarm. There had been a glitch in the system earlier that week; the warning device had gone off unexpectedly, shortly after the satellite experienced a series of minor quakes, not an unusual event for the ancient artificial moon. His technicians never did find the cause of the glitch. But then again, the Event Detection Alarm was the oldest piece of equipment on Moon 39. There was a chance the damn thing was just broken.

So, just go back to sleep. . . . It's not a real alarm. That would be too good to be true.

But then two of his aides burst into his bedroom and informed him that an event *had* been detected on the Home Planets. This was not a false alarm or an unscheduled simulation. One of the worlds below was attempting a space launch. The still-pealing Klaxon in the distance seemed to confirm this.

Xirstix didn't give it another thought. He jumped from his hovering bed, ordered the aides to lay out his best uniform and make ready his sky car.

"But first of all," he told them excitedly, "alert the garrison that this is *not* a drill."

There was already a dozen officers gathered around the Event Detection Alarm when Xirstix arrived at the intelligence center.

He was an imposing figure, six-two, with a cleanly shaved head and matching cheek scars, evidence of a wild and checkered youth. He was dressed in a shimmering combat uniform, shoulder fins and wing projections in place. He always carried not one but two ray guns in a holster tied around his waist. The ray guns were made of reatomized silver. They had cost him a year's salary.

The warning Klaxon was still blaring when Xirstix walked into the central control room. One wave of his hand, and the device fell silent. Those assembled snapped to attention; his officers even added a bow. But he glided past them to speak with the custodian of the usually somnolent event scanner, a lowly tech.

"*Is* this a true reading?" Xirstix asked the soldier.

The man was nervous but confident. "Aye, sir," he told Xirstix. "We have confirmation of a launch, both on instruments and visual, from Planet Thirty-six Minus Eleven."

"That would be Planet France, sir," one of Xirstix's officers whispered in his ear.

Xirstix pushed the toady away from him. He knew each of the Home Planets by name and number, as well as their position around the sun.

"Show me the visual replay of the event," he told the tech.

The man pushed few buttons. The monitor in front of them came alive with a fuzzy aerial shot of the launch site on Planet France. It was located in a thick woods just outside Paris. There were a few dozen people gathered around the heavily camouflaged launch pad. A rocket slowly was rising off the pad.

"Where is this rocket now?" Xirstix asked.

"It's in orbit, sir," the tech replied. "And it appears they may attempt a landing on the system's moon. All they will need is another burn, and they could intercept the moon as it is waxing toward them."

Xirstix could barely contain his excitement. He took a moment to check the scanner numbers himself. Everything was in working order, including the sensor confirming the spacecraft was in orbit. This meant his huge army was about to get a taste of blood.

He turned to his officers and said, "Implement Invasion Plan Alpha-One. I want our lead elements on France in less than two hours."

19

More than a half million men would eventually take part in the invasion of Planet France.

They met little opposition. The BMK had appeared so suddenly and had attacked so quickly, it took just a matter of hours to overwhelm the handful of national police strong points on the near-defenseless planet.

Psychological warfare played an important part in the early going. The BMK's troop shuttles made a horrible noise once they entered the atmosphere; they also appeared as bright, fiery lights during their last stages of entry. On the first night of the attack, the skies above Planet France's largest cities looked like they were raining fireballs. Huge upper atmospheric blasts rocked the planet pole to pole. The population was absolutely terrified. Gigantic, heavily armed aliens were suddenly falling on top of their homes, their schools, their churches. They were carrying very exotic weapons and mowing down anything that moved in the streets. It didn't take long for the planet to go into a collective state of shock.

Of course, this was exactly the reaction the BMK counted on to make the planet's subjugation go that much quicker.

In all, it took just four days, not quite a hundred hours for the invaders to spread out over the countryside and solidify their prize. The planet's tiny national police force had been eliminated; its political leaders tortured, killed, or thrown in prison.

Many of the planet's intellectuals were rounded up and shot; its religious leaders were executed as well. The BMK troops in the cities were encouraged to loot. For any citizen who choose to defy them, ten were executed. Men, women, children, the elderly—no one was immune.

By the fifth day, there was no resistance at all.

On the sixth day, life on Planet France returned to a kind of perverse normality.

The invaders insisted that shopkeepers reopen their stores and essential businesses get back to work. The sidewalk cafés, numerous in every city, were reopened as well. Just about everything looked as it did a week before, except now there were heavily armed space soldiers at every intersection, and the rumors said the entire planet was either being sold into slavery or ground up as food for the brutal, mysterious invaders.

Such talk was running about as thick as the coffee in the city of Le Mans. The invaders didn't like the cuisine, apparently, but business was fine at the sidewalk cafés, busy even, as the newly conquered citizenry met to whisper about what would happen next. In one of these cafés—the *Chez Nous*—sat Hawk Hunter. He was drinking a latte.

He'd arrived during the second day of the invasion, at the height of its intensity. The jump over from Planet America had taken almost an hour, and he'd been forced to enter this atmosphere high and slow, just like his reentries on PA. This meant an anxious ten minutes of descent, much of which he spent dodging the rain of BMK invasion craft still descending on the planet. The slow reentry gave him an opportunity to see the destruction the invaders had wrought. Every major city was in flames. Frightened citizens jammed the roadways, trying to flee the nightmare from space. Mass graves . . .

He'd set down just outside of Le Mans, folded the flying machine into his Twenty 'n Six, and then walked into the city, wearing the clothes of an American farmer as his disguise. The rumpled shirt and frayed pants fit in perfectly with the people numbly walking the streets. Le Mans had been one of the first cities to fall, and by the time Hunter got there, most of the pillage had subsided. He'd found this café open for business, had taken a table in the corner, and had not moved for almost twenty-four hours. The waiters paid him little mind; they just kept the lattes coming and accepted his very PA-looking coins as payment. It was the perfect spy post.

Though more than five hundred thousand troops were down on Planet France, everything Hunter needed to know about the invaders he could tell just from watching the four BMK soldiers standing guard at the nearby intersection. They were wearing old Zanker suits, bulky, ribbed, bubble-top garbs first introduced almost a thousand years before. The bubble helmets had been tinted black, as had the rest of the suit, making the BMK soldiers look anonymous and frightening at the same time.

These soldiers did not appear happy. Not that every occupying force was required to maintain cruel smiles all day long, but these guys were miserable. It was soon evident why. In all the time Hunter had watched them, the soldiers had been given no downtime, no meal break. He'd spotted them popping wrist injections occasionally, essentially doping themselves against hunger and fatigue. A telling sign.

Despite stern appearances, the BMK was not an army that adapted well to occupation duties. They were killers and not suited for anything else. What's more, just watching this foursome, Hunter could tell the invading forces were stretched thin. Since all of the major fighting had already ceased, it would have seemed that at least some front-line troops would have been called back to the city for relief, but that was not the case here in Le Mans.

Reports from other major cities were just about the same. Hunter had managed to carry a squad of CIA men in his Twenty 'n Six with him on this journey. They had fanned out across the landmass, infiltrating the major cities and gathering intelligence on the invaders. The picture they drew was the same as what Hunter saw before him. The BMK shock troops had been brutal during the first phase of the invasion, lazy and sullen once the action had died down. Few would actually be involved in the genocide of the population, scheduled to begin soon. That job was given to special units of soldiers whose superiors had attained favor with Xirstix.

For most of these grunts then, the killing spree was over. From here on out, they were just marking time, just doing a job.

Hunter drained the last of his fifteenth latte and ordered one more for the road.

He'd seen all he needed to. It was time to start picking up his CIA colleagues for the trip back to America. A real war was coming. It would not be fought here on Planet France. This place was lost as soon as the Love Rocket reached orbit. But the war would take place somewhere else; that was a foregone conclusion. And Hunter knew who the enemy would be. Four of them were standing no more than one hundred feet away from him, sweating in their ancient Zanker suits, looking tired, bored, and dopey. The problem was, they were ruthless in battle, and there were more than a million of them. Not real good numbers against planets that literally had no armies, no military equipment, no technology of flight. There were only forty thousand cops in all of America. They were the closest thing to an army the planet had. Hunter wondered if the cops had tried to defend the planet the last time the BMK came calling. He wondered how long such a defense lasted.

But even that could not change what was about to come. There was only one thing worse than allowing the BMK to have its way with the Home Planets; that was not challenging them at all. Knowing what he did now about the circumstances that brought the army of thugs down on Planet France, Hunter vowed to fight them to the death, alone, if he had to. That's how strongly he felt about it. But not only would those odds be overwhelming, he would have to fight this impending conflict with clipped wings because of the two-second problem. If just several short bursts of full ultraoverdrive had caused near devastation on America and (as he now knew) around the entire system, how could he possibly operate against the BMK in the stormy days ahead? In some ways, he had the capacity to cause more destruction than they did.

He'd done some calculations. As he wasn't so sure just how fast his machine could go in full ultraoverdrive, he picked a small fraction—.007—and then set his throttle to go no higher than that number. From now on, his only choice was to fly at about .007 full power, hoping that would cause only .007 the disruption.

But traveling at that fraction, while still very quick, would also mean a big change in the rules. He wouldn't be able to fly ahead of himself and become invisible. He wouldn't be able to appear in two places at once. There would be no chance to destroy the entire BMK fleet as he did the death star's space fighters. There would be no twenty-second sorties like the one he'd flown against the enemy troops on Tonk.

No, bumping down to .007 would be like flying with his air brakes on. And it actually went deeper than that. It made him a lot more human in this place. A superhero who wasn't so super anymore. He would have to make up for that somehow. He knew there were worse things than just being human. He would use his human instincts, his brains, his guile, instead of speed. He would have to figure out how best to hit this enemy, how to fool him. Confuse him. Suck him in. That's what this trip to conquered France was all about. He knew the enemy better now.

He knew something else, too.

Whatever was to come, it was going to be very down and dirty.

20

Pater Tomm was waiting for Hunter when he returned to Andrews Field.

These flights in and out of the isolated field were routine now. Lately, his only welcoming committee had been a black tinted van and a tight-lipped CIA driver. But this time, the priest was on hand, along with some CIA medical personnel to check out the infiltration squad that had accompanied Hunter to the conquered French planet.

The agents had survived their journey back and forth inside the Twenty 'n Six with just a few bumps and bruises; they were loaded into one van, which departed immediately. Hunter folded his plane up and joined Tomm at the second vehicle.

"Was it as bad as we envisioned?" the priest asked, handing him a flask of Seagram's.

"Worse," Hunter replied, taking a healthy slug of the whiskey. He loved the way it burned going down his throat.

"Gordon has arranged a huge meeting," Tomm told him. "They are expecting your report. I fear you will have no good news to tell them."

Hunter took another drink from the flask. "I don't think there will be anything resembling good news for a very long time, Father."

"Well, there is one unusual thing," Tomm told him cautiously. "I was able to talk to the individual representatives from the other Home Planets before you took them home. I checked with Gordon, too, on the damage reports caused that day you went off to recon the sentinel moons. A very odd circumstance has emerged."

Hunter felt his whole body sag. The devastation he'd caused that day throughout the system, though unwittingly, had haunted him ever since. Damage could be repaired, and injuries could heal, but he alone was responsible for the lives that had been lost.

"That's just it," Tomm said, reading his mind. "I checked Gordon's damage report and those of the thirty-five other planets. It's very curious—"

Hunter took a third swig from the flask. "Are you saying you now know how many people I killed that day?"

Tomm had a strange twinkle in his eye. "Yes, I do," he replied. "None."

Hunter stared back at him, the flask halfway to his lips for a fourth time.

"None?"

Tomm nodded. "There were injuries, and there was destruction, but no deaths. Not a single soul lost."

Hunter was dumbfounded. The aftereffects of his time shifting within the time bubble had been catastrophic. He'd seen a lot of the destruction himself. He'd thought the death toll would be in the thousands.

"But how, Padre?" was all he could say.

Tomm just shook his head. "Do you believe in miracles, my son?"

Relief was swelling inside Hunter's chest. It seemed impossible that everyone in the entire system had survived the bout with reversed time. Yet miracles were essentially the impossible coming true. But could that be the only explanation?

"Miracles? I don't know, Father," Hunter finally replied. "That's your department."

The CIA blue room was crowded.

The place had been built big for a reason, but never with this many people in mind.

They were called simply the Space Crisis Group. A hastily picked collection of American government, scientific, religious, and law enforcement bigwigs, they were close to four hundred in all. They'd been whisked here under the tightest security and briefed individually or in small groups by Gordon's people. Then they'd been introduced to Hunter, Zarex, and Tomm and told where the spacemen had come from. They'd been given a demonstration of the spacemen's exotic technology, from losing things into a Twenty 'n Six to seeing Hunter's flying machine make its dramatic entrance. Even the clanker 33418 was finally brought out of the twenty-sixth to show his remarkable talents. Zarex was very relieved to have him back at his side.

All this had been done to convince those assembled very quickly that there was no question that the three visitors *were* from outer space and that they had discovered a grave threat to the people of Planet America and on the other Home Planets as well.

The oval table had been replaced with a smaller one, and a stage had been erected in front of the room's big screen. Five people were sitting at this table: Gordon, the President, Hunter, Zarex, and Tomm. The Space Crisis Group was sitting as an audience in many squeaky folding chairs. Armed guards ringed the room.

The meeting was called to order. Gordon explained now that the team had been briefed on the Moon 39 problem, it was time to talk about how best to prepare the planet should there be an invasion from space. This would be no easy task. Up until two weeks ago, the planet didn't even know what a war was, never mind having a military to fight one.

Gordon gave the microphone over to Hunter. He briefed the crisis team on his spy mission to Planet France. Then he proceeded to drop a bombshell.

"I don't know who," he began, "but someone once said the best defense is a good offense. Once the BMK has finished with Planet France, they will go back to Moon 39, and just as long as Planet America doesn't launch any spacecraft, things will be as they always were. There will be peace, and life will go on. But it certainly won't be *real* peace. That only comes when people are truly free. Free to make up their own minds on where they want their culture to go. If we do nothing, the people of this planet will have everything except what they need the most: the freedom to leave. To go out into the Galaxy. To expand to new horizons.

"These things will never happen unless the BMK is confronted. We are the only ones who can do it. It won't be easy. They outnumber us many times over, and even with help from the other Home Planets, the numbers will always be in their favor. Yet I believe it has to be done. And done now."

That's when someone in back—a cop—stood up and shouted, "My question is: Why are we Americans suddenly taking advice from a bunch of freaks?"

Someone else piped up, "How do we know that *they* aren't in cahoots with these space invaders? They're from outer space, too. They probably all stick together."

Gordon angrily leapt to the spacemen's defense. He began ticking off the contributions they had made—especially Hunter—during the search for truth on Moon 39. But Hunter just lifted his hand, politely cutting Gordon off.

The room got very silent. Hunter stared into his whiskey glass. These were good questions that had been asked. He would have felt uneasy had someone not asked them.

"There was a time not too long ago," he began, "when I thought I would never know where I came from. It's a strange thing, not being able to call someplace your home. I think there is something very human about it. We all need someplace to be from. Now, I will probably never know how I wound up here, in this time and space. But I do know one thing: I believe there is a reason that I came *here*—to America and the Home Planets. I believe that I am *supposed* to be here."

He stopped and contemplated his whiskey glass for a few more seconds. An absolute hush had come over the room.

He went on, "I don't know any other way to explain it other than I *feel* that I am an American. I feel it in my bones. I think that's what drove me across billions of miles of space just to get here. In a way, I've been called home. Not to this place. This system isn't anyone's *real* home. This is our home in exile. Our real home is Earth . . . the center of the Galaxy. Someone back there owes us an explanation as to why the original Americans were sent here. If that means using force to find out the truth, then I think that's the way it has to be. That's just the *American* way of doing things."

More silence. No one moved. No one spoke—for at least a minute.

Finally someone said, "All right then, at least tell us your plan."

Hunter resisted draining what was left of his drink and started gnawing on his lip instead. Yes, he had a plan. It involved a huge gamble, and it wouldn't be pretty. But if they worked quickly, they might be able to let the BMK know that they were going to have to earn their money. No more rolling over. No more bolts out of the blue.

"The first thing we have to do," Hunter began. "Is to start a massive Civil Defense program, especially in our major cities. I will have to leave that to your expertise."

Hunter then asked Gordon to use the screen behind them to display the shot of the American rocket still on the launch pad at the secret base out west, the place called Groom Lake. In a bit of cruel humor, someone in the know had painted the words "Love Rocket Number 2" on its fuselage.

Many of the people in the room were unaware of the rocket's existence. But everyone on hand knew the ramifications of attempting a space launch.

That's why a gasp went through the room when Hunter finally said, "And the second thing we do is launch that rocket."

21

The BMK ships arrived in orbit around America the next day.

Xirstix himself had led the invasion force in. Having controlled the campaign on France from the comfort of his living quarters—as his superiors had instructed him to do so long ago—he'd quickly grown restless, being so far away from the action. When Planet America launched a spacecraft of its own, it came as a pleasant surprise for him. It meant more money, more glory, more blood for his men. And this time, because BMK was now in a two-world war, Xirstix would run things from the battlefield itself.

The trouble started right away though. Three hundred forty-nine troop shuttles left Moon 39. Twenty-seven didn't make it in.

A strange spacecraft had hit them four times on the three-hour voyage. The mysterious craft would suddenly show up, weave its way through the formation, hitting targets, before blinking out again. They had no idea who was operating the craft and worse, they had no way to shoot back at it. The troop shuttles carried no defensive weapons. Losing twenty-seven ships—and twenty-seven thousand men—was a blow to the invasion force. Not a fatal one. But as there was no way to know where and when the enemy craft was going to show up again, the attacks put everyone in the fleet on edge.

A second blow was received shortly after the invasion force reached America's orbit. There would be no troops coming over from Planet France. Why? Because the same mysterious spacecraft had attacked dozens of targets on that planet as well. In one stroke, the unknown attacker had altered Xirstix's entire battle strategy. No occupation troops could be moved off France. The genocide squads could not get their work started, because the troops they needed for gathering the population together for extermination had to be moved closer to the cities as the attacker had chosen to hit the most isolated outposts of the BMK on France.

So, Attack Force Delta—the force heading for America—would have to go it alone, at least in the beginning.

This infuriated Xirstix. He'd expected a problem-free cruise in toward Planet America, just as the invasion of France had been. He was counting on getting his troops on to the new battlefield in a good frame of mind—they were second-echelon soldiers, the first line was on France—and many had never seen action before. Now, with the mysterious attacks, any hope of a replay of France had been lost.

Who had attacked them? Xirstix was absolutely at a loss for an answer. There was no one else out here except the Home Planets and the sentinel moons, and no one on the prison worlds even knew how to fly. The first indications were that the attacker had come from Planet America, but how could a planet who'd just barely put an elementary rocket into space now have a weapon of such mind-boggling power? And if it was from America, why was it attacking targets on Planet France?

It didn't make sense. But there was no turning back now. Xirstix knew he had to face facts: Nearly half the force he thought he'd be controlling was no longer available. They would be tied up, doing nothing but keeping their heads down, seventeen million miles away.

Xirstix's original plan was to concentrate on Planet America's ten largest cities including New York, Chicago, and Los Angeles. He had planned to do this with the troops of Attack Force Delta. The troops from Planet France he wanted to use in a different way. He'd been expecting two hundred fifty attack craft from Planet France. Each one was to be assigned a smaller city or town on America to land in. This was to be done purely for psychological reasons. It was important in Xirstix's mind that in addition to big battles in the big cities, the countryside had to be frozen, bloodied, paralyzed with fear as well. He wanted it to appear as if the alien invaders were falling from the sky *everywhere*.

This important part of his strategy was now in jeopardy. Xirstix couldn't spare the troops of his own force to perform this key tactic; he couldn't cut himself short of soldiers that might actually do some fighting. His psych-war troops were just supposed to frighten the bumpkins and, in a best-case scenario, those bumpkins would simply submit as soon as the invaders showed up and word spread that the invasion of the planet was total and complete.

Now, looking down on Planet America, Xirstix made a fateful decision. He wouldn't send any troops into the countryside. He would use all of his three hundred twenty-two remaining craft to carry out the invasion in the cities alone.

It was clear weather around Planet America when the invasion began. It was just before dawn on the East Coast.

The fiery trails made by the BMK craft across the morning sky could be seen for miles. They caused multiple sonic booms coming in, plus the attack craft themselves had their propulsion units rigged to make as much noise as possible coming through the atmosphere. Once down, the spacecraft were designed to emit strange and eerie sounds, again heightening the frightening aspect of it all.

The first BMK units on the ground were the fleet's shock troops. They wore battle gear that was designed to cause fear and look invincible. Their suits were really part combat uniform, part robotics-assisted devices or RADs. They gave the wearer at least six inches in further height, topped off by a massive battle helmet that gave the illusion of yet another six inches. The battle suit made sizzling, mechanical noises whenever they moved.

The shock troops carried blaster rifles programmed to make heavily amplified noises when fired. Even their ray-gun side arms had been cranked, that is, their beams were brighter, their report louder.

At seven A.M. local time, thirty-two shock troop craft came down in New York City. Xirstix's own personal craft joined them soon after.

• • •

The BMK were professional invaders. Though the army based on Moon 39 was serving under very unusual circumstances, their training essentially remained the same. Fight in the big cities, take out key spots, then spread terror in the countryside. It was a formula that had worked for their peers many times across the Fringe. It was the strategy that had worked just two weeks before on Planet France. There was really no reason why it should not work here.

There were a dozen key objectives the BMK shock troops had to secure in New York City. They included the port, the main TV and radio antennae, and every tunnel and bridge leading in or out of Manhattan. If there was to be any fighting, it would take place at these locations. Usually, the first two hours of an invasion were the most violent. Yet, just twenty minutes after the BMK force had set down, these key objectives had already been taken. More troops landed, and within an hour, the city was declared secured. Casualties to the invading forces were zero. In fact, not a shot was even fired.

This was because there had been absolutely no opposition. The city was empty.

Xirstix had found this news so unbelievable, he took a tour of the city south of Central Park. Gliding along in an ornate sky car, nearly a thousand specially trained combat guards surrounding him, he went up and down every street and alley along both rivers and flew to the tops of the tallest buildings. Long robes flowing, wearing full battle dress from head to toe, it took two hours of Xirstix rushing here and there to convince him that the city was indeed deserted.

What's more, reports coming in from two other landing sites—Boston and Philadelphia—said the same thing. The cities were empty; there had been absolutely no resistance.

How could this be? Xirstix wondered. It was almost as if the people of the planet knew the BMK were coming.

Then it hit him: the mysterious attacker, who had shot down twenty-seven of his shuttles coming in and had attacked BMK targets on Planet France. There had to be a connection. But again, how could a planet that was just barely able to get a rudimentary craft into orbit have such an awesome weapon at its disposal?

Then word arrived that Chicago was not found to be empty.

In fact, the planet's defenders had been waiting for Xirstix's craft and had even shot two of them down.

The news was almost as unbelievable as the lack of fighting in New York.

Xirstix rushed back to his command ship and immediately headed west.

Arriving in Chicago ten minutes later, Xirstix found the situation was near total chaos.

The reports had indicated that Chicago was not a deserted city as New York had been, but this was not entirely accurate. Chicago was indeed empty of a population for Xirstix to conquer, but it was thick with defenders, well-armed fighters apparently made up from the city's police force.

And the reports of two shuttlecraft being shot down—that had been inaccurate, too. It had been *four* shuttles, and they hadn't been shot down by anyone on the ground. The mystery spacecraft had done it.

The first thing Xirstix noticed after arriving over the city was the large number of smoke plumes rising above it. Curiously, these plumes were forming a series of near-perfect concentric rings, each one getting closer to the center of the city. Hovering now just above the lakefront, Xirstix asked his ground commanders why there were rings of smoke around the city. The reply was that the BMK troops were chasing the defenders into an ever-tightening noose; they were retreating toward the center of the city.

The moment he heard that, Xirstix knew something was wrong.

Defenders *never* retreated to the center of a city; the tactic didn't make sense. A retreating force should want to get *out* of an encircled city, not stay within it. Enraged but also uncertain, Xirstix directed his command craft to go right up to the front line of the ongoing urban battle.

His commanders were astonished to see him, of course. The streets around the Loop were littered with bodies and the sudden wreckage of war. The trouble was, the vast majority of the bodies were BMK troops. Many had been taken down by well-hidden ambush nests, dying two or three at a time after being caught in the middle of deadly cross fire in the narrow streets.

Xirstix was furious at the losses the invading forces had suffered.

"But the enemy is retreating," one of his street commanders told him. "We have them on the run."

Then came a report that the last of the defenders had been cornered in a huge sports arena downtown. Xirstix demanded to be taken to the site immediately. Under the nervous eyes of his security troops, he was whisked to the site.

He found his troops had surrounded the arena but that they were also in disarray. The streets were littered with hundreds more dead BMK troops. Most of his soldiers were simply waiting behind cover. Xirstix ordered a unit of sappers to blast holes in the building where the defenders had gone, but again he knew something was wrong. These defenders were a little more savvy than it appeared. Why would they be foolish enough to retreat to a building that the BMK could pulverize in a matter of seconds?

When the BMK troops finally broke into the arena, they found out why. In the middle of the large sports hall there was a large area of distorted air; it looked like a mirage, shimmering, light waves bending as if in a wind.

And enemy troops were running headlong into this distortion and disappearing.

"Shoot at them!" Xirstix screamed at his troops who were standing dumbfounded by what they were seeing.

But it was already too late.

All of the enemy soldiers had escaped.

Meanwhile, the BMK invaders who landed in St. Louis were facing the stiffest fighting of the day.

Twenty-six invasion craft had rained down on the riverside city. Unlike those troops landing in the big cities farther east, this force did not split up into separate forward units. Instead, they landed, en masse, on a huge athletic field and the parking lots surrounding it, just outside the city. This change in orders was the direct result of reports coming in from New York and Chicago. "St. Louis is probably filled with defenders," Xirstix's command staff were telling them. "They know you are coming. Set down in force, assemble, then storm the city immediately."

But the new orders also gave the St. Louis invasion commanders an extra bit of intelligence. If the enemy fights a withdrawing action, no matter how aggressive, pursue at all costs. Identify an arena or auditorium closest to the center of the city and capture it. It is here the enemy will probably be retreating to.

That's what had happened in New York and Chicago. That's exactly what happened here.

The BMK force, twenty-six thousand strong, entered the city and was immediately laid upon by machine guns and snipers. Hundreds of shooters were entrenched within the cluttered urban setting, hitting hard, then quickly retreating. The invaders pressed on, three mobile Master Blasters in their possession. Firing massive blaster rounds on a methodical basis, they took each block in their march forward by simply eliminating everything on and around it.

Within twenty minutes, they had cut a one-mile swath right through the city, finding no citizens except the hundreds who were shooting back at them. Their advance scout units found a large sports arena located not far away from the creeping front line. The BMK unit commanders relentlessly pushed the troops now. Their casualties were already over 50 percent, but soon they were just a block away from the saucer-shaped sports arena. And sure enough, they could see hundreds of the armed defenders running into the huge building. The plan had worked. The BMK commanders giddily ordered their Master Blasters to take aim on the arena.

Then the BMK commanders got a strange order: Stop and remain in place.

Why? The answer arrived overhead a moment later. Like a huge storm cloud, it blotted out the morning sun. It was Xirstix's private command ship. He was here to ruin the party.

The command ship landed in the street next to the sports arena. All of the firing from the defenders had ceased by now. Several thousand of the enemy fighters were inside the building. All the exits were blocked.

A small army of Xirstix's own highly trained security troops poured out of his command ship. They were twice as big and carried twice as many weapons as the standard BMK trooper. They took a few minutes to assemble, then Xirstix himself came bounding down the ramp. He was wearing an enormous battle suit as well, one with huge wings attached to its back and a pair nearly as large flaring off his helmet. The entire outfit was made of highly polished gold.

Xirstix took stock of the situation, used his baton to give the original invasion commanders a flippant salute, then ordered his own troops to rush the arena. They did this, some by blowing huge holes into the side of the structure, others by simply using the massive power provided by their battle suits to literally walk through its walls, leaving a hole ten by ten in their wake.

Sure enough, there was a small cluster of enemy troops on the floor of the place. A wall of gunfire met the special BMK troops once they'd punched inside. Many of the elite soldiers were killed instantly. Just as in Chicago (and they would learn later, New York City), the defenders were disappearing into a large field of shimmering air. But by this time, the BMK had figured out this was a Twenty 'n Six field portal, a large entry-way into the twenty-sixth dimension created by bonding four of the devices together.

There were a hundred or so defenders left when the BMK troops broke in. They doubled their firing, and the sharp gunfight became even more extreme. Suddenly, the inside of the arena was filled with ricocheting bullets, many that could penetrate the BMK armor if they hit the right spot.

Despite the fusillade, Xirstix burst his own way into the building. He had a sonic amplifying device attached to the mouth-piece of his helmet so when he spoke, his voice would take on a frightening, shrill sound. Raising his protective visor now, he screamed for his troops to forget about killing the defenders, just capture the Twenty 'n Six portal before the last soldier stepped through and it disappeared. Only then could the BMK troops continue their pursuit.

But the invaders had taken just a bit too much time preening outside the arena. Though the battle was fierce, the defenders were jumping through the portal faster than the BMK soldiers could fight their way down to get at them. Once Xirstix realized this, he let out a bloodcurdling wail.

It was strange what happened next. Just as the last defender was about to step through the empty space, he turned, aimed his rifle at Xirstix, and fired a single round.

The bullet caught Xirstix in full bellow, right between the eyes.

He was dead before he hit the floor.

22

With the death of Xirstix, a subcommander named Lax
Deaux became head of the BMK invasion forces.

Deaux was Xirstix's cousin; that was the only reason he held
any rank at all in the BMK. Essentially Xirstix's gofer, Deaux
knew nothing about military tactics or strategy or philosophy.
He had no idea of the BMK's order of battle, nor was he privy
to the invasion's plan for world conquest. The commander's
death and the failure of any unit from Planet France to deploy
landed the job right in Deaux's lap. Appropriately enough, he
was asleep while on duty at the time.

Deaux had spent most of his 101-year career holo-whoring,
eating, drinking, and sleeping, in that order. Though only five
and a half feet tall, he weighed a hefty three hundred pounds,
not an ounce of which he carried well. Those who knew him
swore he didn't know which end of a Master Blaster to aim or
which end of an electron torch was up. He'd had a modest staff
of three for nearly fifty years, and he still didn't know their first
names. That was Lax Deaux, a very dim bulb in a very bright
part of the Galaxy.

He was now in charge of nearly a million men.

No sooner had Xirstix's body been placed inside a crude ceremonial rocket and shot out of the atmosphere and into the
nearby sun, when the invasion's field commanders huddled
around Deaux in what was now his command vehicle, trying to

get him up to speed in a hurry at this very critical point in the invasion.

They explained that the American defenders were highly trained guerrilla troops, hitting the BMK at times and places of their choosing and refusing to stand still and make battle. They told him about enemy troops vanishing into Twenty 'n Six field portals and how in the battles in the big cities so far, all the enemy troops knew where to retreat because everyone knew where the city's sports arena was.

Deaux's only knowledge of Twenty 'n Six technology was that it was related in some way to how holo-girls were produced. (They were actually distantly related.) It took the officers nearly two hours to explain to him how the enemy soldiers were able to jump through a screen and literally disappear from the battlefield. Deaux just didn't get it. He just kept asking the same idiotic questions over and over again.

But sometimes idiots open their mouths, and pure genius comes out. That's almost what happened here.

When the briefing finally ended, Deaux simply sat back in his oversized commander's chair and began chewing on his fingernails. "Where do these enemy troops go when they pass through the portal?" he asked.

His officers all shrugged. "No one knows, sir," one explained. "That is the mystery of the twenty-sixth dimension."

Deaux smiled. He had awful teeth.

"I guess what I mean is, where do the enemy troops return to?" he said. "They're obviously returning to this dimension at some other location, a gathering point perhaps?"

The officers all nodded.

"And we can probably expect that they will continue this tactic?" Deaux asked, his first time ever using the word. "Withdrawing to a hiding place of sorts until they can hit us again—and then escape again?"

"True, sir . . ."

Deaux stopped chewing his nails for a moment.

"Well, we must simply find that hiding place then," he said matter-of-factly. "Locate the other side to their Twenty 'n Six field portal, and you may well have them by the throats. Am I right?"

The commanders grudgingly agreed.

"How do we find such a place, sir?" one asked. "This landmass is actually quite large; it stretches right around the planet. It has many, many places in which to hide, especially in the lands west of us. To march out into that vast expanse and try to smoke them out would be a serious task. It might take weeks, and we could never really be sure that we were any closer to their return station."

Deaux bit his nails some more.

"Then send the shuttle crafts out to look for it," he said suddenly. "Draw a hundred men from our advance scouting units for each vehicle, and dispatch them to the countryside. The unit that finds the enemy's return station will be handsomely rewarded with pay raises and elevations in rank. I'm sure such a distortion in the transdimensional fabric can be picked up by some fancy piece of equipment we own. Am I right?"

The commanders all nodded again.

"Then hook them up to the shuttles. Form a grid, and assign each shuttle a square, maybe a hundred miles by a hundred miles. If one of them detects the distorted dimensional field, we can rush the rest of our forces to the spot and crush the enemy to bits."

He looked at his officers.

"Am I correct?" he asked them.

Though they tried, they had no real reason to say no.

"You are correct, sir," one replied, a change in tone betraying a hint of toadyism as well. "In fact, you are *very* correct."

23

The BMK didn't invade Washington, D.C.

Had the original Delta Attack plan worked, then the city would have been swept up by the invaders once New York and Philadelphia had been taken. But when the focus of the battle shifted west, first to Chicago and then to St. Louis, D.C. remained unconquered.

Downtown was empty. Houses, offices, government buildings, the streets themselves, all deserted. Like those people in the other major cities, the population had been evacuated a long time ago.

But the city was still the capital of America. And it was still in American hands.

Tomm and Zarex had stayed behind in the bunker beneath Weather Mountain, along with Gordon and a small army of essential CIA agents. The hope was to hang onto the city for as long as possible but to evacuate if and when the BMK arrived.

By this time, both Tomm and Zarex had their own CIA aides, their own van and van driver. On this night, about twenty-four hours after the first invasion craft streaked overhead, Tomm talked his driver into taking him into the city itself. It was close to three A.M., and the streets were absolutely still. Tomm directed his driver to head for the national cathedral. On arrival, he told the driver to pull around to the back of the big church and kill the engine. Tomm got out, ducked into the shadows, and picked the same lock he had his first trip to the city. Silently, he slipped inside.

It was pitch black inside the massive cathedral. Tomm let his eyes adapt to the darkness as best he could. He had good night vision from all his years of flying in space, but this place seemed extra dark. He studied the altar, the walls, and the ceiling. He walked forward and started searching through the pews. Every once in a while he thought he detected a movement here, a glint of light there, but it always turned out to be his mortal mind playing tricks on him. He was not going to find what he was looking for by eyesight alone.

So he walked to the center of the center aisle and sat down on the very cold floor. Legs crossed, his hands up to his ears, he closed his eyes and began to listen.

It was hard to say just how much time went by. A few minutes? Twenty? A half hour? But then, finally, Tomm heard something. Off to his right, maybe about thirty feet away, in a pew up near the altar. He concentrated on the sound for a few moments, then smiled.

It was the sound of someone snoring.

Just what he was here for.

Tomm carefully regained his feet and started walking toward the sound. It was a light, hushed breathing. Even. Perfectly rhythmic. No surprise there.

He reached the pew and looked down. Below him, cuddled up tightly, snoring away, was a small white form.

"Typical . . ." Tomm murmured.

He reached beneath his collar and took out the brass cross he always kept hanging there. With its longest point, he reached down and gently jabbed the sleeping form. It stirred a bit but kept on snoring.

"It's not as if they've been working so hard," Tomm mumbled again.

He poked the form once more, and this time there was some more movement. It turned over, stretched, and went right back to snoring.

Finally, Tomm put his cross away and shook the form with his hand. Now there was a sudden flash of movement and bright light. In an instant, Tomm found a horrible, drooling, pus-filled face snarling and snorting not an inch from his nose. Tomm steeled himself and swatted the face away. There was another flash. Now a huge set of mechanical teeth snapped at him. Again, Tomm just pushed it away.

"Open yer eyes," Tomm yelled, his voice echoing around the empty church. "I don't have all day for you."

Tomm saw two large eyes appear in the darkness. Wide, dazed, but not the slightest bit frightened.

It was the poof.

"You . . . again?" she asked Tomm.

By the glow of the eyes, Tomm could see the poof as it really was. Not a hellion or a banshee, not quite a jester or a beatific vision. The poof looked mostly like a young, teenage girl. She was pretty, not glamorous, plainly dressed in a short tunic and white tights, her hair pulled all the way back to reveal slightly pointed ears.

The poof was miffed that she had been disturbed. "What are you doing here? How did you find me?"

Tomm just waved these questions away.

"The people of this planet are in trouble," Tomm told the poof. "And I know that you know what that means. If they are in trouble, then the Galaxy, the whole Universe, all of Nature is in trouble."

The poof wearily rubbed her eyes. "So?"

"So you have to help them," Tomm told her. "Them, and all the people in this star system."

She yawned. "What makes you think I would want to?"

"You helped us before," Tomm told her. "In fact, you've been helping us all along."

"I'm sorry." She sighed. "Whatever happens in the normal course of human events, I cannot affect, or—"

Tomm raised his hand and silenced her in midsentence. Her eyes were glowing brighter now. So were his.

"Please, we don't have time for that," he said. "I'm sure you can recite that 'normal course of human events' stuff in your sleep. But I know better. Did you really think nobody would notice that *no one* lost their lives when this system started shaking the other day? My dear, *you are* the normal course of human events."

She smiled, but she was still annoyed. "You seem to be an expert on me," she said. "Why? Just because you're a priest?"

Tomm looked her straight in her huge, glowing eyes.

"No, my dear," he said slowly. "It's because I know what you are."

24

Plain of Stars, East Wyoming

It was a shuttle craft known only as #555 that finally located the elusive American base.

The shuttle had been scouring its eleventh search pattern in forty-eight hours when they reached a place called Fire Rock Ridge just after dawn on the sixth morning of the invasion. Their dimensional distortion detection device had commenced beeping slowly as soon as they passed over the place. Something was affecting the natural dimensional fabric, something very close by.

The shuttle set down about five hundred feet from the lip of the ridge. The hundred special troops disembarked along with the crew and quickly made their way up to the edge of the cliff.

What lay below them was the vast expanse of Ghost River Valley. Long and flat, it stretched unbroken from north to south and beyond the horizon. This part of the valley was known as the Plain of Stars. To the west, not two miles away, was the foot of the Medicine Bow mountain range. Located about half-way between those mountains and Fire Rock Ridge, hidden inside a deep thicket of woods, was a huge military encampment.

Studying the base through long-range viz scopes, the scouts saw many structures, built low to the ground, constructed of melted wood and stone. Their roofs were covered with dirt and tree branches, blending them almost perfectly into the tiny, narrow forest. Barracks, gun emplacements, ammo dumps—the base was also hidden behind a wall of earthen fortifications, one that ran parallel to the western bank of the Ghost River and stretched for miles in every direction. The scouts estimated the encampment housed about fifteen thousand fighters. They had no electron-based weaponry, or at least none the scouts could see. Flying from a crudely cut post located in the middle of the camp was a flag of stars and stripes, colored red, white, and blue.

The scouts were ecstatic. The flag was enough proof for them. They called back to BMK headquarters in St. Louis and issued a one-sentence report: "We have found the enemy."

It was six A.M.

Twenty miles behind Fire Rock Ridge, in the next river valley over, advance elements of the BMK ground forces were approaching from the east.

The largest of these was a motorized artillery column; towing twelve Master Blaster arrays with a fleet of HVVs, a type of military hovercraft that rode a cushion of air about three feet thick.

Intentionally trailing behind the scout shuttles, this column was scheduled to reach the Ghost River area around ten that morning. But then the convoy's commanders learned that the enemy camp had been found just up ahead. This resulted in an acceleration of their original orders.

Their new instructions came right from Deaux's command staff itself. The artillerymen were told to get the twelve Master Blasters up on Fire Rock Ridge as quickly as possible. They were to set up and be ready to fire no later than nine A.M.

One hundred seventy-two miles behind them, was the main element of the BMK's Army Central. Two hundred ninety-four thousand men, they were equipped with heavily armored HVVs and several dozen smaller, single-tube blaster arrays.

They had occupied the city of North Platte, Nebraska, just the day before. The city and the surrounding area had been evacuated nearly a week before they'd arrived.

Having maneuvered west from St. Louis four days into the invasion, Army Central had not been in place in North Platte more than twenty hours when news of finding the American camp arrived. Stopping such a massive force had been no easy task. North Platte could hold fifty thousand people tops; at nearly six times that number, it had been a tight squeeze finding places to sleep and do chow all around. Getting the huge army up and moving again would be just as difficult.

When word reached the Army Central's commanders that the enemy's hidden camp was so close by—actually 190 miles to the west—the first reaction was surprise. They'd expected the crafty enemy to choose a location much more difficult to find. Perhaps among the mountains of the continental divide several hundred miles farther west.

Never did they expect the enemy to make a stand on the long, unprotected plain of the Ghost River Valley. What had just the day before seemed to be turning into a long, drawn-out, tiring affair now took on the light of an early finish. Vanquishing an underequipped, crudely formed enemy force many times less its size was a picture-perfect scenario for Army Central's field commanders.

Like all mercs, they liked their battles to be quick, bloody, and final.

Two hundred miles to the southeast of Ghost River Valley, the BMK Army South was moving along the banks of the Green Tree River.

They, too, had received word of the enemy's location and now excitement was firing through the troops. Though the southern force was only one hundred thousand men, just a third of the Central force, many of the South's soldiers were mountainous terrain fighters. If the Central Army hit the enemy line full force, any enemy troops that survived would undoubtedly flee into the mountains beyond. Army South was perfectly suited to pursue these retreating troops and in essence, slaughter them in the hills.

The BMK South commanders didn't even wait for orders from BMK HQ. They began moving north toward the enemy with great haste.

Back at BMK HQ, still entrenched in St. Louis almost a thousand miles away from the impending battle zone, Deaux's command staff was in disarray.

The news from the scouts atop Fire Rock Ridge was golden, of course, and it really couldn't have been much better from a tactical point of view. The BMK had massive amounts of men and firepower in the area and were quickly closing in on the enemy position. What's more, the potential battlefield—the Plain of Stars—was flatter than the sea at its calmest.

The operation would be textbook. The enemy camp would be bombarded by the huge Master Blaster arrays already speeding toward their forward deployment. After some softening up, a massive ground attack would commence and would not stop until the enemy position was overrun. With only the mountains at their backs, the fleeing enemy troops would be trapped and destroyed long before they reached the first tree line.

It was an ideal situation, and everyone at BMK Headquarters knew it, except for the most important person: Supreme Commander Deaux himself.

Deaux was asleep when the first report from Fire Rock Ridge came in around seven A.M. He was asleep still. Deaux never rose before the sun and was rarely awake by midmorning.

This day would be no different.

By seven-thirty, the advance scouts atop Fire Rock Ridge had settled into their forward observation positions.

These were a line of trenches cored out by electron torches close to the edge of the ridge. Concealed in this manner, the scouts would be able to look down on the enemy position and gather intelligence while waiting for the main forces of Army Central to arrive.

The BMK scouts were equipped with the latest version TVZs—tactical viz screens. These allowed the scouts to breathe in real-time visual images practically right up to the front line of the enemy fortifications. They had three of these devices in the trench and, peering through them, the scouts could see many enemy troops anxiously adding to the ramparts. Like the base's structures, these were constructed primarily of melted stone and wood. If there were fifteen thousand enemy troops within the huge encampment, at least half of them were working on the fortifications. The line of soldiers digging, building, and hauling away dirt stretched for miles.

After observing the situation for twenty minutes, the advance scouts sent off their first report to BMK HQ. It was three simple lines: "The enemy is spread very thin. He has no large guns. His base is located where he has no means of escape."

• • •

The first shots of the Battle of Ghost River came at precisely eight o'clock atop Fire Rock Ridge.

It began as a dull screech coming from somewhere to the north. The BMK advance scouts were so intent on their mission they paid it little mind at first. But then the air itself shook all around them, and the strange noise grew louder and louder. The scouts finally looked up and saw that an airborne object had risen out of the northern hills and was coming right at them.

The scouts didn't know what this thing was. Their top-secret premission briefing had spoken of the enemy's magic weapon, a flying machine that had absolutely nothing in common with anything the BMK had ever flown. The magic weapon was a relatively small aircraft with the power of a space cruiser; this was the only way the BMK commanders could describe it. The strange aircraft had shot down a number of the BMK landing vehicles during the first day of the invasion. It had been attacking targets, both in America and on Planet France, nonstop ever since. This news had been kept secret from the vast majority of the BMK troops. But the scouts were higher in security class, and now they had a need to know.

Oddly enough, though, this wasn't that aircraft.

It was over their position just a few seconds later. Streaking by not fifteen feet off the ground, making a noise loud enough to make one's ears bleed. It was going fast, but not so fast that the scouts couldn't make it out.

It was a robot. A very large robot. It was flying along at high speed, arms tucked back, head up, propelled by miniature rocket burners on the soles of its boots. A thick red beam was flashing intermittently from behind its eye visor. The beams were being directed at the scouts' shuttlecraft, which had been left unattended in a gully five hundred feet below the ridge.

As the scouts watched helplessly, shuttle #555 was rocked by six staccato explosions. The destructo-beam emanating from behind the robot's visor had cut a swath right through the vessel's midsection, and in seconds it was a flaming wreck. Just like that, the scouts had lost their only means of transport off the ridge.

The robot looped around at fantastic speed, then dove on the scouts themselves. This was not typical warfare for these soldiers. They'd been bombarded long range from space before, but they just weren't used to being shot at from machines flying so low. As the robot streaked toward them again, its visor raising itself in anticipation of another volley of destructo-beams, some soldiers panicked. About a third of the hundred men left their positions and fled into the woods nearby.

Those that didn't move, sixty-five soldiers who stayed true to their posts, were all vaporized by 33418's next pass.

By this time, the advancing artillery column was just seven miles away from Fire Rock Ridge, following a narrow dirt road known as Wishbone Pass.

They had been in communication with the advance scouts atop the ridge, and if everything went according to plan, they would soon be using the scouts' shuttle craft to hover-lift each of the Master Blaster arrays up to the cliff.

The commanders of the one hundred-vehicle column were anxious to reach the front. They were well aware of the monetary significance of the upcoming battle. They wanted their part in it to be secure. To do this, they had to reach the ridge and commence the bombardment of the enemy camp as quickly as possible. The more they could pound the enemy before the main forces arrived, the more credible their claim would be that the enemy was in fact subdued by their long guns, and the ground operations were just elaborate mop-ups. This would result in a bigger paycheck for the artillery commanders. Some were predicting the conflict would be over by noon.

Once the column came within five miles of the ridge, the commanders ordered their communications officers to contact the scouts again and get the shuttle-lift operation going.

But this message would never be sent. Not that it would have made much difference; there was no one on the other end to reply, anyway.

The communications vehicle exploded into trillions of little pieces, courtesy of the six blaster rings installed on the nose of the flying machine. It had come out of nowhere, the comm truck no doubt its first intended target. It was moving so quickly that just as soon as it departed to the north, it was coming at them again from the south. It was frightening, strange. The flying machine made no noise, not until it went by you. Then the screech was enough to crack open a skull.

This time, its nose opened up about five miles out. Six blind-

ing red beams shot out in a quick flash. Three headed straight
for the lead truck in the convoy; three did a deflecting maneuver
and veered toward the last truck in the column. Each triplet of
beams hit its target, utterly obliterating them and blocking the
access road irreparably in the process.

The column was now trapped.

Their superiors had told the convoy commanders that if the
flying machine appeared overhead, they should order their
troops to shoot at it. This decree was not based on any evidence
that ground fire could actually stop the aircraft. It was more
along the idea of giving the troops something to do before they
got blasted into salt.

After the machine completed its second pass, it disappeared
off to the north yet again. It was gone just long enough for the
column's commanders to order their HVVs to the ground and
for the troops within to dismount and prepare for action.

These troops were mostly drivers and gun operators. They
were not real terrain combat troops. Yet each was armed with
a blaster rifle and a ray gun as a side arm.

The mystery aircraft appeared once again and, as ordered, the
troops began firing at it with their blaster rifles. There were
about two hundred soldiers in the column. Many now used their
landed HVVs as cover. The combination of two hundred blaster
rifle beams going up at once made for a spectacular sight. The
morning sky was suddenly filled with wild green streaks everywhere.

But it was all for naught. The pilot of the flying machine
simply twisted and turned his way through the columns of lethal
rays, using what appeared to be a minimum of effort and not
losing even a foot of altitude. The six beams erupted from its
nose again. Once more, three landed on vehicles at the head of
the column, three landed to its rear. Massive explosions resulted
as the aircraft again left behind another bone-jarring screech and
departed, this time off to the west. From all indications, its pilot
was intent on destroying the convoy from its farthest points
inward, and there was nothing anybody on the ground could do
about it.

But icing the column was only part of the plan.

The convoy had been arrayed in such a way that most of the
towed Master Blaster units were placed in the middle. The
HVVs carrying security troops as well as the combat engineers

were located at the head and the rear of the column. It was these troops that were now getting pounded into the hard ground as the mysterious aerial machine continued crisscrossing the sky, flying at tremendous speeds, its frightening nose weapon picking off two or three vehicles at a time.

Most of the attention then was drawn to either end of the smoking parade of vehicles. In the middle, where the Master Blasters now lay stalled, the artillery soldiers were firing in vain every time the flying machine reappeared. One cluster of troops had just ceased a barrage when they turned around to realize a small army of enemy soldiers had suddenly landed in their midst. The enemy soldiers delivered a fusillade of blaster fire right into the crowded group of BMK soldiers. Dozens were killed, many more were wounded. In the confusion, more enemy troops appeared and started painting one of the Master Blasters with low-energy beams from their electron torches.

Once the weapon was completely enveloped by the bluish rays, there was a flash, and the huge tubed array blinked out. Stolen, just like that. This happened again and again, more than a half dozen times. The column's soldiers were helpless in trying to stop the raiders from stealing their huge weaponry. The enemy's quick dispersal of massive firepower in a confined area essentially walled off the weapon and its surroundings long enough for the raiders to swipe it by pushing it, end first, through an expanded Twenty 'n Six field. Once the huge gun was gone, the raiders would simply disappear through the field as well. Then it would close up, just like it was never there at all.

The attack on the convoy lasted not ten minutes. Eight Master Blasters were stolen; the rest had been destroyed by the passing flying machine, which never ceased its devastating strafing runs of the battle area. Even after all of the raiders had safely blinked out and the rest of the big weapons were destroyed, the aircraft continued to pummel the convoy until nothing was left. Only then did it leave the area for good.

Just a few dozen BMK soldiers survived the attack. Most were in shock. Many were wounded. There were no officers, no means of communication, and no way to get out of Wishbone Pass except to walk. Those that were able began doing just that, intent on reaching what they believed to be the nearest friendly position: the advance observation posts up on Fire Rock Ridge.

• • •

They finally woke Deaux around nine o'clock.

He immediately threw a fit, kicking the bed clothes off his hovering bunk and threatening to kill the two officers who had roused him by poking his feet with their gun butts.

But waking him had been necessary, the officers pleaded. There were some significant developments he just had to know about. The secret enemy camp had been found. It was in a valley out West that presented a perfect piece of terrain over which the BMK could attack.

Deaux's eyes brightened sleepily at this good news. Then came the bad: The convoy carrying the BMK's full complement of Master Blasters on the planet had been attacked and the weapons stolen or destroyed. There had also been trouble contacting the advance scouts who had spotted the enemy encampment in the first place. All of Attack Force Delta was awaiting Deaux's next command.

The first thing Deaux did was panic. To his way of thinking, the loss of the Master Blasters suddenly meant that he would not have enough troops to vanquish the enemy. That only raw manpower could make up for the deficit of not having any of the powerful multitubed weapons on hand. In a way, he was right. Though he still had almost a half million men on Planet America under arms, many were tied up occupying the empty cities the BMK had so dubiously conquered. Moving all of them west would take days.

What Deaux should have done was simply order half of the Master Blasters on Planet France to be transferred to America with all due haste, and then wait for the BMK troops already in the region of the enemy camp to converge and then attack.

But Deaux decided on another command instead.

His communiqué left BMK HQ shortly afterward. It was foolishly dispatched via a standard communication string with no encryption, no effort at all to make it scrambled. It was directed back at Moon 39.

The message was blunt: The BMK needed warm bodies who could fire a blaster rifle. Deaux was ordering that everyone left on Moon 39—techs, base security troops, space dock workers—be issued a weapon and shipped to Planet America immediately. This collection of primarily logistics troops would constitute yet another army of about seventy-five thousand men. But it would also leave Moon 39 virtually deserted. No matter, Deaux wanted the soldiers sent down anyway.

But there was another problem: All the available troop shuttles were either on America or Planet France. There was no way to transport these rear-area troops. "Deploy six of the moon's dozen space cruisers," the people back on Moon 39 were told. Each could hold about twelve thousand troops. Though it would be a tight squeeze for some of them, the voyage in would take less than an hour.

The people still on Moon 39 were told these reenforcements had to be above the Ghost River Valley battlefield before eleven o'clock that morning, now just two hours away. If not, Deaux would personally disintegrate the head of any officer found responsible for causing even a minute's delay.

25

By the time the surviving artillerymen arrived on foot from the convoy disaster, the scene atop Fire Rock Ridge was total chaos.

Other scout shuttles had landed, and their occupants had found sixty-five dead comrades in the trenches and thirty-three shell-shocked ones in the woods. Deaux's own personal transport craft had arrived as well, along with another dozen shuttle-craft. The huge shuttles had flown west from St. Louis, carrying shock troops and equipment. They were disgorging themselves of cargo and soldiers, then quickly leaving the area and heading back East to pick up more troops.

The BMK's massive deployment west had begun. But as a result, there were now more than twelve thousand BMK troops along the ridge, including the few survivors of the advance scouting unit. The ridge was way too small to hold all these soldiers properly. They were crowded together so tightly, many could not see more than a few feet in any direction. Some were standing, others were sitting on the ground. Still others were asleep, and a few were even suffocating. Their officers didn't know what to do. With Deaux himself on the scene, all orders were coming from behind the sealed hatch of his private, very luxurious Shuttle #1.

It was now about ten o'clock, and Deaux had yet to emerge from his trailer.

•   •   •

No sooner had the artillerymen appeared on Fire Rock when the senior-most soldier was brought into Deaux's command vehicle.

The man was a sergeant major, and he had the unpleasant task of telling Deaux just how eight of the Master Blasters the BMK had been relying on for this battle had fallen into enemy hands, leaving the four others to be destroyed. Deaux did not take his report well.

The BMK leader finally stormed out of his command vehicle, dragging the artilleryman behind him. Against the advice of his security detail, Deaux pushed his way through the crowd of troops and marched the artilleryman right up to the lip of the ridge itself. Gazing down at the enemy's camp, they could clearly see the Americans setting up the eight stolen artillery pieces. Suddenly, an army that had previously fought mostly with ancient rifles and machine guns now possessed eight examples of the deadliest weapon in the Galaxy. Readings from a nearby TVZ scanner said the big ray guns would be operational within the hour.

Deaux was so infuriated, he drew out one of Xirstix's silver-handled ray guns, put it against the artilleryman's forehead, and pulled the trigger . . . but nothing happened. Deaux had failed to hit the weapon's activation switch first. Otherwise the man's head would have disappeared in a cloud to subatomic particles.

Deaux's security troops were able to hustle the terrified man away, but not before Deaux called after them that this man and all of the other survivors from the convoy would be put up on the line, unarmed, for the inevitable BMK attack.

When the long march across the plain began, he said, these men would be right out front, human targets facing the same Master Blasters they'd been carrying to the battle just a few hours before.

Adding more confusion to the scene atop the ridge were the lightning-quick strafing passes still being made by the robot 33418.

The airborne clanker would show up periodically, sometimes approaching from the south or sometimes from over the top of the small mountain to the BMK's rear. He would streak over the BMK position, flying very low, dispensing short bursts from his very narrow-field destructo-beam. The ridge was so crowded with troops, the robot's lethal rays usually found at least a dozen victims with each pass and sometimes a piece of equipment, too. The loss of manpower from these attacks was not great, and Deaux's shuttle was being protected by a crude but effective energy shield (the only one in the BMK's inventory), so he was in no immediate danger. But the harassment factor from the clanker's hit-and-run attacks was tremendous. Those soldiers in the vicinity of the robot's last pass were obsessed with searching the sky, thinking they'd be next.

Yet there was so much confusion on top of the ridge that many of the other soldiers didn't realize their position was being attacked at all.

It was quickly clear that there were too many troops on Fire Rock Ridge and not enough down on the Plain of Stars itself.

Again, a logistics problem had emerged. All of the available troop shuttles were in service carrying soldiers over from St. Louis and Chicago. So a quick airlift down to the valley floor would not be possible. When told of this, Deaux lapsed into one of his dark moods. He ordered his field commanders to have the troops climb down the ridge to the valley below. This would be no easy task; the ridge sat about eight hundred feet above the plain, and its western face was practically sheer rock all the way down. When informed of these dangers, Deaux issued another decree. The first men to climb down should be officers and key sublieutenants only. This way, when the bulk of the troops reached the valley floor, the officers would already be in place to command them. Deaux's field commanders knew this was foolishness, but they had no other choice than to carry out the orders. No matter who went down the cliff first, the purloined Blasters would be operational very soon, and any large deployment after that would be disastrous.

So the commanders gathered what units they could and had their officers step out. They were briefed on the new plan and told to use their electron torches to fashion thick ropes of steel weave. Several hundred of these lines were produced in just a few minutes. The steel ropes were then secured to the top of the ridge by melting their fibers into the cliff rock itself.

Then the BMK officers began the long climb down.

It was just about this time when a message from space came in.

At first, it seemed to carry some good news for the BMK position. One of the space cruisers dispatched from Moon 39 had already arrived in orbit, a full thirty-four minutes ahead of Deaux's deadline. It was carrying 11,500 third-tier troops, fully armed and fitted for combat. The five other ships were on their way in as well.

Deaux was delighted upon hearing this news. Army Central was reported moving quickly to the front, and Army South was approaching, too. Now that the Moon 39 troops were on hand, Deaux believed he'd overcome the loss of the Master Blasters by providing more fodder for them to shoot at once the ground attack finally began.

He ordered the huge space cruiser—it was nearly a half mile long, and shaped like a gigantic wedge—to come down on the Plain of Stars itself to dispatch its troops. With the handful of cruisers right behind it, if all went well, the BMK would have more than seventy thousand soldiers—though not top-notch ones—on the ground within the next few minutes. The ship reported that it would begin its descent immediately.

By this time, the first elements of the BMK officers climbing down off the ridge had reached the plain below. There were more than five hundred steel ropes hanging off the cliff, and the officers were descending at a fairly quick pace. Once on the ground, they could clearly see the Ghost River about a mile and a half away. Two thousand feet beyond that was the enemy's first line of fortifications. When the BMK finally began its advance and its troops reached the river, they would be able to quickly construct bridges with their electron torches to carry them across the two hundred-foot-wide stream. Once they reached the other side, the ground attack would begin in earnest.

Several BMK officers fell to their deaths trying to climb down the sheer rock face. Their bodies were routinely disintegrated after being stripped of their weapons, equipment, and valuables. For the most part, though, the descent went well. Soon there were several hundred BMK officers right where they were supposed to be: on the Plain of Stars, waiting for the rest of their troops to climb down.

Suddenly, the sky above the valley floor opened up.

Even though it was a clear day, a huge bank of black clouds appeared, and a lightning bolt went shooting across the sky. Emerging from the cloud was the first space cruiser dispatched from Moon 39. This made the officers on the valley floor breathe a little easier. The ship was carrying more than eleven thousand men. Once they were put on the ground, the BMK force in the immediate area would almost double in size, with more to come.

But just then came a terrible noise. It was louder than the crack of thunder caused when the space cruiser popped in. This screech was loud enough for the troops down on the plain to drop their equipment and cover their ears. Looking up, they saw a speck of silver falling out of the sun. It was trailing a long plume of white smoke behind it and was twisting through the sky at a very unnatural rate. It was down near the ground in less than a second. Only then did the BMK troops realize this was the enemy's red, white, and blue magic weapon that had been inflicting huge casualties on the Bad Moon Knights ever since they'd landed on this planet.

This time it had announced its arrival with a tremendous sonic boom.

The craft streaked right over the plain, then turned upward, creating another massive boom. Then its nose opened up in a blinding flash, and six blaster beams shot out of it. Their intended target was the space cruiser, which had just come into view. The BMK troops on the plain and up on the ridge watched in horror as the small flying machine began mercilessly blasting away at the suddenly vulnerable starship. There was no way the cruiser could shoot back; it didn't carry any defensive weapons. Nor could the troops on the ground fire at the attacker. It was moving way too fast.

So the BMK troops could only watch helplessly as the strange flying machine began looping around the floundering starship, the deadly ray blasts from its nose never stopping for very long. It took only a few passes before something exploded on the underbelly of the three thousand-foot-long ship. This was followed seconds later by another, even larger explosion on the top side of the gigantic vessel. The cruiser began wobbling in the air not a quarter mile above the battlefield. The mysterious aircraft delivered one long, final blaster barrage to the ship's bridge, then departed at very high speed to the west. A stream of soldiers began pouring out of one of the spacecruiser's jump ports. The ship had tried to unload its troops, even though it was under attack. But it was way too late for that.

There was another titanic explosion, and now the cruiser slowly began to turn over. Gushing huge sheets of flame and smoke, it went completely inverted and slammed into the ground right at the base of Fire Rock Ridge, killing all 11,500 troops on board plus more than four hundred BMK officers who had just climbed down from the ridge top.

Just seconds later, the second and third space cruisers popped in above the battlefield.

Their pilots did not dawdle as the first ship had. They set down immediately on the Plain of Stars, about a half mile east of the Ghost River, side by side. They opened all access ramps and soon thousands of BMK soldiers were streaming out of the starships, running for their lives. Then came another screech. The fourth space cruiser had blinked in. But now another thunderous blast, and the small red, white, and blue craft was back again.

It immediately went for the fourth space cruiser, still breaking out of its cloud about one thousand feet above the plain. The small flying machine hammered away at the bottom of the space cruiser with its six rings of blaster fire. Obviously, a vulnerable spot had been identified on the starship's underbelly. This time it took only two passes by the multicolored aircraft before the spacecruiser's aft section exploded, slamming the huge ship to the ground about a mile south of Fire Rock Ridge. This done, the flying machine whipped around, strafed the troops still pouring out of the two landed cruisers, then climbed straight up and disappeared from sight.

Somehow in the middle of this tumult, the fifth space cruiser arrived and set down about a mile north of the ridge. It began dispensing its troops, but at that exact moment, two of the eight stolen Master Blasters poking out of the enemy's front line became operational. Multitubed barrels level to the ground, their operators opened up on the troops streaming out of the fifth space cruiser. Hundreds of soldiers were vaporized in seconds. The cruiser itself took massive hits on its rear stabilizer legs. Both were blown away, causing the rear end of the huge ship to crumple to the ground. A huge fire broke out on the vessel's bridge, located in a bubble at the opposite end of the ship. A symphony of alarms could be heard going off within the cruiser now, like death bells, tolling away. Finally, the two forward landing struts collapsed as well, and the rest of the mortally wounded ship slammed into the ground.

The sixth space cruiser never appeared at all. It had been shot down by the ascending flying machine soon after entering the atmosphere.

As all this was happening, pure pandemonium broke out on top of Fire Rock Ridge.

The wreckage from the first space cruiser to go down was still exploding, raining pieces of flaming metal down upon those soldiers stuck on top of the cliff. Deaux's personal shuttle had taken off long ago, leaving all but his special security troops behind. This left the surviving soldiers on the ridge with only one option: They began withdrawing the only way possible, down a narrow truck path, which wound its way down the eastern side of the ridge. These troops were strafed endlessly by the 33418 clanker on the way down, though. So much so, that when the majority of the six thousand or so soldiers reached the bottom of the ridge, they started walking east, away from the battlefield.

They had had enough.

It was just about this time that the shuttles sent back to get more troops from Saint Louis and other points east began returning.

They'd appeared above Fire Rock, hoping to set down on top of the ridge as before. But that was no longer viable; the ridge was a sea of flaming wreckage and bodies. Having no other choice, the shuttles began landing right on the Plain of Stars itself. At this point, two more of the stolen Master Blasters came on-line, and now four of the frightening weapons were firing point-blank on the deploying BMK troops. The turmoil that had racked Fire Rock Ridge had moved right down to the valley floor itself. The BMK soldiers from Moon 39 had never encountered anything like this before. They were used to invading helpless planets with little or no opposition at all. Now they were in the midst of what was called in ancient terms a VH-LZ: a very hot landing zone.

The shuttles themselves were nearly five hundred feet long, sleek, tubular, with many windows. Their landing systems were rudimentary, though. These vessels were built to do two things: take off and land. They weren't good at hovering or doing anything that required lateral flight. Their pilots were at a loss on how to find a safe place to set down among the Master Blaster beams, the thousands of battlefield casualties, the bodies, the fires, the smoke, and the wreckage of three enormous space cruisers.

The Plain of Stars was suddenly a very crowded place, and three hundred shuttles needed space to set down. The confusion on the battlefield had now taken over the air above. Shuttles began bumping into each other, then colliding. Some had already landed and were dispensing their one thousand-man contingents; some had not. There were more crashes. The air was filled with blaster bolts and gunfire. And just when it seemed it couldn't get any worse, the flying machine showed up again.

Where the BMK soldiers saw chaos and carnage, the aerial devil saw opportunity. Traveling at an insanely high speed, it wove its way in and out of the scattering shuttles, picking them off one by one with economical bursts from the six-ring blaster in its nose. Once the aircraft made its way down the length of the battlefield, it went into a screaming 180-degree turn and dove into the melee again. Hardly noticed in all the flame and smoke was the clanker, 33418, screaming along in an almost parallel course with the aircraft, firing at individual targets closer to the ground. The barrages from the stolen Master Blasters then doubled as the four remaining weapons came on-line.

It went on like this for what seemed forever. The flying machine and the clanker shooting at anything that moved, the Master Blasters pounding away at the already-burning space cruisers and the surviving airborne shuttles. BMK troops running for cover would find little but flame and destruction at every turn. Some of the more seasoned troops simply located the deepest hole they could crawl into and did so. Others panicked and tried to leave the battlefield altogether. Few of them made it.

The only reason it finally stopped was that about half the fleet of incoming shuttles saw the nightmare they were supposed to fly into and turned around before being sucked into the inferno. The blaster fire died down. The clanker departed the scene, streaking off to the west. The flying machine slowed its speed drastically and flew over the plain, surveying what had been wrought. Finally, it, too, departed the area, leaving behind one last bone-crushing sonic boom.

An eerie calm came over the battlefield now. The wreckage of the starcruisers and dozens of the big shuttles was stretched for seven miles in both directions. Fires everywhere burned out of control. The Ghost River was running with hydraulic oil and blood. The sun could barely poke through the clouds of smoke, it was so thick. Somewhere amid the wreckage, a Klaxon was blaring, with no one around to turn it off. Finally, one of the Master Blasters opened up again, sending a stream of lightning bolts into the vicinity of the noise, silencing it for good.

All was deathly quiet after that.

More than sixty-five thousand BMK soldiers lay dead on the Plain of Stars, killed in a battle that really wasn't a battle at all because the BMK never got to fire a shot. Sixty-five thousand men, lost in just a dozen minutes of confusing carnage. It was the worst death toll for any single action in the mercenaries' thousand-year history.

The trouble was, on Planet America alone, there were still four hundred thousand of them left.

In the midst of the battle, Deaux's command shuttle had escaped to a mountaintop three miles north of the Ghost River Valley, a place called Silverine Peak.

Locked away inside his cabin now, thrown on his hovering bed, Deaux was still shaking from the events down on the Plain of Stars two hours before. His door was locked. He had a pillow over his face. His staff had wisely left him alone.

Attempting to land all of his troops at the same time, in the same place, under fire, had been a monumental blunder on his part. Six space cruisers lost, hundreds of shuttles destroyed, tens of thousands of troops killed. Sure, this was war. People die and things crash. But . . .

Not a shot fired in our own defense! Nothing at all was thrown in the enemy's direction!

That was the real problem here. The history books would paint him as a fool. The ledger books, too.

His career as a top commander, handed to him so easily, was finished.

Just when he had begun to like it, too.

The truth was, things were bad all over. All of the garrisoned cities in the East had been attacked by the enemy's flying machine at least twice just on this day alone. Indeed, it had been attacking them at least once a day just about all week. HVV parks, food warehouses, and ammo dumps were the targets of choice for the aerial devil. Slowly but surely, he was taking away the things an army depends on most.

Worse, and even stranger, the flying machine had been hitting targets on France all day, too. There was little doubt now; the two invaded planets were obviously in cahoots somehow. But no one within the BMK had really been able to make the connection. The fantastic flying machine had something to do with it, though. Why would it appear to aid the causes of both planets? And what drove the man who flew it? And where did he come from? Deaux's commanders had even produced a time line showing that, during the disaster on the Plain of Stars, whenever the red, white, and blue craft wasn't overhead shooting at them, it was off attacking targets in Saint Louis, Chicago, Philadelphia, and New York. The plane was spotted moving at incredible speeds as it dashed back and forth between target areas. Add in the missions over France, and whatever time it took to fly between the two planets, and it was apparent that the flying machine had never stopped moving. Day and night, for nearly a week, it had been in the skies over both planets attacking the BMK with impunity.

"When he is not here, he is there," Deaux had murmured when shown the report. "But he is always somewhere."

Deaux had other problems, too. There were no more Master Blasters on Planet America—at least none in BMK hands. Deaux had foolishly dismissed the idea earlier of sending for six of the multitubed arrays from France. Now these weapons were hiding in caves near Paris for fear that if they moved, the enemy's secret weapon would find them and bomb them. Deaux did have several hundred smaller Faster Blasters on hand, but even put together, they didn't add up to one whole big boy.

The BMK in America was also running out of supplies. They'd been dwindling rapidly even before the flying machine intensified its attacks. The BMK simply hadn't planned to be engaged for this long against opposition. Usually on these forays, the army came with enough stuff to last a week and a half. That's when the extermination squads were normally done with their work. The planet would be fried, and the troops would all return to Moon 39. Obviously, this campaign was going to take a little longer than that. But it was getting so bad, Deaux would have to order all his troops to half rations soon.

So he was feeling very low at this point, which made the

message his officers came bearing such an unexpected surprise.

"The enemy wants to talk," one of the commanders told him, one of three who'd dared knock on his cabin door. "We've just pulled down a message string from them."

"Talk?" Deaux asked, not quite getting it. "Talk about what?"

"About this war," the lead officer said. "About the future of the conflict. It's called a truce meeting."

"But what is there to say?" Deaux asked them. "We all know what's happened so far."

"It's considered a very Five-Arm thing to do," the lead officer explained again. "Which makes us wonder exactly who we are fighting against over there. To talk to your opponent at a crucial point in the battle: Soldiers who are steeped in myth feel a sort of compulsion to do this. It's a ritual. But some valuable information can be gained from it, too."

Deaux was still confused. "Well, who goes to talk with them?"

"You do, sir," was the reply.

"Alone?"

"You can bring three warm bodies with you," he was told, "but no weapons of any kind. That's the tradition, and it's as old as the truce meeting itself. You will meet on a neutral spot at an agreed-upon location, under a green flag. As your advisers, we urge you to go and see what they have to say."

Deaux suddenly became excited. He sat up, wiped his eyes, and straightened his uniform.

"Is there a possibility they might want to surrender?" he asked his commanders.

The officers all shrugged.

"Anything is possible," the lead officer finally replied.

The truce meeting took place on another peak located halfway between Silverine and the Plain of Stars.

Deaux was transported to the summit by a specially adapted HVV. With him were three of his biggest bodyguards. None of them were carrying weapons. Deaux was holding a green flag.

He had assumed that four enemy soldiers would be on hand when he arrived. But instead, only one person was waiting for him at the top of the windblown peak. He was holding a green flag in one hand, a large brass cross in the other.

A priest . . .

Deaux climbed out of the HVV and walked to within six feet of the diminutive monk.

"Are you lost, Father?" Deaux asked him snidely.

The priest just shook his head slowly. The wind was making his cassock crack like a whip.

"I am the one they choose to speak to you," he said.

Deaux handed the green flag to one of his security men and imperiously snapped off his gloves.

"So then, speak, Father. I'm a very busy man."

"This war is unnecessary," the priest told him simply.

"And why is that?"

"Because it's not your battle to fight," the priest replied. "You've been duped. Whoever is paying you has made a fool of you and your men and has been for centuries."

The wind began howling now. Smoke from the battle scene below was wafting up toward them, swirling in the mountain crosswinds. It was suddenly very cold.

"Father, I'm sure you are a more learned person than me," Deaux said. "So forgive me, but I don't understand what you are talking about."

The priest finally lowered his green flag to the ground.

"Answer me this," he began again. "When was the last time you were paid for this mission?"

Deaux didn't reply. Paid? He couldn't remember back that far.

The priest went on. "When was the last time you heard from your families? Or saw your superiors? You must have a command structure somewhere in the Galaxy. When did anyone from there visit you last?"

Again, Deaux could not reply. Besides Xirstix, he'd never seen any superior officers on the sentinel moon. For years the rumor around the base was that their superiors always visited in secret, which explained why they were never around. But Xirstix had once confided to him that it had been decades since the last real contact. Yet there was a reason for that: What they were doing out here was *so* secret, regular communication would have jeopardized the security of the mission. Or at least that's what Xirstix had been told.

"Don't you get it?" the priest asked him now. "Just like everyone else in this system, you're stuck inside a time bubble. You think you've been out here for just a few decades, but it's really been centuries. It is only noticeable to someone from the outside looking in. But take it from me, back where I'm from, those uniforms, those weapons, those little wings—they went out of date hundreds of years ago. The people who stuck you out here are probably all *dead* by now. Of old age, I'm sure. And that means there is *no money* waiting for you."

Deaux remained mute. His eyes darted back and forth, for him a sign that he was approaching something that passed as deep thought.

"I was told I'd be out here for fifty years," Deaux finally croaked. "I was told that it would be an isolated post, but I would be paid handsomely once my tour was done."

"Have you ever heard of Holy Blood, my son?"

Deaux shook his head no.

"It is a magical substance that keeps you alive a long time, so a friend of mine tells me," the priest said. "He thinks you were all given a bit of it and then sent way out here to serve for centuries, not decades."

"Nonsense!"

"Oh, really? Then why do you think they never came back to finish the other ninety-nine sentinel moons?"

Deaux was stopped dead in his tracks. He had no answer to that question.

"We could prove it to you, if you let us," the priest offered.

Deaux's face turned red. "I did not come up here to be educated by you," he snapped. "What you seem to forget here, Father, is, time bubble or not, I've got you at an advantage on the field—more than twenty to one! My job here is to crush you. That means you will be crushed."

"Even though there is a chance that what I've said here is correct? That you've in effect given up your lives out here? That your families are all dead? Your loved ones gone, assuming you even had loved ones? Think about it, man. It makes sense. Sure this is a secret place. Highly secret. It was built that way. And they didn't want anyone back there to know about it. They knew they had to keep their prisoners under lock and key, but they also had to keep the prison guards quiet, too. How best to do that than put them all in a time bubble and allow the years to pass like water dripping on stone. From that perspective, what's the point of all this?"

"What's the point?" Deaux roared back. "What do you want

me to do? Just walk away, just on your say-so?"

"Yes! Exactly . . . Just walk away. Leave this planet. Leave the system. Pop out of the bubble and go do whatever it is you people insist on doing. No one will even know you've gone. Not for decades—and that's only assuming they'll actually come out here looking for you again someday, which they probably won't."

Deaux had had enough. He was starting to think too much, and it hurt. He wanted to go.

"Father, you are dulling my senses, and I have to be sharp for my victory celebration tomorrow. So my best to you and your Heavenly Creator or whoever, but I have things to do. . . ."

The priest just shook his head sadly.

"Hear one more thing then," he said. "Honor binds me to tell you that my friends will have a secret weapon if and when you clash again. They will not hesitate to use it on you if you persist. This secret weapon will kill many of your soldiers. So many, that at the end of the day, it just won't be worth it for you."

"If your secret weapon is that flying maniac," Deaux retorted angrily. "We'll get around to destroying him eventually. I won't lie and say that his attacks haven't been . . . *noticed.* But he can't do it alone."

A very dark moment came now. "That flying machine is a weapon of awesome standards," the priest replied sternly. "But that is not the secret weapon of which I speak. This is something more brutal, and for your men, unstoppable."

"*Please,*" Deaux sniffed. "I have nearly a half million men still under my command. You have fifteen thousand, tops. Now, really, I thought you wanted to talk—not bluff."

"It is not a bluff. We want to make a deal. You and your army go back to where you came from. You leave us alone. We leave you alone. We never have to meet again."

Deaux couldn't help it; he laughed in the priest's face. Even his security guards were laughing.

"You're bold, if anything, Father. I have to give you that. But your friends have sent a fool in their place. No matter what mumbo jumbo you want to fill my head, the facts are still these: Your friends have the smaller army, it is *their* planet that has been invaded. Their cities are under *our* domination."

He signaled for the HVV to come and pick him up.

"I have more important things to do than stay up here talking to a delusional priest," he said.

The HVV appeared, and Deaux climbed aboard.

The priest called after him, "Just think of the lives you could save, my son. *Please . . .* "

But Deaux was already gone.

27

They were called *whistles*.

They were an ancient device that would produce a shrill, piercing sound when manipulated by breath. Every BMK field commander carried one; so did every officer down to the rank of captain. Through the centuries, their predecessors had discovered that if one blew hard enough, the whistle's song could be heard above all types of battle.

At precisely six A.M. that following morning, just as the fog was rising off the Plain of Stars, more than four thousand whistles went off at once.

It was enough to wake the dead.

Several good things had happened for the BMK during the night. The three hundred thousand-man Army Central corps had arrived. They'd encamped on the other side of Silverine Peak and had infiltrated onto the Plain of Stars throughout the night. The one hundred thousand men of Army South were just a few hours away as well.

It was also reported that the enemy's flying machine had been attacking targets over on Planet France for most of the night. The respite had been a help. It had allowed the fresh BMK troops to consolidate, get into position, eat a little, sleep a little.

Their main infantry troops, Army Central's sixteen divisions of foot soldiers, were now arrayed all along the Ghost River

Valley, hidden behind the mountains of wreckage from the day before. The wreckage actually worked to their advantage, too. It had perfectly masked the assembling points for the soldiers throughout the night.

Set within Army Central's rank was a division of combat engineers. They would go out first, just before the main attack began, their goal being to reach the river and start zipping up their mobile field bridges. Leading the engineers across the wreckage-strewn killing ground would be the hapless, unarmed artillerymen.

On either side of the main line was the mounted infantry, combined about forty thousand strong, riding in heavily armored HVV hovercrafts that glided three feet above the ground. Behind them, a line of small single-tube blaster arrays, sometimes called Faster Blasters because they fired 0.983759 quicker than the big arrays. They, too, were towed on hovering platforms and could be ready to fire in seconds. Behind all this, eight more divisions—eighty thousand men—were held in reserve on the other side of the hill.

The blowing of the whistles meant troops forward.

The foot soldiers of Army Central beat their chests once, creating a thunderclap that echoed up and down the river valley. Then they started walking, slowly at first, but with each step picking up speed. The combat engineers broke ahead of their ranks and, pushing the unlucky artillerymen before them, scrambled through the still-burning wreckage, heading for the river. On the flanks, the motorized infantry began to move as well, the slight whirring made by every HVV creating a sound like the wind rushing through trees.

Breaking out of the wreckage, the trembling artillerymen unwillingly leading the way, the engineers were the first to see the enemy, waiting behind their lines, about a mile away. The glint of several thousand rifles pointing in their direction grew stronger with each second in the rising sun; meanwhile, the Master Blasters towering over everything had an illumination all their own.

Most of the wreckage from the day before had fallen close back to the ridge. The engineers would have preferred it if the debris led right up to the riverbank; the artillerymen heartily agreed. But, it was more or less a clear sail now up to the river— about five hundred feet of open ground. A perfect killing ground for the enemy troops. Crossing it would be a chore.

The engineers surged on, pushing the artillerymen in front of them, expecting the worst at any moment. Yet nothing came. The enemy did not shoot at them. This was strange. Certainly they could see them. Were they saving ammunition? Why? Master Blasters rarely ran out of power. And a single electron torch could produce a couple thousand bullets a minute. Why then were they holding their fire?

Whatever the reason, the engineers took advantage. They pushed the artillerymen aside now and ran full out for the eastern bank of the river. There were more than ten thousand CEs; each one seemed to reach the riverbank at the same time. Some dove right in the water, not quite believing they had made it this far without so much as a scratch.

Behind them was the tremendous noise of almost one hundred thousand soldiers now running at close to full speed, breathing in and out as one, racing for the riverbank just as the engineers had done before them. Many of the artillerymen were trampled to death in this stampede. Others just fell down, covered up, and hoped for the best.

The engineers crawled to the river's edge, now, about a six-foot drop from either bank. They quickly began unzipping their bridges. Basically, these were structures made of ions, which assembled themselves in a kind of hovering runway about twenty feet wide. Both ends of the near-invisible structure could move back and forth, absorbing as many soldiers as quickly as possible and carrying them across the divide. The engineers were able to deploy about four thousand bridges in a matter of seconds. Just seconds after that, the first of the infantry reached the riverbank and went charging across.

And that's when the Americans opened up.

It was the engineers, still lying low near the water's edge, who had the best look at the battle.

No sooner had the Army Central troops hit the bridges when all eight Master Blasters and thousands of rifles and machine guns opened up on them at once. The Americans' fusillade hit the BMK foot soldiers point-blank, head-on. The Master Blasters disintegrated all soldiers found within their beams. There were no bodies to trip over, just tiny piles of salt. But for those soldiers hit by the ballistic piece of metal called a bullet, death could be a horrible thing. Severed arms, legs, arteries. Hearts exploding, throats torn away, skulls blown off.

The roar of weapons and death quickly reached a crescendo and stayed there, nearly overwhelming everything else. The engineers remained below the riverbank, staying in place as ordered, and thankful for it. But then the bodies of those BMK soldiers hit by bullets just coming off the bridges began falling back into the Ghost River. Soon so many dead and wounded soldiers were hitting the water, the sound of their splashes almost overcame the ear-splitting blast of the enemy's multitubed master arrays.

Through all this, the CEs could hear other noises as well. The whooshing sound made by the 33418 clanker strafing the length of the plain back and forth once again. Above that, the unmistakable screech of the enemy's magical flying machine. It had suddenly appeared overhead as well. The engineers could see it streak over the riverbank, back and forth, its nose blaster always open, always spewing six bright red beams. Sometimes flying right behind it, lower, slower, was the robot, destructo-rays from its eye blasters bouncing in every direction.

Five minutes, six minutes. Seven . . .

The BMK infantry kept coming, and the Americans kept firing. The dead soldiers were not falling back into the river so much any more only because a large wall of bodies was preventing the corpses from flopping backward any farther. The engineers could also hear the oddly calm whir of the HVVs. The hovercrafts would streak right over the river in formations of twos and threes, their smaller Faster Blasters firing full bore. But soon after the CEs lost sight of them, they would hear the sound of the hovercraft either being disintegrated or simply shot out of the sky.

In the midst of all this, some of the engineers saw something else. Through the smoke and fog of war, a strange craft popped in, just for a moment, above the battlefield. Unlike just about every other spacecraft in the Galaxy, this craft was not shaped like a triangle or a wedge. Instead, it was shaped like a saucer. It hovered high above the river for just a few seconds, wobbling a little bit as if whoever was inside was watching the battle and not quite believing what they were seeing.

Then, just as suddenly as it appeared, the saucer-shaped craft blinked out.

All of the firing died down after that.

More than a minute of silence passed before the first few brave CEs dared to climb up and look over the riverbank to see what had happened.

Most would wish they hadn't.

What lay before them were the remains of Army Central's infantry divisions. Three miles in both direction lay piles of bodies, horribly shot up, among small hills of salt. Salt was also blowing in the wind.

No one was moving; only a few muffled cries could be heard. Smoke covered most of the battlefield, but behind the enemy's stone and wood lines, the glint of thousands of rifles still pointing eastward was quite evident. Five of the Master Blasters were on fire and smoking heavily; only three had survived the battle between them and their smaller cousins. The killing field was also littered with hundreds of crashed HVVs.

From what the engineers could see, not a single BMK soldier had made it to within ten feet of the enemy line.

The eerie astonishment of the scene was just as quickly broken by the sound of another muffled thunderclap. The engineers turned around to see another wave of BMK soldiers running right for them. It was Army Central Two, the eight reserve divisions that had been hiding behind the hill.

Eighty thousand soldiers, stretched along a seven-mile front, hit the ion bridges seconds later. The firing went up full roar again. The engineers fell back into the water. After all, this is where they were supposed to stay. In a replay of the carnage just minutes before, the flash of blaster beams and the rumble of gunfire mixed and rose as one into a deep, monstrous growl. The air was thick with spent cordite, disintegrated atoms, fresh blood.

This time, the bodies weren't piling up near the edge of the river as they had when the first wave charged into oblivion. Did this mean the reserve soldiers were going farther and possibly beginning to overwhelm the enemy's fortifications? Not one of the engineers dared stick his head up to find out.

There was no reason to look into Hell if you didn't have to.

At this moment, three miles away, the advance elements of Army South entered the Ghost River Valley.

These soldiers were hardened veterans of numerous bloody

campaigns, many of them on tough, mountainous planets. But they had never seen anything like this. The wreckage alone on the Plain of Stars seemed to stretch right up to the sky. Bodies and white splotches of burned salt were everywhere. Flames and smoke were so thick, they blotted out the sun. A death pall covered the east side of the valley.

To the west, over the river, was the enemy encampment and a fierce battle in progress. The Army South commanders trained their TVZs on the action. The BMK strategy was clear: The first wave of BMK soldiers had been essentially sacrificed to wear down the defenders. Then the reserves were thrown in, further weakening the American line. The reserve divisions were battling close but were not yet on the enemy's fortifications.

The Army South commanders knew this only meant one thing. They had arrived at precisely the right time.

They started rushing their troops forward. Troops normally used to marching into war were now stuffed onto overcrowded HVVs and sent speeding toward the battle. Somewhere up in the mountains to the east, they knew Deaux was looking down on them. First there was Army Central. Then Army Central Two. Now came Army South. One hundred thousand men hitting the line at just the right moment.

Of such things are victories won.

The first wave of Army South soldiers hit the wavering front line just seconds later. The wave of overcrowded HVVs streaked over the last of the reserve divisions and penetrated the enemy line itself. But there was a surprise waiting for them here. The American trenches were empty. The remaining Master Blasters were in flames, wrecked on purpose. The last of the American army was going over the hill to the west.

"Pursue them!" Deaux bellowed now from his position on high, his voice carrying over the battlefield via a sonic bell. "We've finally got them on the run!"

It was, of course, Deaux's hubris that had him send his army after the Americans.

None of them had any idea what was on the other side. The location of the American encampment had been selected just for that reason. The topography was such that there was no line of sight from the battlefield on the Plain of Stars to what lay beyond the hill.

What was on the other side was an old, abandoned highway bridge, about a half mile long, which crossed a large ravine. Its roadway then flowed down through a narrow pass and ended in a canyon known as Carson Sink. The canyon was about a half mile square.

Just as the first Army South soldiers reached the east end of the highway bridge, the last of the American soldiers were fleeing into the pass. The Army South troops charged across the bridge, many on HVV hovercrafts, many on foot, some officers literally pushing their soldiers through the gap. Once this massive pursuit was set in motion, there was no quick way to stop it or even slow it down. Obsessed with the high-speed movement of troops, it would be Army South's final undoing. They'd managed to move nearly one hundred thousand troops two miles over rough terrain, across a long bridge, and into the open area beyond in an astoundingly short amount of time.

Quite a feat—but that area beyond, Carson Sink, was surrounded by high cliffs. And as soon as the last BMK soldiers had streamed into it, the flying machine appeared overhead and bombed the pass, sealing the canyon.

It was a trap. And Army South had fallen right into it.

When Deaux arrived in the canyon in his customized shuttle craft, his officers greeted him with worried expressions and much nervousness. They knew they'd been fooled. The withdrawing Americans had simply rushed through their Twenty 'n Six field portal again, leaving the BMK soldiers in one of the most indefensible situations imaginable.

These officers had to explain this now to Deaux, but even before the words could come out of their mouths, there was a collected gasp from the thousands of troops milling nervously around them.

Everyone was looking up, pointing to the canyon ridge that surrounded them. Dark figures were appearing atop this high ground, groups of twos and threes popping in all along the line.

The daylight was still dim—it was not yet 7:30 in the morning—so it was nearly impossible to make out just who or what was staring down at them from these highlands. They appeared to be soldiers, but they weren't the ragtag American fighters. They were long gone. These soldiers were bearing huge combat weapons, and they themselves looked enormous.

And there were thousands of them. Tens of thousands. *Hundreds* of thousands. And more were popping in with each passing second.

Finally, Deaux was able to get a working TVZ scope and focused on the ridge closest to his position. That's when he realized these weren't soldiers at all. Not typical ones, anyway.

They were robots. Combat robots. The TVZ was telling him there were more than a half million of them encircling the canyon.

"So that's why the Americans didn't destroy the bridge," Deaux mumbled now, stepping back into his shuttle with a small coterie of security troops. He gave his shuttle pilot two thumbs up.

The pilot got the message right away. He engaged the shuttle's controls and they quickly lifted off, leaving nearly one hundred thousand BMK troops behind.

Clanker 33418 was standing at the top of the highest peak above Carson Sink, looking down into the canyon.

He was facing east. The sun was reflecting off his visor. He was slightly larger than the battle robots; he stood out among them all. On either side of him were two smaller, thicker 'bots. One was green, one black.

They were, of course, the dead souls of Myx, the ancient robots called back to life again and transported here by purely magical means. But this time they had been resurrected not to fight each other—a simple adjustment of the aggression programs—but those soldiers now caught in the canyon below. They were just waiting for the word to proceed. His chest whirring with all kinds of sounds now, 33418 lowered his head and did one final scan of the canyon. There were 99,416 individuals down there.

Every one of them had to be destroyed.

Clanker 33418 turned to the robot on his left, lifted his visor slightly, and sent a red beam into the smaller 'bot's viz lens. That robot shuddered a bit, then turned and transferred the same red beam to the robot on the right. This robot sent it on to two more. And they sent it to two more, and two more, over and over and over again, until in a chain reaction of red beams, the entire army of robots had been given their final orders.

With no ceremony, no hesitation, they began marching down into the canyon.

Pater Tomm and the poof popped in where 33418 had been standing moments before.

The battle below was just beginning. The robots were wading into the terrified soldiers, most of whom were too afraid to even raise their weapons and fire. Now the soldiers were being crushed, trampled, shot, electrocuted, and disintegrated in a disturbingly methodical manner. If for some reason one of the robots was hit just right by blaster fire and disabled, it took just a few seconds for it to rebuild itself and come back to life again. The robots had been designed for eternal combat. There was no stopping them. The BMK soldiers never had a chance.

Looking down on the bloodbath, the poof became quickly disgusted.

"To be involved in such an enterprise goes against my privilege as an eternal soul," she said. "And it is your fault, Father. I broke just about all the rules of Nature getting these gas cans here for you. And now they are participating in a slaughter."

"Think of it as a cleansing," Tomm told her. "Or the misery the people of this Galaxy will not have to endure now that these dark souls are being dispatched. I gave them their chance. I warned them of our secret weapon."

He took a drink from his flask. It contained only coffee, his new jones.

"Some things are just necessary, my child," he concluded.

The poof put her hands on her hips and began to glow red. She was wearing her jester's costume today.

"First of all, you can spare the 'child' stuff from now on," she hissed at him. "I'm older than you by at least a couple eons."

Tomm just smiled. "Don't be so sure of that," he told her. "I stopped counting long ago."

They watched in silence for a few moments as the ring of robots closed in tighter around the shrinking mass of helpless soldiers. The physical aspect of the battle was overwhelming, with thousands of men and robots moving at once. The screams were bone-chilling, the crunch of robot steel against flesh and bone unnerving. Most of the BMK officers had fled to the center of the crowd, prolonging their lives by just a few more minutes but giving them witness to the slow horror that would eventually reach them, too. Some took their own lives instead; some shot comrades and then themselves. Some even dug holes in the ground and stuck their heads into them, one last act of madness.

The canyon's dusty surface was now soaked with blood.

"This deed will soon be done," the poof said. "But the demons we have let out of the bottle here will be impossible to stuff back in."

"Why are you so sure that they are demons?" Tomm asked her. "Maybe it's a squadron of angels that has been released. Or shouldn't I use that term, considering present company?"

"Don't be so dramatic, Father," the poof told him. "You can't possibly disagree that *all* of history is a painful march, good or bad, on both sides. It is. Believe me, I should know."

She began to cry softly. "That canyon is filled with a bit of history now. And something has been started here that won't stop. It's necessary, I suppose, for the people of this planet, of this system. Certainly they've been wronged. But what is to come will not be a peaceful enterprise."

Tomm just shook his head as the killing below approached its peak.

"I guess you're right." He sighed heavily.

"I'm always right," she said. "Just remember that."

It took more than an hour for it to be finally over.

Hunter wanted no part in watching it. He'd had enough of the killing, enough of all the death.

He set down on top of the devastated piece of high ground that was once Fire Rock Ridge, so weary he could barely climb out of his cockpit. He'd hadn't stopped driving bombing missions on Planet America or Planet France for nearly a week. Now all he wanted was a drink and to go to sleep.

He crawled underneath his aircraft into the shade, out of the bright, warm sun. He retrieved a flask from his boot pocket; it was filled with Seagram's. He uncorked it and downed the entire container in one long, noisy gulp. He felt the warm liquor burn its way down his throat, into his stomach, and then to all parts of his tired body. He'd been waiting for this moment for what seemed like forever. He lay back on the hard ground and started to close his eyes.

That's when he saw a small party of soldiers waving to him from the next peak over.

They were carrying a green flag.

It took Hunter twenty minutes to drunkenly climb up to the peak, his arms and legs weary, his throat dry. With the pint of whiskey still speeding its way through his veins, everything that happened next appeared to him in a kind of dreamy slow motion.

At the top of the peak, he found Deaux with three of his security men waiting for him. None of the guards appeared armed. Hunter had left his weapons back with his plane.

"So you're the devil who's been flying that infernal machine," Deaux said to him. "Interesting concept—a small aircraft with the power of a starcruiser."

Hunter boozily waved him off. He wished the others were here. But no matter. If this was a surrender party, he wanted to get on with it.

"Make your proposal quickly," Hunter said to Deaux. "For I am honor bound to offer you your lives once you've surrendered."

Like the mythical battle on Myx, it was time for the winning side to be magnanimous.

But Deaux had other ideas. It took Hunter a few moments to realize the BMK commander had pulled out a hand weapon. The three security guards saw what happened and quickly blinked out. Even they wanted no part of breaking such a long-standing rule.

So now it was just Hunter and the chubby little man with a very big ray gun.

"This is not how these things are supposed to go," Hunter told Deaux calmly.

"I just wanted my good name in the history books," Deaux babbled, aiming the ray gun right at Hunter's forehead. "And to get paid, of course. That's all. However, you just didn't beat me on the battlefield, *you embarrassed me.* Made me look foolish. Now, that won't get me into the annals of time, nor will it get me my just reward. But killing you? The demon pilot. Here and now? That will accomplish both things."

Before Hunter could even move, Deaux pulled the trigger—but nothing happened. He'd forgotten to unlock the firing mechanism again. But he quickly rectified his mistake.

He aimed the gun once again at Hunter and started to pull the trigger a second time.

Suddenly there was a flash, and a moment later, Deaux was minus his head. What remained of it was floating away in a cloud of subatomic ash. His body stayed upright for a moment, but then it fell over in one great heap.

Hunter staggered back a few steps. He was astonished. Someone had just saved his life. But who?

He turned around to find an ancient man in an ancient space combat uniform, holding two huge smoking ray guns and a cracked smile.

It was his savior. The Great Klaaz.

Hunter couldn't believe it.

"Brother Klaaz!" he roared. *"How . . . ?"*

Klaaz put his guns back into his holsters. "Let's just say a poof told me how to get here," he cackled.

But suddenly there was another flash. And a moment later, five men were surrounding them. They, too, had huge ray guns. But they were not BMK. These men were dressed in black uniforms with red trim and two lightning bolts on their collars. They also smelled heavily of slow-ship wine.

They were Solar Guards. Specifically, the members of the shadowy Post-Fringe Five Mission.

"You spent a lot of time getting here for nothing," one sneered at Hunter as another relieved Klaaz of his ray guns. "And you've managed to uncover the greatest secret since the Big Generator. We're just going to have to deal with that."

"How the hell did *you* get here?" Hunter asked them incredulously.

They all looked at Klaaz. "We followed him after our little visit to his new planet," one said. "But actually, Major Hunter, we've been looking for you for quite a while. You're a deserter from the Empire forces; you're a wanted man. Plus you've stuck your nose into something here that just cannot be known. By rights, we should bring you back for trial. But considering the circumstances and the fact that you have resisted arrest, it appears an execution is in order here, for you and your accomplice."

The Solar Guards aimed their weapons at both of them, but then there was *another* flash. Suddenly, the five gunmen were cut in half by a fusillade of blaster rays. Again, Hunter spun around to see his unknown saviors.

He found Erx, Berx, and Calandrx standing behind him, holding three smoking guns.

Erx pointed at the dead Solar Guards.

"And we followed them . . ." he said.

28

So the war was won.

Those BMK troops left back in the cities of the East would be allowed to leave. It was a very Five Arm thing to do. They had to evacuate the Home Planets system immediately and never come back. The fact that the only vessels to be made available to them would be the hundred or so working shuttles left, the chances of them returning to anywhere was low.

Once they were gone, the people of America could return to their cities and towns from their exile in the wilderness of the countryside.

The planet would be theirs again, except this time, they would be free.

The small group of warriors sat atop Silverine Peak now. Night was falling. They were numb. Drained. Grateful.

Hunter scanned the tired faces. It seemed a fitting cast for this, the end of the first great adventure. Tomm was there, of course, drinking only coffee from his flask. Could his contributions to this epic ever be fully appreciated? Probably not. Zarex, lighting a fresh cigarette from the burning end of a nearly spent one. He had been the genius behind selecting Ghost River Valley as the site of the dramatic showdown; he'd also led the army of policemen and armed civilians in building the fortifications on the Plain of Stars and the brilliant, if intentionally temporary, defense of the same.

Senior Agent Gordon was also on hand. He and his men had served as target-spotters for Hunter, both in America and over on Planet France. Hunter's continuous air raids had prevented more troops from moving west to help the BMK armies in Wyoming; they'd also postponed the genocide squads from taking any action on France.

The big surprise, Erx and Berx, were there too, exuberant even after their long search for him. An even bigger surprise: Calandrx, Hunter's mentor, was also present, pleased just to be in outer space again. The old warrior Klaaz, the first hero to save the day, was sitting by a roaring campfire, in deep discussion with the holo-spy.

Even the poof was on hand, slinking around the cliff rocks nearby.

Behind them, watching over them all, was the clanker 33418.

On the valley floor below, the immense robot army of Myx.

Tomm looked around and nudged Hunter. He said, this time with a twinkle in his eye, "What a merry band are we . . ."

The night grew longer, and the swirl of stars overhead grew brighter. No surprise, Erx and Berx had brought gallons of slow-ship wine with them. At the moment, Hunter was enjoying a half and half cocktail: half slow-ship, half Seagrams. The result was mind-blowing. Or was it mind-opening? It was hard to tell. In any case, many things began running through his head.

What would come next? They would have to liberate Planet France. But first, they would have to get out to Moon 39, to lay claim to the deserted base and the six ion-ballast starcruisers still in dock out there. The robots of Myx would do the fighting on France; the starcruisers would get them there.

Then what? Find a way to pop the system's time bubble? Possibly. But if they could simply come and go, once they had made it out beyond the star system's boundaries, there might be an advantage in keeping these planets just as they are. Educate the people certainly, but keep the uncomplicated life intact. Could these two things coexist in what might soon become a very violent, very different Galaxy?

Maybe. Maybe not.

But it might be interesting to try.

• • •

Hunter reloaded his drink, then moved farther up the cliff, quietly slipping away from the others.

He reached the mountain's summit and sat on top of a rock at its peak. Gazing out on the great ocean of stars before him, he was once again astounded by the unusual celestial display. This place had been built as a prison, true. But it had also been situated in an area of space that allowed for the most spectacular view of the entire galaxy, a place where all of the heavens could be seen at a single glance. Hunter found this very strange. Was the breathtaking vantage point built-in by design? Or was it just a happy coincidence?

He gulped his drink and more questions came flooding in. Why were the original Earthlings allowed to live? Why didn't their ancient jailers simply liquidate them three thousand five hundred years ago and be done with it? Another huge question: How were the Specials involved in all this? Their ancestors had ruled the Galaxy for thousands of years. The present Royal Family must have at least been aware of the Home Planets—after all, the Solar Guards were. Was there a connection between the Specials and the people who originally built this prison system more than three millennia before? Could they be one and the same?

Oddly, the Americans had come upon a small, if tantalizing clue on that: It emerged from a discussion Gordon had conducted with the holo-spy right after the big battle. Zarex had shown Gordon how to tap deeply into the projection's memory banks in order to learn everything he could about the people of the original Earth, minutiae included. Gordon asked the holo-spy for the most obscure fact she knew about the mother planet and the forced deportation of its people. Her reply? It came in the form of a rumor she'd picked up while training for her still-born mission, but it had the potential for a real bombshell. All along Hunter and the others had just assumed that every country from the original Earth was accounted for out here in the prison system, that some unknown outside entity had forced them off the planet. But according to the holo-spy's memory banks, this might not be so. The rumor was that one of Earth's countries might have actually been spared the forced deportation. For some reason, its people never made the journey out here, beyond the edge of the galaxy. The holo-spy had never heard this country's name or where it was located on "old" Earth, and her knowledge of it ended there.

But how could one country avoid being taken off Earth? Perhaps because they were the ones in charge of the deportation in the first place? Could this "missing" country be responsible for locking up the rest of Earth's original inhabitants? Hunter knew if this proved even a little bit true, then the real villains in this might well be the people from this mysteriously-absent country.

He gulped his drink again. In the end though, no matter how or why, only one thing was for certain: Earth belonged to the ancestors of the people of the Home Planets. It had been taken away from them at the height of an empire that was as great as the present one. The question was, how could such a crime be redressed? Certainly not by compromise, or accommodation or reparation. There was no way that a deal would make such a monumental injustice just go away.

No, the only way to properly right the wrong was to take it all back. Earth. The original Solar System. The entire Milky Way. Everything. Piece by piece if necessary. And it couldn't be just a war against the Solar Guards. They were just the flunkies here. The whole imperial structure would probably have to go. Top to bottom.

Did this mean then that the United Planets were destined to fight the Fourth Empire? To bring it down by force? Hunter almost laughed out loud. The Fourth Empire was quite possibly the largest enterprise in human history. They owned the secrets to Supertime, the Big Generator and the Holy Blood. How could their little band of planets, with no real army or weapons or spacecraft, ever hope to take down something so huge? It would be an impossible campaign, even with their horde of fierce combat robots. But in Hunter's mind, there was no other choice. *They had to do it.*

And that meant a final dealing with Emperor O'Nay, God Himself or the closest thing to it. Leader of trillions of troops, with the support of billions of planets.

The father of Xara . . .

Another complication.

Hunter gazed deeper into the massive ring of swirling stars now, his hand going to the pocket where he kept his American flag wrapped around the faded photograph of the pretty blonde whose name he did not know. At least now he realized why he'd been drawn here, to this time, to this place in the universe. He was an American. And someone, somehow, somewhere, had bent the rules of Nature to get him here just so he could participate in the great crusade ahead.

But who brought him here? Who had the power to do so? That was another mystery for another time. He tapped his pocket three times, thought of the woman in the photograph, and then, strangely, of Ashley. Where was she right now? At this very moment?

He drained his flask then looked down at his hands. Even though it felt like they were shaking slightly, they were actually very calm. He looked back up at the great wash of stars and squinted and searched like always but then . . . suddenly, there it was. Shining like a bright blue jewel amongst the clutter of the One-Arm. The magical place.

The new goal.

Home . . .

The real one.

Hunter smiled . . .

Yes, this time, he really could see Earth.

Billions of Miles Away

On a very simple, pastoral planet, hidden yet not hidden, in a very ordinary star system, there was a small cottage built on a hill, which looked out on grassy fields and a river beyond.

Inside the cottage, in the bedroom, an ancient form lay on a Sears Roebuck four-poster bed, sagging with a Sealy mattress, a tiny RCA radio emitting nothing but static on the bed stand nearby.

The man on the bed was dressed in a spacesuit nearly five thousand years old. The suit was remarkably intact; indeed just like its owner, it was enjoying an unprecedented long life, now approaching its sixth millennia.

The helmet was still firmly in place around the man's head; his hands were still covered by Velcro-sealed gloves, his feet shod with the bulky, self-heating magnetic boots. On his left shoulder was a patch bearing the letters NASA. On the right, a flag consisting of red and white stripes with a blue field of stars.

The man was an astronaut—literally, an ancient astronaut. He was more than five thousand years old. No one knew how he had managed to reach such an advanced age, least of all himself.

Two female attendants cared for his needs day and night. These were few. He needed no food, no water, just air, apparently. He was alert, though mostly sleepy, and he would talk, but only from behind the thick faceplate on his helmet.

Now, one of the female attendants—a nurse was the ancient term—entered the bright, sunny room, lifted the window, and let the warm breeze blow in from the meadow below.

"What is new?" the astronaut asked in his slightly mechanical voice.

The nurse leaned over him and whispered, "You received a message from an old friend of yours today. A very old friend . . . Pater Tomm."

A slight ripple went through the astronaut's body. He'd been waiting a long time to hear those words.

"And what did my very old friend have to say?" he asked the attendant.

The woman came even closer to his earpiece.

"He said to tell you, *'Something is coming. . . .'*"